U0092428

Merlin
Merlin
Merlin

Michael Skupin

for

John Mc Namara

Introduction: Many Merlins

American Medievalist is the subtitle of a 1975 study of Ralph Adams Cram (1863-1942). This is paradoxical from a Houstonian perspective, since the best-known Houston work by that legendary architect is the administration building of Rice University, which is not medieval at all, but moorish. It is also paradoxical from an architectural perspective, where the term "Gothic" is more common to describe the style that was, after all, Cram's trademark. The author of the study, Douglass Shand-Tucci, does make the case for the use of "medievalist," and even more fully in his subsequent book, *Boston Bohemia 1881-1900*, the first volume of his in-depth biography, where he deals not only with Cram's architecture, but also his writings, membership in antiquarian societies, and most relevant to this study, his editorship of *The Knight Errant*. "The doughty Cram...swings his sword at the world generally," wrote fellow Bostonian and poet Louise Imogen Guiney, who composed a poem for the inaugural issue of this "as Medieval as possible" little magazine that began its one-year life in April 1892.[1] It had a Kelmscott Press look, and consciously so, as Cram would later make plain: "For some of these volumes Goodhue [Cram's partner] made his wonderful initials and decorations based on the art of William Morris." It also had a Kelmscott Press philosophy, being "not only an expression of the most advanced thought of the time (the word [Cram does not specify which word] meant then something radically different from what it means to-day), but, as well, a model of perfect typography and the printer's art."[2] As for the

---

[1] Shand-Tucci, 1994, 340
[2] Cram, 1969, 85

content, the first stanza of Guiney's "The Knight Errant," what Cram called her "poem of salutation; one of the best things I think this dear Irish genius ever wrote,"[3] will give an idea of the tone.

> Spirits of old that bore me,
> And set me, meek of mind,
> Between great dreams before me
> And deeds as great behind,
> Knowing humanity my star
> As first abroad I ride,
> Shall help me wear, with every scar,
> Honour at eventide.

Guiney did more than contribute poetry; she also recruited talent, introducing Cram "to several of her more Bohemian companions, including those three 'vagabonds' Richard Hovey, Bliss Carman and Tom Meteyard, so called because of their having collaborated on the then celebrated series of Vagabondia books."[4]   All three made important contributions to *The Knight Errant,* Meteyard as an illustrator, Canadian poet Carman as a writer, but it will be Hovey (1864-1900) who will be important to this study: he had written a Merlin play, *The Quest of Merlin* (1891), and would go on to write an extended cycle of Arthurian dramas.

The doughty Cram was not one to be behindhand.

> Not being afflicted with an inferiority complex, and acting under a strong, if evanescent, emotional stimulus, I decided to do, in poetic form, and for our own racial epic tradition, what Wagner had done in music for the Teutonic sagas – a blank-verse trilogy on the Arthurian Cycle; so, writing

---

[3] Cram, 1969, 87
[4] Shand-Tucci 1994, 340

furiously, I produced the first of these dramas in the space of a few months, calling it 'Excalibur.'[5]

The play will be discussed at some length in this study, but three preliminary observations should be made.

First, although Cram implies that opera composer Richard Wagner (1813-1883) was his inspiration, this will be seen to be true in only in a superficial way; the Master of Bayreuth cast a long shadow in those days, and was a background influence on many authors to be examined in the first chapter of this study, but only in superficial matters like setting and tone: a visually-oriented poet might come away from a performance of the *Ring* with visual impressions like brandished swords, and assume that he was a Wagnerian because he wrote a drama where a sword was brandished (perhaps with vague indications in the stage directions that there was to be some kind of musical heaving going on). In point of fact, Wagner's operas are powerful for musical reasons, specifically his development of the *leitmotiv* as a means of unifying and intensifying the drama. I will use *leitmotiv* in its dictionary sense, of a melody that is associated with a character or an idea. The "Siegfried" theme (melody) is first heard in a straightforward, lusty version played by a solo horn, and it establishes the young Siegfried as a rowdy adolescent; it is repeated with great variety of mood throughout the subsequent action, culminating in a full symphonic version at Siegfried's death in his maturity. It will be seen that Edwin Arlington Robinson deduced the poetic possibilities of this device, not, I would suspect, in any bookish way, but simply by repeated hearings of the Wagner operas. I find no evidence that any of his contemporaries did: invoking the name of Wagner does not make them Wagnerians.

Second, it should be pointed out that, although Cram's *Excalibur* fell by the aesthetic wayside long ago, it is now easy to find, thanks to The Camelot Project, a website of the University of Rochester, which

---

[5]   Cram 1969, 93

is a collection of Arthurian texts, pictures and lists that includes not only well-known works like Tennyson's *Idylls of the King*, but also those that have not stood the test of time, which would include most of the works to be examined in this study, since the whole Merlin genre has fallen by the wayside. The accuracy of the texts included is exemplary, as comparison with the out-of-print originals will show, and the site is very valuable as a source of leads and ideas that can be followed up on using the inter-library loan resources of the library. It will be cited in this study as "Rochester," and — *caveat lector!* — *only* as "Rochester." The same will be true for IBDB and IMDb, the Internet Broadway Database and the Internet Movie Database. A website *is* a website, after all, and, although all three of these are eminently cyber-navigable with their indices, links and searches, they do not lend themselves to traditional author-page-and-line citation practice, so none will be attempted on short works; for longer works, I will include "guideposts" like stanza numbers and act-and-scene numbers as they seem helpful.

The third preliminary point that needs to be made is that, although *Excalibur* is in the Arthurian mainstream insofar as Merlin is depicted as an aged counselor of the king, Cram's play is outside the mainstream in a crucial detail: the importance accorded to the sword. The sword is clearly more important than the young king who wields it. After the young king's first triumph on the field, he proclaims:

> King Arthur: Give me no honour, lords;
> What brought I, save the brawn of rugged arms?
> If ye would glorify the holy thing
> That won the day, look on this awful Sword
> That hews untramelled victory, whoe'er
> May hap to wield him.   Hail Excalibur,
> And heap your thanks on Merlin, not on me.

This is a technocrat's touch, the glorification of the gadget; not surprisingly, we also find the other side of the coin, distrust of human weakness.   Arthur is, in fact, a great disappointment, because he has "bartered England for an harlot's kiss."   Merlin, having cast Arthur's horoscope (II.3), had ordered the king to "Swear on thy knighthood and the holy Cross / That thou wilt cast away all love and lust," because "Who plays with either perils all things else."   Merlin practices what he preaches, having just withstood the wiles of a seductress, but the impetuous Arthur insists on following his heart, with the disastrous results that Merlin has predicted.   The young King's success depends on his acquiescence to Merlin's word: Arthur is thus little more than Merlin's puppet.   In the last scene of that work, Merlin sighs,

> Oh, what a thing is man,
> When he has cast away the flimsy guise
> The world bestows to veil his nakedness.
> And I must work with such unhandy tools
> As these to carve a kingdom.

Merlin, in other words, is something of an architect.   *Excalibur,* wrote Cram, "fell perfectly flat, and has dropped wholly out of mind.   All the same, I still hold to a private conviction that it is the best thing I ever wrote and some day it may be discovered."[6]

Twenty years later, during his 1915-16 tenure as head of the Architecture Department at M.I.T., there occurred another revealing episode in Cram's long and distinguished career, his commission to stage a pageant to celebrate the fiftieth anniversary of that institution. He was given "twenty thousand dollars for expenses, a body of two thousand students," and a free hand.   "The general idea was the triumph of man over the forces of nature," and the allegorical content was as thick as anything in the fourteenth century.   Cram describes the spectacle in his autobiography:

---

[6]   Cram 1969, 94

Water and steam mains were brought in for particular effects, lighting pits sunk in the central area, and batteries of searchlights of different colours were ranged along the parapets of the buildings...[A] throne was raised for His Excellency the Governor, with flanking thrones for the Mayors of Boston and Cambridge. At the river end of the area there was a semicircle of six thrones for personages representing Earth, Air, Fire, Water, Steam, and Electricity, with, in the centre, a female figure, the Time Spirit, in a sheath gown of gold tissue... We started off with a Dance of Primitive Man – some forty naked youths, elegantly browned. From this howling mob Prometheus emerged...Then came, as I remember, dances of all the Elements, with liberal use of steam, water fountains, electric lights, and coloured fires where required.   Then we had the "March of Time," a thousand men on each side of the Governor's throne...[Many, many other allegorical figures followed]   It was all very symbolic and optimistic"[7]

And where was Cram himself?   "As director of the whole affair, I appeared as Merlin..."

As dominating as Cram was in his day, his literary work will be of only secondary importance in this study.   I mention his efforts to show that Merlin was not the exclusive property of scribblers.   Active minds from other disciplines made detours to deal with this subset of Arthuriana: John Veitch (1829-1894) was a professor of logic in Scotland who wrote a ruminative, introspective drama *Merlin*; Lambert A. Wilmer (1805-1863) was a crusading American newspaper editor remembered for defending the posthumous reputation of his friend Edgar Allan Poe, whose contribution to the continuum is a drama set in the New World, on the banks of the Hudson, and Wilfred Scawen Blunt (1840-1922), an eccentric patrician who wrote Merlin lyrics

---

[7]   Cram, 1969 215-216

using Arabic verse techniques, but with eccentric patrician themes. Although the music of opera composer Henry Hadley is only incidental to this study, the libretto Hadley used is relevant, being by Ethel Watts Mumford (1878-1940), a well-known playwright, short story writer, and wit of her day.

Her name brings us back to literature, and in fact most of the Merlin-inspired efforts to be examined in this study were not labors of love by architects on holiday, but were the work of poets plying their craft, like Richard Hovey, and like the two central authors of this study, Edwin Arlington Robinson (1869-1935) and Laurence Binyon (1869-1943). Yet common to professional writers and occasional writers alike is the way that Merlin inspired them to produce works that were utterly different from their trademark styles. Robinson had been a miniaturist until the publication of his book-length *Merlin* in 1917; Binyon's literary work, although wide-ranging, had always been mainstream until he wrote the nightmarish and exotic *The Madness of Merlin*; and until he wrote the bombastic *Quest of Merlin,* Hovey's themes had been those common to dapper young college men at the turn of his century: wanderlust, merrymaking, and the avoidance of gainful employment. Mumford was no exception in that her melodramatic foray into Merliniana was also utterly atypical of her work up to 1907, when *Merlin and Vivian* was premiered. She had co-authored insouciant works like *The Cynic's Calendar of Revised Wisdom* (1904), its sequel *The Entirely New Cynic's Calendar of Revised Wisdom* (1905), and *The Auto Guest Book: being the maxims of Punbad the Railer, garaja of the Pun-job, vice-roysterer of Notsopoor* (1906). There is not a trace of insouciance, however, in the grimly serious libretto she wrote for the operatic *Merlin and Vivian,* set to music by Henry Hadley: she portrays Merlin as helplessly under Vivian's spell, bewitched by a magic ring. When Vivian receives it from Morgan-le-Fay, she sings, *forte, deciso,*

> Give me the ring of Love and Hate!
> My hand shall be as the hand of fate;

He shall find Death when he seeks a mate,
Morgan-le-Fay![8]

She is the conventional stock mezzo-soprano Jezebel. Hadley's setting is also conventional, being purely Wagnerian villain-music, with the orchestral part alternating between forceful unisons with the soloist and chordal outbursts, rushing scales leading to downward-tramping bass lines, minor chords, diminished chords, key changes, every trick in the book of the composer of that era. Unfortunately for Hadley, these same techniques were soon to be done to death by thousands upon thousands of accompanists of the silent movies of the day. I do not know if Henry Hadly ever saw the slender volume called *Musical Accompaniment of Moving Pictures: A Practical Manual for Pianists and Organists and an Exposition of the Principles Underlying the Musical Interpretation of Moving Pictures,* by Edith Lang and George West (Boston: Boston Music Company, 1920), but if he did, he must have died a little. Beginning on page 20 is do-it-yourself melodrama music of exactly the kind in his *Merlin and Vivian.* The crowning irony was that it had been reprinted by G. Schirmer, the same company that had published his opera in 1907!

We must not get ahead of ourselves, however. The fact is that Hadley did write his opera in 1907, not 1920, and G. Schirmer did see fit to publish it, and its Wagnerian echoes still sounded fresh. Ralph Adams Cram would have approved. Speaking of his first hearing of Wagner, he wrote, "It is really not too much to say that with the 'Ring' operas, heaven opened for me. Then and there I became a besotted Wagnerite, and have remained so to this day, holding stubbornly to my idol when later my musical companions rejected him in their superiority and, after many years, witnessing his reinstatement in much of his old glory."[9]

---

[8]   Hadley v
[9]   Cram, 1969, 8

Hovey's *The Quest of Merlin* is equally besotted, featuring norns, "valkyrs," a visit to Valhalla, and bacchants à la *Tannhäuser.* There is also a scene where Merlin encounters Titania, Oberon and the fairies à la Goethe's *Faust.* This may remind the reader of Cram's M.I.T. spectacle, but it is important to remember that Hovey was no amateur: he had already earned not one niche, but two in English literature, and distinguished ones at that. The works of Maurice Maeterlinck were introduced to American readers through his translations, which, for accuracy and taste, are models of the translator's art. The three Vagabondia books are models of craftsmanship and sparkle. In Jessie B. Rittenhouse's *The Younger American Poets,* a fascinating time capsule published in 1904, it is the chapter on Hovey that has pride of place, and it is Hovey's picture that faces the frontispiece. He had a large readership, including, as will be seen, yet another besotted Wagnerite, Edwin Arlington Robinson.

Yet for Hovey, Merlin proved to be a Circe. Consider two passages from *The Marriage of Guinevere: A Tragedy.*[10] In Act II, Scene 1,

> Dagonet: She cries "boy" too loudly. Oh, la la! Ostriches, ostriches!
> Morgause: Come, let's to tennis.

Tennis? And in Act III, Scene 3 we read

> Merlin: What, were you in the pillory, Dagonet?
> Dagonet: Long enough to feel an imaginary ruff about my neck still.

A charitable reader may wish to believe that Hovey was being tongue-in-cheek, that no writer of his reputation would be guilty of Arthurian ostriches, Arthurian tennis and Arthurian ruffs, but with the

---

[10] Rochester

exception of a witty bacchanal in *The Quest of Merlin,* there is nothing tongue-in-cheek about Hovey's Arthurian plays; they are ponderous, elephantine—Wagnerian.

Stark Young (1881-1963) would enjoy enormous success in New York as a theater critic, playwright and novelist, but his venture into Arthuriana, *Guenevere* (1906), written during his years as a professor at the University of Mississippi, is pure fustian.   It is hard to imagine that the following passage was the work of the polished, urbane Young. From Act II:

> Arthur: There's foulness in thy words, I like it not.
> Mordred: 'Twere best forgotten all. Why should we credit Vile
> slander. Thou knowest—
> Arthur: I had some warning of this same thing once From
> Merlin, the wizard, long before I took The daughter of
> Leodograunce to wife.But when I saw her I did heed
> him not.[11]

It is equally hard to imagine the busy journalist and editor John Reade (1837-1901) veering from his usual subjects, nostalgia for his native Ireland and praise of his adopted Canadian home, but so he did with "The Prophecy of Merlin," set after Arthur's last great battle, after Bedevere has just thrown Arthur's sword back to the Lady of the Lake; he collapses, weakened by his wounds.   Merlin appears and tends to him, and as part of his bedside manner, prophesies.   His prophecies sound increasingly familiar, until the sequel to his account of three ancient queens, in which he gives away Reade's game.

> And she, the fourth fair tenant of the throne,
> Heir to the ripe fruit of long centuries,   450.
> Shall reign o'er such an empire, and her name,
> Clasping the trophies of all ages, won

---

[11] Rochester

By knightly deeds in every land and sea,
Shall be VICTORIA.[12]

From the standpoint of technique, it would have been more efficient to write a praise-poem as a praise-poem instead of the roundabout expedient of embedding it in a prophecy, but it must be conceded that Reade was following ancient precedent: Virgil has a eulogy in the form of a prophecy in the sixth book of the *Aeneid,* when one of the souls of Roman heroes-to-come is identified as the recently-deceased nephew of Augustus.   Lines 868-886 are a lament for what might have been, expressed as fear for what might happen: Anchises says

> *heu, miserande puer, si qua fata aspera rumpas,*   882
> *tu Marcellus eris.*
> ("Alas, pitiable boy, if you can break harsh fate, you will be [a] Marcellus."   The second of these two lines contains an artful ambiguity: Marcellus was the name of   Augustus's nephew, thus, "you will be Marcellus," but it was also the name of a Roman general mentioned in line 855, *insignis spoliis Marcellus opimis,* ["Marcellus, famous for the highest honors"], and thus "you will be [a second] Marcellus.")

Although uncommon, this device is not unknown in English poetry: Shakespeare's *Henry VIII* ends with one, a "prophecy" about the baby Elizabeth (V.5.14-62), almost certainly written post-mortem, which means that, for all its huffing and puffing, the play fizzles out with a recapitulation of yesterday's news.   The Bard knew better, as can be seen in the joking prophecy of a prophecy in *Lear* (III.2.95), which is also one of only two references to Merlin found in his poetry.

> Fool: This prophecy Merlin shall make, for I live before his time.

---

[12] Rochester

George Darley (1795-1846), a Dubliner whose professional life was spent in London, also used this device on Victoria's behalf, in "Merlin's Last Prophecy."

> Rapt Merlin sings: "where a strengthless woman
> This sceptre holds with a firm strain,
> That Land, maugre East and Western foeman,
> Shall rule both East and Western main..."[13]

Again, the "Last Prophecy" is very different from the bulk of his work.   Darley lived well on the income from two of his books, *A System of Popular Geometry* and *Familiar Astronomy*, which brought him money enough to travel through the museums of Europe, and thus led to a secondary career as an art critic.   His lighthearted play *Sylvia, or The May Queen* was a commercial and critical success.[14]   Yet his belletristic work, his criticism especially, is frequently marred by bitterness and jealousy.   "I am an involuntary misanthrope, by reason of an impediment which renders society and me burthensome to each other."[15]   He had what was then called a "hesitation:"   a stammer, evidently a severe one.

In contrast to these stodgy affirmations of the status quo, the subject of Merlin could also inspire wildness, exoticism, like "Merlin's Youth," where the wizard *en herbe*, "dark-haired and dark of eye, / Ever the first to court a danger shown," is not seeking wisdom, but pursuing a girl.   This young daredevil has just swum in the dark of night through rough water to where this beautiful Yberha ("pronounced nearly to rhyme with the Italian word *guerra*," the poet informs us) is, and finds her alone, in the middle of a magical rite.   In the fourth stanza he offers her his company and his protection.

---

[13]   Rochester
[14]   Darley, 1979, 22
[15]   Darley, 1892, viii

> Proud of my power, shamed of my nakedness;
> Not caring what this maid with golden tress
> Thought of my sudden speech.[16]

Yberha is contemptuous of Merlin's offer. She calls up a wolf pack to test him.

> And round the wolves were seated. Panting tongue,
> Sharp teeth in cruel jaw, that hungry hung
> Under the gleaming eyes; and all the air
> Was noisome with their scent.

One of the animals is the wolf whose mate and two cubs Merlin has recently killed. It recognizes Merlin, and is about to lunge at him, but is stopped by Yberha's spell. The tension of the scene in the ninth stanza is remarkable.

> She struck her little hand across his ears—
> "Down, rascal! Hast no manners for my friend?
> Kiss, dog, where I have kissed."—I saw him bend,
> I felt his mouth drip hot and hungry tears
> Over my feet; and then from foot to head
> He slavered me—whose cubs I had laid dead—
> With teeth, and shining eyes, and hair bristling in hate and dread.

The University of Rochester's Camelot Project website gives the author of this fine poem as George Bidder, but this proved to be a pseudonym. It should be noted immediately that this is a daring pseudonym, since the fame of mathematician, architect and engineer George Parker Bidder (1806-1878) in Victorian England was equal to that of Thomas Edison in the United States; his son, also named

---

[16] Rochester

George, was a famous London attorney; there were two other contemporary George Bidders of some reputation as well. Establishing the poem's authorship proved to be a merry chase. Eventually the answer came via e-mail from Robert Sharp, the archivist of Britain's National Museum of Science and Industry.

> The author was not George Parker Bidder I, the engineer, nor his son GPB II the barrister, killed after being knocked down by a tram in 1896…Oddly, it was someone later known as Mary Porter…She appears to have written songs, poems, many religious pieces and even some novels, being active between about 1889, when she wrote the novel *Westminster Cloisters*, and 1938…[She was] also styled Mrs. Horace Porter and even M. Bidder. It seems likely that she was born Mary Bidder but called herself George Bidder before marrying Horace Porter and writing the bulk of her works as Mary Porter.[17]

We have another example, then, of how the Merlin theme inspired a writer to produce a work atypical of her norm, since "Merlin's Youth" is about a sensual, reckless lover-boy who learns magic as an afterthought.

Just as England had many Bidders, Scotland had many Buchanans, and many of them were named Robert, so tracking down the author of "Merlin's Tomb" was another turn in the House of Mirrors; the results were instructive, however. The poet's father (also named Robert Buchanan) was an Owenite pamphleteer and lecturer, and like father, like son. Young Robert (1841-1901) is remembered in literary criticism for his article "The Fleshly School of Poetry," which provoked celebrated counterattacks from Swinburne and Dante Gabriel Rosetti. In his time he was a successful dramatist, but the bulk of his work is poetry, splendidly vigorous agitprop, identified as being in the

---

[17] Sharp

socialistic Owen tradition by titles like "The Lords of Bread" and "The Cry from the Mine." He was a poet of modernity, of the here and now, a celebrator of the new woman; yet when he came to write a Merlin poem, the results were utterly atypical of his *oeuvre*: Merlin is neither a sinister exploiter nor one of the *damnées de la terre,* but a mere illusionist, who

> can bid the bright noontide
> Turn to a midnight gloom,
> And toothless crone seem bonny bride
> To mock the gay bridegroom.

Nor is Viviane the independent and admirable woman that Buchanan elsewhere extolls. How does she get Merlin's spell? She sleeps with him.

> Ne'er loved the Lady Viviane,
> It seemed so fondly well,
> And long I ween ere morning dawn,
> She learned that fatal spell![18]

Buchanan included only a few of his medieval poems in his complete works, and none of his Arthurian ones; to one biographer this suggested "that the poet, or possibly...his posthumous editor, came to feel that they were unworthy,"[19] but this is too severe. As poems, they can stand with Buchanan's other early works; the problem with them is that their tone and message are completely uncharacteristic of Buchanan's work at any other stage in his career.

Let us pause to recapitulate. The Merlin story attracted a great deal of talent; and when dealing with Merlin many writers produced works that were completely different from their norm. Interest in a seer is not surprising, since an important theme of the late nineteenth

---

[18] Rochester
[19] Cassidy 84

and early twentieth century is the dilemma of the visionary, the scientist-visionary with disturbing theories or the artist-visionary with a disturbing aesthetic.   It is logical that the image of a seer in the toils of a Jezebel would resonate, since the increasing presence of women in many fields was an unsettling development that called for commentary.

Merlin, then, was an appropriate subject for the times, but it is only a subset of Arthuriana, which in turn is only a subset of medievalism.   Why medievalism in modern times?   The answer to that question might have to do with a utopian sort of nostalgia, contrasting the past, frequently portrayed as a golden age, with the crass, materialistic present.   Cram wrote,

> I suppose—at least I shall assume—that, for the major part, we realize that there is a marked difference between the art of the last hundred years and that of the five preceding millennia; a difference in motive, in approach, in the agencies of production, and in the quality and content of the results obtained.   I shall also assume that the most of us would be glad if the elder ways, as above, could be brought back, and this whether we are content with the contemporary showing, or profoundly discontented.[20]

This sort of nostalgia is not limited to Cram; one feels it between the lines in other authors as well, and it is important to understand it as a background influence.   There is a limit, however, as to how broad a study can be, and medieval or Arthurian questions are impossibly broad. Speaking of his research in Arthuriana, James D. Merriman, writing in the *Philological Quarterly,* states that, "Over the years I have managed to locate and examine nearly a hundred works by more than sixty authors."[21]   Yet Merriman's area of interest is quite limited: he is concerned with the nineteenth century, or, as he wittily puts it, "to

---

[20] Cram, 1969, 300
[21] Merriman 246-7

Arthur's triumphant return to Victorian England."[22]   Since that time, Arthurian and medieval themes have inspired such a flood of creative work, especially given their success in media that did not even exist then, television and film, that it would be beyond the scope of any one study even to catalogue it all.

This study will have a very narrow focus, on the subset of the Arthurian tradition where the central character is Merlin.   This will specifically involve a close reading of Edwin Arlington Robinson's *Merlin* and *The Madness of Merlin* by Laurence Binyon.   These fine works will illustrate the very different ways in which the Merlin story could be adapted as to tone, message, and aptness for the times. Robinson wrote in the shadow of World War I, and Binyon wrote in the shadow of World War II, but "the times" will of necessity refer to somewhat earlier works known to the readers of those days.   The reader, after all, *is* a reader, with expectations based on previous readings.   The readers of Robinson's *Merlin* knew Tennyson's version of the tale, and critics of the day were quick to point out Robinson's innovations.   In turn, Binyon's readers not only knew their Tennyson, but their Robinson as well, and they recognized Binyon's novelties in his very unconventional drama.   Tennyson's Vivien is a she-devil, pure and simple, who wheedles, rages and weeps until Merlin gives her the spell that will destroy him; she has no discernable motivation: she is simply malicious.

By contrast, Robinson's story is replete with subtle touches that keep the reader off balance.   Dagonet says, for example, that Merlin is hexed, that Vivian is an enchantress who sings:

> To Merlin, till he trembles in her arms
> And there forgets that any town alive
> Had ever such a name as Camelot.[23]

---

[22] Merriman 253
[23] Robinson 1937, 239-40

The reader later finds, to his surprise, that Dagonet is wrong, however: Merlin is in fact free to leave Vivian at any time.   He says to the gate-keeper of Vivian's pleasure-garden, thanking him for relaying a verbal message, and alluding to the loud clanging of the gate,

> "I like you and I like your memory,"
> Said Merlin, curiously, "but not your gate.
> Why forge for this elysian wilderness
> A thing so vicious with unholy noise?"—
> "There's a way out of every wilderness
> For those who dare or care enough to find it,"
> The guide said...[24]

Binyon has no temptress at all, but a benefactress.   As will be shown, his *The Madness of Merlin* is not only non-Tennysonian, but non-Arthurian.   Analysis of the two works requires very different approaches.

The Robinson *Merlin* will involve, first of all, sifting through a secondary literature of very uneven quality.   Up to about 1920 Robinson was considered avant-garde, and so was noted only by connoisseurs like critic-poet Amy Lowell and critic-editor Harriet Monroe.

Next comes a series of adulatory biographical potboilers inspired by the take-off in Robinson's career that began in the 1920's and culminated in the best-seller status of *Tristram* (1927).   So great was his success that Stark Young, writing to Allen Tate two years after Robinson's death, a college Arthurian no more, but a New York literary insider, would hint at a cabal: "You may or may not know the extent to which the Van Doren clique or claque—then ruling the waves—put over *Tristram* by making it the Book League (?) book. EA's best friend, executor etc. is an old friend of mine.   I've heard the ins and outs."[25]   Young is referring to "the Van Doren Trust," the

---

[24]   Robinson 1937, 262
[25]   Young, 1975, 688

brothers Mark and Carl Van Doren and their wives, who were very influential in New York publishing in the Twenties,[26] and to the Literary Guild, which made *Tristram* its book of the month selection when it appeared in 1927. Also appearing in 1927 was Mark Van Doren's study of Robinson, which is mostly boosterism: Robinson's Arthurian poems have "no equal, I think, in all of the poetry since the Middle Ages which has treated those themes...to Mr. Robinson [the Arthurian setting is] a scene, a background, against which the symbols wherethrough he interprets human motive may be grandly projected...Mr. Robinson, starting from Camelot, has attached his imagination to the farthest walls of the human world."[27] If this be evidence for a 1927 cabal, what of it? *Tristram* is Robinson's masterpiece. One only wishes, reviewing his career, that the cabal had begun its machinations sooner. Whether the adulatory potboilers were the cause or the effect of Robinson's belated fame is beyond the scope of this study. Suffice it to say that as biography or as analysis they are not very informative.

After them, though, comes silence. Chard Powers Smith, a man of letters in his own right, besides being the most sympathetic biographer imaginable (in his account of his first meeting with Robinson he refers to E.A. as "God"[28]), concedes that

> Soon after Robinson's death in '35, the modern movement of artistry in poetry which he had introduced denied him. By the beginning of the War, his prophetic affirmations were not only unread but unknown. Of his great poems only the tragic negations *Eros Turannos* and *Mr. Flood's Party* survived, and chiefly he was and is known for his clever, thumbnail dramas such as *Richard Cory* and *Miniver Cheevy.* No obliteration of a prophet could be more complete.[29]

---

[26] Kunitz 1143
[27] Van Doren 66-7
[28] Smith 8
[29] Smith xii

In the late 1960's, at about the time of the centennial of the poet's birth, some critics roused themselves for Ellsworth Barnard's centennial critical anthology (1969), and Coxe (1969) and Franchere (1968) published their studies. Beginning in the 1970's, Colby College came to specialize in Robinson criticism, but there has been no Robinson revival. Tellingly, these studies are almost all about Robinson's all-too familiar short lyrics; the book-length poems, of which *Merlin* was the first, typically receive only cursory mention. It is by no means uncommon for a survey to devote less space to *Merlin* than to, for example, "Miniver Cheevy." Just as much an issue as quantity, however, is quality, since the commentary on the longer poems seems to proceed from the assumption that a long poem is the result of mere garrulousness: the readings are uniformly careless, and miss not only the intricacies and subtleties of *Merlin,* but even its sturcture. I hope that I may be proven wrong, but to the best of my knowledge, this study appears to be the first ever to present an accurate time line of the plot of the epic, one that takes into account Robinson's not-especially-daring use of flashback, and that takes at face value the narrative as it stands on the page.

Binyon's case is the mirror image of Robinson's. Both men were born in 1869, but other than that they had little in common: Robinson labored in obscurity until middle age; Binyon, as is made clear in Hatcher's definitive biography, had been discovered early (his school nickname was "the Bard"),[30] and early on became a citizen of "Little London," the ultra-smart Oxbridge elite where everyone of importance knew everyone else, and which guaranteed lifelong readership and respectful reviews for his verse. The verse dramas he wrote were staged forthwith, produced with first-rate talent in respected theaters, and newspaper coverage of their premieres was extensive. These connections also put him in touch with money: looking for a Maecenas for his first drama, *Attila,*

---

[30] Hatcher 6

[I]n July 1906, Binyon approached the 26 year old Lord Howard de Walden...One of the richest men in England, he was just embarking on his career as a patron of the arts... [Binyon wrote to Charles Ricketts, the play's designer] 'I have now met him, & told him I wanted 3000£. Though taken aback, he did *not* say "You be damned", but thought "something might be arranged."'[31]

The production set new standards for opulence.

It climaxed in the famous all red final scene with Attila, the tributary kings gathered for his wedding feast, Ildico's attendants, and the dancing girls all in blood red among red pillars and against a red backdrop, and amid this sea of blood Ildico, preparing to murder Attila with his own sword, standing like a sword herself in a silver and white wedding dress with a long silver train, her hair ornamented with horns and shells, her arms entwined with golden snakes.[32]

The differences go on and on: Binyon was multitalented, and was respected not only as a poet and dramatist, but as an art historian and interpreter of Oriental painting and its Buddhist background. He had a position at the British museum, acquiring Oriental art works and collaborating with distinguished Orientalists. Binyon was a patriot, what would today be called a propagandist for the British Empire as a civilizing and pacifying force; Robinson was a recluse, a bachelor; Binyon was known as "a poet of marriage."[33]

It could be said that Binyon and Robinson have in common the fact that their poetic legacies consist of only a few short "hits," despite the fact that the bulk of their output consists of ambitious, long-winded

---

[31] Hatcher 149
[32] Hatcher 150
[33] Hatcher 154

works.   Binyon's case is extreme: his monument boils down to only
four lines of poetry: not even a complete poem, but one stanza from

> ...his 1914 war elegy 'For the Fallen'.   Recited annually at
> Remembrance Day services for the dead of two world wars,
> carved on thousands of tombstones and war memorials, its
> central stanza is so familiar as to be virtually anonymous,
> wholly absorbed into the ritual substructure of British cultural
> life:
>
> > *They shall not grow old as we that are left grow old:*
> > *Age shall not weary them, nor the years condemn.*
> > *At the going down of the sun and in the morning*
> > *We will remember them.*
>
> Eighty years on, these ritual cadences continue to fulfill a
> need.[34]

The reason that the other six stanzas have not stood the test of
time, in my opinion, is the same for the oblivion to which the rest of
Binyon's corpus has been consigned: his vocabulary is a little fussy,
a little stilted, and the rhymes are a little too clever; Binyon never
really refined the ore until his last poems and the poetic drama *The
Madness of Merlin* (1943, although not published until posthumously
in 1947), when the poetic prissiness was finally burned away, in my
opinion, by the grimness, the ugliness of the times: the British national
agony of the Blitz, Binyon's personal trauma of his narrow escape
from Greece just before it fell, his knowledge that his one-time protege
Ezra Pound was broadcasting propaganda for the Fascists, and his
witnessing of the witch hunt sponsored by the British propaganda
machine that, as an exercise in morale building, systematically ruined
the reputation of literary icon P. G. Wodehouse (who was accused of

---

[34] Hatcher v

treason while wasting away in a German concentration camp), simply left no room for archness. Binyon came close to saying as much in 1941, when speaking of metrical technique:

> It may be the infection of the moderns, but I think it is something in the air these troublous times; somehow the traditional movement of blank verse doesn't seem to correspond to one's needs: it is too smooth.[35]

The source for Binyon's *The Madness of Merlin* is the medieval Latin *Vita Merlini*. The relationship between the modern drama and the medieval poem is subtle: it is partly a translation, partly a reworking, but is also a continuation and an amplification of the original story, picking up where the former work leaves off, and adding episodes to the main line of its narration. The *Vita Merlini* is thus everywhere and nowhere. In addition to a literary translation, I have done a close translation of this work, so that the reader can see the *Vita Merlini* fresh, as Binyon, a first-rate Latinist in a generation of first-rate Latinists, saw the *Vita Merlini*.

Laurence Binyon's *The Madness of Merlin* and Edwin Arlington Robinson's *Merlin* show how far the sources could be stretched as to tone, message, and aptness for their times; they also illustrate how divergent the approaches could be. These two versions of the Merlin legend are worth discussion not only for their place in the Arthurian tradition and for their period interest, but also for their intrinsic merit. Robinson and Binyon were recognized as major poets by the discerning readers of their era; poetry has since come to be defined in terms of shock value and eccentricity, but the pendulum will surely come unstuck some day.

---

[35] Binyon, 1947, xi

Table of Contents

Robinson's *Merlin* and its Context

Que diable faites-vous dans cette galère? is how Harriet Monroe, the influential editor of *Poetry,* began her review of Edwin Arlington Robinson's *Merlin* shortly after the poem's publication in 1917. Monroe's review is an interesting time capsule, because at the beginning of the twenty-first century the *galère* of the beginning of the twentieth has been forgotten. Monroe and other critics, however, saw Robinson, the pure artist, as joining a rather crowded club: *"Que diable faites-vous dans cette galère?* one might ask Mr. Robinson when one finds him trying to resuscitate Merlin and Vivian and King Arthur, and others of that overworked and much over-poeticized crowd."[1] Friendly reviewers made the same point: in the March 31, 1917 *Boston Transcript,* an otherwise unidentified "D. L. M." included the caveat, "Today our poetry-reading public has been thoroughly saturated with Arthurian lore." Monroe finished her article with a restrike: "It is queer what a fascination those old tales have for the most indigenous poets! One would have pronounced Mr. Robinson immune—now that he has had a light case of the fever perhaps he will be."[2] We have introduced the important members of the *galère* in the previous chapter; this one will be concerned with those in which Merlin is the aged seer, a group which I will call the Tennyson continuum.

The influence of Tennyson on Arthurian literature may be gauged by examining the other reviews that greeted Robinson's *Merlin.*

---

[1] Monroe, 1917, 211
[2] Monroe, 1917, 213

They invariably compare Robinson's verse to Tennyson's, sometimes implicitly, but more usually explicitly, as did Stark Young in his review for the *New Republic.*

> The inevitable and commonplace observation, of course, wherever the Arthurian material appears, involves Tennyson... Tennyson's verse—often beautiful, nearly always musical, often diluted for mild intelligences, and sometimes saccharine—and the secure popularity of his central conceptions of the legend, have established almost a monopoly for him...But the fad of despising him is very often carried so far that it becomes only another recognition of his importance.[3]

Young's article itself is a recognition of that importance in that the thrust of his review is concerned with demonstrating that *Merlin* is, in fact, Tennysonian, and therefore un-Robinsonian in the sense that Robinson had abandoned his trademark style.   Young offers a novel thought experiment to clinch his argument: he splices a passage from Tennyson's "Holy Grail" onto one from Robinson's *Merlin* and challenges his readers to tell where one starts and the other stops. Young's review is unique, then, in producing a literal continuum to illustrate a literary one.

Stark Young ought not to be censured for the perfunctory nature of his review: it is, after all, a review.   A fuller study of *Merlin,* however, will involve other parameters of traditional analysis: the state of the genre as Robinson and his readers knew it; Robinson's innovations relative to that genre; Robinson himself, since much of his poetry is autobiographical, despite his repeated statements to the contrary; *Merlin* as seen by the reviewers of the day and as seen by the critics of the Robinson centennial; an examination of the symbolism and imagery of the poem.

---

[3]   Young, 1917, 250

The present study will add a new parameter to the question, a close look at the internals of the poem with an eye to two techniques which, to my knowledge, have never been discussed, what I term leitmotivs and jolts.

The word "salamander" will illustrate the first of these two devices. At the beginning of the poem an old warrior tells his comrade "That all your certainties have bruises on 'em, / And all your pestilent asseverations / Will never make a man a salamander—"[4] 1,193 lines later, Merlin's lover will muse about a primordial time "When the world was young / And you and I were salamanders."[5] It will not do to go into a possible symbolism of "salamander," since the word is used only twice in the poem, and in mutually exclusive senses, that of the fireproof creature of classical mythology in the first instance, and in the second, the Darwinian common ancestor splashing happily about in the primordial slime. What we are left with is simply the word and its echo.

Merlin's dark-haired lover Vivian wears red, and so appears "crimson and black" during their first evening together; at the end of the poem Merlin looks over Camelot and sees "crimson and black." Again, the contexts, the beginning of a romance on one hand and the ending of a civilization on the other, cancel each other out, and we are left with simply the words and their echo, although the more frequent occurrence of this leitmotiv means that there will be not one echo, but many, each one varied and made more expressive by Robinson's poetic skill.

Eventually, the echoes reach a poetic critical mass which gives the poem an auditory power that may not be appreciated in these days of silent reading. Harriet Monroe's dismay at Robinson's choice of subject may have distracted her from this parameter in 1917, but her comments in her 1926 critique of Robinson's *The Man Who Died Twice* show that she sensed that there was more to the poetry than the flicker of visual symbols:

---

[4] Robinson, 1937 (*Collected Poems,* to be abbreviated *CP*), 242
[5] *CP*   278

...in honor of his tragic agony the poet tolls deep bells and beats muffled drums...It is quite wonderful what the poet has done with his simple instrument of blank verse, piling up splendid chords that seem to reverbrate [sic] through cathedral aisles as he records disaster...

The poem is itself a symphony. Never has Robinson rolled out such magnificent harmonies as in the superb climax of this poem.[6]

It will be seen that *Merlin* is germinal in this respect, and that its final scene is in fact a finale in the musical sense.

The second device, what I call jolts, refers to Robinson's insertion of surprises to wake the reader up. This can involve an abrupt insertion of detail or a laboriously-prepared crack-the-whip that can take hundreds of lines to set up. Examples of this technique will be cited in due course, as it requires more space to illustrate. For now, it is enough to observe that Robinson's craftsmanship in this regard would seem to have fallen on stony ground in this age of skim-reading: I have never seen it commented on in the Robinson literature.

First things first, however: Stark Young's monoparameter thought experiment, that of a continuum *sensu stricto* that illustrates a continuum *sensu lato*, is worth examining, so let us answer it unequivocally: Robinson certainly does belong in the Tennyson continuum: his fondness for Tennyson and his familiarity with the *Idylls of the King* antedate the composition of *Merlin* by at least twenty years. Consider this passage in a letter written at age twenty-five to a boyhood friend:

June 10, 1894

In reading Tennyson the other day, I came across a little poem in blank verse dedicated to the Princess Beatrice, in which he speaks of her marriage as "that white funeral of the single

---

[6]   Monroe, 1932, 9-10

life." A Poet Laureate is worthwhile when he says things like that. And, speaking of Tennyson, how would it do to read him some this summer? His greatest charm lies in the fact that one can read him over and over again without tiring of him. I have read *Maud* aloud three times, and am quite ready to do so again—or listen to you. Perhaps the best way to read a long poem like that is alternately. The metre, like the poem, is hard (in a certain sense) and strange. And there are always the *Idyls*.[7]

It is tempting to amend the last word to "idylls," making the reference Arthurian, but Robinson's word has one "l," so it will be taken to refer to *English Idyls and Other Poems,* which contains its own Arthurian poems. In any case, the poet's feelings about Tennyson are clear enough.

Robinson's *Merlin* is an ideal touchstone for a survey of what is the majority of the Tennysonian Merlin *galère* of his day, but this is because it is so utterly different, both in matter and manner, from the poetry of his contemporaries. Since *Merlin* is to be our reference point, let us make it our starting point.

Beginning with the bare bones, *Merlin* can be described as written in unrhymed iambic pentameter, 2,629 lines in length. Elsie Ruth Dykes Chant took a closer look in a meticulous master's thesis written in 1930; some of her findings are of interest primarily to stylometricians (the number of syllables in the poem is 26,904), but others are arresting. The number of rhythmic irregularities is vanishingly small: trochaic substitutions, that is, trochees for iambs, 90 [0.3%]; anapests for iambs, 112 [0.4%]; hexameter lines, 3; "...and in *Merlin* he writes a defective line in which there are only nine syllables."[8] This evidently refers to "Climbing, climbing, climbing,

---

[7] Robinson, 1947, 163
[8] Chant 33

all the time."[9]   In Robinson's defense, however, it should be pointed out that the previous line is hypermetric, and when read straight through, the extra syllable, the "them" of the previous line, is in effect an upbeat, as if it were "millions of / Them, climbing, climbing, climbing,   all the time;" Lines with unstressed syllabic endings number 482, a remarkable 18% of the poem.   Chant compared Robinson passages with other poets, concluding that

> In comparing the blank verse of Robinson with that of Browning and Tennyson, the results show that the trochaic substitutions and the run-on lines average about the same. However, the percentage of anapestic substitutions was much greater in Robinson's work, as was the percentage of feminine endings.   It would seem that Robinson's blank verse is much freer and more flexible than that of the other two poets, and that his freedom and flexibility are largely gained by his greater use of feminine endings.[10]

Continuing with the bare bones, we see that the poem is in seven numbered sections.   A closer look reveals that these sections are not in chronological order, which would be IVa, V, I, II, III, IVb, VI and VII .   Robinson will use flashbacks, even flashbacks within flashbacks, as jolts to keep the reader awake.   Section I is a dialogue between knights Gawaine and Dagonet concerning the return of Merlin to Arthur's realm after ten years in Vivian's pleasure-garden in Broceliande, and their forebodings as to what has prompted his return. In the second section knights Lamorak and Bedivere, later joined by Kay, converse about the crisis of the Arthur-Guinevere-Lancelot triangle, and how it is being exploited by Arthur's bastard son Modred. The third has a pessimistic audience between Arthur and Merlin, followed by an even more pessimistic one between Arthur and

---

[9] *CP*   274
[10] Chant 27

Dagonet.   Section IV begins with Arthur's regret at Merlin's decision to return to Broceliande, which merges into Vivian's misgivings about Merlin's return.   Merlin punctuates his return with a three-line "marker," which, as will be seen, is a structural leitmotiv.   Merlin, assuring her that he will not be called for again, says "Be glad or sorry, but no kings are coming. / Not Arthur, surely; for now Arthur knows / That I am less than Fate."   A flashback begins, to a period ten years earlier, recounting Merlin's first arrival at Vivian's pleasure-garden, their courtship and romance, and their idyllic life until Dagonet arrives with a summons from Arthur, which Merlin obeys.   His departure ends Section V.   Section VI begins with a paraphrase of the three-line "marker," although elaborated, as any leitmotiv should be.   "No kings are coming on their hands and knees, / Nor yet on horses or in chariots, / To carry me away from you again... / King Arthur knows that I have done with kings..."   Merlin has returned to paradise, but things are not the same.   Vivian is jealous of the attraction that the outside world, Arthur specifically, had for Merlin, and her suspicions lead to quarrels. After two more years, Merlin has a prompting that he must return a second time to Camelot.   In fact, Arthur's court is a shambles, owing to bloodshed during Lancelot's rescue of Guenevere from the stake and the demoralizing effects of the invariably fruitless quest for the Grail. He leaves Broceliande for good.   Section VII takes place at Merlin's Rock again; Bedivere is trying unsuccessfully to persuade Gawaine against a war of revenge.   After they leave, Merlin and Dagonet talk, decide that there is nothing that can be done, and walk off into the night.

We note that the poem is dedicated to one George Burnham, but this last bare bones observation must leave us unsatisfied, since it leads us to questions of context — historical, biographical and literary. How did *Merlin* fit in with the rest of 1917?   How did Edwin Arlington Robinson fit in?   What was George Burnham to him, or he to George Burnham?

None of these questions have straightforward answers, because Robinson was not only reticent about his work, but he was also reticent about his reticence, insisting that his poetry was impersonal, objective, dispassionately realistic.   We will see that this was not at all the case, and James G. Hepburn has detailed this pattern of behavior, in his "E. A. Robinson's System of Opposites," using a phrase from one of Robinson's letters.[11]   This is a euphemism, since a "system of opposites" cannot boil down to anything other than a pattern of evasion. True, Robinson did not lie, but he did fib: he did not create a phony persona, as Joaquin Miller did, but his denials of any personal, subjective content in his poems were not true, either.   *Merlin* is replete with Robinson's personal experience, but those experiences will have to be found one by one in the accounts of his contemporaries. Hepburn puts a good face on this secretiveness by suggesting that it was a defense mechanism related to a lack of self-knowledge: "A poet, of course, is not required to see himself and his poetry clearly...Any stratagem is permissible to protect poetic self-confidence from despair or self-consciousness."[12]   Yet there was nothing mysterious or hard to understand about the crises in Robinson's life: as will be seen, they were of the humiliating and public sort that anyone would want to keep secret.

Robinson's reticence about his work notwithstanding, his circle had no reticence at all, and the results are frequently like the blind men and the elephant.   Returning to the question of *Merlin*'s dedicatee: Who was George Burnham?   Robinson biographer Chard Smith gives a thumbnail vita:

George Burnham was a pure spirit who reinforced the mystical side of E.A.   At seventeen he had run away from home and progressed around the West from frontier job to frontier job, until one January night in Wyoming, having taken the wrong road, he had both feet frozen, crawled into a settlement, declared that he was not going to die, and presently had them

---

[11] Hepburn 266
[12] Hepburn 274

amputated.   As a cripple with two wooden legs he had
returned East to study law at Harvard while E.A. was a student
there in the early nineties.   They became close friends and
roommates, both then and later in New York, where Burnham
practiced law until he quit the profession, concluding that it
was suborned by the corporations...He himself was a Hindu,
and in accounting for E.A.'s mysticism, Burnham's Brahma
must be accredited at least equally with Emerson's Oversoul.[13]

Smith's 1965 account, however, is not the official biography; that
was written by Hermann Hagedorn, and published in 1939, only four
years after Robinson's death.   Hagedorn had authored an in-depth
biography of Theodore Roosevelt, had published a slangy,
rabble-rousing booklet called *You Are the Hope of the World!*, a pep
talk for the youth of America on the eve of World War I, and was an
occasional poet.   In the Robinson biography, however, his style is
prolix and imprecise: what Smith said in the first seven lines above,
takes Hagedorn a full page.   He was also addicted to purple prose, as
is shown in the conclusion of his description of Burnham:

> Robinson leapt to him as to a magnet.   His sensitive
> imagination cried out at the picture of Burnham's suffering
> and sacrifice, and all the compassion of his nature went in a
> flood to this hapless man so arbitrarily picked out by fate for
> punishment.   What did it mean?   Here was clarity of mind, a
> keen sense of justice; here was spiritual nobility, if the word
> had any meaning.   He brooded over his new friend's agony
> and made it almost his own.[14]

This paragraph leaves the reader with no doubt about Hagedorn's
thoughts, but it is an open question if it really tells about Robinson's.

---

[13] Smith 36-7
[14] Hagedorn 66

It is by no means atypical of Hagedorn's style, which is emotive and impressionistic throughout his book; this, however, is completely wrong for understanding Robinson, where accuracy with biographical details is crucial. Take, for example, the circumstances surrounding the departure from his home town of the great love of Robinson's life with her new husband, as far as the young poet knew, forever (in fact, she would later return). Scholarly digging reveals that the couple went by train; their destination was St. Louis, Missouri; the train pulled out at 4:00 p.m.; from Gardiner to St. Louis is 1,500 miles.[15] The opening to Robinson's "Cortège" is no longer obscure. "Four o'clock this afternoon, / Fifteen hundred miles away: / So it goes, the crazy tune, / So it pounds and hums all day."

To be sure, the reticent Robinson gave no hint of this during his lifetime, and so until Smith's 1965 study, his poetry was simply regarded as impenetrable. Amy Lowell, in her 1922 dunciad *A Critical Fable,* writes, "I mean, and I rather imagine you know it, / Edwin Arlington Robinson, excellent poet, / And excellent person, but vague as a wood / Gazed into at dusk…"[16]

Lowell, a true child of her time, explains this vagueness in the then-trendy Freudian terms: the poet has a complex. "…his quaint, artificial control / Is a bandage drawn tightly to hold down his soul."[17]

Even as sympathetic an observer as Chard Smith was led astray by his Freudian preconceptions, and concluded early on that Robinson had inhibitions. Smith writes of his astonishment at finding that Robinson had not been inhibited at all, merely secretive, or, to use a milder word, reticent.

> Nine or ten years later, soon after E.A. died, I was talking with Ridgely [Torrence, an old friend of Robinson's], trying to persuade him to do the official biography. In what

---

[15] Nivison 175
[16] Lowell, 1922, 26
[17] Lowell, 1922, 27

connection I don't know, I suddenly asked him, "Was E.A. celibate all his life?"   "Hell, no," said Ridgely.   "Was there one great love?"   "Yes," he said.   "It started back in Gardiner, and he fought it out in the *Octaves*.   It ended along about '08 or '09, and after that E.A. took the veil."[18]

Thirty years later Smith would write that the "system of opposites" was not so hard to understand, after all.

> On the score of discretion this outward obscurity was necessary, in the autobiographical poetry, to disguise the main characters, usually the same two or three characters, for they were his much loved, closest kin.   For the purposes of disguise he used no cryptology, no code that can be broken by some verbal key so as to reveal who is who and just what happened when.   The only key is foreknowledge of the main situations in the actual drama.   When they are understood, then each poem contributes to the understanding of the characters, especially the dramatist-actor himself, and to the development, climax, resolution, and implied preachment of his play.[19]

Having brought up the importance of biographical details for understanding Robinson's poetry, it is logical to deal with them in some detail.   For this study, however, it will not do to ask, What kind of man was Edwin Arlington Robinson?   Since *Merlin* was published in 1917, it is more to the point to ask what kind of man he was then. In 1917 he was a hopeful man, a man who had reason to believe that he was on the threshold of success.   A year before, after many years of wandering in the literary wilderness, he had finally had a success that was not merely a *succès d'estime, The Man Against the Sky*.   He had become a regular guest at the MacDowell Colony in Peterborough,

---

[18] Smith 57
[19] Smith 64

New Hampshire, the summer retreat for creative artists, "presiding, it is said, with gracious hospitality at the large table where American artists forgather for retreat and creative work,"[20] and so had a home base, an artistic family, as it were, that gave him something to look forward to in the summers.

In the years prior to 1917, however, Robinson had been a sad man, having suffered family tragedy, ill health, poverty and failure. Unfortunately for his reputation, his most frequently anthologized poems were written during this period, so for most readers he is known as a downbeat poet, the pessimist who wrote "Richard Cory." Robinson's life will merit a closer look, not only to understand *Merlin*, but also because it intersected with the careers of other authors relevant to this study.   Born in 1869, he grew up in Gardiner, Maine.   He was the youngest of three brothers, and his family was prosperous.   He attended Harvard from 1891-93, then returned to Gardiner until 1899, when he permanently moved to New York City.   This bare bones account, however, needs fleshing out.   Robinson's adolescence and his Harvard years were clouded by an intensely painful chronic mastoid infection caused by a blow to the ear by a high school teacher who caught him daydreaming in class, this in the school year of 1881-82.[21]   There must have been a grim irony in his signing his letters E. A. R., when he was suffering from the agony of an acute earache, one that lasted literally for years, "that thenceforth impaired his hearing and was a continuing menace to his brain and life.   The necessity of living with this threat deepened the gloom of his gathering interpretation of the world."[22]   In July, 1891 young Robinson "was in Boston having his ear treated.   The drum was destroyed and the bone diseased, and the advice was that he should have regular treatments in the hospital there."[23]   The pain must have been intermittent rather

---

[20] Romig 17
[21] Smith 388
[22] Smith 81
[23] Smith 110

than constant, since Robinson played the clarinet, an activity impossible with an acute earache, but it was a nagging problem. In a letter dated October 6, 1895, he apologizes to his boyhood friend Harry Smith for not writing, because "[m]y ears have been knocking a good deal, but I don't [like] to say too much about them – especially in letters – so will let that matter drop."[24]   Robinson's college days were clouded by this condition, since this letter was written three years after leaving Harvard.

Robinson suffered not only from earache, but from heartache.   In 1888 he had met the great love of his life, Emma Shepherd; in 1890 she married his older brother Herman, a businessman, which caused great tension between the brothers up until just before Herman's death in 1909.   After he died, according to Smith, Robinson still had hopes of marrying Emma, and proposed to her at regular intervals, the last occasion being in 1927, when he was fifty-eight years old.

Robinson's Harvard days were a happier interval: he grew intellectually, and made lifelong friends.   There was one area, however, where he was unsuccessful: getting noticed.   The publications available to students were dominated by golden boys from illustrious families, and by a relentless and flamboyant self-promoter named William Vaughn Moody (1869-1910).   Robinson was very much on the outside looking in on this clique.   "None of Robinson's poems was accepted by the *Monthly,* whose poetry columns he was not far wrong in thinking a monopoly of its editors.   During that academic year 1891-92, three-quarters of its verse was written by…the editorial staff, Moody appearing in almost every number."[25]

Nor did Robinson make an impression on William Lyon Phelps, who would become a well-known scholar, critic and pedagogue of the era, but who seems not to have known that Robinson had been a fellow-student of his at Harvard.   In his autobiography he wrote, "I never saw Robinson until Yale gave him the honorary degree of

---

[24] Robinson 1947, 231
[25] Neff 26

Doctor of Letters in 1922,"[26] this despite the fact that Robinson had mailed him a copy of *The Torrent and the Night Before* (1896; his first book, self-published in a run of only 300-odd copies, and therefore a book collector's grail).   "I have no recollection of reading this book, and none of acknowledging it; but I must have done both, for the next year (1897) I received a bound volume of 123 pages, called *The Children of the Night...*" (another book collector's grail).[27]

Robinson's leaving Harvard was not his idea: the money ran out. The Panic of 1893 abruptly and decisively reduced his family's income, so he was forced to return to Gardiner, where he was confronted with a series of crises.   These are worth recounting, as biographer Chard Powers Smith makes a convincing case for Robinson's poetry being dominated by these traumas, that he in effect kept writing the same poem over and over again.   There was the continual presence of his Beatrice, Emma Shepherd, still married to his brother Herman, but with a difference: the Panic had caused Herman's business interests to collapse; Herman began to drink heavily.   His mother died in 1896 (his father passed on in 1892, while Robinson was at Harvard).   His oldest brother, Dean, a physician, died in 1899 after years of mental and physical misery as a result of addiction to self-prescribed morphine. Robinson moved to New York only to face poverty, as the last recorded payments from his family's estate are from 1901.   Herman's alcoholism made him unable to provide for Emma and their children, which led Robinson to try unsuccessfully to become the family's breadwinner, one suspects for psychological reasons as well as economic ones.

According to Smith's scenario, characters like Flammonde and Richard Cory were inspired by the charming and successful Herman; "How Annandale Went Out" is an explicit account of Dean's sudden death of a morphine overdose;   Emma's divisive beauty was the model for a variety of Robinson's heroines, but most especially

---

[26]   Phelps 695
[27]   Phelps 694

Guinevere; the collapse of the family fortune would be transmuted into the fall of Camelot.   Smith's analysis runs counter to the older view of Robinson as an utterly dispassionate, totally objective analyst of human nature.   Robinson himself encouraged this view, as we shall see, but it will not stand scrutiny: the coincidences are irrefutable, and their persistence shows how psychologically "stuck" Robinson was in the not-at-all-Gay Nineties.

In "Captain Craig," much is made of the old derelict's choice of music for his funeral, of his insistence that it be Handel (from the oratorio *Saul*), not Chopin (presumably the famous funeral march from the B-flat minor piano sonata).   The closing lines of that poem are memorable.   "And all along that road the Tilbury Band / Blared indiscreetly the Dead March in Saul."[28]

Captain Craig: A Book of Poems was published in 1902; in 1915, in the play *The Porcupine,* Larry, the protagonist, is playing the violin offstage; the reader will recall that Robinson was an enthusiastic amateur clarinetist.

> Alma: Poor Rachel!   I wonder if she will ever laugh again.
>
> Stuart: Probably not—unless Larry makes her.   That fiddle of his might be of some assistance if he would only stick to the Dead March in Saul.[29]

Robinson's older brother Dean, it will be recalled, had died in 1899.   A family memoir records that "He was a Knight-Templar, and at his funeral the commandery marched in uniform to the 'Dead March' in *Saul*."[30]

Smith mentions an interesting detail in his description of Emma: "Being lightsome and nimble in all her gestures, she used her fingers when talking, and sometimes paused suddenly and looked at them."[31]

---

[28] *CP* 169
[29] Robinson, 1915, 8
[30] Nivison 181
[31] Smith 89

Not surprisingly, Guinevere (in *Lancelot*) does the same: "She looked away at a small swinging blossom, / And then she looked intently at her fingers."[32]   Not only once: "Observing her ten fingers variously, / She sighed, as in equivocal assent."[33]   Not only in *Lancelot*; in the play *Van Zorn* (1914), the stage directions for Mrs. Lovett also recall this mannerism: "[She stops and looks angrily at her fingers],"[34] and "[Mrs. Lovett sits and frowns, and looks at her hands]."[35]

Robinson's memories would not only provide poetic inspiration and impetus, but could also form a mental block.   *The Porcupine* is an instructive example of this: Larry is visiting his half-brother Rollo, amid scenes of great tension (shades of E.A. and Herman); Rollo is married to Rachel, but she does not love him (perhaps wishful thinking on E.A.'s part projected onto Herman and Emma); Mrs. Hoover does not love her husband Stuart, either (the same projection); Stuart is pursuing Alma, the protagonist's sister (another triangle); Rollo is pursuing Mrs. Hoover (still another); Rachel is trying to work up the courage to tell Larry that he, not his brother, is the father of her child (more wishful thinking on E.A.'s part, perhaps).   This is the same story told no less than seven times, evidence of obsession; and, fatally for the play, Robinson is so stymied by this recreation of his trauma that he is only able to resolve two of the subplots, and then only by the puniest of theatrical clichés: *deus ex machina* and death.   Larry writes Mrs. Hoover a check (so that she can start a new life in New York), and Rachel takes an overdose of medicine as the curtain falls. It is not necessary to be a psychologist to see how pitifully "stuck" Robinson was in this painful episode in his family's history.

The present study will build on Smith's view, but will ask a technical question: where did *Merlin* come from?   It appears

---

[32] *CP*   372
[33] *CP*   415
[34] Robinson 1914, 74
[35] Robinson 1914, 76

abruptly in Robinson's collected works, without any poetic antecedents whatever.   Until *Merlin,* Robinson had been a miniaturist.   In Amy Lowell's *A Critical Fable* she speaks of "His tight little verses an inch in diameter,"[36] and there is an element of truth there: with the exception of one long poem, "Captain Craig" (1902), the majority of his poems had been spare, tightly-written thumbnail sketches like "Richard Cory."   In fact, it is misleading to say that "Captain Craig" is a long poem, in the sense of a unified narrative: it is rather a long series of miniatures with bridges.   The fact that Robinson's next volume, *The Town Down the River* (1910), consists of nothing but "tight little poems an inch in diameter," shows that "Captain Craig" was a one-time experiment.   *The Man Against the Sky* contains one longer-than-average poem, "Ben Johnson Entertains a Man from Stratford," but it is only about one-fifth the length of "Captain Craig." Then, without any poetic antecedents whatever, comes the book-length *Merlin,* extroverted, almost operatic in tone, and unhurried, almost symphonic in movement.

This study will hold that *Merlin* is the breakthrough, the resolution of Robinson's mental blocks.   He found a vehicle where he could work through his anguish without shutting the reader out.   Both *Van Zorn* and *The Porcupine* catalogue those mental blocks: as dramas, they are insipid; for understanding *Merlin,* however, the plays are the thing.

Let us take up our account of the biographical highlights of Robinson's life where we left it, in 1901 and in increasing poverty, the payments from the estates of his father and his brother Dean dwindling to zero.   "Beginning in that fall of 1902, Robinson had no apparent means of support for about a year," recounts Smith, but also notes that Robinson may have been financially down, but not artistically out: "He tried to save up money for a new pair of pants, but when he almost had it he happened to pass the Metropolitan and spent it all on *Tristan*

---

[36] Lowell 1922, 28

und Isolde."[37]   This event would seem to be another example of Robinson's "system of opposites, since he had written to his long-term correspondent Edith Brower in 1899 that "I find that I am not a Wagnerite, after all,"[38] but in elaborating this statement, he betrays a detailed knowledge of the Wagnerian operas.   Many years later, musician friend Lewis M. Isaacs recalls Robinson's wish that he bring musical scores with him to Peterborough, but that since one guest "has endowed the place with the piano score of *Die Meistersinger...*you need not bring that with you.   You might bring *Tristan* and *Götterdämmerung* and anything else you like,"[39] and that "Wagner was the most reverberating corpse that ever was buried.   He just won't stay quiet, which must annoy his many undertakers."[40]

It would have been *Das Rheingold,* specifically the underworld scene, which would have been more apropos in those early years, as Robinson's poverty led him to find work on the construction of the New York subway system from the fall of 1903 to the summer of 1904.[41]   Moody, with whom he had reestablished contact, wrote in a letter dated December 1, 1903 that "Robinson is not much use for purposes of comradeship these days.   He is working, at a very dreary job, poor chap, and is too tired after he gets through to do much but roll into bed."[42]   For once, Hagedorn's purple prose is appropriate.

> The work was simple, too appallingly simple.   He checked the workmen in, in the morning; and out, at night; and, in the dreary hours between, paced the dark tunnel, heavy with the odor of damp clay and sickening gases, checking the loads of material as they were dumped at the gaping tunnel-mouths.

---

[37]   Smith 208
[38]   Robinson 1968, 90
[39]   Isaacs 502
[40]   Isaacs 501
[41]   Smith 388-9
[42]   Moody, 1935, 172

The ground was soft and wet, with unexpected mud-holes which the smoky kerosene lantern did not always reveal.[43]

We may ask ourselves if there is any memory of this in the stage directions to *The Porcupine,* where Larry is described thus: "He is dressed in a nondescript costume consisting chiefly of a blue pea-jacket and a pair of dingy rubber boots, into which a pair of old trousers are tucked."[44]

How much had Robinson advanced professionally since his arrival in New York City? In 1904 Jessie B. Rittenhouse published *The Younger American Poets,* a fascinating time capsule showing who was who in that year. Robinson is not even mentioned, even though Richard Hovey, Robinson's friends Ridgely Torrence (1874-1950), and Josephine Preston Peabody (1874-1922) are given a chapter and a photograph each, as was George Santayana (1863-1952), who had been a graduate student at Harvard during Robinson's enrollment there. Hovey's picture is facing the frontispiece. Fifteen other biographical chapters are devoted to other more or less forgotten bards, although it should be stated forcefully that their oblivion is more of a commentary on changing tastes than a reflection on the excellence of the poets: an unsystematic sampling reveals that some very good poetry fell by the wayside, and that is a pity. Rittenhouse gives considerable space to a discussion of Hovey's Arthurian dramas, including *The Quest of Merlin,* and this in the lead chapter, since Hovey is given pride of place. Moody is not included with "great regret" because of "circumstances incident to the copyrights."[45] One of the poets who is included, Madison Cawein (the last syllable is a homonym with "wine"), in addition to being an occasional Arthurian, is worth noting for his observations about Robinson in his correspondence. Cawein (1865-1914) was a Kentuckian who had achieved a national reputation,

---

[43] Hagedorn 1939, 202
[44] Robinson 1915, 13
[45] Rittenhouse viii-ix

thanks to the sponsorship of William Dean Howells.[46] Cawein's specialty was nature poetry, written with such an intimate knowledge of wayside flora (his father had been a herbalist) that it is hard for the city folks of today to follow him; a pity.   This familiarity with nature also affects his Arthurian poems.   Merlin is portrayed as the Tennysonian greybeard; "But still he sits there drowsing with his dreams; / A wondrous cohort hath he; many as gleams / That stab the mottled mazes of a beech;"[47] but this presupposes that the reader knows something about beech trees.   Another poem, coincidentally titled "The Knight-Errant," which will recall Louise Imogen Guiney's contribution to Ralph Adams Cram's medieval magazine, begins by assuming that the reader will know what a witch-elm is and what the top of a thorn tree looks like.   "The witch-elm shivers in the gale, / The thorn-tree's top is bowed; / The night is black with rain and hail, / And mist and cloud."[48]

Although Cawein was firmly based in Louisville, he visited New York from time to time, and was received cordially.   Writing to fellow-Southerner R. E. Lee Gibson on November 20, 1905,   he says, "We were at Richard Watson Gilder's last Friday for dinner; after dinner the people poured in—poets especially... William Vaughn Moody, the poet, who so many say is our greatest writer, and Edward [sic] Arlington Robinson, whom the President praised in the *Outlook,* were also there"[49]   Three years later (April 23, 1908) Cawein still had not grasped that Robinson's first name was Edwin: "Ridgely Torrence and Edward [sic] Arlington Robinson were the only other poets I saw after the banquet.   Both are interesting young men."[50]   Young men?   Both Moody and Robinson were born in 1869, only four years after Cawein.   He may have been revealing an opinion he had expressed to Gibson the previous year (May 26, 1907):   "Moody

---

[46] Rothert 85
[47] Cawein, 1889, 3
[48] Cawein, 1911, 100
[49] Rothert 254
[50] Rothert 275

and Torrence and Robinson are all right.   But what are we to say
about Edith M. Thomas [who also has an article in Rittenhouse] and
Florence Earle Coates [who are] worthy of serious and great
consideration? ... [Why not] Joaquin Miller, by far our first poet living
now, or ... James Whitcomb Riley?"[51]   Cawein had nothing against
Robinson, and years later would be his guest in New York,[52] but it is
obvious that he was not in awe of Robinson at all.   Cawein evidently
impressed Robinson, since Otto Rothert's biography of Cawein was in
Robinson's library at his death.[53]

For many years thereafter, Robinson lived on loans from his
friends; the fact that he eventually paid back every penny shows that
his debts weighed on him.   "[E]ven while he accepted and returned
affectionate loyalty for all this help and support, he was restive under it,
for he never soothed himself with the notion that as a poet society
'owed him a living.'   It was not until the very end of his life that he
entirely outgrew his shame for his long period of indigence."[54]   His
distress was temporarily relieved in 1905 by no less than President
Theodore Roosevelt, who arranged for a sinecure with the New York
Custom House until 1909, when his administration ended, and who
used the Bully Pulpit to champion Robinson's work, which at that time
included *The Children of the Night* (1897, a reworking of poems which
had been self-published in 1896 as *The Torrent and the Night Before*)
and *Captain Craig* (1902).

It is hard for a modern reader to understand why Robinson's work
would need any championing at all, since it included poems like
"Richard Cory," "Luke Havergal" and "Reuben Bright," all of which
are now anthology staples.   The neglect of Robinson's poetry is
understandable, however, when considered in the context of what other
poets were writing.   It is fortunate that one early poem of Robinson's

---

[51]   Rothert 263
[52]   Rothert 436
[53]   Humphry 43
[54]   Smith 35

can be compared apples-to-apples with a poem by Trumbull Stickney (1874-1904), one of the fair-haired boys who dominated student publications at Harvard.   He had dashing good looks, an impeccable ancestry, and—very important in those classically-oriented days—had acquired Greek and Latin as a child from his father, a classics professor.   After Harvard, he and his friend George Cabot Lodge, another fair-haired boy, went to Paris.   Stickney was the first non-francophone student to receive the prestigious *doctorat ès lettres* from the University of Paris.   His friendship with Henry Adams would seem to have completed his preparation for a literary career, both in education and connections, but he died young.[55]

"Turning an ode of Horace" was a very common task for serious young men of that era, and both Robinson and Stickney happen to have translated the same ode (I, xi) at about the same time, and both made it a sonnet.   Whittle dates Stickney's version from 1892.[56]   Robinson's "Horace to Leuconoë" was written before 1896, since he included it in *The Torrent and the Night Before,* published that year; Smith, evidently relying on Robinson's recollections, dates it as early as the winter of 1888-89, "the only work from this time to make the permanent record."[57]

First, Horace's original, for which I have prepared a close translation.   "Babylonian calculations" is understood to be astrology; in line 5, the poet has the winter "wearing out" the sea by driving it against the rocks; "pumice" is used for "rocks" because Horace prefers a specific to a general; "tend to the wine" refers to pouring wine through a strainer to remove sediment, a common housekeeper's chore, and therefore similar to "go on about your business."

*   *   *

---

[55] Whittle, 1972, xxi-xxxi
[56] Whittle 268
[57] Smith 101

Tu ne quaesieris – scire nefas –
quem mihi, quem tibi
finem di dederint, Leuconoë,
nec Babylonios
temptaris numeros.Ut melius
quicquid erit pati,
seu plures hiemes, seu tribuit
Iuppiter ultimam,

quae nunc oppositis debilitat
pumicibus mare
Tyrrhenum.Sapias, vina liques,
et spatio brevi
spem longam reseces. Dum
loquimur, fugerit invida
aetas:carpe diem, quam minimum
credula postero.

You should not seek – to know is
taboo – the end
The gods will have given to you or me,
Leuconoë, nor should you try
Babylonian calculations.How much
better to endure whatever will be,
Whether Jupiter has granted you
several winters, or [just this] last one
[to live],
Which now weakens the Tyrrhenian sea
[by dashing it] against the pumice.
Wise up!Tend to the wine, and into a
little space
Curtail your long[-range] hopes.
While we talk, jealous time
Steals away.Seize the day, trusting
as little as possible in what is to
come.

*   *   *

The translations:
(Stickney)   (Robinson)
Horace   "Horace to Leuconoë"
To A. S.   (From The Torrent and the Night Before)

Ask not, Leuconoë, for thou
must not know,
Ask not the gods thy fated end
and mine,
Nor try the art of Babylonian
sign:

I pray you not, Leuconoë, to
pore
With unpermitted eyes on
what may be
Appointed by the gods for you
and me,

Better endure whate'er the gods bestow!
Have Jove allotted thee a length of days,
Or if this very winter be thy last,

Which, while the rocks stand fortified and fast,
Vexes the sea that laves Etruria's bays,
Drink still and drink and clear the ruby wine!
And with a moment's joy cut short the thread
Of hope.For as we converse emptily
Has jealous age sped on to his decline;
Pluck the day's flower while yet unwithered,
And trust thy least to that which is to be.[58]

Nor on Chaldean figures any more.
'T were infinitely better to implore
The present only: — whether Jove decree
More winters yet to come, or whether he
Make even this, whose hard, wave-eaten shore
Shatters the Tuscan seas to-day, the last —
Be wise withal, and rack your wine, nor fill
Your bosom with large hopes; for while I sing,
The envious close of time is narrowing;—
So seize the day, or ever it be past,
And let the morrow come for what it will.[59]

*   *   *

The first difference that the modern reader may note is the artificiality of Stickney's diction, observable in almost every line: "thou" in the first line, "thy" in the second, "whate'er" in the third, "thee" in the fourth, "thy" in the fifth and fourteenth.   There is also an

---

[58] Stickney 268
[59] *CP*   91

intrusiveness into the original's simplicity: instead of "long-[range] hopes," there is a "thread of hope;" the wine is now "ruby wine;" "seize the day" is "Pluck the day's flower."

Against this, the only archaisms Robinson offers are, "I pray" and "'T were." A survey of the works of his contemporaries is in order to understand just how revolutionary this was—and how fatal it was for the acceptance of his poetry.

Josephine Preston Peabody was a friend of Robinson's, a successful author while he was at his nadir. In January of 1907 she wrote in her diary, "I spent the day reading through 'The Wayfarers' [a volume of her poetry] and noting the alterations that I must make; i.e., mostly the 'Ye's' and such things, with here and there a dreamy word where a live one should be."[60] And yet Peabody was too good a writer not to know that something was wrong. In a letter dated August 11, 1911, she tells her husband that she "Read Dictionary: — Roget's Thesaurus: — Greek dictionary; — Anglo-Saxon primer, to see if anything will make English feel less like a dead language."[61]

The poets were not the only ones to know that something was wrong. Edmund Wilson wrote of the once-omnipresent Moody that

> Moody's verses slip by as smoothly as some thin ethereal syrup; his colors have the shimmer of a soap-bubble film. You begin by being delighted, but you end by being annoyed. With all the sureness of Moody's touch, he has some fundamental deficiency of taste. *The Daguerrotype,* which ought to be moving, goes on and on for so long that it finally begins to sound maudlin. The *Ode in Time of Hesitation,* which ought to be hard-hitting and bitter, is so diluted with conventional rhetoric:
>
> The proud republic hath not stooped to cheat

---

[60] Peabody, 1925, 203
[61] Peabody, 1925, 247

And scramble in the market-place of war, etc.—

that you almost end by sympathizing with the imperialists, because they at least get down to brass tacks.[62]

One recalls Peabody's search for something that would "make English feel less like a dead language." From today's perspective, the language was not dead, but deadened, with the poets themselves doing the deadening. Consider this line from "Astarte," a sonnet published in 1897 by Ridgely Torrence, lifelong friend of Robinson.[63]

That pois'nous curved mouth I still can trace;

What a difference an apostrophe makes! For a thought experiment, let us imagine this line as it would have looked had Torrence written the plain, garden variety trisyllabic poisonous.

⏝   — ⏝ —   ⏝   —   ⏝ — ⏝ —
That poisonous curved mouth I still can trace;

A Petrarcan sonnet is supposed to be in iambic pentameter, and that is what the line is. The only quibble with the line, from the standpoint of rocking-horse rhythm, is that *curved* is on a weak beat; in point of fact, from the standpoint of actual poetic praxis, this is no fault, since it gives the line an attractive, syncopated "kick;" Elsie Ruth Dykes Chant would have called it a trochaic substitution. Torrence, however, wrote "pois'nous," as if it were disyllabic, and this results in a second artificiality, a disyllabic "curvèd."

⏝   —   ⏝   — ⏝   —   ⏝ — ⏝   —
That pois'nous curvèd mouth I still can trace;

---

[62] Stickney ix
[63] Clum 28

What a difference an apostrophe makes.   The line is now artificial, stilted, thanks to *curvèd*, but the stiltedness must have been the poet's intent, since he went out of his way to achieve it.

Yet Horace had it right: *Naturam expelles furca, tamen usque recurret* (Epistles I.x.24):   Though you drive nature away with a pitchfork, she will rush right back.   In this case, the conflict was between the stilted diction of the day and "plain Saxon," represented by Edwin Arlington Robinson.   Robinson's first defender on this charge was none other than Trumbull Stickney, who

> was one of the few to raise his voice in defense of Edwin Arlington Robinson's *Captain Craig,* in a review in the [Harvard] *Monthly* for December of 1903.   Of the author he writes that "the honesty and simplicity of his mind, the pathos and kindness of his heart, and above all the humor with which his imagination is lighted up continually, have made me begin life over again and feel once more that poetry is part of it, perhaps the truth of it."   To those who complain of the author's "plain Saxon," Stickney insists the "the test of all forms of expression lies not in their resembling other forms, but in their proving adequate to the thought."[64]

No one was a more consistent practitioner of the stilted style than Stickney's friend George Cabot Lodge, as witness the first speech in Act I of his drama *Cain* (1902).   Eve speaks: "The rapt silence! The dark twilight!   — It dawns! / The multitude of the ineffable stars / That lamped the viewless parapets of heaven, / Melt in the light like pearls in golden wine..."[65]   Yet in moments of anguish, even Lodge wrote plain Saxon, as he did when Stickney died.

With tearless eyes we kept steadfast

---

[64] Whittle, 1973, 68
[65] Lodge 1:235

His vigil we were sworn to keep:
But, when he left us, and at last
We saw him pass beyond the Door,
And knew he could return no more,
We wept aloud as children weep.[66]

Old habits died hard, however. When it came time to write
Lodge's elegy, Theodore Roosevelt's effort was completely
conventional.

He lived detachèd days;
   He servèd not for praise;
      For gold
      He was not sold;
Deaf was he to the world's tongue;
   He scornèd for his song
      The loud
      Shouts of the crowd.[67]

Detachèd, servèd, scornèd, thee's and thou's and a few of
Josephine Preston Peabody's "ye's"—that was poetry.

Therefore, Robinson's writing was not poetry. Nor had it ever
been: "Robinson's language from the beginning was prosy – not
elegant or precious – and it offered the illusion of the colloquial..."[68]
Even during his lifetime his contribution would seem to have been
forgotten. Harriet Monroe's 1917 review of *Merlin,* as we shall see,
is full of complaints about its dowdiness; but then, in her very next
review, she complains that the now-forgotten opus by one William
Alexander Percy that she is criticizing

---

[66] Lodge 2:71
[67] Lodge 1:xvi
[68] Davis x

is full of everything that I most dislike and resent in poetry: from words and phrases imitative of a bygone diction or manner, like *guerdon, methinks, of yore...*and hundreds more such minor derelictions, to the mortal sin of sacrilegious misuse of a great name and an ancient tradition.[69]

Evidently Monroe failed to make the connection between Robinson's work and the deflation of that old-time diction.

Some thought that the old-fashioned diction was just fine, and resented its absence in *Merlin*, as did the reviewer for *The Dial,* Odell Shepard, the same Odell Shepard that years later would author *The Lore of Unicorns* and, still later, would be lieutenant governor of Connecticut.[70]   In 1917 he had only just begun what would be a long and distinguished career at Trinity College, but was already a man of strong opinions.

And where are the jostle and press, the flashing color and sonorous din which five centuries of English poetry, going back to "Gawayne and the Green Knight," have made us feel we have a right to expect?   They are sicklied o'er with the pale cast of thought.   Where is that Merlin who loomed so hoary and hirsute upon one's childhood, the king-making, empire building, cloud compelling Merlin?   "Gone, faded out of the story, the seafaring friend I remember."   We do not so much object that he should commit spiritual suicide, if only he had been allowed to "do it beautifully."   But this perfumed, purple-frocked, groomed, and barbered Merlin, with vine-leaves in his hair!   One feels defrauded of a birthright.[71]

Amy Lowell, on the other hand, felt that Robinson was an old fogey.

---

[69] Monroe, 1917, 213
[70] Kunitz 1275
[71] Shepard 340

In reading [*Merlin*], we feel that Mr. Robinson was hampered by the weight of tradition hanging about his subject...There is too much of the fustian of the antiquary; too little of the creative vision of the poet...In "Merlin," we turn over the pages of a beautiful picture-book, a portfolio of old, rare prints. They have nothing to do with us, nor we with them.   They are charming, but remote, and — they are only pictures.[72]

Lowell's discussion of *Merlin* is noteworthy not only for its point of view and its length (fourteen pages), but also for the fact that it is included in her book *Tendencies in Modern American Poetry,* published in October, 1917; *Merlin* had appeared but six months earlier, in March of that year, which makes Lowell's analysis commendable for its timeliness and evident speed of composition. She liked the old, terse Robinson better than the new, expansive one.

This is, as its name implies, a re-telling of the Arthurian legend, and one cannot help a slight feeling of disappointment that this re-telling is neither so new nor so different as one might have expected.   For some reason, the author seems here to have abandoned his peculiar and personal style. Instead of a vivid, modern reading of an old theme, instead of the brilliant psychological analysis applied to history and legend...we find in this book only a rather feeble and emasculated picture, tricked out with charming lyrical figures, it is true, but lifeless and unconvincing.   Merlin is no great wizard, swept into Vivian's toils by a fascination which no man, not even he, can resist; he is a vain, weak old man, playing at a pastoral.[73]

---

[72] Lowell, 1917, 65-6
[73] Lowell 1917, 63-64

The anonymous reviewer in *The Catholic World,* on the other hand, takes a middle position between Lowell's disappointment and Shepherd's indignation.

> The reader whose knowledge of this old tale is derived for [from?] the *Idylls of the King* will find Mr. Robinson's treatment of the Arthur-story arrestingly modern in method. The author of *Merlin* has worked in the tradition of the most realistic, least conventional, of the modern poetic schools, and the result has little in common with the symbolism and stately harmonies of the Tennysonian line. Especially in diction is the heroic strain abated – the wording of the poem is every-day, terse, conversational, at times lapsing into a state of almost ludicrous "undress." Yet the experiment succeeds, on the whole; the reality of the medium helps to establish the reality of the story conveyed.[74]

The modern reader may find that this is going too far, since *Merlin* does have its share of archaisms, "mazard," "sore" in the sense of "very," "hautboys" and the like. The *World* review, however, is instructive: what is intrusive to us was not even noticeable in those days, accustomed as the readers then were to a high concentration of thee's and thou's and ye's.

    The Yale Review critic was the most perceptive, in the sense that he realized that the innovations in *Merlin* were not just experiments or novelties, but represented an important development in poetry.

> This is unlike any Arthurian poem we have ever read, and it deserves to be ranked with the best verse the legends of Uther's son have inspired.
>
> The characters are not figures in armor; they are men and women no further removed from us than the characters in

---

[74] Anon. 1917, 255

Meredith's "Modern Love." Of all our modern writers, Mr. Robinson most resembles Meredith, never in his technique or in his choice of subjects, but in the solidity of his work and in the sense of intellectual force. Much of our contemporary verse is painfully thin; here the foundations are dug deep...Each volume of Mr. Robinson's deepens the conviction that he is our foremost American poet. In laying down "Merlin," we have but one criticism to offer: it is too soon ended.[75]

A pause is in order to survey the opinions of critics cited so far: Harriet Monroe and "M.," that Robinson was straying into an overworked subject unsuited to his talents; Young, that Robinson was leaving his trademark style behind for one aimed at "mild intelligences" (and we will later see that Phelps, too, feared that Robinson was trying to be a poor man's Tennyson); Lowell, that Robinson had produced, some beautiful passages notwithstanding, a flat modernization; Shepherd, that Robinson had offered a drab treatment of a subject that demanded color and extroversion; "Anonymous," that Robinson is a modernizer; and Reed, that Robinson was an excellent poet in the Meredith tradition who had brought the men and women of old closer to our time. The overall emphasis is on *Merlin's* style, psychology and visual appeal.

Again I call attention to Harriet Monroe's contrasting review of *The Man Who Died Twice,* with its sensitivity to the aural appeal of the poem, and maintain that, in Robinson's poetry, it is the aural element that is its cornerstone, as can be seen from a revealing occasion recorded by biographer Chard Powers Smith. Robinson was in his cups.

Somewhere along in his second half-pint he began to read me Wordsworth, probably the first among his three favorite

---

[75] Reed 863

non-dramatic poets, the realistic, rustic triumvirate that included Crabbe and Hardy.   I suppose others heard him read, but I suspect my experience was unique in duration and in the alcohol-released naturalness of his technique.   To call it bad reading was to misconstrue it.   It was not reading at all. Rather it was the delighted, voluptuous ejaculation of one word and then another, with rhythmless pauses between in which he would look across at me with challenging eyes—"Get that?   Get that?"   And once he added, "You're too damned young to get that!"

So he read me "one word after another," emphasizing the key sounds of each, ignoring utterly the meter, the line structure, and the cadence...I think I saw the unique phonetic and semantic foundation of Robinson the poet, the exacting, perfectionist labor that went into both his packed single words and his elaborate circumlocutions.   I understood how it was that in an age that, following him, was emphasizing conscious craftsmanship, he remained preeminent.[76]

An illustration of that craftsmanship may be found by looking at the way "gold" recurs with variations in *Merlin,* mutating in an arch from sadness to joy to sadness, exactly matching the mood of the poem.   Early on, the imagery is of gold that is lacking: Arthur scolds Merlin, "the seer, the founder, and the prophet," for having thrown away "the gold of your immortal treasure / Back to the God that gave it, and then laugh / Because a woman has you in her arms..."[77]   Merlin warns Arthur of bad news in his "golden horoscope of imperfection."[78]   In the middle, the Broceliande episodes, gold is physical and abundant.

---

[76] Smith 27-8
[77] *CP*   251
[78] *CP*   252

> Merlin smiled / To see himself in purple, touched with gold, /
> And fledged with snowy lace[79]
> A golden cup that for a golden moment / Was twinned in air
> with hers[80]
> Surrounding her, shot glory over gold / At Merlin[81]
> At the end / Of this incomparable flowing gold[82] [referring to wine]
> He stared a long time at the cup of gold[83]

After the collapse of Merlin's paradise and Arthur's kingdom, gold is just spare change.   The Fool, preparing to abandon Camelot, goes off to pack, saying "I'll assemble certain gold / That I may say is mine."[84]   Finally, it is nostalgia, as when Merlin recalls "Vivian, when her eyes looked into mine / Across the cups of gold."[85]

Returning to our thread, it is worth recalling not only Robinson's position with regard to the generation that followed him, but also to the generation that preceded him.   According to biographer Chard Powers Smith, Robinson's break with the preciosity of Victorian poetic diction is observable in his very first published poem,

> the sonnet *Thalia*.   It is juvenile, but clearly Robinson.
> Much of it is banal, but not with the stereotyped banality of
> Victorian sentimentality.   There is not a hint of a "poetic
> subject," not a breath of "poetic diction."   It is all honest
> feeling and honest expression.   In the whole listening
> empyrean, there was in March, 1890, not one person except
> Robinson himself, twiddling his clarinet, who knew that
> "modern American poetry" had begun.[86]

---

[79] *CP*   268
[80] *CP*   276
[81] *CP*   276
[82] *CP*   276
[83] *CP*   277
[84] *CP*   308
[85] *CP*   309
[86] Smith 104-5

We may quibble that young Robinson's use of classical allusions as shorthand ("Pollio capers with Terpsichore") is backward-looking, but the broader our survey of the poetic status quo, the more striking Robinson's simple modernity is. Smith expresses this more fully in his preface.

Robinson was preceded by Poe, with the dubious support of Emerson, in the repudiation of the Victorian moral standard of criticism with its limitation of "poetic subjects" to maidenly and sentimental ones. And he was preceded by Whitman in the substitution of the vernacular for Victorian "poetic language." But he was the first to dramatize common experience at once in the language of common speech and in the standard verse forms.[87]

An additional quibble with Smith would be the fact that an aspiring writer of Robinson's day had two choices, not one: in addition to the "poetic language," dialect was a permissible medium of expression.

> Fritz: Ach, nein, nein, cheer up yourself…What is der brod…Yesterday's?
> Tomasso: Si, si, me no lika today's bread. It is too—too—hot.
> …Harry: Why do you stay [in America] then, if you make no money?
> Tomasso: Ah, signore, I didna come for money.
> Fritz: Ach, lieber, what den? [*Striking at a fly.*] for lof?

This from future drama critic Stark Young's 1912 one-act play *Addio,*[88] whose *Guinevere* we have already cited. Robinson's friends Ridgely Torrence and William Vaughn Moody wrote plays in dialect. Torrence's Negro plays enjoyed a *succès d'estime,* and Moody scored a solid hit, a two-year Broadway run, with *The Great Divide*

---

[87] Smith ix
[88] Young 1912, 15

(beginning in 1906, which gives context to Robinson's poem "The White Lights [Broadway, 1906]"), in which the New Englanders talk like New Englanders and the cowboys talk like cowboys, this as opposed to his earlier *The Masque of Judgement,* written in "poetic language," which had been merely a *succès d'estime.*

Robinson at this time was hungry for any kind of *succès* he could get. He decided to become a playwright, not only for the reason advanced earlier, that the theater gave him a vehicle for working out his emotional problems, but also because there his aesthetic principles held sway: he had seen firsthand that plays with thee's and thou's and ye's simply did not do as well as those written in plain Saxon. There was also the fact that Broadway in the first decade of the twentieth century was the way to fame and fortune in the same way that Hollywood is today. Robinson needed to alleviate not only his own poverty, but also the financial woes of Emma and his nieces, the consequence of Herman's business failures and alcoholism.

The play was the thing. Consider these entries from the diary of Josephine Preston Peabody concerning *The Piper,* entered in the Stratford Prize Competition in England. She was in the hospital after the birth of her second child.

> February, 1910. L. [her husband Lionel] let me see a letter that he had, knowing that the things of this world could not then occasion me suspense of any size. News from Stratford that 'The Piper" is one in Seven – Final Seven out of 315 plays.
>
> March 5, 1910   A Letter: and a Shock.   News from Stratford – via Ireland – that 'The Piper' is *One of TWO* – the Two Final Plays.
>
> March 10   'The Piper wins!
>
> March 11, 1910.   Cables, telegrams, motors, callers, letters, flowers all day long.   'Tis much like waking up to find one's self famous.
>
> A dizzying dream.   Benign and patriotic cab-driver calls after Lionel in the street, 'Professor Marks, your wife's ALL RIGHT.'

March 15. And still it keeps on – this delicious, unhoped-for thing that people (and papers) take it as an honor for the country, and a Banner for the cause of womankind. Oh – oh – and I wanted to be something or other for these in some manner, some day![89]

On January 12, 1907, Moody wrote to his wife that

Torrence and Robinson have the dramatic fever acutely. Torrence has just finished a three-acter [*The Madstone*] which he is to read to me tonight...Robinson thinks the play is a big thing. He (R.) has also one in first draught, called *Ferguson's Ivory Tower,* the ivory tower, I believe, being Art. It would be wonderfully good luck if they both pulled it off.[90]

The ultimate source for this fever may have been another member of this circle, Percy MacKaye. On November 20, 1905, Moody writes of plans to dine with him. "I hear he has plays up both sleeves and shakes them out of his boots when he goes upstairs."[91] This is not surprising: his father was playwright and empressario Steele MacKaye (1842-1894), remembered in theater history for his innovations. He had opened the Madison Square Theatre in 1879, "and presently remodeled it according to his advanced ideas of technical equipment. He installed an elevator stage, overhead lighting (installed personally by Thomas A. Edison), folding seats (to which he later added attached hat- and coat-racks, and a modern system of ventilation)"[92] He also established the first school of acting in New York City, later known as the American Academy of Dramatic Art. The Chicago World's Fair was to witness his masterpiece, "a mammoth theatre to seat 10,000 persons, and which he hoped would embody all his artistic and technical accomplishments and

---

[89] Peabody 1925, 226-7
[90] Moody 1935, 319
[91] Moody, 1935, 242
[92] Hughes 235-6

aspirations....Scene changes were to be accomplished by sliding stages with electric motor power, and the curtain was to be of light." Steele MacKaye's aspirations at the high tide of his career, however, were blighted by the Panic of 1893[93] the same crash that had forced Robinson, at the beginning of his career, to leave Harvard.

We note that it is just possible that Moody passed on to Robinson his *bon mot* about MacKaye *fils*, at least the first part, about having plays up both sleeves and shaking them out. Note the following exchange in *Van Zorn.*

> Otto: [*After a pause*]   Well, Phoebus, I can't speak for Farnham.   But there was a time when the rest of us would have said that you had empires up your sleeve. [*Impressively*]
>
> Lucas: [*Looking at his sleeve*]   Then they must be there yet. I've never shaken them out.[94]

MacKaye, for his part, recalled those days.

> Beginning with our group-onset, Robinson put aside all his poetry for several years working incessantly at two plays, *Van Zorn* (first entitled *Ferguson's Ivory Tower*) and *The Porcupine* (both afterwards published), only one of which, *Van Zorn,* was produced years later by Henry Stillman, with Wright Kramer as Van Zorn, for a week's run at the Brooklyn Y.M.C.A., Feb. 26, 1917.[95]

The venue may have been humble, but the production must have been good: Wright Kramer had been appearing on the Broadway stage since 1900, and since 1902 had been in the "stable" of big-time

---

[93] Hughes 236-7
[94] Robinson 1914, 19
[95] Moody 1935, 31

producer Charles Frohman.[96]   In 1915 he had been in two films as
well.   His New York career, in which he was director and producer as
well as actor, would extend to the early 30's; he ended his career in
Hollywood, keeping busy with minor roles: he can be seen as Senator
Carlton in *Mr. Smith Goes to Washington*.[97]   Henry Stillman's equally
varied Broadway years would be 1919-1936, not beginning until two
years after the ill-fated *Van Zorn*.[98]   The reviewer in the February 27
Brooklyn *Eagle* "noted that a small audience called the actors forward
five times at the end, and he agreed that they deserved the kudos."[99]
These two professionals, however, could not save this amateurish play.

Phelps expresses a minority opinion in his autobiography, that
"His original play *Van Zorn*, is not only very fine as drama and as
literature, but it exhibits a side of his talents usually unknown; it had
the bad luck to appear in 1914."[100]   This is far too kind.   Even
confirmed lovers of Robinson's poetry have never liked *Van Zorn* and
The Porcupine.   More common are assessments such as Cary's:

> The familiar axiom that every comedian wants to play Hamlet
> finds its counterpart in the heart of many a poet and novelist
> who longs to be a playwright.   Flaubert and Henry James,
> among countless others, broke their lances in futile efforts to
> create dramas acceptable to theatre-goers of their day.   And
> so it was with Robinson.   He embroiled himself for at least a
> decade in writing, revising, and trying to market *Van Zorn* and
> *The Porcupine*.   They were unanimously rejected by
> producers who squirmed uneasily under the heavy weight of
> their psychological themes.[101]

---

[96] IBDB
[97] IMDb
[98] IBDB
[99] Moody, 1935, 31
[100] Phelps 697
[101] Cary, 1963, 237

This is still too kind.   The plays are insipid, pure and simple, so much so that it is hard to believe that they were written by Robinson.   Far more common is the view in Franchere.

> Certainly this play [*Van Zorn*] does not come off well.   Its characters move on and off the stage stiffly and sometimes without sufficient motivation.   Their lines are often written as if to be read and never spoken; and the prose style is somehow reminiscent of the later Henry James, lacking even a hint of the warmly colloquial language we expect to find in comedy.... Villa Vannevar's announced unconventionality, when it appears at all, seems to be more in the clothes she wears than in her actions or her speech; and only at the moment when she realizes that she is making a mistake in her plan to marry Farnham does she move the reader.[102]

Note that the article speaks of "the reader" and not "the audience."   Hagedorn puts a good face on the event by saying, "The characters were like exquisite engravings talking."   Be that as it may, his account of Robinson's reaction to the play's premiere is worth noting.   "The production excited Robinson out of all proportion to its significance.   He suffered agonies during the first performance, his face red and tears of excitement in his eyes."[103]   This, however, is itself is a clue.   The fact that Robinson's obsession with the stage was a ten-year detour from his poetry, which itself had been a lifelong obsession, shows how hungry he was for some kind of success.   This study will maintain, however, that Robinson's detour was not a total loss, that in his ten years of wrestling with drama he learned lessons that he was able to apply to *Merlin*:   once he had found the right vehicle, the flat dialogue and crabbed intrigues of his stage works would reappear transmuted into convincing turns of plot and extroverted, bravura discourse.

---

[102] Franchere 48
[103] Hagedorn 1939, 321

When all was said and done, however, Robinson's theatrical efforts did not bring him what he wanted, fame and fortune. Moody had gotten both, but was quite cavalier about his theatrical success. One would even call him a snob, judging by this letter to his wife.

> Monday, Jan. 21 [1907] I went last night to the annual dinner of the 'American Dramatists' Club' at Delmonico's. The dinner and the wines were good, and dear old Bronson Howard presided; but here the mitigation ended. The guest of honor was Charles Klein, whose dishwater *Lion and Mouse* is just rounding its five-hundredth performance (consecutive run) in this city, with five road companies going full steam. This furnished the keynote of all the speeches, which, taken together, constituted a more naïvely blatant mumbo-jumbo ritual before the shrine of 'Success' than I would have thought possible in a civilized gathering. The idea that any other standard of judgment existed than that furnished by the box-office tally-sheet never for one instant, even by innuendo, lifted its head, throughout two hours and a half of speech-making. All plays and all playwrights were by tacit consent ranged in a hierarchy of merit according to the amount of cash receipts they represented, little Klein, with pathetic face and winking eyes, heading the august line, in which even I, God help me, had for the nonce my quasi-conspicuous place! O, fie on't! Why not write a play to show up in its true colors this success-madness? It is certainly a dreadful organic disease in our society, an impostume that cries to heaven to be lanced, and lanced deep.[104]

If Moody's *hauteur* were shared with his intimates as well as with his wife, which, although I cannot prove, I strongly suspect, recalling MacKaye and his sleeves, how galling this must have been for the

---

[104] Moody 1935 321-2

unsuccessful playwright Robinson! Cary suggests that "In an oblique sense, Moody contributed vitally to Robinson's development. He was a providential obstruction, the irritant rock Robinson needed to thrust his blade against—and so sharpen it."[105] Eventually, though, enough was enough. On November 15, 1918, in the New York *Evening Sun* appeared a poem called "Broadway," not to be confused with the earlier "The White Lights (Broadway 1906)." Robinson stated that it had been printed without his knowledge,[106] and it is not included in his *Collected Poems.* It is revealing, however; the first stanza is the best. The Great White Way is now

> By night a gay leviathan
> That fades before the sun—
> A monster with a million eyes
> Without the sight of one—
> A coruscating thing with claws
> To tear the soul apart—
> Breaker of men and avenues,
> It throbs, and has no heart.

Robinson had evidently given up on the theater. Yet his artistic, financial and emotional needs had not changed at all: he wanted a big, paying audience; he needed a mask behind which he could reenact his personal traumas; he needed a vehicle where he could speak his own language.

Robinson had his epiphany, but unfortunately the man who witnessed it was the always-imprecise Hagedorn, who states that "one day" in "1916" [Laurence Perrine, best known as the author of the textbook *Literature: Structure, Sound, and Sense,* a classroom staple for many years, but also the author of important articles on Robinson, suggests that it was actually 1915], during one of his "frequent visits,"

---

[105] Cary 1962 183
[106] Cary 1974, 184

the poet, allegedly enthralled by the poem Hagedorn was working on, "suddenly asked for a copy of *Morte d'Arthur*[107] Other borrowings are better attested: "Robinson borrowed the two-volume Temple edition of Malory from his friend Louis V. Ledoux in April 1916 and did not return it until July 1924."[108] He also had Ledoux send him S. Humphrey Gurteen's book *The Arthurian Epic,* a summary of the French prose romance known as the *Vulgate Merlin.*[109] This is why, although Robinson follows certain details of this romance, "there is no need to suppose...that Robinson had actually read the Vulgate *Merlin.* It is a huge tome, not readily available, written in Old French, and the story of Merlin and Vivian, as told there, is scattered and almost lost amidst tedious and interminable accounts of wars and battles."[110] Ledoux adds two reminiscences: that "Robinson used to have him or his wife read to him occasionally [William] Morris's "The Defense of Guinevere" and "King Arthur's Tomb;"[111] and that "Robinson disliked the [Richard] Hovey treatment and made 'disrespectful remarks' about it." Robinson apparently took Hovey seriously enough, however, to send to Ledoux from Peterborough in late May 1917 for Hovey's *Launcelot and Guinevere.* Ledoux filled the order."[112]

Yet for all the vexations occasioned by biographer Hermann Hagedorn's lapses, in this instance he may just be right about the role of "The Great Maze" in the genesis of *Merlin,* except, that is, for its happening in 1916. The poem is a retelling of Agamemnon's return, with nothing Arthurian about it; yet of all the poems examined in this study (outside of the Robinson canon itself) it is the closest in manner, although not in matter, to the diction of *Merlin.* Ægisthus addresses Agamemnon.

---

[107] Perrine 1972, 346
[108] Perrine 1972, 337
[109] Perrine 1972, 337
[110] Perrine 1972, 314
[111] Perrine 1972, 341
[112] Perrine, 1972, 345

                                                     Mockingly
Ægisthus laughed.   "Let us be dignified
By all means, if it seems more proper.   Listen.
When you went off to Troy ten years ago,
You said that you would stay a month, two, three,
No more than three."
                              "I was mistaken."
                                          "True."[113]

Hagedorn, too, was capable of plain Saxon.   "The Great Maze"
is replete with passages that bear comparison to Robinson's
blank-verse epics, both in style and in dramatic effect.   An especially
affecting moment is Agamemnon's death: Ægisthus and
Clytæmnestra are hiding in the dark, waiting to kill him; Agamemnon
has come to apologize, and is groping around, calling out.

Where are you hiding,   Clytæmnestra?   Speak.
I have not come to blame you.   I who love you,
And did you grievous wrong, how should I blame you?
Life is a great maze, Clytæmnestra.   You
And I were lost in it a while.   But look,
Love is the thread of it, love is the key.
We shall not walk in mazes any more.
Speak to me!   Come to me![114]

This poem could have triggered Robinson's epiphany.   Be that as it
may, the stage is set for an examination of *Merlin* in the context of
other works in the genre, and for an examination of the internals of the
work and how they build to a finale.
    Although the poet uses a broad palette of rhetorical devices, there
are only three that relate to his readers' familiarity with the Tennyson

---

[113] Hagedorn, 1916, 38
[114] Hagedorn, 1916, 81

continuum: (1) Robinson relies on his readers' expectations, so as to obviate the need for digressive descriptive or background passages; (2) Robinson ignores his readers' expectations by adding new episodes like the two drinking scenes and the shaving of Merlin's beard; and finally, (3) Robinson deceives his readers' expectations, as he does with the very first lines of the poem, where Gawaine is accosted by Dagonet.

> "Gawaine, Gawaine, what look ye for to see,
> So far beyond the faint edge of the world?
> D'ye look to see the lady Vivian,
> Pursued by divers ominous vile demons
> That have another king more fierce than ours?[115]

Such was the reputation of Vivian (Vivien in the *Idylls*) that the mention of "demons" is almost superfluous.   This is very subtle artistry on Robinson's part.   The reader will go through the first seven hundred lines of his *Merlin* with the Tennysonian villainess in mind, only to find that Robinson is playing crack-the-whip: his Vivian is in fact a flapper, a jazz baby, pert, but by no means evil.

Tennyson's Vivien is relentlessly evil, and her force of personality dominates the other characters completely.   After she has induced the brothers Balin and Balan to kill each other in "Balin and Balan," her gloating does not lessen her squire's puppy-love.   "'And, Vivien, tho' ye beat me like your dog, / I too could die, as now I live, for thee.' / 'Live on, Sir Boy,' she cried.   'I better prize (575) The living dog than the dead lion: away! / I cannot brook to gaze upon the dead.'"   In "Merlin and Vivien" her motivation for seducing Merlin is thin, "As fancying that her glory would be great (215) According to his greatness whom she quenched."

Cram calls his temptress Nimue.   Her evildoing is more credible: Morgan wants Excalibur for an incantation, and Nimue is the agent she dispatches (II.2).

---

[115] *CP*   235

> Morgan: Ha, Nimue!
>   I need thee, girl: art ready to my hand?
> Nimue: As restless sword that clamours for the fray
>   Within the sluggard sheath of errant knight.

What chance does Merlin have against her wiles?   He starts strong (III.3):

> Merlin: Mock me not!
>   I am no lusty knight...
>   ...Lightly get ye hence,
>   I am aweary.
> Nimue: Nay, I leave thee not.
>   …My lord, my love, look deep into mine eyes
>   And see my secret!

The stage direction adds: (*Soft music.*)   Merlin wavers, then is mesmerized; he snaps out of it in time, however.

> Merlin: A mocking spell
>   Is over me: my heart has ceased to beat:
>   My brain is in disorder.   Help me, God!
>   My craft is broken!
>   (He makes the sign of the cross: the vision vanishes.)
>   Damn thee, witch of hell!
>   I know thee now!

Merlin "hurls her down from the battlements, then slowly descends and seats himself by the table."

Mumford's operatic Vivian is also Morgan's agent, but is more successful.

> Vivian: I shall be wise as thou art wise,
>   And in my hand he shall be as clay;

> I will lure his heart as the fowler lures,
> Who calls the bird but to maim and slay.[116]

There is no seduction in Mumford: Merlin is hexed by a magic ring, in full view of Arthur's court, who exclaim, *Allegro agitato,*

> Chorus: The magic gold holds fast and strong!
> He may not tear it from his hand!
> About his heart and through his soul
> Rush the dark spells of Fairyland![117]

Despite the *animato* warnings of the Chorus of Knights, he follows Vivian off to Fairyland, to "a glade surrounded by giant trees, in the centre of which a hill whereon, at the bidding of Merlin, the Spirits will build the Palace of Joyousguard."[118]   Mumford is alone in this use of the toponym, which ordinarily refers to Lancelot's castle. After a year has passed, Vivian has learned all of Merlin's magic. The stage direction announces that "Merlin though able to read the future for others, was blinded to his own doom."   She has him drink from "the cup of death," then entombs him in a magic shroud.

> Vivian: From my hair a shroud I spin,
> Wrought of magic and of sin;
> Merlin, all I learned of thee,
> Yet know naught to set thee free!
> Here in stupor shalt thou lie,
> Till a thousand years go by,
> But one thought for company:
> Thou liest here for love of me,
> Love of Lady Vivian. (Merlin is sealed within the tomb.)

---

[116] Hadley v
[117] Hadley vii
[118] Hadley viii

Merlin's last words, *in modo patetico,* are, "I forgive thee, Vivian."[119]

Tennyson's Vivien, by contrast, may be behindhand in motivation, but is more than a match for Mumford's Vivian in her execution: she relies on no magic ring, as in Mumford; she does not fail to get her man, as in Cram.   She begins by imploring ("Merlin and Vivien").

> There lay she all her length and kissed his feet,
> As if in deepest reverence and in love.   218
> ...And while she kissed them, crying, "Trample me   223
> Dear feet, that I have followed through the world,
> And I will pay you worship; tread me down,
> And I will kiss you for it;"

She whispers sweet nothings.

> "O Merlin, do ye love me?" and again,
> "O Merlin, do ye love me? " and once more
> "Great Master, do ye love me?" he was mute.   235

After another 661 lines of her scolding and wheedling and cajoling, finally

> The pale blood of the wizard at her touch   897
> Took gayer colours, like an opal warmed.

Merlin, "overtalked and overworn," lets his guard down and dozes off.

> Then, in one moment, she put forth the charm   915
> Of woven paces and of waving hands,
> And in the hollow oak he lay as dead,
> And lost to life and use and name and fame.

---

[119] Hadley x

Robinson's transformation of the oak elicited Monroe's condemnation. "… He puts Merlin and Vivian through new paces, quite domesticates them at Broceliande...but there is little magic in his touch upon any of these familiar figures."[120]

> Here's an oak you like,
> And here's a place that fits me wondrous well
> To sit in.   You sit there.[121]

Hovey's Nimue is too decorous to maneuver Merlin into an oak. She is continually chaperoned, as it were, by her superior, Argente, and does nothing more than try to distract Merlin from his quest, his desire to know the future, by nothing more emotional than an appeal to the effect that the spirit world is his true home.

> Nimue: Here, here, O Merlin,
>   Delight awaits thee,
>   Soft lips that smite and sweet hands that kiss,

Merlin's head has no difficulty controlling his heart, and his reply is decorous.

> Merlin: A brittle anchor is thought;
>   But the storm bellows and ramps and the gods in heaven
>   are earless.
>   Weak as it is, I cast it out to the tide.

At this, Nimue does take "no" for an answer.

> Nimue: Be it so, then.   I summon my ministers…
>   But, oh, my master and lord!

---

[120] Monroe 1917, 211
[121] *CP*   287-8

> Thou shalt hear in the teasing of leaves stirred by the wind,
> In the lisp of the lake through the reeds and the swan's harsh cry,....a message of me;
> For I wait for thee—there in the reeds.

She returns Merlin to Camelot herself. "The ground opens and flames appear. Through the opening a car rises, drawn by dragons. Nimue enters the car and extends her hand to Merlin, who follows her. The car rises into the air and disappears in the distance."

Wilfred Scawen Blunt, "minor poet and amateur of nationalist movements"[122] gave the readers of 1914 a Nimue with a touch of Araby: "To Nimue" is Koranic in form in the sense of having long lines and rhyming AAA, BBB... It is a monologue; the speaker is Merlin. The tenth of its eleven three-line stanzas is worth quoting:

> And she came and sat at my feet, as in days ere our grief began.
> And I saw her a woman grown. And I was a prophet no more, but a desolate voiceless man.
> And I clasped her fast in my arms in joy and kissed her tears as they ran.

Blunt had, in fact published some Arabic translations, but his role was actually versification of his wife's work, as she was the linguist of the two.[123] The readers of 1914, however, probably did not look beyond the poem's by-line: Blunt, in his youth, had personified what in our times has been called the Hollywood radical, being theatrically handsome and enormously wealthy (inherited from his aristocratic family), yet at heart a preachy, shallow butterfly flitting from cause to noble cause. By 1914 the playboy had become a curmudgeon, and this mars the rest of "To Nimue." The fourth stanza:

---

[122] Hourani 87
[123] Assad 93

I will not love without love.   I despise the ways of a fool.
Let me prevail as of old, as lover, as lord, as king, or have
done with Love's tyrant rule.
I was born to command, not serve, not obey.   No boy am I in
Love's school.

Blunt is cited for two reasons in this study: first, because his
characterization of Merlin as misanthrope, or perhaps, his
misanthrope's self-characterization as Merlin, is relevant to how
Merlin was understood in 1914.   Second, because of the contacts that
Blunt's wealth and status brought him.

> In 1914, W. B. Yeats, Richard Aldington, Ezra Pound and four
> other poets of the new generation traveled down to his country
> home to dine with him and present him with a poetic address
> written by Pound and marking their admiration…
> No profound meeting of minds seems to have taken
> place…But at least the food (roast peacock in its feathers) was
> worthy of the occasion, and he was touched by their
> gesture.[124]

Yeats' "Time and the Witch Vivien" will be seen to have left its mark
on *Merlin.*   William Morris, whose "The Defense of Guinevere" and
"King Arthur's tomb" have already been alluded to, had visited Blunt
in 1896, as his diary records, and Arthuriana was in vogue.

> [May 30]   Swinburne's new poem was reviewed yesterday in
> all the papers.   Morris thinks it poor stuff and not worth
> doing, as the story, 'Balin and Balan,' was quite perfect in its
> prose form in the 'Morte d'Arthur.'   'It would not do,
> however,' he said, 'for Swinburne to hear me saying this, for
> he would never forgive me.'   Swinburne, it appears, is the

---

[124] Hourani 89

most sensitive and jealous of men, and cannot bear the smallest criticism...Tennyson, Morris says, was the same, and never forgave him for having disapproved of his bowdlerization of the 'Morte d'Arthur' in the 'Idylls of the King.'[125]

In addition to this overview of other Merlins, the opening lines of Robinson's *Merlin* are worth citing for their poetic importance.   The setting of Merlin's Rock will recur in the final scene, and the repeated "Gawaine, Gawaine" will recur as an echo in line 10.
Dagonet pursues his questioning:

> Or think ye that if ye look far enough
> And hard enough into the feathery west
> Ye'll have a glimmer of the Grail itself?[126]

It may not be stretching a point to find a Tennysonian echo in the "glimmer of the Grail," even though "Merlin and the Gleam" does not mention the Grail specifically.

> *I* am Merlin,
> And *I* am dying,
> *I* am Merlin
> Who follow The Gleam.

Dagonet will appear in both the opening and closing scenes of Robinson's *Merlin,* and is thus important for the poem's symmetry; he is also important because, like the other minor characters, his reactions to Merlin help to delineate Merlin; and finally, because Robinson relies on the reader's preconception of Dagonet's character in order to goad the reader forward by toying with that preconception.   He is introduced as

---

[125] Blunt 1921, 229
[126] *CP*   235

> ...Dagonet, whom Arthur made a knight
> Because he loved him as he laughed at him,[127]

From the standpoint of the poem's structure, however, we see that Robinson is already setting up echoes that will recur more than two thousand lines later: "And was with Arthur when he made him knight,"[128] "Who laughed at him because he was a fool,"[129] and a deft stroke that lets us know that Dagonet will allow himself to be the object of fun, but not of pity: "Had you been so, I doubt if Arthur's love, / Or Gawaine's, would have made of you a knight."[130]

Far richer, however, is the mutation of the leitmotiv "fool." Dagonet begins his speech by "Presuming on his title of Sir Fool;"[131] Gawaine replies, "I'll not forget I had it of a knight, / Whose only folly is to fool himself,"[132] which is inverted three pages later with Gawaine speaking "with admiration for the man / Whom Folly called a fool,"[133] and again echoed in the very last scene by "the knight who made men laugh / And was a fool because he played the fool."[134] In between there are some remarkable elaborations suggested by the word. Gawaine sharply observes, "If I be too familiar with a fool, / I'm on the way to be another fool," [135] which in turn is echoed when the distraught Arthur muses, "Poor Dagonet's a fool. / And if he be a fool, what else am I / Than one fool more to make the world complete? / 'The love that never was!'. . . Fool, fool, fool, fool!"[136] Dagonet himself has a remarkable rhapsody in the final scene "so should I have been / A king, had I been born so, fool or no: / King Dagonet, or

---

[127] *CP*   235
[128] *CP*   301
[129] *CP*   312
[130] *CP*   310
[131] *CP*   237
[132] *CP*   237
[133] *CP*   239
[134] *CP*   282
[135] *CP*   238
[136] *CP*   256

Dagonet the King; / King-Fool, Fool-King; 'twere not impossible. / I'll meditate on that and pray for Arthur, / Who made me all I am, except a fool. / Now he goes mad for love, as I might go / Had I been born a king and not a fool. / Today I think I'd rather be a fool."[137]   On the last page of the work he says, "'Say what you will, I say that I'm the fool / Of Merlin, King of Nowhere, which is Here...And on the morrow I shall follow you / Until I die for you.   And when I die...I shall die a fool.'"[138]

The traditional analysis, involving antecedents, will also add to the picture.   Perrine suggests that "Robinson might have got his conception of Dagonet either from Tennyson or likelier from Richard Hovey, but it is hardly necessary to go to either of these for explanation."[139]   A priori not from Tennyson, as can be seen in the opening lines of "The Last Tournament" in the Idylls: "Dagonet, the fool, whom Gawain in his mood / Had made mock-knight of Arthur's Table Round," neither knighted by Arthur, nor even a real knight, as in Robinson.   Tennyson's Dagonet spends most of his time dancing. Nor is Hovey's too-clever-by-half Dagonet a prototype.

> Guenevere: How now, sir? You look soberly.
>
> Dagonet: I? I am as merry as a skull, and that is always grinning, as you would see if you could but look beneath the skin.
>
> Guenevere: A grim jest, sirrah.
>
> Dagonet: Ay, it is ill jesting at a wedding. Aristophanes himself, who first wore motley, would go hang for lack of a laugh. For your good unctuous jest must have a soil of light hearts or it will not grow; and there is a predisposition at weddings to solemnity...So no more jests from me, my lady,

---

[137] *CP*   303
[138] *CP*   313-4
[139] Perinne 1974, 339

till you have done with eating green cheese,
which is excellent diet for the moonstruck—but I
prefer Stilton.[140]

Tennyson's stock epithet for Dagonet is "little."   Sophie Jewett
(1861-1909) wrote an attractive poem in which Dagonet is a dwarf,
jealous of the long-limbed knights of Arthur's court.   Although Prof.
Jewett (she taught at Wellesley) is remembered today for "God's
Troubadour," her story of St. Francis of Assisi, it is relevant here to
note that she was also the author of "a critical edition, published in
1901, of Tennyson's 'The Holy Grail,' with an Introduction that makes
careful comparison of the modern poem with the Perceval Romances
and with the medieval stories of the early history and quest of the
Grail."[141]   "The Dwarf's Quest: A Ballad" also dates from 1901.
Dagonet may lack the physical attributes to go grailing, "Yet ice and
flame were in his breast; /   He hid his curling lip, /   And wept for
fierce desire to quest / With the great Fellowship" (39-41).   He prays,
and is told that a vision of the Grail waits for him as well as for
Galahad.   Dagonet travels far, and chances on Lancelot, lying
wounded and unconscious at a crossroads.   He stops to aid him.
"That night Past midnight, when the moon was set, / And utter dark
the night, / Round Lancelot and Dagonet / There shone a sudden
light." (101-104) Lancelot does not regain consciousness, so only
Dagonet sees the vision.   Lancelot's wounds are healed by the
Grail's power.   "'He will awaken whole and strong (145.)   As ever
he hath been; / He need not know his trance was long, / Nor what the
fool hath seen.'"
    Stark Young's Dagonet is not a fool, but Guinevere's youthful
page.   Early in the drama he is a combat courier: the Queen's party
is ambushed by Mordred and his henchmen, and Dagonet is entrusted
with the mission of bringing Lancelot.   Guinevere is abducted before

---

[140] Rochester
[141] Jewett xii-xiii

her protector arrives. In Act II the lad tells us that Lancelot has
broken into Mordred's stronghold and wrought havoc

> until Sir Mordred came and yielded
> Him in terror, and granted the queen's release.
> Colgrevaunce. You saw it, boy?
> Dagonet. Yea, did I. Some day my Jesu grant
> That I may be a man, even such a knight
> As our Sir Launcelot, and serve some lady
> Like the queen.[142]

Young's Dagonet will also appear as Arthur's messenger when the
King visits Guinevere in the nunnery after her disgrace.

Robinson's portrayal of Dagonet comes not so much from what
he says as from the different ways the other characters react to him.
To Gawaine, Sir Fool is harmless: "And as for making other men to
laugh, / And so forget their sins and selves a little, / There's no great
folly there.   So keep it up, / As long as you've a legend or a song,"[143]

Hovey's Dagonet has songs aplenty, and they are more like the
insouciant Vagabondia lyrics than the bombastic rant of the rest of his
Guinevere. He mocks a knight: "For there are worser ills to face /
Than foemen in the fray; / And many a man has fought because— / He
feared to run away. / Ri fol de riddle rol" (IV.3).   He mocks
courtiers.   "With ribald chalkings on his coat /   Sir Pompous struts
the street, And wanton boys put walnut-shells /   On stately Tabby's
feet. /   Ri fol de riddle rol" (I.3).   He returns to Camelot with a jape.
"Merrily canter on through life / And joy shall be your store, /   But
if you ride a trotting nag / Your buttocks will be sore. / Ri fol de
riddle rol" (I.3).

Robinson prepares for Merlin's entrance with much more care
than he did for any of the characters in his dramas.   In *Van Zorn,* the

---

[142] Rochester
[143] *CP*   237-8

title role is introduced in only three exchanges to the effect that he is rich. When he appears, all the set-up he gets is

> Otto: You may come in, for I know your name. Your name
> is Van Zorn, and I've seen you before.[144]

Merlin's appearance, on the other hand, is set up for four hundred and fifty-odd lines, not only with intense conversations between the principals, but with background noise as well.

>   It was heard
> At first there was a ghost in Arthur's palace,
> But soon among the scullions and anon
> Among the knights a firmer credit held
> All tongues from uttering what all glances told—
> Though not for long.[145]

With words like "scullions" and "anon," it is hard for a modern reader to understand why Robinson's first audience was struck by the modernity of his style. To our ears *Merlin* is quite liberally garnished with archaisms. Yet we must take the poet's contemporaries at their word: this was a great change, or rather, *even* this was a great change.

> Gawaine, this afternoon...
> Had sauntered off with his imagination
> To Merlin's Rock, where now there was no Merlin
> To meditate upon a whispering town
> Below him in the silence.[146]

---

[144] Robinson 1914, 26
[145] *CP*   235
[146] *CP*   235-6

"To Merlin's Rock...to meditate upon a whispering town..." will be echoed in the opening of Part VII as "By Merlin's Rock," where Dagonet goes "to meditate on human ways... gazing down on Camelot."

Gawaine recalls a conversation he had with Merlin long ago, in which he says "'Long live the king;'"[147] this will be transmuted into Sir Kay's verdict in Part II, that "the King I saw today / Was not, nor shall he ever be again, / The King we knew.   I say the King is dead; / The man is living, but the King is dead;"[148] an echo that is even more direct in form, yet opposite in meaning is Arthur's comment, "God save the King, indeed, / If there be now a king to save."   The jealous Vivian will say, "'Long live the king, but not the king that lives in Camelot;'"[149] then, suggesting that Arthur is replaceable, "'The world will say its prayers and wash its face, / And build for some new king a new foundation. / Long live the King!'"   With a satisfying symmetry, Dagonet has one last echo, as he dismisses Gawaine and Bedivere after their last dialogue: "Farewell. / I'll sit here and be king.   God save the king!"[150]

Returning to Gawaine's conversation with Merlin, Merlin remarked that "You are young,/ Gawaine, and you may one day hold the world / Between your fingers...,"[151] which will be transmuted into Dagonet's plea in the last scene: "Gawaine, you have the world / Now in your fingers—an uncommon toy."[152]

Merlin's entrance is not even an entrance; this understated, offstage introduction is a contrast to Hovey's stage directions: "A low, foreboding roll of thunder.   MERLIN   appears on a jutting crag [in a cave], with a forked wand in his hand. – The flame flashes into sudden brilliancy, sharply defining the rocky walls of the cavern, but at once sinks back into its former weak and flickering indistinctness..."

---

[147] CP 248
[148] CP 248
[149] *CP* 293
[150] *CP* 303
[151] *CP* 236
[152] *CP* 302

His first words are addressed to the Norns, a specifically Wagnerian touch: "Hail! / Ye monstrous Glooms! / Formless Forms! Known and Unknown! / To what avail/ Through strifes and storms,/ Athwart the Sea that bellows and booms / In the ear / With the threatening of dire dooms, / Strove I once alone / In the starless vast of the night of fear, / Dread Queens, to behold your throne?"[153]   An additional Wagnerian touch is a reference to Odin in Merlin's next speech.

In Ralph Adams Cram's *Excalibur* Merlin makes an entrance in "impenetrable darkness," predicting that the Pendragon line will bring about a Christian realm.

> A kingdom passes; now a kingdom's king
> Shall raise a kingdom for the King of kings.

The lights come up gradually as he speaks; "faintly visible, poised in mid-air" he compels Morgan to yield Excalibur.   The stage directions would seem to prefigure his M.I.T. spectacle.   "Merlin is illuminated with a dazzling radiance.   Four shafts of light shoot upward, downward, and to either hand, as he draws Excalibur, brandishing it aloft in the light."

There are no such special effects in Robinson's *Merlin*.   Monroe understood his subtle manner perfectly.

> In the longer poems we have, as a rule, monologue and dialogue, the characters unfolding their perplexities, or recording their action upon each other, in long speeches which are not talk, as talk actually ever was or could be, but which are talk intensified into an extra-luminous self revelation; as if an X-ray, turned into the suffering soul, made clear its hidden structural mysteries.
>
> Robinson's method is thus akin to that of the psychoanalyst who encourages confessional monologue, or uses dialogue, as

---

[153] Rochester

a probe to strike through the poison of lies and appearances and reveal the truth.[154]

Yet Monroe is of the opinion there is such a fault as too much subtlety.

Again [Robinson] pushes it to the other extreme of too detailed analysis in speeches of too great length...Perhaps the temptation to excess is strongest in the two legendary poems *Merlin* and *Lancelot;* here it is emphasized by the academic traditions of conventionalized archaistic speech. Not that Robinson adopts an archaic style, or forswears all modern significance, in his use of the perpetually typical old tales; but to me at least his modern instinct and habit of mind seem out of place in Camelot, as if a tweed-suited and felt-hatted American were trying to possess the Vatican gardens and the Borgian suite of Pincturicchio-decorated chambers.[155]

Nor is this the only peculiarity the reader must face: Robinson's idiom is "an old language, reborn, sometimes abstract and involved, usually sparing of metaphor, though the imagery when it occurs is crucial, perhaps the more so because of its very compression and sparseness."[156]   The language must be vivid, so as to be memorable when used as a leitmotiv, as above.   What follows is a mild example of what I have called a jolt.

<blockquote>
Gawaine,
Remembering Merlin's words of long ago,
Frowned as he thought, and having frowned again,
He smiled and threw an acorn at a lizard:[157]
</blockquote>

---

[154] Monroe 1932, 5
[155] Monroe 1932, 5-6
[156] Coxe 252
[157] *CP* 236

Where there are acorns, there must be oaks, and where there are lizards there must be concomitant lizard flora and fauna, but Robinson has not established any of this, or any kind of setting at all. The reader knows that there is a rock, Merlin's Rock; it may be assumed that he has a "default" mental picture of the rock's background; yet unless this background includes oaks and lizards, Robinson's belated announcement of these details must occasion a jolt, or at least an abrupt readjustment of the reader's mental picture. Amy Lowell, in her 1917 study, praised this technique. In the context of "Richard Cory" she writes,

> In four words, "one calm summer night," is set a background for the tragedy which brings the bullet shot crashing across our ear-drums with the shock of an earthquake...Mr. Robinson has carefully studied that primary condition of all poetry: brevity; and his best effects are those gained with the utmost economy of means...This creating an atmosphere with a back-hand stroke is one of the most personal and peculiar traits of Mr. Robinson's style.[158]

The trait is good when it enhances the poem, as with "Richard Corey," but in *Merlin* it gives the reader a jolt. Most of the settings in *Merlin* are minimal. What color is the lizard? What sound does the acorn make when it hits? Robinson's writing is always spare, which Smith characterizes as

> the quality of Robinson that all critics emphasize, namely his indifference to outward, physical paraphernalia, his almost exclusive concern with the psychological and spiritual problems of people in that inward world where each of them represents universal man or woman. The neglect of outward description has several significances. For one thing, it immediately directs the reader's attention away from

---

[158] Lowell 1917, 32-3

irrelevant surfaces into the essential drama and the larger
poetry.   Also, it conceals in most cases the concrete
experience of the poet in the interest of the universal situation.
Certainly the paucity of sensuous symbols often contributes to
his famous obscurity.[159]

The paucity of sensuous symbols has another effect that neither Lowell
nor Smith mention: by suddenly filling in the gaps with unexpected
images, like the lizard, the poet can play crack-the-whip, not so much
disorienting the reader as waking him up, forcing him to focus on the
details of the poem.   The jolt the reader feels at Robinson's very
intellectual ambush—no other word will do, as laboriously set up as it
is—in part II[160] is the sort normally found in the great chess masters.
Robinson's elephantine joke there means that part II of *Merlin* is as
much a flashback as the Vivian scenes, but I have never seen it
identified as such in the critical literature.

By contrast, there is no paucity of sensuous symbols at all in the
way that Hovey sets up his Merlin's entrance.   "Interior of a cavern in
the bowels of the earth, beneath Mount Hecla.   Huge rock-fragments,
amid which twists tortuously a great root of the tree Yggdrasil.   A
flickering flame, by the light of which are seen the NORNS, colossal
but shadowy shapes, about a gigantic but indistinct loom.   Dull, heavy
sounds, out of which arises a strange music, which resolves itself
continually into imperfect harmonies, which leave the heart in unrest.
A sense of striving and struggle beats through the music."   Again we
note the visually-oriented artist's vividness with sights and vagueness
with sounds.   Robinson's artistry is such that the tension is achieved
through dialogue, as is the delineation of Merlin's character.

Gawaine continues:

"There's more afoot and in the air to-day

---

[159] Smith 64
[160] *CP* 247

Than what is good for Camelot.   Merlin
May or may not know all, but he said well
To say to me that he would not be King.
Nor more would I be King."[161]

John Reade's Merlin certainly did know all: he could even
predict the telegraph: "For words shall flash like light from shore to
shore, / And light itself shall chronicle men's deeds" (216-217)
Steamships, as well: "Great ships shall plough the ocean without
sail." (218)   Even the erection of the Crystal Palace: "A palace shall
arise / Beneath the guidance of the Blameless Prince, / The crystal
image of his ample mind, /   The home of what is best in every clime"
(338-41). Reade's Merlin, unlike Robinson's, has not entered time, and
so is ageless.   "To me what was and that which is to come / Are ever
present, and I grow not old / With time, but have the gift of endless
youth."   Merlin's prophetic gift is bittersweet.   "As one who stands
beside a placid stream, / Watching the white sails passing slowly down,
/ And knows a fatal whirlpool waits them all, / And yet, the while, is
powerless to save,— / So watch I all the ages passing by / Adown the
stream of time into the gulf   / From which is no return. Alas! Alas!"
(88-91)[162]
Returning to Robinson's *Merlin,* Gawaine falls silent.

Far down he gazed
On Camelot, until he made of it
A phantom town of many stillnesses,
Not reared for men to dwell in, or for kings
To reign in, without omens and obscure
Familiars to bring terror to their days;
For though a knight, and one as hard at arms
As any, save the fate-begotten few

---

[161] *CP* 236
[162] Rochester

That all acknowledged or in envy loathed,[163]

Why is Camelot "a phantom town?"   What are "many stillnesses?"
Who are "the fate-begotten few?"   These phrases are tangled,
elusive, even though Robinson seems not to have thought so.   In a
letter dated June 24, 1917 he wrote to a long-time correspondent that
"I'm glad to know that you like *Merlin*—if you do—although I am
sorry that you are having such a hard time with him.   For once in my
life I thought I had written something that would read straight along,
and even now I don't quite see how it can be read in any other
way."[164]   The modern reader will also have a hard time, and, as with
any obscure writing, has to decide whether these arabesques are
worth slowing down for and disentangling, or whether they are like
Gawaine's lizard, simply decorative nuggets.   Robinson's
contemporaries took these arabesques seriously, and recognized them
as a characteristic of his style, as can be seen, first, in Amy Lowell's
critique of *Merlin.*

> There is one curious mannerism in Mr. Robinson's work, and
> one which is the absolute opposite of the ballad quality of
> which he is at times too fond.   The mannerism consists in the
> obscuring of a thing under an epithet, more or less artificial
> and difficult of comprehension...   In less skillful hands, such
> a mannerism would be unbearable, but Mr. Robinson often
> manages to convey with it a subtle symbolism, to underlay the
> fact of his poem with a cogent meaning, tragic, ironic, cyncial,
> what he pleases.   Doubtless the method contains hidden
> germs of danger; it may easily degenerate into artificiality.
> But, so far, Mr. Robinson has not allowed it to degenerate, and
> employed as he employs it, it is valuable.[165]

---

[163] *CP* 236-7
[164] Robinson 1968 143
[165] Lowell 1917, 46-8

Jules Bois, a foreign follower of the American literary scene, and a MacDowell Colony neighbor of Robinson's for several summers, in his enthusiastic 1926 study, was less than enthusiastic about this device, informing French readers that the American poet

> a...une retenue, une façon parfois si elliptique de s'exprimer, qu'il faut s'y reprendre à deux fois pour pénétrer dans ses arcanes. Ceci est la seule critique sérieuse que je me permettrai de lui adresser...Presque jamais il n'est direct. Il suggère, il fait entendre. Il est évasif et rempli d'implications, où le lecteur ordinaire risque de se perdre. Mais ces ombres au tableau ne font que lui donner plus de lustre.[166]
> ("has...a holding-back, a way of expressing himself sometimes so eliptical, that it takes two times to penetrate into his arcana. This is the only serious criticism that would permit myself to make...He is almost never direct. He suggests, he hints. He is evasive and full of implications, where the ordinary reader comes close to getting lost. But these shadows only give the picture more luster.")

In Robinson's defense, we should recall that the same criticism could have been made of Horatian phrases like "Babylonian calculations," or tangled sentences like "Whether Jupiter has granted you several winters, or [just this] last one [to live], / Which now weakens the Tyrrhenian sea [by dashing it] against the pumice." It has been observed that the education of serious young men of Robinson's generation was classically-based, which led to what the French call a *déformation professionelle* ("occupational warping") that was hard to outgrow; in the Latin authors, having to read a passage twice is not uncommon. What is sauce for Horace's goose is sauce for Robinson's gander.

---

[166] Bois 372

Both Lowell and Bois were right, as far as their observations went, but they ignore a very basic question, that of tempo.   It will not do to skim over Robinson's poetry, because to Robinson, and to his generation, poetry was to be savored, as attests Smith in his account of the tipsy Robinson's reading of Wordsworth.   Is there a paucity of sensuous symbols in Robinson?   Not when the poetry is read slowly, and preferably aloud.

In any case, there is no paucity of sensuous symbols in the following lines.

> He felt a foreign sort of creeping up
> And down him, as of moist things in the dark,— [167]

One wonders if "moist things in the dark" is a reference to Robinson's subway days. "Robinson is not only adept at visual and auditory types of imagery, but he also has a power of realising and transferring abstract impressions, especially impressions of darkness."[168]   Another passage involving this leitmotiv of creepy things will occur over a thousand lines later, where Vivian's

> listening skin
> Responded with a creeping underneath it,
> And a crinkling that was incident alike
> To darkness, love, and mice.[169]

Gawaine replies to Dagonet.

> "Sir Dagonet, you best and wariest
> Of all dishonest men, I look through Time,
> For sight of what it is that is to be.

---

[167] CP 237
[168] Chant 48
[169] CP 270

I look to see it, though I see it not.[170]

Robert Buchanan's Gawain does see what is to come.   In "Gawain's Ghost" he appears to Arthur in a dream the night before the last battle (as he does in Tennyson's "The Passing of Arthur" 31-37), and warns him to delay the fight.   There is a reference to his former gallantries: he appears thanks to the intercession of the fair damsels whose champion he has been.   "These once on earth were ladies, / Belied, but chaste and true, / For whom, upon their slanderers, / My sword did battle do; / And they have won me grace on high, / By favour and by prayer, / To come this night to redd thee / To-morrow's fight beware."[171]

Gawain himself has dreams in Act II of *Sir Gawain and the Green Knight: A Play* by the Reverend James Yeames (1843-1931). Gawain is watched over by none other than Merlin as he is tempted in his sleep.

> Merlin: Sleep, sleep well, my son! But, sleeping, thou shalt have strange dreams, and see visions of mystic meaning. The time of thy fiery testing is at hand, and I will strive to fit thee for the hour of trial.

The first dream is of fame.   As it ends, Merlin reappears.

> Merlin: Methinks Gawain is strong for e'en so subtle and mighty a tempting.   Crown and Kingdom! Fame and Glory! Aye, but the price!   Yet (looking down upon the sleeper) thou mightest be royal,—if thou couldst be disloyal!

Gawain passes the other two tests as well.   He wakes.

---

[170] *CP* 237
[171] Rochester

> Gawain: Then, 'twas not all a dream! Was it thou who camest
> to me as in vision, in such strange guise? Dost thou
> read my future?
> Merlin: Nay; only that I see great trials awaiting thee. In what
> shape the ordeal shall come, I know not. Be on thy
> guard, my son! Forget not the Vision of the Holy
> Grail, and to thyself be true![172]

Most of Yeames' writings "have a religious theme, also covering such subjects as mission services and temperance" (Sharp). This Methodist minister, then, is yet another author drawn out of himself by the Arthurian tales.

Robinson's Gawaine has no Merlin to counsel him, and so he only sees what is there.

> I see a town down there that holds a king,
> And over it I see a few small clouds—
> Like feathers in the west, as you observe.[173]

Robinson's development of this is a straight crescendo: Dagonet "knew more, / In a fool's way, than even the King himself / Of what was hovering over Camelot;"[174] in Broceliande, the sunset reminds Merlin of "A thing that was a manor and a castle, / With walls and roofs that had a flaming sky / Behind them... / Above the roofs of his forsaken city / Made flame as if all Camelot were on fire;"[175] "he drank no more. There came / Between him and the world a crumbling sky / Of black and crimson, with a crimson cloud / That held a faroff town of many towers...;"[176] "A crumbling sky that held a crimson cloud / Wherein there was a town of many towers / All

---

[172] Rochester
[173] *CP* 237
[174] *CP* 256
[175] *CP* 266
[176] *CP* 277

swayed and shaken, in a woman's hand / This time, till out of it there spilled and splashed / And tumbled, like loose jewels, town, towers, and walls, / And there was nothing but a crumbling sky / That made anon of black and red the ruin / A wild and final rain for Camelot;"[177] and the last line of the poem is "And there was darkness over Camelot."[178]

Gawaine continues:

> And I shall see no more this afternoon,
> Than what there is around us every day,
> Unless you have a skill that I have not
> To ferret the invisible for rats."[179]

This will be echoed in Dagonet's soliloquy in the last scene: "Your fool sees not / So far as Merlin sees: yet if he saw / The truth—why then, such harvest were the best."[180] Gawaine is skeptical of Dagonet's deadpan denials, and wonders to himself, in a combination of the "fool" motiv and the "seeing" motiv, "'Poor fool!'" he murmured. "'Or am I the fool? / ...God knows what he knows, / And what his wits infer from what he sees / And feels and hears. I wonder what he knows / Of Lancelot, or what I might know now, / Could I have sunk myself to sound a fool...'"[181]

Returning to the traditional analysis, with reference to the "rat" imagery, Tennyson's Vivien refers to herself as a rat in "Merlin and Vivien." Before going after Merlin, she insinuates herself into Guinevere's retinue and starts malicious gossip, principally against the Queen and Lancelot. "Ah little rat that borest in the dyke 110. Thy hole by night to let the boundless deep / Down upon far-off cities while they dance— ...For Lancelot will be gracious to the rat, 118. And our

---

[177] *CP* 308
[178] *CP* 314
[179] *CP* 237
[180] *CP* 304
[181] *CP* 241

wise Queen, if knowing that I know, / Will hate, loathe, fear—but honour me the more."
Robinson's Dagonet is dismissive of invisible things and of rats.

"If you see what's around us every day,
You need no other showing to go mad.[182]

What does Merlin see?   "The man who sees / May see too far, and he may see too late / The path he takes unseen."[183]   This idea is elaborated both in content and poetic variation as "The man who saw / Too much must have an eye to see at last / Where Fate has marked the clay; and he shall delve, / Although his hand may slacken, and his knees / May rock without a method as he toils; /...I see the light, / But I shall fall before I come to it; / For I am old."[184]   Merlin also sees the past: "I saw too much when I saw Camelot; / And I saw farther backward into Time, / And forward, than a man may see and live, / When I made Arthur king."[185]
Robinson piques the reader's curiosity about the returning Merlin.

"To mention lesser terrors,
Men say his beard is gone."[186]

Another example of the inadequacy of Hagedorn's biography is found in his account of Robinson's first meeting with Isadora Duncan. First of all, the account is undated, except for the statement that Isadora was "fresh from European triumphs."   A glance at a Duncanology places this in December, 1908, but it is irksome to have to do Hagedorn's work for him.   Equally irksome is Hagedorn's myopia in his account of the party where Duncan and Robinson met.   "At two in

---

[182] *CP* 237
[183] *CP* 294
[184] *CP* 295
[185] *CP* 297
[186] *CP* 238

the morning she began to send her guests home, all except Robinson and Torrence, an attractive young couple from Canada, and a devoted slave who had that day, for love of her, shaved off his vast and virginal beard."[187]   Given Robinson's way of seizing on commonplace events and elaborating them, is it not likely that this is the origin of the *Merlin* beard episode?   And would not this indicate that the germ of the Merlin-Vivian passages was the Robinson-Duncan encounter?   That Vivian was partly based on Isadora?   And as such, should an alert biographer not have seized on this loose end, and asked Robinson for clarification?   As it is, we will never know.

Regardless of where he got the idea, Robinson made Merlin's beard a thread that goes throughout the poem.   He arrives in Broceliande "Cloaked like a monk, and with a beard," [188] a very full beard: "Merlin—whose advance, / Betrayed through his enormity of hair / The cheeks and eyes of youth—," much to Vivian's chagrin.   "'O, that hair?'" / She moaned, as if in sorrow: "'Must it be? / Must every prophet and important wizard / Be clouded so that nothing but his nose / And eyes, and intimations of his ears, / Are there to make us know him when we see him?'"[189]   Merlin has predicted to Arthur that he would be "By love made little and by a woman shorn, / Like Samson, of my glory."[190]   At Vivian's insistence, he does have his beard shaved off, and Vivian is unrepentant: "'Be never sorry that my love took off / That horrid hair to make your face at last / A human fact.   Since I have had your name / To dream of and say over to myself, The visitations of that awful beard / Have been a terror for my nights and days— / For twenty years."[191]   A final, touching echo reveals that he is through with Vivian for good: he is letting his beard grow back, although he is no longer ageless: he now has "an old face / Made older with an inch of silver beard."[192]

---

[187] Hagedorn 1939, 230
[188] *CP* 264
[189] *CP* 265-6
[190] *CP* 260
[191] *CP* 274
[192] *CP* 304

Dagonet suspects that Merlin's return means that trouble is coming, and uses a phrase that will find an echo at the very end of the poem: "Time swings / A mighty scythe, and some day all your peace / Goes down like so much clover,"[193] which will recur as Dagonet's fears of war: "Wherefore a field of waving men may soon / Be shorn by Time's indifferent scythe, because / The King is mad."[194]

Equally elaborate is the development of the burial motiv, but not at first.   Robinson begins by deceiving his reader's expectations.

> he told the King one day
> That he was to be buried, and alive,
> In Brittany; and that the King should see
> The face of him no more.[195]

This plays to the reader's expectations, that Merlin was hexed, as in Mumford, or entombed, as in Tennyson.   Accordingly, the poem's first readers must have discounted the following lines, which do not follow the main story line; they may have even been read as hearsay. Robinson is leading the reader on: the reader will find, to his surprise, that they are, in fact, perfectly true.

> Then Merlin sailed
> Away to Vivian in Broceliande,[196]

The echo of these lines will come after Merlin's audience with Arthur: "Over the waves and into Brittany / Went Merlin, to Broceliande."[197]

> Where now she crowns him and herself with flowers
> And feeds him fruits and wines and many foods

---

[193] *CP* 238
[194] *CP* 303
[195] *CP* 239
[196] *CP* 239
[197] *CP* 260

Of many savors, and sweet ortolans.[198]

This is the set-up of still another Robinsonian crack-the-whip, but only if the reader knows that an ortolan is a bird (of the finch family); the *volte-face* will not come until over a thousand lines later.

And there are players of all instruments—
Flutes, hautboys, drums, and viols;[199]

Indignor quandoque bonus dormitat Homerus said Horace ("I am bothered whenever good Homer nods," *Art of Poetry* 359), and the modern reader may be bothered whenever good Robinson nods, committing here the sin of gratuitous archaism. An "hautboy" (pronounced "oh boy," etymologically *haut* ["high"] *bois* [wood{wind}]) is a rare instance of Robinsonian preciosity. It is nothing more mysterious than an oboe, and it would have been better if he had simply written "oboe," since "hautboy" is not an archaic word the way "shawm" is; it is simply a distraction, as if he had written "flutes" as "floutes."

A contemporary parallel is found in Buchanan's "Merlin's Tomb," where "the Lady Viviane" boasts of the spells she has learned. "And I can wake ærial strain / The moping mood to cheer, / As viol, lute, orpherien, / Did mix sweet music near 40."[200] It is irksome to note that good Buchanan nods twice here, committing not only Robinson's sin of phony antiquarianism, but the additional sin of redundancy: an orpharion (the usual spelling) is nothing more mysterious than a sister instrument of the lute, the difference being the lack of the extra bass strings that on the lute serve as resonators. It is as if Buchanan had written "twelve-string guitars and guitars."

---

[198] *CP* 239
[199] *CP* 239
[200] Rochester

> and she sings
> To Merlin, till he trembles in her arms
> And there forgets that any town alive
> Had ever such a name as Camelot.[201]

Perrine's observation is very much to the point:

> To Tennyson Robinson owes nothing at all in story or detail, but perhaps a great deal in impetus, if mainly by a resolve to do it differently.   Like Tennyson, Robinson saw in the story a symbol of the surrender of the intellect to the senses.   But Robinson's sense of psychological realities made him rebel against Tennyson's crude allegorical treatment.   Tennyson, revolted by the idea of sensuality, embodied it in a symbol stripped of all attractiveness.   His Vivian is so repulsive that she is simply incredible, and Merlin's succumbing to her is inexplicable.   Robinson bent his efforts to make Vivian first and foremost a woman—and an enchanting one.   Insofar as he made her and Broceliande also a symbol, he made them represent the sensuous life in its full attractiveness.   The surrender of the man of intellect to this life is convincing because its beauty is felt by the reader.   Robinson's treatment of the Merlin-Vivian story is in reaction against Tennyson's.[202]
> So Vivian holds him with her love, they say,
> And he, who has no age, has not grown old.
> I swear to nothing, but that's what they say.[203]

The question of Merlin's age is an example of the persistence of a preconception.   Robinson, as we will see, repeatedly refers to Merlin as neither young nor old, until the Vivian episode, when he enters time.

---

[201] *CP* 239-40
[202] Perrine 1972, 318
[203] *CP* 240

"Whatever I am," he says at their first meeting, "I have not lived in Time until to-day."[204]   The critics of his day, and often those of our day, however, read right over this detail.   Charles Cestre, who championed Robinson's work to French readers, writes that

> Le *Merlin* est l'histoire d'un amour fragile, fugitif, dont les partenaires sont un viellard souriant et bon, brûlant d'une dernière flamme, et une damoiselle transportée pour un temps d'admiration et de tendresse quasi-filiale.   De telles liaisons ne peuvent durer.[205]
>
> ("The *Merlin* is the story of a fragile, fleeting love, where the couple are a graybeard, smiling and good, ablaze with a last flame, and a young lady carried away for a time by admiration and by an almost daughterly tenderness.   Relationships of this sort cannot last.")

In point of fact, this relationship lasts for ten years, and I am at a loss as to where Cestre comes up with his blandly grandfatherly Merlin, since the poem is clear that the Vivian episode is the transition from agelessness to an unquiet age.   Robinson himself was not very helpful in preserving this distinction, as we see in a letter to his long-time correspondent Edith Brower:

> 2 November 1920
> On the whole, I am not displeased with your final preference for *Merlin,* for I am inclined to believe that my best work is there, though the subject matter of *Lancelot* is infinitely more appealing.   If you think it is easy to make anything beautiful out of an amorous Merlin in his dotage, just try it for a hundred lines or so.[206]

---

[204] *CP* 265
[205] Cestre 193-4
[206] *CP* 239-40

> And you must know that Love, when Love invites
> Philosophy to play, plays high and wins,
> Or low and loses...
> But Vivian, she played high.   Oh, very high!
> Flutes, hautboys, drums, and viols,--and her love.
> Gawaine, farewell."[207]

The seductive powers of music are also mentioned in *The Porcupine.*

> Stuart: She found out that I had some property, and then she
> found that she could lead me wherever she liked with
> her shape and her face and her infernal music.[208]

In any case, "In his *Merlin* Robinson has almost done away with the supernatural.   Vivian's charms are the magic which hold Merlin in Broceliande, not any mysterious spell of waving arms and mysterious passes."[209]   I would only quibble with the word "almost."   The only element in the poem that could be called supernatural is Merlin's observed agelessness before Vivian and his self-announced aging after Vivian, and even here Robinson does not spell out what he means. This is not a question of the poet being cryptic; he simply states that Merlin has "entered Time," and leaves it at that.

Sometimes Robinson is cryptic, as he is with Gawaine's exit:

> And later, when descending to the city,
> Through unavailing casements he could hear
> The roaring of a mighty voice within,[210]

In what sense is a casement unavailing?   This is more than just one of Robinson's thought-provoking turns of phrase like "phantom town,"

---

[207] Perrine 1972, 318
[208] *CP* 240
[209] *CP* 265
[210] Cestre 193-4

"many stillnesses," and "the fate-begotten few." This is the set up of the "back-hand stroke" that will occur almost two hundred lines later.

> Confirming fervidly his own conviction:
> "It's all too strange, and half the world's half crazy!"— [211]

Turns of phrase with "half" are common with Robinson. In 1915, in an autobiographical sketch, he wrote, "I might add that certain superficial critics who have called me a pessimist have been entirely wrong in their diagnosis. In point of fact, one has only to read my books to wish that half the world might have half my optimism."[212] In *The Porcupine,* we find

> Larry: [*Tapping his boots*] Rachel, when I ran away from
> home, I was just about half crazy.[213]

In Van Zorn,

> Villa: They think I'm a fool for marrying Weldon Farnham—
> when he doesn't more than half want me.[214]

Gawaine's closing lines are

> He scowled: "Well, I agree with Lamorak."
> He frowned, and passed: "And I like not this day."[215]

No attentive reader could be satisfied with these two lines. Agree? Agree with what? One agrees with something that has been said; yet this is the first time Lamorak's name has been mentioned. How can

---

[211] *CP* 241
[212] Robinson 1975, 68
[213] Robinson 1915, 70
[214] Robinson, 1914, 69
[215] *CP* 241

there be a "said" without a sayer?   Passed?   Passed what?   Until
he springs his trap, Robinson is playing poker.

Part II is another conversation.

> Sir Lamorak, the man of oak and iron,
> Had with him now, as a care-laden guest,
> Sir Bedivere, a man whom Arthur loved
> As he had loved no man save Lancelot.[216]

Algernon Charles Swinburne (1837-1909) will be of interest later,
for his portrayal of Merlin, but it is worth noting that his *Tale of Balin*
has a Lamorak, too.   Swinburne's knight has no "oak and iron" to
speak of, however.   Bedivere has already been noted in John Reade's
"Prophecy of Merlin," as the seer's "straight man," the naïve questioner
who sets up Merlin's pronouncements with his naïve questions.

> Like one whose late-flown shaft of argument
> Had glanced and fallen afield innocuously,
> He turned upon his host a sudden eye
> That met from Lamorak's an even shaft
> Of native and unused authority;...
> And each man held the other till at length
> Each turned away, shutting his heavy jaws
> Again together, prisoning thus two tongues
> That might forget and might not be forgiven.[217]

"The most important respects in which Robinson's Arthurian
trilogy differs from the *Idylls,* and rises superior to them, is in
Robinson's provision of believable, complex characters, rather than
allegorical abstractions and paper cut-outs."[218]   Even by the poet's

---

[216] *CP* 241
[217] *CP* 242
[218] Perrine 1969, 417

usual standards, though, this passage is a tour de force: he has roughed out two characters in only thirteen lines.   Unlike the short, early poems, however, the characters will continue to develop, in a steady revelation of telling details.   Smith is quite correct when he observes that

> It is in the other category of greatness, that of size of population, that Robinson is preeminent among poets in English except those who wrote for the stage.   His 233 fully drawn characters are approached only by Chaucer's 188 – the latter at a cursory count.   Browning, with less than a hundred, follows far off – as indeed do Goethe and Hugo, whose works are notably populous in their respective off-stage poetic literatures.   In Robinson you are in the presence of a world which for size and completeness of portraiture is hardly equaled elsewhere in modern poetry except among the playwrights.   In the double epic *Merlin* and *Lancelot,* he gives us a general statement of the meaning of life that will stand with those of Milton and Blake, of Wordsworth and Shelley and Whitman.   But in his presentation of many people and their multitudinous dilemmas, he is almost alone.[219]

Amy Lowell, on the other hand, in her 1917 study complains that "Mr. Robinson is constantly desiring a larger canvas than his fugitive poems permit.   He has tried plays, now he essays a narrative poem. Yet for some reason he seems never to have realized the different technique necessary for these more sustained efforts.   He still remains the poet of the fleeting instant."[220]

Then Bedivere, to find a plain way out,

---

[219] Smith xiv
[220] Lowell 1917, 66

> Said, "Lamorak, let us drink to some one here,
> And end this dryness.   Who shall it be—the King,
> The Queen, or Lancelot?"—"Merlin," Lamorak growled;[221]

This is the first of two drinking scenes in *Merlin,* the second being in Vivian's pleasure garden.   For the reader of 1917, they must have been incendiary, not in spite of their decorousness, but because of it. Temperance agitation had brought that movement to the threshold of Prohibition, which would take effect in 1919.   There was a literary side to this agitation, and, not surprisingly, the play was the thing: *Ten Nights in a Bar-Room and What I Saw There,* Timothy Shay Arthur's 1854 best-seller which "did for the temperance movement what *Uncle Tom's Cabin*...had done for the abolition movement—popularized and sentimentalized it," [222] had been dramatized by one William Pratt in 1854, and "Come Home, Father" ("Father, dear father, come home with me now...") had been set to music in 1862 by none other than Henry Clay Work, whose prestige in that day was similar to Andrew Lloyd Webber's in ours.   *The Drunkard, or The Fallen Saved* made its debut in 1874.

Stark Young's 1906 *Guenevere* has a drunk scene at the opening of Act III, where two witnesses to Mordred's plot are too inebriated to give their testimony, which not only disturbs the dignity of Arthur's court, but also creates tension: all are awaiting the appearance of the Queen for her trial; these two have exculpatory evidence, but are incoherent.

> (Enter Cador and Breuse, drunk.)
> Arthur: 'Tis out of form and reverence that ye come
>   Thus here, muddled with wine.
> Cador: 'Tis out of form and reverence what we have
>   To tell the king. 'Tis somewhat for thy ears.
> Arthur: Speak, then.

---

[221] *CP* 242
[222] Flexner 356-7

Cador: Last night before the feast, in a dark place—
Some say the dark is devilled—before the cups
At the feast, I heard two speak together.
Arthur: What said they, good fellow?
Cador: Thou heardst it, Breuse, what was't? I cannot think.
My lord, I wake not early thus all days.[223]

In Hovey's bacchanal, Merlin is overcome: as the revellers
exeunt, "Merlin attempts to follow, but falls tipsily."
What was E. A. Robinson's relationship to The Bottle? It is
useless to go to Hagedorn, as he cannot even get his story straight. In
the context of Robinson's loneliness in New York City, he writes that
the poet's sensitive soul was so oppressed by all the urban anguish that
"he could not resist dropping in at the bar of the Fifth Avenue Hotel,
for a whiskey. It was astonishing how that one glass lifted the whole
burden." [224] A mere three pages later, however, he writes:
"[Robinson's] drinks cost him more than his food, since he was
alcoholically so unimpressionable that he had to drink deep before he
felt the desired effects."[225] Which is it? "That one glass," or "drink
deep?" Smith's account rings true:

> E.A. was unique among drinkers in that he had the greatest
> capacity anyone ever heard of, and yet he never became an
> alcoholic…He loved liquor…, took it "not for the taste but for
> the effect, " and yet, at least during my eleven years'
> acquaintance with him, he could do without it at any time.
> He never drank before dinner time, and he took frequent,
> considerable jaunts on the wagon.[226]

---

[223] Rochester
[224] Hagedorn, 1937, 198
[225] Hagedorn, 1937, 201
[226] Smith 33

Two telling remarks by Robinson are worth mentioning: in a 1920 biographical sketch he wrote, "My 'principal hatreds,' or two of them, are prohibition and free verse,"[227] and during an evening ramble with Smith, he said, "When I was young, there was a devil in all of my family.   But I knew that liquor was not the devil that would get me. Poetry was the devil that would get me."[228]

They toast the absent wizard, and, having cooled down, speak their minds.   Lamorak begins, telling Bedivere that all his talk will not make

> ...a slippery queen a nun who counts and burns
> Herself to nothing with her beads and candles.[229]

Robinson relies on the reader's knowledge of Tennyson here: the queen will, in fact become a nun, however improbable that may seem to Lamorak at this time; and the references to fire will recall the drama of her being rescued from the stake by Lancelot.   There are other "fire" references, however.   To Lamorak, Guinevere is Arthur's "easy Queen, / Whom he took knowing she'd thrown sparks already   / On that same piece of tinder, Lancelot, / Who fetched her."[230] Dagonet will later allude to the damage she has done when he tries to coax Merlin into interceding with the King, beginning with "Lancelot, the other day / That saved this pleasing sinner from the fire / That she may spread for thousands.   Were she now / The cinder the King willed or were you now / To see the King, the fire might yet go out."[231] To Lamorak, she is simply the easy Queen.

> That's how I speak; and while you strain your mazard,

---

[227] Robinson, 1975, 69
[228] Smith 34
[229] *CP* 242-3
[230] *CP* 245
[231] *CP* 308

Like Father Jove, big with a new Minerva,[232]

The reader may strain his mazard as to the aesthetics of these lines: the archaism is abrupt, and the Jove-Minerva business seems a throwback to Pollio capering with Terpsichore, which was itself old-fashioned when Robinson wrote it back in 1890.   Lamorak continues as if nothing had happened.

The story is that Merlin warned the King
Of what's come now to pass; and I believe it...[233]

Lamorak will go so far as to say that Arthur acted to spite Merlin: "Because the King—God save poor human reason!— / Would prove to Merlin, who knew everything / Worth knowing in those days, that he was wrong."[234]   Lamorak's interjection will echo through the poem, a minor leitmotiv.   Merlin will observe to Blaise, "God's pity on us that our words have wings / And leave our deeds to crawl so far below them;"[235]   Gawaine will exclaim in fury at Lancelot's bloody rescue of Guenevere, which resulted in the death of his "two brothers, whom he slew / Unarmored and unarmed —God save your wits!"[236]; in the last scene, Bedivere in despair will say, "God's mercy for the world he made, I say."[237]

The King, if one may say it, set the pace,
And we've two strapping bastards here to prove it.
Young Borre, he's well enough; but as for Modred,
I squirm as often as I look at him.[238]

---

[232] *CP* 243
[233] *CP* 243
[234] *CP* 245
[235] *CP* 269
[236] *CP* 299
[237] *CP* 301
[238] *CP* 243

Modred will later kill Lamorak,[239] as the old warrior predicts: "If Modred's aim be good / For backs like mine, I'm not long for the scene."[240]

In Tennyson's "Guinevere" Arthur expressly denies fathering Modred, referring to him as "the man they call / My sister's son—no kin of mine..." (569)   "For I was ever virgin save for thee," (554) he tells Guinevere.

Cram is specific as to Arthur's wild oats, beginning   in Act II, Scene 1 of *Excalibur.*

> Merlin: Thou art a boy,
> And therefore prone to vain and wanton things;
> But like a torrent raging lawlessly,
> I'll turn thine ardour in an wholesome course

(Like the "water and steam mains" of Cram's M.I.T. pageant, perhaps?)

> Until it serves God's ends...
> I find thee enmeshed
> Within the springes of a wanton girl.

The young king's irresponsibility continues in Act II, Scene 3. Arthur, provoked by jealousy, has dueled with Lancelot, and has impetuously proposed to Guenever.   He meets with Merlin, who shows him his horoscope, and warns him that Guenever will bring him humiliation and strife.

> Merlin: Listen: in the seventh house,
> Yea, even in the cusp thereof, in square of Mars,
> The Great Malefic, grim implacable,

---

[239] *CP* 300
[240] *CP* 249

> Frowned on thy birth, and therefore shalt thou swear
> To have no part in love forevermore…
> King Arthur: Save thy words,
> For here I act alone.

Cram uses Arthur's infatuation with Guenever to account for the birth of Modred: in Act III, Scene 3, "Morgan le Fay in the guise of Guenever is seated on a splendid throne." She seduces him, and induces him to give up Excalibur.

(Robinson, too, has Modred conceived as the result of a deception.

> Your son, begotten, though you knew not then
> Your leman was your sister, of Morgause;[241]

as Merlin notifies Arthur in their audience.)

Cram's Merlin, by swearing Arthur to monogamy (since it is too late for absolute chastity), is able to conjure the sword back. Angelic voices sing, and their metaphors are once again architectural. "The Holy Grail / the Sword and the Table / fix the foundation / of God's Holy City. / Guard thou Pendragon's inheritance / Build thou the City of God."[242]

Robinson's *Merlin* is not so jubilant: it begins with forebodings and ends the same way. The poem's first reviewers understood its autumnal tone. "Edwin Arlington Robinson's 'Merlin' shows Camelot on the eve of the war that ends all; a kingdom in decay is tottering to its end. Here is no pomp of chivalry, no tournament, no dance or feast, but the end of the Round Table."[243] Bedivere predicts,

> And we shall have, where late there was a kingdom,
> A dusty wreck of what was once a glory—

---

[241] *CP* 252
[242] Rochester
[243] Reed 863

A wilderness whereon to crouch and mourn
And moralize, or else to build once more
For something better or for something worse.[244]

This autumnal quality seems to have escaped the poet himself.
Robinson wrote to Edith Brower on June 24, 1917,

> But as I have long given up pretending to know anything
> about myself or my work, you needn't mind what I say, only, I
> wish you wouldn't call the poem "sad" for I'm — if it is
> anything of the kind.   There is nothing especially sad about
> the end of kings and the redemption of the world, and that is
> what Merlin seems to be driving at.[245]

What the poet says, however, does not square with what he wrote:
the middle part of *Merlin*, the Vivian intermezzo, is certainly idyllic,
with its themes of love and luxury; and if the outer sections are
contrastive, then they must be sad, regardless of what Robinson said.

This is not to say that an author's stated intentions are to be
ignored: only that Robinson's are.   The maxim is, *falsus in uno,
falsus in omnibus.* False in one thing, false in all, and we have already
noted that Robinson was consistently false, or, if you will, cagey,
evasive, about the autobiographical elements of his work.   Smith
gives numerous examples:

> With respect to the material of Robinson's verse, he was
> forever protesting too much that all of his work was
> "objective" – though he admitted that it was sometimes
> touched by "personal coloring."   In 1897, writing to his
> friend Harry Smith about his first book, he denied that there
> was much of "me" in it.   In 1917 he informed Lewis

---

[244] *CP* 244
[245] Robinson, 1968, 153

Nathaniel Chase that "I do not recall anything of mine that is a direct transcription of experience." And about the same time he told Esther Bates that he "precipitated his own characters."[246]

Josephine Preston Peabody, in April, 1900, writes of "E. A. Robinson exhorting me to drop 'philosophizing' and twittering at infinities and to write about things objective."[247]

Yet all the while Robinson was writing poetry that was extremely subjective, full of autobiographical details and workings-out of his personal traumas.   In addition to Hepburn's "System of Opposites," W. R. Thompson's "Broceliande: E. A. Robinson's Palace of Art" is a well-considered analysis of many important elements in of *Merlin,* but the reader should be reminded of the variable that Thompson includes:

> Critics, more often than not beguiled by thematic echoes from other poems in the Robinson canon, have forced *Merlin* into a preconceived contextual pattern of the poet's work without regard to that poem's particularity.   What is purposed here, then, is an examination of what the poet achieved in the light of what he attempted.[248]

But how does the reader know what Robinson attempted?   The only one who knew what he attempted was Robinson himself, and we have seen that he did not "level" with his readers about his poetry.   He did not even level with his intimate friends.

Kay concludes:

> ...how the King persuaded or beguiled
> The stricken wizard from across the water

---

[246] Smith 62
[247] Peabody 1925, 131
[248] Thompson 231

> Outriddles my poor wits.   It's all too strange."
> "It's all too strange, and half the world's half crazy!"
> Roared Lamorak, forgetting once again
> The devastating carriage of his voice.[249]

Here is the crack-the-whip that Robinson has so patiently set up. The "unavailing casements" that Gawaine observed at the end of part I[250] are of no avail when it comes to muffling "the devastating carriage" of Lamorak's voice, which is what Gawaine heard on that page, and which he, recognizing Lamorak's voice, agrees with.   We suddenly find that the opening of book II has been a flashback, that it began some time before we thought it did: not at the end of part I, but at whatever time it was so that the line "It's all too strange, and half the world's half crazy" of part I lines up with the line "It's all too strange, and half the world's half crazy" of part II.   They are the same line, first as overheard by Gawaine, then as spoken by Lamorak.   The laboriousness with which this jolt was set up is evidence for the deliberateness of the other jolts in *Merlin*.

The beginning of Part III would support Kay's pessimism.

> King Arthur, as he paced a lonely floor
> That rolled a muffled echo, as he fancied,
> All through the palace and out through the world,[251]

The poem that Hagedorn said inspired *Merlin*, "The Great Maze," has a similar description of a restless Agamemnon.

> Troubled, bewildered, lonely, sick at heart,
> With bowed head, Agamemnon, king of men,
> Strode down the corridor.   The house was mute

---

[249] *CP* 247
[250] *CP* 241
[251] *CP* 249

Save for his footsteps.[252]

Laurence Binyon's drama *Arthur* was performed in 1919, but was written before the war; it is also in the Tennyson continuum (unlike *The Madness of Merlin*), and is so relevant to Robinson.   The sixth scene has

(Arthur pacing up and down.   Enter Gawaine.)
Gawaine: Does not the King sleep?
Arthur: Gawaine, there are things
Will not be put to sleep: thoughts in the blood...[253]

And later,

Arthur: Heaven knows my heart
Has nothing willing in it: slow and heavy
Moves my thought thither where the fear is, slow
And heavy as sea-tides against the wind.[254]

Note the understated entrance Robinson has given Arthur, in contrast with Mumford's setting in Part II of her opera, where the curtain rises on the "Hall of the Knights of the Round Table: King Arthur presiding, with Merlin, his chief councilor, at his right hand. The knights are assembled and the feast is in progress."   *Con spirito*, *forte*, Hadley's music is foursquare, with trumpet calls and a men's chorus (the knights) singing in block harmony, that is, with no polyphony; the trumpet calls give the scene a resemblance in tone to the triumphal march in *Aida.*

Hail, all hail!

---

252 Hagedorn 1916, 28
253 Binyon, 1919, 76
254 Binyon 1919, 79

Let the hall resound
To the ringing mirth
Of the Table Round!

We note that Mumford's verse is ideal for a libretto: the words are vivid, and the lines are short enough to give the composer some flexibility as to the setting.

Robinson's Arthur is similar to Binyon's in his hopelessness, his inability to hear

What Fate's knocking made so manifest[255]

There are more than a dozen references to fate in *Merlin,* a fact not lost on the anonymous reviewer in *Catholic World.*

An undefined but terrible power called fate is the chief factor of the poem...This taste of futility and desolation lingers longest after the poem is read, and puzzles most as to its meaning.   A faint promise is half given, in the end, that catastrophe will be the teacher of men, and that the world will finally profit by these mistakes and sins. But it is hard to reconcile this tentative afterthought of hope with the strong sense of fatalism   in the poem; the sense that a will before which the human will is powerless, has caused each act and directed each disaster.[256]

The reviewer is misled by taking Robinson's references to fate at face value.   Although Robinson uses the word "fate" frequently, there is nothing fatalistic about *Merlin* whatsoever.   Arthur is reaping the whirlwind: Merlin warned him not to marry a woman who did not love him, but he did so anyway.   Modred's plots advance because Arthur turns a blind eye to them.   Merlin goes off to Broceliande because he sees that the dominoes have started to fall, and that he has done all he can.

---

[255] *CP* 249
[256] Anon., 1917, 255

It might be easy to assume, from the theme of Nemesis in the poem (as Arthur said of Merlin, his "Nemeis had made of him a slave") that the sage does nothing but let events take their course.   This is not the case.   He acts vigorously a number of times.   After his first visit to Broceliande, for example, he reproaches Arthur...he also warns the King against Modred, and bids him not to let his enemies take the Queen and kingdom.   Moreover, he is a free agent;   he leaves Broceliande when he wishes, and returns to Camelot the last time in agony of mind to do what he can for Arthur's realm. When he tells Vivian of the dangerous state of affairs in Camelot she reproaches him bitterly in a powerful scene. Merlin is in despair.   Yet his place is in Camelot.[257]

Robinson's use, overuse and misuse of the word "fate" is a flaw in *Merlin.*   Since the plot is driven by perfectly plausible cause and effect, Robinson's harping on fate makes no sense at all.   Although this contradiction cannot be excused, it can be explained: as is often the case, the plays are the thing.

Van Zorn exhibits exactly the same flaw, except that there Robinson uses the word "destiny."   Amy Lowell's analysis is a good starting point.

> So far as [the dialogue] and the action are concerned, the play is one of half tones.   The swift vigour of the author's character poems is completely lacking.   Those brief, virile dramas scattered throughout his books have lent no cutting edge to this long play...
> One reason for this vagueness of the actual actors lies in the fact that behind all they do and say is the real drama, and the hero of it is Fate.   It is Fate who shakes the lives of the characters into place and will not be denied... Van Zorn is

---

[257] Starr 114

chosen as the interpreter of this Fate.   He is at once its tool, and its avenging sword.[258]

It is true that Robinson talks about destiny (not Fate, as Lowell writes); he talks about it incessantly, as a survey of the play will show.

> Otto: [*With affectionate disgust*]   You?   You haven't done anything.   Destiny, or something or other, has done it for you.
> Farnham: [*Laughing*]   But I don't believe much in destiny. I believe in work.[259]

*   *   *

> Farnham: As for poor Mr. Lucas, this man [*Looking at Van Zorn*] will tell you that he is in the hands of Destiny—gin-rickeys and all.[260]

*   *   *

> Van Zorn: Whether he takes one way or the other, will depend upon events.
> Farnham: [*With a short laugh*] Why don't you say Destiny, and be done with it?
> Van Zorn: Very well—we'll call it Destiny.[261]

*   *   *

> Farnham: More Destiny I suppose.   We can't beat Destiny.

---

[258] Lowell,1917, 49
[259] Robinson, 1914, 5
[260] Robinson, 1914, 41
[261] Robinson, 1914, 47

Van Zorn: Certainly not.   But Destiny can beat *us,* and it can
make us do better than we have done in the past.[262]

*   *   *

Otto: [*After shaking hands, rather suddenly, with Villa and
Lucas*]   Farnham, old man, the more I think of this,
the better I like it.   There's a—there's a kind of
destiny about it.

Farnham: [*Patting Otto's shoulder*]   Otto, we can always
look to you for the right word.   [*Wearily, with a
mild trace of venom*]   I've been trying to think of
that word "destiny" all the evening.[263]

In point of fact, however, *Van Zorn* is not a play about destiny at all,
but a play impelled by a *deus ex machina,* Van Zorn himself, who is
neither destiny's interpreter, nor its tool, nor its avenging sword; he is a
busybody, albeit a beneficent one.   He saves Lucas from despair by
writing him a check (shades of *The Porcupine*), he prevents him from
committing suicide by taking away his small vial of poison (again,
shades of *The Porcupine*), and he prevents a potentially unhappy
marriage by pointing out to the bride-to-be that the marriage would be
potentially unhappy.   This is not destiny, no matter how often
Robinson may use the word, but meddling, pure and simple, and the
more Robinson uses the word "destiny," the more put off the reader
becomes: after all, if the playwright has not thought the drama
through, why should the reader put himself out to do so?

   Merlin's "fate" is nothing more than an undigested holdover from
Van Zorn's "destiny;"   Lowell and the anonymous reviewer in the
Catholic World were right to sense that something was wrong, but
missed the nub: Robinson is sending a mixed message, the dialogue

---

[262] Robinson, 1914, 51
[263] Robinson, 1914, 150

saying "fate" or "destiny" while the plot says the opposite. The plot of *Van Zorn* is feeble, and the incongruity of the "destiny" business makes the bubble burst. *Merlin* is written with such verve, however, that the "fate" business is not a distraction, or at least is rationalized as a sort of reaping what one sows.

Arthur's audience has begun with

> ...Merlin, once the wisest of all men...
> ...the fond, lost Merlin,
> Whose Nemesis had made of him a slave,
> A man of dalliance, and a sybarite.[264]

These lines recall the Merlin poems of Ralph Waldo Emerson.[265] "Sybarite" recalls Emerson's "Merlin I:"

> By Sybarites beguiled,
> He shall no task decline.

"Nemesis" echoes "Merlin II:"

> And Nemesis,
> Who with even matches odd...

Robinson was unequivocal: "Emerson is the greatest poet who ever wrote in America. Passages scattered here and there in his work surely are the greatest of American poetry. In fact, I think that there are lines and sentences in Emerson's poetry that are as great as anything anywhere."[266]

King Arthur senses the alteration in his friend, and feels that Merlin is lost to him.

---

[264] *CP* 249
[265] Gilman 136
[266] Robinson, 1975, 126

And on the King's heart lay a sudden cold:
"I might as well have left him in his grave,
As he would say it...
...This Merlin is not mine,
But Vivian's..."[267]

Merlin is still the seer, however:

Then Merlin, as one reading Arthur's words
On viewless tablets in the air before him:[268]

It is interesting to compare Merlin's effortless knowledge with the huffing and puffing in Hovey's opening scene. The Norns have answered the seer's inquiry with a riddle, and offer no explanation, saying, "There is no wit in us to make this clear." He responds:

Merlin: Not in you?
Where then? In myself?
[He strikes his own forehead with the wand. – A black formless mark appears on his brow. – He falls in a swoon]

Hovey's Merlin is not only Wagnerian, but Faustian. Consider the song the Norns sing while the scene changes:

Over the Loom
Brooding and bending
Weave we the ending,
Self-decreed doom,
A robe for repayment.

---

[267] *CP* 249-50
[268] *CP* 250

Compare this with the song of the first spirit that Goethe's *Faust* conjures up:

Geburt und Grab,		("Birth and death,	
Ein ewiges Meer,	505	an eternal sea,	
Ein wechseld Weben,		a changing hubbub,	
Ein glühend Leben,		a glowing life,	
So schaff' ich am sausenden		so I create at the humming	
Webstuhl der Zeit		loom of time	
Und wirke der Gottheit	510	and make Divinity's	
lebendiges Kleid.		living garment.")	

Not only is the poetry reminiscent of *Faust,* but the stage directions, too, provide special effects of a learnèd kind. As the Norns sing, the light fades to black, and according to the stage directions there is "a confused sound, like a low rumbling. Then a clear tenor voice is heard singing: *'Nonne anima plus est quam esca; et corpus plus quam vestimentum?'* ("Is not the soul more than food, and the body more than clothing?") – A ray of light breaks through the darkness..." The scene is revealed to be "a grove, with a Greek temple in the background. Merlin lies, still in his swoon upon the ground". Sylphs start to sing.

> The fleet wind's footing
> Is light on the roses.
> Wherever he goes is
> The lilt of his luting,
> Sweet, sweet.

Not only does Hovey out-Swinburne Swinburne in this passage, but the refrain "Sweet, sweet" corresponds to the bacchants' refrain *Ich dufte süss, ich dufte süss* ("I smell sweet, I smell sweet") in *Tannhäuser.* There is even a rainbow bridge à la *Das Rheingold.* Nor does Hovey limit himself to Wagner; Greek mythology furnishes a second cast of thousands, and opportunities for some very elegant writing: it is rare to find a well-written Sapphic stanza in English, but Hovey turns out four of them, all idiomatic and accentually correct. Aphrodite is addressed as traveling

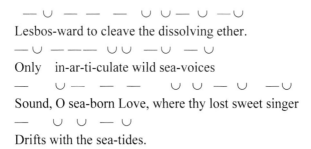

Lesbos-ward to cleave the dissolving ether.

Only   in-ar-ti-culate wild sea-voices

Sound, O sea-born Love, where thy lost sweet singer

Drifts with the sea-tides.

Argente, the Lady of the Lake, finally appears, and informs Merlin that he is in Avalon.   Finally he can ask his questions.

> Argente: Seeks Arthur, then, a queen?
> Merlin: He would be wed.
> Argente: Beware lest he find a queen, but not a wife!
> Let him not marry her, Merlin!
> Ah, woe!   I see a great woe in the land!

The oracle and its explanation continue.   The prognosis is bad, but Merlin resolves to make the best of it, out of loyalty to Arthur.   Before he leaves Avalon, he expresses a wistful longing to Nimue:

> Merlin: O Nimue, had it been but possible,
> That thou an earthly maiden, I a lad…
> But Arthur waits for me,
> And what should I, an old man, have to do
> With dreams of a completion for myself…

They depart in a chariot drawn by dragons.   Not so with Robinson's Merlin, as Mark Van Doren noted.

> "Merlin," like the two poems which come after it, dispenses with the fairy tale element so conspicuous in most versions of the Arthurian material.   Mr. Robinson is not interested in the legend that Merlin, miraculously born and early endowed with powers of prophecy, foretold all that would happen to Camelot and its king in the way that fortune tellers foretell events.[269]

Robinson's Merlin is, in fact, real-time, and his dialogue is low-key. Lowell finds this a fault.   "Merlin comes, but his power is gone, he has nothing to suggest, no vigour to impart.   He tells the King what the King knows already."[270]   Perhaps, but the way he tells him is worthy of scrutiny.

> "Now, Arthur, since you are a child of mine—
> A foster-child, and that's a kind of child—   [271]

This fits the Tennysonian expectations of the readers of the day.   In "The Coming of Arthur," the newborn Arthur is "Deliver'd at a secret postern gate / To Merlin, to be holden far apart / Until his hour should come" (214).   Merlin gives the child to an old knight and his wife, bringing him to court and having him crowned "thro' his craft" (234). Merlin works as a faithful counselor.   "And there I saw mage Merlin, whose vast wit / And hundred winters are but as the hands / Of loyal vassals toiling for their liege" (279-81).

Robinson's Arthur, however, is not satisfied with his counselor. He is uneasy about Merlin's dapper new look: "When he returns to

---

[269] Van Doren 67
[270] Lowell, 1917, 70
[271] *CP*   250

Camelot, beardless, arrayed in purple silk, Arthur at first feels that the old Merlin has gone."[272]   He is also displeased at Merlin's initial evasiveness.   He insists, however, that Merlin be candid.

> … I have sinned and erred and heeded not
> Your counsel…you yourself—God save us!--
> Have gone down smiling to the smaller life
> That you and your incongruous laughter called
> Your living grave.[273]

"We see Arthur suffering from too little light, and Merlin from too much."[274]   Merlin warns the king to beware of Lancelot and Modred, and that his loveless marriage must be maintained.

> Let that be all, for I can say no more;
> Not even to Blaise the Hermit, were he living,
> Could I say more than I have given you now
> To hear; and he alone was my confessor.[275]

Vivian's attendant is also named Blaise, and Robinson will have Merlin comment on the coincidence.[276]   Poetically, the repetition is a unifying echo; to look for anything more is risky.

> Since the name *Blaise* appears nowhere in the original materials of Arthurian legend, one can only speculate as to Robinson's purpose in settling on it.   The most likely figure from whom he might have appropriated the name is Blaise

---

[272] Pipkin 10
[273] *CP* 251
[274] Kaplan 88
[275] *CP* 253
[276] *CP* 267

Pascal, whose thesis it is that matters relating to faith are beyond the scope of human reason.[277]

This is going too far.   In fact, the name is straight out of Tennyson's "The Coming of Arthur," although the orthography is not.   "Merlin's master (so they call him) Bleys, 152   Who taught him magic; but the scholar ran / Before the master..."
Arthur's audience is over, but nothing has been resolved.

The King was long awake.   No covenant
With peace was his tonight; and he knew sleep
As he knew the cold eyes of Guinevere
That yesterday had stabbed him,[278]

His misery is an echo of a scene in *The Porcupine*.

Rollo: [*Clutching Larry's arm*]   But you cannot ever imagine what an inferno it was for me when I found that I had married a porcupine instead of a woman.   [*He goes backward a few steps and wipes his forehead.*]
Larry [*Worried and puzzled*]: Do you call Rachel a porcupine?
Rollo: I don't know what else to call her.   Whatever she is, she is something that isn't human.   Whenever I go near her now, she seems to wear an armor of invisible knives.   And I tell you, Larry, they cut.   They cut deep.[279]

Evidently Guinevere's eyes are extremely expressive: Sir Kay says, "All I know of her / Is what her eyes have told the silences / That

---

[277] Thompson 246
[278] *CP* 256-7
[279] Robinson, 1915, 55

now attend her;"[280] Lamorak pities Lancelot, "For by my soul a man's in sorry case / When Guineveres are out with eyes to scorch him."[281] Arthur is also worried by the effect that Vivian is having on his friend,

> for now he knew that Modred, Lancelot,
> The Queen, the King, the Kingdom, and the World,
> Were less to Merlin, who had made him King,
> Than one small woman in Broceliande.[282]

The way that Merlin makes him king is the dramatic high point of the first scene in Cram's *Excalibur,* a scene strongly reminiscent of the opening of Wagner's *Lohengrin,* where an urgent military undertaking is held up by a damsel in distress appealing for justice.   In *Lohengrin* the *deus ex machina* is the title role arriving on a swan; in *Excalibur* it is young Arthur, in the matter of the drawing of the sword from the stone.   The setting is the funeral of Uther Pendragon.   The enemy is at the gates, and the need for a king is urgent.   The nobles cry out—Launcelot is among them—for an intercession, and various petty kings jostle to extract Excalibur, but in vain.   Merlin presides calmly. All clamor for a king to lead them, but Merlin's aplomb is unshaken.

> Sir Launcelot: Merlin, art thou leagued with them
>   That shatter England?
> Merlin: No, Sir Launcelot.
>   The king shall come.

Young Arthur bursts in with the news that the enemy is on the walls, and is appalled to find that no leader has been chosen.

> Arthur: What shame is this?   Shall men dispute a sword

---

[280] *CP* 245
[281] *CP* 246
[282] *CP* 258

> Nor use their own to save a kingdom?　Fools!

Cram's imagery is consistently macho.

> Arthur: The devil makes men women, now may God
> Make men of boys, England is fallen else!
> …Your arms are women's arms, that like your hearts
> Halt quaking!

Merlin is disappointed in the lack of response.

> Merlin: Now do I know that I must work alone
> To save this land and give it back to God.

Cram's resolution is not macho, but mawkish.　Merlin kneels by Uther's coffin and prays.　The stage directions:　(*The dead king lifts his hand, removes the crown from his brow, and with it crowns Arthur.*)
That settles the matter.

> Over the waves and into Brittany
> Went Merlin, to Broceliande.[283]

These lines are liminal in two senses:　first, because they mark the beginning of the Vivian episode, which will occupy parts V and VI. In this context, it is worth noting the deftness of Robinson's transition, as opposed to the corresponding passage in Tennyson's "Merlin and Vivien," where Merlin is manipulated while in a depressive fog, what the poet calls a "mind-mist" (299).　"Then fell on Merlin a great melancholy; / He walked with dreams and darkness, and he found / A doom that ever poised itself to fall…" (186-8).　Vivien takes advantage of his gloom.　"So leaving Arthur's court he gained the

---

[283] *CP* 260

beach; / There found a little boat, and stept into it; / And Vivien followed, but he marked her not... (195-7). And touching Breton sands, they disembarked. / And then she followed Merlin all the way, / Even to the wild woods of Broceliande" (200-2).

Robinson's transition lines are also liminal in terms of his place in the Merlin genre. Up to now, Robinson's *Merlin* has been analyzable by comparison and contrast with other Merlins. From this point on, however, Robinson leaves his predecessors behind by dealing successfully with two themes that the genre had never dealt with at all: Woman and Age.

Robinson's Vivian is credible, consistent, and carefully delineated. Not one of the other Vivians, Viviens or Nimues examined in this study has had any personality at all: they are nuanceless stock characters, women who were never girls, as un-human as forces of nature.   They pop into the story, move the plot forward, and then pop out again.   The mainstream Merlin was likewise a stock character, the old man who had evidently been born old, like St. Joseph or Santa. Centuries of writing by dozens of authors had not advanced the delineation of either character a whit since Plautus, except that the stock *senex* was now named Merlin and the stock *meretrix* was now named Vivian.   This is where Robinson's talent for characterization puts him head and shoulders above his predecessors.   We learn about Vivian's girlhood, about her changing feelings toward Merlin, about her fears for her Eden that is slipping away.   We see Merlin changing from cocksure intellectual to introverted epicure, and then to dispassionate man with a mission.

On June 24, 1917 Robinson wrote to Elizabeth Brower, a fan from his earliest days as a poet, and a correspondent of many years, speaking of Merlin, that "He is also a suffragist, as you must have noticed."[284]   The reader in the early twenty-first century may not realize the extent to which Robinson was playing with fire in his portrayal of Vivian in terms of the early twentieth, that is, as "barred by her sex from an active part 'in a world that men are making.'

---

[284] Robinson 1968, 143

Where women are excluded from political and practical affairs, they tend to lavish all their talent and interest on winning and holding men… For Vivian it is only Merlin, 'the master of the world,' whose love and service can be 'her school, her triumph, and her history.'[285] For the reader of 1917, woman suffrage was a hot topic, comparable to the temperance agitation of the day.

The critics of the day, however, did not particularly like Robinson's Vivian. Not only did Lowell find her uninteresting, as we have noted, but Monroe asked "what does Mr. Robinson make of the witch-lady of old romance? Alas, we become too familiar with her, with the usual consequence."[286] For critics of the era of the Robinson centennial, however, Vivian was fascinating.

> Volatile as quicksilver, she has no set, inflexible attitudes. Though the first visit of Merlin frightens her, she receives him with frankness and informality. Expressing hatred easily— she hates King Arthur and she poisons those she hates—she is also capable of giving Merlin a kind of love he has never known, adoration for his greatness, and deep affection. To her Merlin is a means of self-realization in the fullest sense. As she says,[287]
>> In an age
>> That has no plan for me that I can read
>> Without him, shall he tell me what I am,
>> And why I am, I wonder?"[288]

Cochran makes much of Vivian's exclusion from active participation in world affairs because of her gender,[289] but it is interesting that her argument consists mainly of quotations from *Merlin,* especially when

---

[285] Perrine 1969, 425
[286] Monroe 1917, 212
[287] Starr 112
[288] *CP* 263
[289] Cochran 1988, 53

Vivian asks Merlin to "Tell me a story about the world, / And the men in it, what they do in it, / And why it is they do it all so badly,"[290] which suggests that Robinson's expression of the issue is sufficient as it stands.[291]   As a leitmotiv, in the last scene Merlin will recall Vivian, "whose unquiet heart is hungry / For what is not, and what shall never be / Without her in a world that men are making, / Knowing not how, nor caring   yet to know / How slowly and how grievously they do it." Vivian will use this theme for her and Merlin, making Broceliande a place "where two disheartened sinners may forget / A world that has today no place for them."[292]

Still, the Broceliande episode is first and foremost a love story. "*Merlin* is the story of a reciprocal love between two persons of intelligence, charm, and comparable temperament.   The relationship, which lasts for ten years, is unmarred by sexual infidelity on either side. For Merlin there is no other woman but Vivian; for Vivian there will never be another Merlin." [293]   "Possibly Robinson's greatest achievement in creating the character of Vivian lies in providing Merlin, as never before, with a woman who can not only satisfy the craving of his lost youth for beauty but who can also stimulate him intellectually."[294]

Robinson's treatment of Merlin's aging is related to the Broceliande idyll: he is of "indeterminate age" when he arrives, but at his first meeting with Vivian he declares, "Whatever I am, / I have not lived in time until to-day."[295]

> In Broceliande Merlin and Vivian not only shut out the world, they also attempt to shut out time.   Living for the present, Vivian has a horror of growing old.   She shudders at

---

[290] *CP* 288
[291] Cochran 1991, 55
[292] *CP* 291
[293] Perrine 1969, 425
[294] Starr 113
[295] *CP* 265

everything that suggests old age or death. Merlin's shaving of his beard on his arrival in Broceliande symbolizes not only the sacrifice of his powers of intellect but also his attempt to regain and retain youth. Broceliande, though it contains infinite variety, is devised as a defense against change. Vivian hopes that she and Merlin may live there in a timeless present, perpetually young.[296]

Finally, however, the attempt proves unsuccessful; and this is the most important difference between Robinson and his source. The source is a romance, and the laws of romance enable Merlin and Vivian to keep eternal love-tryst   in their enchanted castle.   In Robinson, psychological and moral realities govern.[297]

Still, things begin well enough when Merlin arrives.

> The birds were singing still; leaves flashed and swung
> Before him in the sunlight; a soft breeze
> Made intermittent whisperings around him.[298]

Hagedorn's brooding Agamemnon enters a garden:

> The garden greeted him with music.   There
> Leaves rustled very softly; and so full
> Of cadenced melody the insects filled
> The warm, sweet air, that all the song they made
> Seemed nothing else than singing silence...[299]

Back to Robinson:

---

[296] Perrine 1969, 427
[297] Perrine 1972, 321
[298] *CP* 261
[299] Hagedorn 1916, 28-9

Of love and fate and danger, and faint waves
Of many sweetly-stinging fragile odors
Broke lightly as they touched him;[300]

Amy Lowell conceded that this passage had its beauties. "For once [Robinson] seems to have allowed his lyricism free play, and the result makes the reader hope that he will never again felt it necessary to curb it...I can recall few such images as "leaves flashed and swung, or "many sweetly-stinging fragile odors broke lightly as they touched him," in the earlier books.[301]

And Merlin, having entered, heard the gate
Clang back behind him; and he swore no gate
Like that had ever clanged in Camelot,
Or any other place if not in hell.[302]

We have already noted the exchange between Merlin and Blaise, the gatekeeper, but Robinson's artistry does not stop there, leading to a variation with real pathos. When Merlin complains to Vivian about "that most evil sounding gate of yours, / Which has a clang as if it shut forever," Vivian replies, "If there be need, I'll shut the gate myself."[303] Eventually their love affair does end, and Merlin departs, escorted by Blaise, and the episode is punctuated by an understated touch that is pure Robinson. "For long there was a whining in her ears / Of distant wheels departing. When it ceased, / She closed the gate again so quietly / That Merlin could have heard no sound of it."[304] Hagedorn [305] reports that Robinson loathed James Russell Lowell's "The Vision of Sir Launfall," but it is interesting to note the

---

[300] *CP* 261
[301] Lowell 1917, 69-70
[302] *CP* 262
[303] *CP* 267
[304] *CP* 298
[305] Hagedorn 36

opening line of part III of that poem: "The drawbridge dropped with a surly clang."

Merlin and his guide walk

> Down shaded ways, through open ways with hedgerows,
> And into shade again more deep than ever,
> But edged anon with rays of broken sunshine
> In which a fountain, raining crystal music,
> Made fairy magic of it through green leafage,
> Till Merlin's eyes were dim with preparation
> For sight now of the lady Vivian.[306]

Lowell writes: "The description of the magician's eyes as 'dim with preparation' is one of those sudden stampings of emotion into fact which make Mr. Robinson's work so poetically, so actually, true."[307] More important to the continuity of the poem is the introduction of the color green, which will be a thread all the way through the Broceliande episode.

> He saw at first a bit of living green
> That might have been a part of all the green
> Around the tinkling fountain where she gazed
> Upon the circling pool...[308]

Robinson would appear to be breaking a pledge he had made as early as 1896, when, in a letter dated October 28 of that year, he vowed that his poetry would have "no tinkling water nor red-bellied robins."[309]

> In *Merlin* he used, among other natural images, the very words that he had earlier dismissed from his poetic credo: tinkling water!

---

[306] *CP* 262
[307] Lowell 1917, 71
[308] *CP* 263
[309] Baker 4

He speaks of "rays of broken sunshine," of a "fountain raining crystal music," of "all the green / Around the tinkling fountain where she gazed / Upon the circling pool...." Indeed, nature is the idyllic background for Merlin and Vivian in Broceliande.[310]

This is more than just Robinson getting carried away. It recalls William Morris's *Arthur's Tomb,* a favorite of Robinson's, as we have seen. "The stars shone out above the doubtful green 61 Of her bodice, in the green sky overhead; / Pale in the green sky were the stars I wean, / Because the moon shone like a star she shed."[311]

In Hovey's bacchanal, maenads serenade Merlin (as they "caress him and ply him with wine") with color imagery: "Thought is gray and life is green— / These are what men choose between."

The fountain recalls the setting of Yeats' "Time and the Witch Vivien:" *A marble-flagged, pillared room. Magical instruments in one corner. A fountain in the centre.* Another similarity will be noted presently, the reference to carp. This would seem to be another bit of unfinished business from the plays. W. B. Yeats was in America in 1914, and was in fact principal speaker at a banquet organized by Harriet Monroe in honor of young Vachel Lindsay.[312] It will be recalled that 1914 was the year that *Van Zorn* was published, when Robinson's "dramatic fever" was at its most acute. Yeats, the successful dramatist, must have been very much on Robinson's mind, as can be inferred from this odd speech in *Van Zorn.*

> OTTO: Do you remember my last book?...Sometime, therefore, when you are old and full of wrinkles...some far-off winter evening, for example, when you sit by the fire, with your cat in your lap...[313]

---

[310] Franchere 84
[311] Rochester
[312] Monroe 1932, 132
[313] Robinson 1914, 23

The resemblance to Yeats' lyric is unmistakable.

> When you are old and gray, and full of sleep,
> And nodding by the fire, take down this book,

The mention of age makes the following lines pertinent. We have observed that the mental picture of the aged, Tennysonian Merlin was so firmly set in the readership of the day that even respected critics were led astray by this preconception. Yet Robinson is unequivocal; Merlin is not old until the end of the poem, and ages only because he has "entered time" as the result of his Vivian episode, or, better put, he had "kept his youth until he abandoned knowledge and the world to follow passion to Vivian's garden at Broceliande."[314] The reader will recall that Vivian has induced Merlin go clean-shaven. After Merlin's beard has been "reaped," he looks in the mirror and sees

> a stranger, falcon-eyed,
> Firm-featured, of a negligible age,
> And fair enough to look upon, he fancied,
> Though not a warrior born, nor more a courtier.[315]

There is no youth in Hovey's Merlin; in the bacchanal the dryads ("half-seen in the trees"), describe him thus: "See the queer old fellow / With the moss-gray beard! / His eyes are bleared / And his skin is yellow. / Prying and peering— / Hits! Hark! / He can hardly see,/ For his eyes grow dark; / And the voice of a tree / Is too fine for his hearing."
Robinson's Merlin can certainly see.

> "Are you always all in green, as you are now?"
> Said Merlin, more employed with her complexion,

---

[314] Stovall 13
[315] *CP* 298

Where blood and olive made wild harmony
With eyes and wayward hair that were too dark
For peace if they were not subordinated;[316]

Whatever role Isadora Duncan may have had in inspiring
Robinson's Vivian, it could not have been her appearance: she did
not have dark, wayward hair, and was physically no waif. There was
one member of the Robinson circle who did resemble Vivian, the
Broadway actress Alla Nazimova, although by 1917 she was famous
enough to be referred to as simply Nazimova. This is another
unknowable, as there is even less of a paper trail than in the case of
Duncan. The only evidence I can offer will be in the reader's mind after
seeing Nazimova's films, especially *The Brat*. She could have inspired
not only Vivian's appearance, but her "quicksilver" mannerisms.
... if I go in green, why, let me go so,

And say at once why you have come to me
Cloaked over like a monk, and with a beard
As long as Jeremiah's. I don't like it.[317]

Tennyson's Vivien, on the other hand, makes a great show of
liking Merlin's beard, "...then adding all at once, / 'And lo, I clothe
myself with wisdom,' drew / The vast and shaggy mantle of his beard /
Across her neck and bosom to her knee..." (252-5)
Robinson's Vivian continues:

I'll never like a man with hair like that
While I can feed a carp with little frogs.

This would seem to be another echo of Yeats' "Time and the
Witch Vivien."

---

[316] *CP* 263-4
[317] *CP* 264

> Vivien: Where moves there any beautiful as I,
> Save, with the little golden greedy carp,
> Gold unto gold, a gleam in its long hair,
> My image yonder?   (1-4)
> How still it is!   I hear the carp go splash,
> And now and then a bubble rise.   (62-3)

Robinson's Vivian concludes her denunciation of the beard with panache: "I'm rather sure to hate you if you keep it, / And when I hate a man I poison him."

It is hard to imagine Isadora Duncan or Nazimova being the model for polished banter like this. The word "poison" recalls Robinson's remark about Amy Lowell: "She should have lived in Renaissance Italy. She'd have enjoyed poisoning people. A grand talker. But always slaying six or eight people in an evening."[318] She had slain Robinson in *A Critical Fable,* and had gone on to slay Frost, Sandburg, especially Pound, and others in it, too.

Robinson's Merlin calls Vivian's bluff.

> "You've never fed a carp with little frogs,"
> Said Merlin; "I can see it in your eyes."—
> "I might then, if I haven't," said the lady;
> ...I'm cruel and I'm cold, and I like snakes;[319]

It has been observed that E. A. Robinson was the first poet to use the word "Yonkers" in a poem; this may be the only time in literature that a female character saucily declares that she likes snakes. This is playfully anti-Tennyson, as compared to the Victorian writer's use of "snakes." Beginning with line 30, Mark says, "Here are snakes within the grass; / And you methinks, O Vivien, save ye fear / The monkish manhood, and the mask of pure / Worn by this court, can stir

---

[318] Robinson, 1975, 142
[319] *CP* 264

them till they sting." Beginning in line 236, where the temptress has been groveling at Merlin's feet, Tennyson writes, "And lissome Vivien, holding by his heel, / Writhed toward him, slided up his knee and sat, / Behind his ankle twined her hollow feet / Together, curved an arm about his neck, / Clung like a snake;" And just for good measure, the poet in line 885 has Vivian wearing snake-shaped hair ornament. "She paused, she turned away, she hung her head, / The snake of gold slid from her hair, the braid / Slipt and uncoiled itself..."

Robinson's other snakes are flat, almost pro-forma. Modred is a snake, or a worm.[320] Leaders like Arthur find it difficult to proceed "Unbitten by the serpents they had fed."[321] Vivian challenges Merlin, "Why do you look at me as at a snake / All coiled to spring at you and strike you dead?"[322]

All is gaiety and banter at first.

Embroidering doom with many levities,
...They mocked their fate with easy pleasantries[323]

> The love of Merlin and Vivian...is primarily a love of the senses, enhanced by wit and mutual admiration. Though for both it serves a real need, it is not something that overmasters them; rather it is a game which they voluntarily choose to play, and which they play with a calculated artfulness. In the traditional story of Merlin's enchantment and burial in Broceliande, the succumbing of the wizard to a woman, there was an obvious symbol of the surrender of the intellect to the senses. Robinson emphasizes this, as Tennyson had also done, but with much more sweetness and subtlety. He makes Merlins' defection understandable by showing the full attractiveness of the temptation.[324]

---

[320] *CP* 246
[321] *CP* 250
[322] *CP* 290-1
[323] *CP* 265
[324] Perrine 1969, 426

Merlin's beard is the first topic of conversation, and we have noted Vivian's despair at the hirsuteness of prophets and wizards. "Praise heaven I'm not a prophet! Are you glad?"[325]   This itself will elicit an echo: Vivian, wondering about possible rivals, "If they were all at hand. Praise heaven they're not" receives an answer from Merlin, "If they were in the world—praise heaven they're not—"[326]

> Like her predecessors Vivian is determined, against all the pressures from Camelot, to get what she wants. Again like her sisters, this seems not to be sensual delight—though she is by no means insensitive to it and appreciates physical attractiveness enough to make Merlin shave his beard—rather it is Merlin's *wisdom* that she seeks. But in a departure from earlier versions it is not his incantations that she wishes; like her predecessors she is a relentlessly ambitious woman, but unlike them she has a good mind which she wants to improve.[327]
>
> 'When this great Merlin comes to me,
> My task and avocation for some time
> Will be to make him willing, if I can,
> To teach and feed me with an ounce of wisdom.'[328]

She has already gleaned a little from Merlin as "A moment's worth of wisdom there escaped him, / But Vivian seized it, and it was not lost."[329]   Merlin's perspective is different, as we see at the end of the poem, when he tells Dagonet that he will not go back to Broceliande. "I shall not go back. / We pay for going back; and all we get / Is one more needless ounce of weary wisdom / To bring away with us."[330]

---

[325] *CP* 266
[326] *CP* 274
[327] Starr 112
[328] *CP* 267
[329] *CP* 265
[330] *CP* 311

Her eye must be fed, however, and so Merlin is given a make-over.

> ...Merlin smiled
> To see himself in purple, touched with gold,
> And fledged with snowy lace.— [331]

No black, because Vivian

>   abhors
> Mortality in all its hues and emblems—
> Black wear,[332]

Evidently, clothes make the man, as far as Robinson was concerned: in *The Porcupine* Rollo, the protagonist's unhappy half-brother "is dressed in black, with a frock coat, throughout the play, and his manner is marked by a singular lack of magnetism."[333] (On the occasion of the first romantic evening with Merlin, she wears red, which reviewer D. L. M. found remarkable. "...clad in the living green which delighted the heart of the mediæval lady, Vivian awaits Merlin. So far we have the mediæval setting. Then with a direct modern twist, he gives her crimson—modern vampire-wear—when she lures Merlin. In Mallory red is the color of the Grail and is worn by Galahad to symbolize his spiritual purity."[334] The poem's first audience did not read Merlin in isolation at all, but with its predecessors in the genre in mind. When Vivian is said to dislike "long argument, and all the cold / And solemn things that appertain to graves—,"[335] the latter line recalls Tennyson's Vivien saying, "I cannot brook to gaze upon the dead." This led Phelps to be on his guard.

---

[331] *CP* 268
[332] *CP* 268
[333] Robinson 1915, 10
[334] M. 1917
[335] *CP* 268

I confess that I made two errors in estimating his work. I thought that when *Merlin* appeared, he was on the wrong track, that he had better let those legends alone.   It seemed to me as if he were trying to dilute Tennyson; and to dilute Tennyson won't do at all.   My second error was my belief that the value of Robinson's work was analytical and intellectual, rather than emotional.   In 1918, I wrote,

> It is of course possible that Mr. Robinson wished to try something in a romantic vein; but it is not his vein.   He excels in the clear presentment of character; in pith; in sharp outline; in solid, masculine effort... He is an excellent draughtsman; everything that he has done has beauty of line; anything pretentious is to him abhorrent. He is more map-maker than painter.

> Then, to my amazement and delight, he proved me wrong by producing in 1927 his masterpiece, *Tristram.*   It is not only his best poem, it is the best poetic version of that immortal story that has ever appeared in English.   It glows with passion and is radiant with beauty.[336]

Could it be said that any of the "tight little poems an inch in diameter" in Robinson's early *oeuvre* glowed with passion and were radiant with beauty?   *Tristram* is the culmination of Robinson's extroversion, but the poet's letting-go began with *Merlin,* and particularly with the Vivian episode, as was noted by literary all-arounder Ben Ray Redman (1896-1961).

> There is, indeed, an almost barbaric splendor in this part of "Merlin," a lavish sensuous beauty and a rich sensual passion that incarnate the dreams of no merely "cerebral" poet.   This

---

[336] Phelps 1939, 697-8

time, at least, Robinson has completely "let himself go," and the result is magnificent. Then the glory fades, from the poet's eyes as from the eyes of Vivian and Merlin, and we hear a misunderstood man asking a misunderstanding woman:[337]

"What reading has a man of woman's days,
Even though the man be Merlin and a prophet?"[338]

Going back to that first evening, though, there is nothing barbaric about the way Merlin compliments Vivian. "Yes, you are like a tree, —or like a flower; / More like a flower to-night."[339] The word "flower," bare and nuanceless as it is, may strike the reader as at variance with this passage, which is lavish with descriptive detail. Yet Robinson explicitly identifies himself with the author of the most famous bare and nuanceless flower in all literature, this in a letter to his long-time correspondent Edith Brower that, "The one man with whom I have a sort of internal affinity seems to me to be Heine, but no one else seems to have thought of it." This letter is dated only a few months after *Merlin* came out, in August, 1917.[340] Heine's poem begins

Du bist wie eine Blume, ("You are like a flower,
So schön und hold und rein. so beautiful and sweet and pure")

Heinrich Heine (1797-1856) may have attracted Robinson's attention because he too wrote "tight little poems an inch in diameter," but another parameter may be just as likely: Robinson the music-lover could have been drawn by the musical setting of *Die Lorelei,* or by *Dichterliebe* ("poet's love"), an extended cycle of poems set to music

---

[337] Redman 79
[338] *CP* 290
[339] *CP* 271
[340] Robinson 1968, 143

by Robert Schumann, in which the poet explores a disastrous infatuation (reminiscent of Robinson's own love for Emma Shepherd). Although his letters that mention foreign authors usually refer to French ones, he certainly would have been able to read Heine in the original: Heine is not difficult, and Robinson's German studies at Harvard would have given him the necessary language background to read him.   It is amusing to note that in his correspondence Robinson playfully refers to William Vaughn Moody as "von Moody."

Robinson will amplify his description of Vivian, calling her "a flower of change and peril."[341]

Vivian moves away from Merlin's embrace, indicating the dinner which will lead to the second drinking scene.

> "Are you to let me go again sometime,"
> She said, -- "before I starve to death, I wonder?
> If not, I'll have to bite the lion's paws,
> And make him roar."[342]

This may be another echo of *Van Zorn.*

> Villa: If you look at me like that much longer, Auntie, I'll say
> bow-bow; and then I'll put both my paws on your
> shoulder, and then I'll bite you.   [*She snaps her teeth
> and laughs*][343]

In any case, Vivian is quite the coquette.

> She told him, with her chin propped on her fingers
> And her eyes flashing blindness into his:
> "I put myself out cruelly to please you,

---

[341] *CP* 271
[342] *CP* 272
[343] Robinson, 1914, 72

And you, for that, forget almost at once
The name and image of me altogether.
You needn't, for when all is analyzed,
It's only a bird-pie that you are eating."[344]

Evidently the "sweet ortolans" referred to earlier:[345] yet another Robinsonian jolt, only for the attentive reader. Vivian also serves wine, as we infer from Merlin's growing expansiveness.

My dear fair lady—
And there is not another under heaven
So fair as you are as I see you now—
I cannot look too much at you and eat;
And I must eat, or be untimely ashes,
Whereon the light of your celestial gaze
Would fall, I fear me for no longer time
Than on the solemn dust of Jeremiah—
Whose beard you likened once, in heathen jest,
To mine that now is no man's.[346]

I take the verbal infelicities in this speech to be Robinson's way of expressing the effects of the wine, described as "...this incomparable flowing gold,"[347] which may be another clue that the Vivian episodes were inspired by Robinson's meeting with Isadora Duncan: what kind of wine is golden? According to Hagedorn's account, "Champagne flowed like brooks in spring...She kept Robinson at her side and pushed the others into an adjoining room, accompanied by a half dozen bottles of champagne."[348]

Vivian returns Merlin's compliment.

---

[344] *CP* 272-3
[345] *CP* 239
[346] *CP* 273
[347] *CP* 276
[348] Hagedorn 1939, 231-2

> "You are the only one who sees enough
> To make me see how far away I am
> From all that I have seen and have not been;"[349]

Shepard singled this passage out for censure.

> Mr. Robinson's habitual obscurity has never seemed less
> justified than it does in the present poem. There is no
> discoverable reason why Vivian should choose to ensnarl her
> meaning in the [preceding] tangle of words...
> Here there is no great depth or intricacy of meaning, but merely
> a failure to make words do their work. Neither does this
> devious verbiage individualize the speaker, for it pervades the
> entire poem. In other places the reader is perplexed by such
> things as the inordinate length of a sentence, ingeniously tortured
> sentence structure, or the trick of the transferred epithet...
> Eventually we ask the man who assumes a mysterious and
> cryptic air for some commensurate enlightenment. In reading
> this poem, we do not get it... He resembles his own Merlin, who
> has much to say about what he has seen and known without
> giving much notion of what it is, and who seems to rely upon our
> remembrance that he has been impressive in other scenes.[350]

Again we note the novelty that the readers of 1917 saw, not only
relative to other writers, but to Robinson's own previous work.
Shepard's was not the only opinion, however.

> I have dwelt at such length upon the purely emotional
> elements in "Merlin" and in "Lancelot" for the simple reason
> that Robinson is usually written of as an unemotional poet.
> We have heard too much of the man's astringent irony, of his

---

[349] CP 280
[350] Shepard 341

cold detachment, and his cerebral complexity; too much of his philosophy, and his precise psychological patterns. Such descriptive terms are accurate enough, but they describe the poet by half, and only half his work. There is another Robinson, who has been ignored by the critics; and the fullness of his expression may be found in the tales of Guinevere and Lancelot, of Vivian and Merlin. His voice is heard fleetingly in the earlier poems, infusing them with life and human poignancy; but in these two it is dominant, and for that reason they are, I think, the greatest of all his creations. In them the balance of the heart and mind is perfect. He has not thought himself back into the period when men believed in wizardry. He has brought the legendary figures of Camelot forward into the living present and made them one with the men and women of all time. Although he shares none of Miniver's illusions regarding "iron clothing," the world of Arthur has furnished him with his most congenial theme and has called forth all his powers. Perhaps he may find another like it, but he has not found it yet.[351]

Robinson deals not only with the first flush of love, but with its end.

> Again the frozen line of irony
> Was on her mouth. He looked up once at it.
> And then away—too fearful of her eyes
> To see what he could hear now in her laugh
> That melted slowly into what she said,
> Like snow in icy water: "This world of yours
> Will surely be the end of us."[352]

---

[351] Redman 81
[352] *CP* 291-2

The intrusion of the crisis at Camelot disturbs the *rêve à deux*.[353]
Vivian starts to talk about "this world of yours."

> Don't tell me, Merlin, you are growing old.
> Why don't you make somehow a queen of me,
> And give me half the world? I'd wager thrushes
> That I should reign, with you to turn the wheel,
> As well as any king that ever was.[354]

The thrushes may be an echo of the William Morris poems that Robinson enjoyed. In "Arthur's Tomb" we find, line 283, "...the thrushes sang / In the lonely gardens where my love was not," and in line 325, "The thrushes sang in the lone garden there." In "The Defense of Guinevere," lines 105-6, Morris wrote, "No minute of the wild day ever slips / From out my memory; I hear thrushes sing."

Hovey's Merlin also has a thrush in his final speech:

> Merlin: O Nimue, had it been but possible,
> That thou an earthly maiden, I a lad,
> With nought to know of to forbode beyond
> The thoughts that stir the thrushes in the coverts.

So much for the thrushes. There still remains "this world of yours," and the world will not be denied. Merlin will return to Camelot. Nor will time be denied. "Later Merlin comes to terms with his destiny, in what is perhaps the most moving passage in the poem, a soliloquy charged with the imminence of death, indeed with the burial of his 'poor blundering bones,' and yet also illumined by courageous acceptance of what must be, and by the 'light' which leads him."[355]   On that subject, the passage has a powerful figure for fate, so memorable that the critics we have cited may be forgiven for having

---

[353] McCoy 100
[354] *CP* 292
[355] Starr 114

fate on their minds when they wrote their reviews. Robinson is speaking of the end of a man's life.

"Then Fate will put a mattock in his hands
And lash him while he digs himself the grave
That is to be the pallet and the shroud
Of his poor blundering bones...[356]
Time has won.
Tomorrow I shall say to Vivian
That I am old and gaunt and garrulous,
And tell her one more story: I am old."[357]

"The affair ends, as an affair; however, its aftereffects are powerful. The stated ideal combines the themes of many Arthurian romances, in which love of woman or love of God may lead the seeker toward achievement."[358]   What Robinson has given us, then, is a story of happiness in the long run, despite the immediate consequences of human weakness.   Tennyson's vision in "The Passing of Arthur" is autumnal.   "Then spake King Arthur to Sir Bedivere: 181 The sequel of today unsolders all / The goodliest fellowship of famous knights / Whereof this world holds record...184 I perish by this people which I made,— 190   Though Merlin sware that I should come again / To rule once more..."

As for Robinson's version, we may wish that half the world had half his optimism.

We pass, but many are to follow us,
And what they build may stay; though I believe
Another age   will have another Merlin,
Another Camelot, and another King.[359]

---

[356] *CP* 295
[357] *CP* 295-6
[358] McCoy 100
[359] *CP* 302

Binyon's *The Madness of Merlin*

and its Predecessors

"I cannot help thinking that the historical Merlin was a far higher personality than this representation embodies," wrote John Veitch in 1893, only one year after Tennyson's death, analyzing the seduction scene in "Merlin and Vivien." "The enchanter and bard of the sixth century was no commonplace Solomon to fall before vulgar temptation."[1]

Veitch, as mentioned earlier in this study, was professor of logic and rhetoric at the University of Glasgow. He authored weighty volumes on Descartes, and a book-length biography of Sir William Hamilton, his counterpart at the University of Edinburgh, with whom he had worked as co-author and translator. Accordingly, it is not surprising that his criticism of the Merlin of the *Idylls* should be especially trenchant.

Veitch puts his finger on two flaws that Tennyson's sonorousness cannot quite drown out: first, that the tale is in fact about a "commonplace Solomon," or, as it has been expressed in the previous chapter, about the stock *senex* being bamboozled by the stock *meretrix,* the moral of the tale being nothing more profound than that there's no fool like an old fool. It matters not a whit what the name of the old fool is: call him Merlin, call him Solomon; nor does the setting matter: it could be in England, it could be in Hollywood, but when all is said and done, the reader is left with the clichés and truisms of the

---

[1] Veitch, 1893, 1:238

May-December genre. The second flaw becomes evident with Veitch's insistence on the historical Merlin as a benchmark. There must be a limit as to how far an author can stray from a historical figure and still invoke that person's name, and, as Veitch's summary of the Merlin tradition will make plain, the Tennysonian continuum has almost nothing to do with Celtic legend. On the other hand, the non-Tennysonian writers discussed in this chapter were mindful of the historical Merlin, and were respectful of the details of the Celtic tradition — the exception being Wilmer A. Lambert, whose drama could just as easily have been titled *Prospero*:   except for *one word* at the very end of the play, there's no Merlin in his *Merlin*.   Laurence Binyon's *The Madness of Merlin* (*MM*) contains the most thorough integration of the traditional material, but the works of Ernest Rhys (remembered as the long-time editor of the "Everyman" books), Mary Porter (as she will be henceforth referred to in this study, rather than by her *nom de plume,* George Bidder), and John Veitch himself, are accurate in their allusions to the Celtic elements, and are not contradictory when they elaborate or innovate.   Veitch offers a succinct overview of this Merlin legend in his *History and Poetry of the Scottish Border.*

There were apparently at least two men of the name Merlin. The earlier of the two was called Merlin Ambrosius, Aurelius Ambrosius, Myrdin Emrys... But the Merlin of Upper Tweeddale is a somewhat later and a different personage. He was called by the Welsh Myrddin Wyllt, or Merlin the Wild, Merlinus Sylvestris, or Woodland Merlin, and Merlinus Caledonius. He was reputed the son of Morvryn, and he had had a sister Gwendydd, a name meaning the Dawn [literally, Welsh *gwen*, "white," and *dydd*, "day," pronounced like the English "doth"], whiteness, or purity, and redolent of the nature-worship and the poetry of the time...It was Merlin Caledonius who was present at the battle of Ardderyd ["Arthuret" is a good anglicization, and is the one Binyon uses] in 573. He was on the side of the defeated pagan Cymri [i.e. Welsh; the first syllable is pronounced "come"] under Gwenddoleu [which could be anglicized "Gwentholy"]. Gwenddoleu himself was slain, as was also the son of his sister Gwendydd. The nephew, indeed, was said to have fallen somehow under the hand of Merlin himself. After this disastrous battle, Merlin fled...and passed the remainder of his life, reputed insane...[2]

Veitch's "Merlin" is a chamber drama, having only three characters, Merlin, his sister, and "his early love." Merlin's opening soliloquy is, to use Veitch's description of Gwendydd, "redolent of the nature-worship and the poetry of the time," as it is a dawn hymn. The sun is referred to as "the lord of day" (16), "lord of light" (17), "lord of happy melody" (27), referring to bird song, and "sovereign of the sky, / The symbol of the God who is unseen" (36-7). Although Merlin is humble before the sun, he recalls the high ambitions he used to have, "To know the soul of things has been my quest, / To feel the beating of the inmost heart / That pulses through the world..." Veitch's characterization is already superior to that of Wilmer's, in that the latter's Merlin is incapable of development: when a character is omniscient and omnipotent, what development is possible? Veitch's Merlin holds our interest because his personality is in flux, now philosophical, now dynamic, and with a background motif of despondence over the defeat at Ardderyd. He wanted "To stand supreme in mystery of might; / To lead the battle on to victory;" (71-2) but the battle was decided by the appearance of a blindingly bright cross that demoralized the pagan army and led to its rout. Veitch's writing is direct, effectively conveying a variety of emotional states; yet Veitch the professor peeps through, as when Merlin's ruminations veer off into Buddhism, "the creed of that far Orient, / Whence my race has sprung—to Nirvana's shade, / The formless state where

---

[2]   Veitch, 1893, 1:224, 230

nought is marked or known, / No sense, no thought, pain, pleasure, or desire..." (93-6)   The passage goes on for another twenty-two lines. I find this digression on Merlin's familiarity with world religions to be nerdy and jarring, and fatal to the drama's momentum: from this point on, the dialogue of the work resembles the text of an oratorio, in that there are lengthy speeches, each with a set, unvarying mood, but without the variety of conversational exchanges or interruptions. Merlin's speeches are in iambic pentameter, the others, except for the last, are in ballad-like quatrains.

Gwendydd appears and sings, appealing to Merlin to shake off his depression; Merlin replies that he cannot, because the misfortune is not only personal, but national.   His speech identifies the conflict as between pagans and Christians: "The Bard dishonoured, worthless priest extolled, / The kingless Cymri trampled on the plain." Gwendydd sings again, extolling the beauties of nature and pointing out that Merlin should be inspired by them, but is not.   This does hit home: Merlin rhapsodizes about his past life, and about his past love.

> Merlin the Wild, in his wanderings, was haunted by a female form, known originally as Hwimleian, or Chwifleian, meaning "the gleam." ... There can be no doubt that the Hwimleian of the bard Merlin, the haunter of his life among the hills, the inspiraton of
> 'The fosterer of song among the streams,'

became the Vivien or Nimiane of the mythic Merlin and of the mediæval romances.[3]

Hwimleian enters and sings of nature responding to sunlight; Merlin speaks of his desire for happiness; Gwendydd suggests that he see a priest, but Merlin refuses to have anything to do with "the ally of our foes," asking Gwendydd to lead him to his fountain again.   Merlin foresees that his hour is come, and, sure enough, "rustics" enter,

---

[3]   Veitch, 1893, 1:235-6

herdsmen who blame him for bad weather and agricultural mishaps, and drag him to the Tweed. "Raising his head once from the current ere he sinks," Merlin looks forward to being with Hwimleian after death. Hwimleian, "in the air over the stream," announces that she and Merlin are now one, and that they will work "In high endeavor after nobler good" on a spiritual plane.

Veitch's drama is too static for theater, but his verse is successful because of its directness, and because it deals squarely with serious questions: the psychological condition that was then called melancholia, what would later be called battle-fatigue, and what we would now call post-traumatic stress disorder; the relationship between outer Nature and inner psychology; the sufferings of the sufferer's family and friends.

Mary Porter's "Merlin's Youth" has been cited for the exoticism and wildness of its first two parts, and none of what has already been quoted would seem to have anything at all to do with Veitch's summary, but in Part III Porter brings echoes of the legend to her tale: there is a battle. Young Merlin fights alongside the father of the object of his affections, the beautiful witch Yberha. (20) "Bloodily waged the battle. I was light / Of spear and swift of foot, and through the fight / Passed like a wandering death. With heavy blows / Of axe on target, edgéd stone on hide, / My cousins fought in phalanx, side by side; / And over all the voice of Yberha's father rose..." As in the legend, a kinsman is killed. In this case it is the father. Merlin takes his place and leads his side to victory, but all for nothing: Yberha blames him for her father's death. (24) "Smooth coward! whole of skin, / You have come well forth from all this bitter strife, / And saved, at least, one traitorous, worthless life— / Maid's body, with a weasel's heart within! // There lies my father, stricken by your guile." Despite his cousins' vouching for his courage and leadership, Yberha rejects Merlin. She vows to wed one of the cousins. Merlin, embittered, goes into exile and devotes himself to magic. (29) "I made strange spells in the night, and spell on spell / I learned, till all the world obeyed me well; / And one, with weaving paces and with waving hands, / You wot of, I made then; and spelled those twain, / Her and her sotted lover..." After hexing Yberha and his cousin, however, Merlin settles down to live as a recluse, but one whose craft sways the destinies of nations. (30) "And I live on in power, power of men, / To wield their kings and councils..."[4]

The reader leaves Porter's poem with admiration for its sweep, the momentum with which she develops her character from amorous daredevil to loveless hermit, and for the boldness of her imagery (the slavering wolves, for instance). Yet one cannot help remarking Porter's phrase "with weaving paces and with waving hands." and how it echoes "Of woven paces and of waving hands," line 966 of "Merlin and Vivien." How pervasive Tennyson was, even with poets working from a different set of premises and in a different tradition!

Lambert A. Wilmer's *Merlin* is an exception. The play appeared in three installments, each of a single act, in the columns of the Baltimore *North American* for August 18, 25, and September 1, 1827.[5] The drama thus antedates the *Idylls of the King,* and so is *ipso facto* non-Tennysonian, but there are other factors that make it *sui generis* among Merlins: first, Merlin is superhuman, as he announces in the beginning of Act I, scene 1: "I can the nimble lightning bind, / And chain the sharp and whistling wind... / To me futurity unveils / And destiny submits her scales: / The gloomy caves of hell I tread, / And hold dire converse with the dead!"

He even hears prayers, as he informs the spirits he invokes: "I call you from the regions of the air, / By the soft influence of a virgin's prayer—"

The second factor that sets Wilmer's *Merlin* apart is that its aesthetic context is firmly anchored with two Poe works, *Tamerlane* and *The Pirate.* Lovers of the poetry of Edgar Allan Poe may be forgiven for not knowing *The Pirate,* since it is not by that Poe at all, but by his brother, William Henry Leonard Poe. *Tamerlane* was

---

[4] Rochester
[5] Wilmer vii

published in Boston about July of 1827, *The Pirate* in Baltimore on November 27, 1827,[6] and so these two works bracket Wilmer's. Besides being contemporary, however, the internals of all three pieces would seem to reflect Edgar Poe's desperation at the two disasters of that year, his confrontation with John Allan over his gambling debts and the break-up of his engagement with Sarah Elmira Royster.

> Wilmer represents his hero as considering suicide. This I think was a "touch from life," for W. H. Poe represents his pirate as seeking death in vain. Edgar Poe had written John Allan, on March 19, 1827, "If you fail to comply with my request [for money]—I tremble for the consequence," a clear hint of suicide. I think Edgar's wild language had terrified his brother. As for the suicidal tendency of Poe—it really was not serious...In retrospect, one can always say that a man who did not kill himself, nor seriously attempt suicide, had no strong suicidal tendency. But this would not have been clear at the time, and one feels that Wilmer, genuinely moved by the situation, made *Merlin* a poetical plea against suicide, taking the excellent position that a situation may right itself.[7]

The editor of the modern edition of *Merlin* points out echoes of one poet's work in the other's.

> It is not absolutely impossible that in *The Raven* itself (into which Poe poured an immense amount of reminiscence), we have an unconscious or half echo of what is perhaps the best passage in... *Merlin*, I, iv, 17, 19; "And now, when [death] no doubt would be most welcome,...Like other friends he leaves thee in thy need," and the tenth stanza of *The Raven;* "Other

---

⁶ Wilmer v
⁷ Wilmer vi-vii

friends have flown before—On the morrow *he* will leave me,
as my Hopes have flown before" [8]

The theme of suicide is related to the character Alphonso, who,
returning from India, is shipwrecked and despairs of ever seeing the
fair Elmira again in her home "on the banks of the Hudson," which
means that Wilmer's work is also *sui generis* in having an American
setting, although it is not clear if this is the primary setting: the
Merlin scenes occur in "Merlin's cave," and the Alphonso scenes
occur on "the sea-shore," but the author does not specify which side of
the Atlantic is meant; it matters little, however, since distance is not
important in the play, as is made clear in Merlin's orders to the spirits
he has sent to guard the young lovers, in Act II, scene 1.   "But I must
hence away, / To Lapland's freezing clime, to bring a root, / None but
myself doth know:—Till I return, / Which shall be ere the evening sun
descends..."   To Lapland and back before sunset!   Merlin does make
the journey, and the root is efficacious against the Furies who are
creating all the unhappiness for Elmira and Alphonso, and the young
lovers are reunited.

Wilmer's *Merlin* is of only period interest from a literary point of view:
its plot is fatuous, its poetry is uninspired, its characters are unconvincing,
and its moral is trite.   There is one detail in the final speech of the drama
that is arresting, however: Merlin says, "With charms of force, a brazen
wall I'll rear / Around Cairmardin..."   "Cairmardin" is an indication that
Wilmer had some knowledge of Merlin lore, even though he did not avail
himself of it: a commonly-encountered etymology of the name "Merlin"
is that it is a back-formation from this toponym, in Welsh Caerfyrddin.
"Caer" is the regular Welsh word for "stronghold," and is pronounced
to rhyme with "wire;" the rest of the word is pronounced as if it were
"burthen" with an initial "v."   Welsh for Merlin is "Myrddin,"
pronounced as if it were "burthen" with an initial "m."   The argument
turns on a point of Welsh phonology, where an initial "m" mutates to a

---

[8]   Wilmer ix

"v" in compounds.   There is a "v" (written "f" in Welsh) in Caerfyrddin, and it is in a compound, so, runs the argument, the elements of the toponym may have been Caer+Myrddin, "Merlin's Stronghold."

"Merlin's Town" is how the toponym is rendered by Ernest Rhys, whose credibility on this point is enhanced by the fact that he grew up there.   The opening chapter of his autobiography is titled "From Islington to Merlin's Town,"[9] and he spoke of it as being "designed by nature to be a small boy's paradise," where young Rhys explored local landmarks like "Merlin's Hill," "a curious grotto...said to be Merlin's grave, but I imagine it had been the opening of a drift into a long deserted lead mine," and "an ancient tree in the last stages of decay which was known as Merlin's Oak."[10]   Small wonder that he would grow up to write a Merlin poem, "The Death of Merlin," and one in the Welsh tradition.   True, there is an echo of the Tennysonian plot in "The Sailors' Song," 'Marvelous Merlin is wasted away / With a wicked woman:—woe might she be! / For she hath closed him in a crag / On Cornwall coast.'   This idea, however, is cited only to be immediately dismissed by the shipmaster.   (IV) 'A fair sea-tale! What woman could, / With all the red witchery of her blood, / Enchant the Enchanter that is lost?   The "Shipmaster's Song" has Merlin suffering a different kind of fate.   "Marvellous Merlin is wafted away / In a sailing island, on a ship of glass; / Far over the edge of the world he's blown / By Annwn's blast."   Annwn (pronounced "on-noon") was a warrior-poet, like the historical Merlin.   The shipmaster, shaken by an apparition involving this moving island, goes to meet Morial, a priest who has just finished giving the Last Rites.   "'From demons save my soul,' began   / The Shipmaster: 'Hark ye, it blew / The blackest blast that ever I knew, / Under Enlli Isle: and we fell afeard, / For the Isle was adrift, and we barely cleared."   "Enlli Isle," Rhys would later write, "is now known as Bardsey Island."[11]   (VI) "'Like a

[9]   Rhys, 1940, 1
[10]   Rhys, 1898, ix
[11]   Rhys, 1940, 14-15

ship of glass as white as milk / With mast of ebon and shroud of silk, / She sailed away.   But see in black / Stands Merlin midships, round his head / A ring of white-fire, —while the rack / Streams by o'erhead: and the long-drowned dead / Stand up to see.   But he never looks back: / Though the hounds of Annwn are on his track." (VII) "'Oh, the dead cried out, and the sea-worms leapt, / For her keel drag'd fathom deep, and swept / Gulf dark with demons in her wake! / ...Good Morial, take / Off Satan's curse for Christ his sake!'"   The following day the shipmaster has forgotten the apparition: the weather is fine, and so his vessel sails, the sailors singing.   Priest Morial, however, is more deeply affected.   He begins to write a chronicle of Merlin's life, and becomes obsessed with it.   (IX) "Oh, then to all else Morial died, / Save scroll and desk, and wall beside..." He is both fascinated and repelled by the story, but sums it up thus: *Merlinus mortuus, deo laus* ("Merlin is dead, praise to God"), which is the poetic expression of the idea that John Veitch laid out in prose, that a crucial element in the Merlin legend is his symbolizing the Celts' pre-Christian religion, that after the Battle of Ardderyd in 573 the   defeated   Merlin   was   "a   heart-broken   and   despairing representative of the old Druidic nature-worship, at once the poet and priest of   the fading faith, yet torn and distracted by secret doubts as to its truth."[12]   Rhys does not belabor the point, but rather moves his poem quickly to a close: a vision comes to Morial, one that beckons him to the Nine Oaks that mark Merlin's grave.   Merlin awakes. 'Crist Celi,' next he cries, with hands / Heaved trembling up, and forthright stands.'

"Crist Celi" (literally, "Christ of Heaven") is an echo of the *Vita Merlini* (*VM,* "Life of Merlin").

Celi Christe deus quid agam	87	"O Christ, God of heaven, what will I do?"

---

[12] Veitch, 1893, 1:230

Parry's note on this line is relevant: "Celi Duw" [Welsh for "God," the second word rhyming with "see you"] came to be a very common title of the Deity in Welsh, the "coeli" losing completely its original meaning and being considered quite equivalent to "God."[13]

The oaks turn to druids, who sing that "Marvellous Merlin's awake with the day," and that "Wild Merlin's awake."   The poem ends exuberantly, with hopes for a Welsh awakening.

"Let us have the courage of our imperfections.   I know...that my Merlin is too mediæval and too long,"[14] wrote Rhys in the dedication to the first edition of *Welsh Ballads,* in which "The Death of Merlin" first appeared.   This is sham modesty, since the vigor, the glee with which the poem was written is evident in every line; in Rhys's later autobiography *Wales England Wed* the reader may detect a note of enthusiasm more consistent with the mood of the poem: "Long years afterwards I wrote a ballad called *The Death of Merlin,* into which I worked some of the wild traditions I had heard as a boy."[15]   The enthusiasm evidently continued into his days as editor and publisher: the precursor of the Everyman Press was the Camelot Press, and one of its first publications was a *Morte d'Arthur,* complete with the stilted diction that was *de rigeur* then: "'That wot I will,' said the King, 'but it shall so heavy me their departing, that I wot well that there shall be no manner of joy remedy me.'[16]   Rhys's account of the book's reception is instructive, as it involves two of the authors already mentioned in this study, a further illustration of the intimacy of "Little London:"

> After his lecture William Morris told me he had got hold of the Camelot *Morte d'Arthur,* and was delighted with it, and then he asked me to stop to supper...[T]he guest who

---

[13] Parry 119
[14] Rhys, 1898, ix
[15] Rhys, 1940, 15
[16] Rhys, 1906, 161

particularly caught my eye was a tall, pale, exceedingly thin young man, with a raven lock over his forehead...He was introduced to me after supper, as a young Irish poet, Willie Yeats...[17]

Yeats subsequently published a volume of Irish fairy tales with Rhys, although not as "Willie," and their relationship would last for years. Rhys was also on intimate terms with Laurence Binyon, whose main source of income was his post at the British Museum, where Rhys did research.

> In winter the atmosphere of the Reading Room was very trying.   There was a queer fusty odor that seemed to come partly from the old calf bindings of the books on the reference shelves and I am afraid from the human bindings of the habitués of the room, some of whom, poor things, could not afford hot baths.   One day Laurence Binyon met me in the lobby outside, and I complained of the miasma.
> "Ah well," he said, "you see it is eighteenth-century air, it has never been moved since then."   This went pretty near the truth.[18]

Whereas Malory had brought Rhys success as publisher, Binyon had enjoyed success with his treatments of the same material as dramatist and as poet, not only in the already-cited *Arthur,* but also in his *Odes.*

> The success of the volume was 'The Death of Tristram', a three-part in which Isoult and the dying Tristram are briefly reunited for an ecstatic *Liebestod.*   More dramatic than either Arnold's 'Tristram and Iseult' (1852) or Swinburne's *Tristram of Lyonesse* (1882), praised by Wilfrid Gibson for raising its

---

[17]   Rhys, 1940, 91-2
[18]   Rhys, 1940, 86

Arthurian subject 'above the ruck of Sham-Medievalism', the poem creates a rhetorical world heightened and ritualistically remote and yet, in its better moments, passionately physical.[19]

Like Rhys, however, Binyon had personal ties to the Welsh tradition. Binyon was of Welsh descent on both sides of his family: "Binyon" is anglicized *Ap Einion* , and "he was aware that some Lloyds [his mother's side of the family] wishfully traced their ancestry back to Arthur."[20] Gordon Bottomley, editor of *MM,* adds a reminiscence as to the point where Binyon abandoned the Tennysonian continuum:

> So far as I remember it was soon after the publication of his play *Arthur,* and its production at the Old Vic in 1923, that he felt there were great opportunities waiting in a handling of the Merlin theme for its own sake, and not as an episode of Arthurian legend; and that his thoughts had been turned to this by having lately learnt of another Merlin in the North, who had had prophecies recorded in his name. A special attraction of this was that he might develop such a plan into a consideration of the ardours and agonies, and doubts and dilemmas of our contemporary life, by reference to the timeless factor common to all generations.[21]

The references to prophecies indicate that this "Merlin in the North" was the *Vita Merlini* ("Life of Merlin," to be abbreviated *VM).* John Veitch offers an overview, which begins, "In the twelfth century, a Life of Merlin in Latin hexameters appeared—(*Vita Merlini Caledonii,* 1150). It is attributed to Geoffrey of Monmouth."[22]

---

[19] Hatcher 115-6
[20] Hatcher 1
[21] Binyon, 1947, vi
[22] Veitch, 1893, 1:234

Here I must interject a quarrel with the normally circumspect Veitch, beginning with his "1150." In the *VM* literature, 1150 is one of the few dates that have *not* been proposed: 1154 is mentioned more often, usually as a *terminus ante quem*, on the grounds that Geoffrey died in that year, but that milestone is relevant only if one assumes that Geoffrey was in fact the author. I concede that the scholarly consensus has taken Galfridian authorship of the *VM* as a given, and that in the year 2009 there would be fewer dissenters than there would have been in 1893. I do dissent, for reasons I will set out in another book, and thus I will write "the *VM* poet" where Veitch and others will write "Geoffrey of Monmouth." If the reader objects that this is a quibble, I agree: the authorship of *VM* is irrelevant to the present study, since it will be seen that both Binyon and Veitch treat *VM* as a self-contained literary entity, one comprehensible without considering how it fits in with Geoffrey's other work, or whether or not it does. There is, after all, a vanishing point in every inquiry, beyond which that inquiry is fruitless or goes astray; for Veitch and Binyon that vanishing point will be the text of the *VM* as it was available in their day, and taken at face value, *in sich,* as it were, without regard for its medieval *Sitz im Leben.*

We return to Veitch's overview:

> By this time the mythic element had grown in great measure round the historic character. Geoffrey represents Merlin, and, doubtless on the ground of local tradition, as frequenting a fountain in the wilds of the Caledonian Forest. The fountain is on the summit of a mountain; it is shaded by hazels, and girt round by low copse-wood, or shaws. There Merlin was in the habit of sitting and gazing on the wide expanse of woods around him. He watched the sportive movement of the creatures of the wilds, seeking thus to soothe the phrenzy of his brain.[23]

---

[23] Veitch, 1893, 1:234

Veitch the poet treats these issues in a thought-provoking way; his prose analysis is more penetrating.

> Whatever we may think of this solution of these early days, the problem dimly felt then is even now a pressing one for us. We must now still ask how we are to reconcile or to interpret harmoniously the impressions of nature—the scientific sense of what it presents to us, the imaginative sense of what it suggests to us, its literal and its symbolical aspects—with the supersensible personality which every normal human heart must feel somehow pervades it.   How are we to conciliate natural feeling with supernatural emotion? was the question of the reflective nature-worshipper among the Druids.   It is not less the question for every reflective man in this nineteenth century; and I am afraid we are not much advanced beyond the sun-worshippers of a thousand years ago on the Tweeddale hills.[24]

Laurence Binyon in his last years might be thought of as the sort of person least likely to make this kind of advance: in 1939 he turned 70, and could look back on a lifetime of success as a mainstream poet and dramatist, and as an explicator of the aesthetics of Oriental painting to western art-lovers.   He had published translations of Dante's *Inferno* and *Purgatorio* to great critical acclaim, and, when not occupied with his garden, his orchard or his grandchildren, was finishing up *Paradiso.*   Yet it was 1939.   As Binyon's biographer puts it, "In his study overlooking the garden and orchard he tracked Dante's ascent from Hell through Purgatory to Paradise, while the world followed a precisely opposite course."[25]   Binyon underwent a remarkable metamorphosis in the last four years of his life, and he wrote poems utterly unlike anything he had written before.   Consider

---

[24] Veitch, 1893, 1:240
[25] Hatcher 279

these lines from "The Burning of the Leaves," which was first published in October, 1942.

> Now is the time for the burning of the leaves.
> They go to the fire; the nostril pricks with smoke
> Wandering slowly into a weeping mist.
>   Brittle and blotched, ragged and rotten sheaves!
> A flame seizes the smouldering ruin and bites
> On stubborn stalks that crackle as they resist...
> Now is the time for stripping the spirit bare,
> Time for the burning of days ended and done...[26]

The first element in Binyon's transformation involved his feeling firsthand the stresses of the time.   His retirement was interrupted.

> On 13 December [1939] the British Council telephoned to ask if he would consider going out to Athens for four months as a stopgap Byron Professor of English Literature on a few days' notice.   Despite his age and the uncertainties of travel in a disintegrating Europe, he did not hesitate...Arriving in Athens on the Orient Express in early January, the Binyons moved into a small suite at the Hotel Grande Bretagne, where he hastily wrote a series of fourteen lectures on English poetry from Wordsworth to Eliot and Auden, a valedictory celebration of the craft and tradition he had followed for sixty years.   With enthusiasm for English surging in Athens since the outbreak of war, the lectures were packed with students from among the 5,000 enrolled at the English Institute.[27]

Binyon was scheduled to return to England in May, but the war had made travel next to impossible:

---

[26]   Binyon, 1944, 1
[27]   Veitch, 1893, 1:234

On 16 May, a day after the collapse of Holland, the Binyons were flown by flying boat to Marseilles, where they were held up for two days by a mistral, while to the north the Allied armies began withdrawing from Belgium and the Germans entered Brussels. They arrived back in England in time for Dunkirk and the fall of France.[28]

He wrote to Bottomley that "the agony of France at this moment haunts me all the time. When I was in France in 1917 & 18 I saw the hideous destruction & can never forget it: & to have to endure it again & much worse, is hard for us in England to imagine."[29]   Binyon had in fact been a medical orderly at the front in those years.   He wrote poetry based on this experience, but, with the exception of the four-line stanza of "For the Fallen" already cited, none of it can be included with the great poetry inspired by that terrible event: on the contrary, the reader is left with the impression of flatness.   Binyon accepts the rightness of the British cause, but lacks the debonnaire persuasiveness of Rupert Brooke; he is affected by the suffering he sees, but conveys nothing of the bitter anger of Wilfred Owen; and despite undergoing the same experiences as Robert Service, who was also a medical orderly, Binyon never comes close to the vividness of Service's *Rhymes of a Red Cross Man* in his poetic account of his wartime experiences.

Binyon's 1918 lecture before the British Academy, "English Poetry in its Relation to Painting and the Other Arts," contains nothing that suggests that World War I had brought him any kind of epiphany at all.   The opening of the lecture, in fact, is trite.   "All the arts of man spring from a single well of inspiration.   They spring from the deep impulse and desire to create an ideal world more true to our real selves, more adequate to our innate conceptions, than anything we can achieve in actual existence."[30]   If this sounds like repression in the

---

[28] Veitch, 1893, 1:234
[29] Veitch, 1893, 1:240
[30] Hatcher 279

psychological sense, it would appear to have been temporary: seven years later, in the middle of   a short work on poetics, he would interject, "There was no need to look outside Europe, or to some other planet, for the barbarians.   They were all within ourselves."[31]

World War II would provide him with an entirely new set of wartime experiences, but instead of being in a remote and romantic foreign setting, they were at home, an incessant, menacing background to his work and his family.

> Lectures took him to London several times during the height of the Blitz, where more than 250,000 Londoners were bombed out of their homes.   From Westridge [Binyon's country home], 50 miles away, they could see flashes of anti-aircraft fire during the nightly raids.   With babies and young children under their roof, even Westridge was not safe. War-planes droned overhead, and bombs occasionally dropped on nearby fields and farmhouses...
>
> The extended family, often including eleven adults and children, were absorbed in a 'daily round of small things', gardening, salting beans, making jam, canning fruit, and selling greengages [a hybrid plum] and plums to raise money for the Red Cross.   By the autumn of 1942 the orchard was yielding two tons of apples and plums, and with income tax taking half Binyon's pension, they lived frugally, living mainly off home-grown vegetables...
>
> The enforced isolation of their life on the downs was a godsend to Binyon's poetry.   He completed the *Paradiso* in April 1941, and returned to his other major project of these final years, *The Madness of Merlin,* a long dramatic poem which had been in gestation for at least thirty years.[32]

---

[31]   Binyon, 1944, 1
[32]   Hatcher 286-87

It was inevitable that this long-term project would come to the fore: the two key elements in the Celtic Merlin's tale, it will be recalled from John Veitch's synopsis, are wartime trauma and rural retreat, and these matched Binyon's own experiences precisely and pervasively: Binyon had become Merlin.

In addition to describing Binyon's emotional state during the genesis of *MM*, it necessary to take a closer look at the poem that was its catalyst, the *Vita Merlini*. In a nutshell, *VM* is a Latin epic of 1,529 lines in dactyllic hexameter. Its style is allusive, musical and virtuosic. It is allusive in that it abounds in echoes of Vergil and Ovid; it is musical in that the *VM* poet delights in echoes of a more literal kind, repeated words and homonymic syllables; it is virtuosic in the sense that it undertakes difficult technical tasks, such as versifications of prose essays on scientific topics.

The *VM* poet's allusiveness is shown from the very opening of the poem.

Fatidici Vatis rabiem, musamque iocosam
Merlini cantare paro.

A prophet-bard gone mad, the laughing muse
Of Merlin I'm preparing to sing.

The *VM* poet's familiarity with Ovid, particularly the *Heroides,* has been mentioned in my *Anonymity in Western Literature*; this very first line of the poem hints at a familiarity, not only with Ovid, but with Vergil. One is struck by the similarity of this phrase with the one in *Aeneid* (*A*) VIII.340: *vatis fatidicae, cecinit quae prima futuros* ("[in honor of] the soothsayer-bard [the nymph Carmentis] who first sang of future [events]"), and other Vergilian and Ovidian echoes will be noted. (It is to be noted on the other hand that the *VM* poet uses *vates* to refer to himself in line 7.) A cautionary note is in order: the *VM* poet employs Ovidian and Vergilian turns of phrase, but for his own purposes, as if they were tiles lifted from one mosaic and embedded in another. Consider the phrase in line 22, *Jura dabat populis.* It is evident that the VM poet was much taken by this phrase in *A* I.507

iura dabat legesque viris ("She gave decrees and laws to men"), since it inspired several lines in *VM.* Yet the Vergilian context is that of a queen (Dido) ruling over men; in the *VM*, however, there is only one instance where that is the case, of the otherworldly nine sisters in 916-7, *Illic iura novem geniali lege sorores / Dant his* ("There nine sisters give decrees to them by gentle laws"). The other cases involve men: *His duo iura dabunt* 652 ("Two will give decrees to them"); *Pacis amator erat populo nam iura feroci / Sic dabat* 696-7 ("He was a lover of peace, for he gave decrees to the fierce people"); 1131 *Iura dedit populo regni diademate sumpto* ("He gave decrees to the people, having taken over the crown of the kingdom"). The *VM* poet was also much taken by the phrase *furor arma ministrat* ("[their] rage supplies [them with] weapons"), in *A* I.150, both by its vividness and because *ministrat*, having a short syllable and two long syllables, is a useful word in filling out the parts of a dactyllic hexameter line where a spondee is called for. That the *VM* poet was susceptible to shortcuts *metricis causa* is shown by his use, or rather, overuse, of *ergo,* both in terms of frequency and semantic infelicity; I submit that he liked the word simply because it is a spondee.

Even without leaving the first line, there are two other thought-provoking words: *rabiem* and *iocosam.* The author uses *rabies* once in a figurative sense: 580 *rabiem britonum* ("mania of the Britons"). The other occurrences of the word are literal: 1150 *sese cognovit rabiem* ("he recognized his insanity"); 1257 *multo rabie corruptus* ("torn by much insanity"); and 1417 *corripuit rabies miserabilis* ("pitiable insanity seized"). A synonym is *furia,* as in 208 *Merlinus furiasque suas miratur et odit* ("Merlin is amazed at his madness and hates it").

As for *iocosam,* there are jocular moments in the *VM,* such as the implausible divinations that in fact come true, but they are few and far between. The greater part of the story is taken up with sober scientific matter and the anguish of mental illness. Rather than take this phrase literally, it is more likely an Ovidian echo. In *Tristia* we find both *musa iocosa mea* (2.354) and *musa iocata* (3.2.6). I reiterate my contention that the fact that the *VM* poet grafted the words of Ovid and Vergil onto his work does not mean that he also had their contexts in mind. Discussion of the *VM* poet's use of classical sources will call for what the French call *le frein vital* ("the vital rein"), knowing when the literary vanishing point has been reached, and knowing when to stop.

The failure to do this lands Siân Echard, author of *Arthurian Narrative in the Latin Tradition* in severe difficulties. Her discussion of *musa iocosa* is accurate as far as the original context is concerned.

> The phrase is odd, but it does occur in another, perhaps helpful, context. In book II of the *Tristia,* Ovid offers a defense of his own work: "Believe me, my character is far from my songs: / My life is virtuous, although my Muse is jocose. / The greater part of my work is lying and fictive; / It allows itself more latitude than does its author. / Nor is the book an indication of the spirit, but an honest game; / You will find in it many things suited to the delight of the audience."[33]

So far, so good; what gets Echard into trouble later is her application of the context to Geoffrey of Monmouth.

> The potentially playful – or tricky – nature of this writing is also emphasized. One thinks of Walter Map's complex presentation of his *nugae,* of John of Salisbury's assertion that , while all he writes might not be true, it is nevertheless useful, even William of Renes's presentation of his *Gesta* as a *ludus* is suggested here.[34]

Bracketing the question this way proves nothing: Ovid was facetious before *VM,* and Walter Map would be facetious afterward, but that does not mean that *VM* is facetious. The Ovidian smirk is not

---

[33] Echard 217
[34] Echard 217

characteristic of the other occurrences of *iocosa* in *VM*; on the contrary, the word is consistently used in its simple sense, of hearty fun: 141. *cursusque iocosque ferarum* ("the running and play of wild animals"); 201-2. *iocosis / Adfatur verbis* ("he addressed with joking words"); 261. *letusque iocatur amanti* ("and happy, he joked with his lover"); 335. *sic regina iocando* ("the queen in jest [said]"); 532. *vatemque iocosus adorat* ("laughing, he adores the bard"); 1364. *verbis iocosis* ("with joking words"); 1392. *ut moveat risusque iocosque loquendo* ("so that he might provoke laughter and joking by his speech").

Despite this, Echard insists that the Ovidian origin of these two words in the first line of *VM* are the key to the whole.

> In any case, the invocation of the musa iocosa at the opening of the Vita Merlini seems to show Geoffrey declaring that what follows is a game of sorts, something amusing, for a select group of listeners who will get the joke – Map's arguti, perhaps.[35]

This gives more importance to the first line of the poem than to the following 1,528.   Echard herself has difficulty with the way her assumption plays out.

> But if this is a game or a joke, it is a joke of a very peculiar character, most peculiar in precisely those passages which have claims to inspiration by the musa iocosa.[36]

The peculiarities only obtain when the *VM* is conceived of a priori as comedy.   Echard alleges more contradictions:

> Thus far we have been discussing the mingling of references to laughter with material which seems ill-suited to jocosity.

---

[35] Echard 218
[36] Echard 218

Another jarring aspect of the Vita lies in a structural deployment of a similar technique; abrupt shifts in narrative material and tone are characteristic of the piece from the outset. Despite the jocose muse, the poem opens, as we have seen, with references to fate; a string of formal laments follows as Merlin flees into the woods.[37]

Letting the poem unfold on its own terms obviates these so-called contradictions, which, I repeat, obtain only when one puts too much weight on the single phrase *musa iocosa*. In fairness to Echard, it is to be noted that her interpretation, although more thoroughgoing in degree, is nevertheless foursquare with the scholarly consensus: Parry (31) translates *musa iocosa* as "a humorous poem," Clarke (53) as "an entertaining tale," and Vielhauer (42) as *in unterhaltender Form* ("in an amusing manner"). They thus commit the translator's sin of hyperfinesse, and it is the source of their subsequent critical tangles. Let us eschew obfuscation: *musa iocosa* is a laughing muse, and the *VM* does have laughter, many different kinds of it, and much of it is not light-hearted at all.

For the remaining word, *vates,* the entry in the *Oxford Latin Dictionary* proposes an etymology that introduces themes that will recur in our discussion. *Vates* is

> [of Italo-Celtic origin, cf. Ir. *fāith* 'bard', Welsh *gwawd* 'song of praise'; cogn. also w. Goth. *wods* 'frenzied', 'possessed']

Leaving the Irish word for later comment, we note that although Gothic may not be germane to our topic, Old English certainly is: we may take it as a given that the *VM* poet heard the Old English *wōd* ("mad") used by his Saxon neighbors, and may have noticed its similarity to *vates.* As to whether or not the *VM* poet would likewise have recognized the Welsh *gwawd,* either in the *OLD*'s sense of "song

---

of praise" or in its modern meaning of "satire," that is another matter;
Geoffrey of Monmouth probably would have, since *HRB* sometimes
betrays a Welsh accent, as when Merlin scolds Vortigern's *magi:*

> *Nescientes quid fundamentum incepte turris impediat.*
> *laudavistis ut sanguis meus effunderetur in cementum* (*HRB*
> 382).
> ("Ignorant of what hinders the foundation of this tower, *you*
> *have praised* that my blood be poured into the mortar.")

Praised?   No; the magi had *declared* that this grim expedient would
stabilize   the   foundation.   Geoffrey's   *laudavistis*   is   a   Welsh
"fingerprint:"   it is plausible that an original *datganu* ("declare") in
Geoffrey's *vetustissimus liber* could have been read as *da* ("good") +
canu ("sing," often in praise).   The Latin of the *VM,* however, is quite
correct, and betrays no accent that I can detect.

The *Oxford Latin Dictionary*'s mention of "Ir. *fāith* 'bard'" brings
up the question of an Irish "fingerprint," which is a very elusive matter.
The Irish connection is everywhere and nowhere: there are obvious
similarities   between   *VM*   and   *Buile   Suíbhne   Geilt*   (*BSG,*   "Mad
Sweeney"), since both are tales of a king who goes mad.   Certain
elements in the *VM* would be linked if Irish etymologies were to be
brought to bear: Merlin prophesies; Merlin laughs; the root cited by
the *OLD* above connects the two, since a *fáith* or *fáidh* is a prophet,
and *fáithbhim* means "laugh."   Yet the absence of a cut-and-dried,
follow-the-dots relationship between the Irish tradition and the *VM*
calls for caution in dealing with specific similarities: when is a
similarity an antecedent, a borrowing, a quotation, or an element that
was simply in the air when *VM* was written, an idea from a common
Celtic background?

In addition to *VM*'s allusiveness, it has a harmoniousness, this in
the aural sense; one could even say that the *VM* poet's ear admitted a
very un-Vergilian jingliness, usually in the form of juxtaposed echoing
syllables.   Consider lines 26-7.

Dux venedotorum peredurus	The leader of the North Welsh,
bella gerebat	Peredur, was <u>waging</u> war
Contra guennoloum scocie qui	Against Gwentholy, who <u>ruled</u>
regna regebat.	<u>the realms</u> of Scotland.

Although twenty-first century reading habits may draw the eye to the half-rhyme at the end of the couplet (*regebat, gerebat*), it is the *regna regebat* that is more common:

Tresque ducis <u>fratres fratrem</u>	34.	As did <u>three</u> <u>brothers</u> of the
per bella secuti		leader who had followed their
		<u>brother</u> through the wars,

Tres and *[fra]tres, fratres* and *fratrem.*   There is also   *concor<u>dant</u> cum <u>dant</u>* 94,("help, since they grant"), *sine fronde...sine fructu* 96 ("without foliage, without fruit"), *loqui vellet <u>secum</u> <u>secum</u>que* 113 ("to speak to him [and sit] with him"), would be a preliminary list of only the simplest types.   There are more involved examples as well:

Rotabit que domos <u>sacro</u> <u>sacer</u>	637.	And a <u>holy</u> man will turn the
imbre <u>sacerdos</u>		Houses <u>holy</u> by <u>holy</u>
		sprinkling,

The poet has echoes from one line to another:

Hec fratrem <u>flet</u> et illa virum	187.	She be<u>wails</u> her brother and
communiter ambe		the other her husband;
		together both
<u>Fletibus</u> incumbunt et tristia		They spend their time in
tempora ducunt		<u>weep</u>ing, and pass the time
		sadly.

Lines 170-2 have a triple echo.

O diros gemitus lugubris	170. "Oh, the desperate groans of
<u>Guendoloene</u>	sorrowful <u>Gwendolyn</u>!
O miseras <u>la</u>cr<u>i</u>mas	Oh, the pitiful <u>tears</u> of <u>tear</u>ful
<u>la</u>crimantis <u>Guendoloene</u>	<u>Gwendolyn</u>!
Me <u>miseret mis</u>ere morientis	I <u>pity</u> the <u>pit</u>iful, dying
<u>Guendoloene</u>	<u>Gwendolyn</u>!

Binyon transmutes this into a triple echo involving Merlin when the Minstrel sings: "It is the tears of Guendolen that fall./ It is the voice of Gwyndyth that laments, / Wife and sister, night and day: / Merlin, Merlin, Merlin is their cry, / Merlin the loved, the lost."[38]   Binyon repeats this triple echo in Scene VIII.   Merlin's wife, in anguish over accusations of his cowardice, asks, "Could Merlin, noble Merlin, my Merlin / Have flung his sword away upon the moor?"[39]   The saintly Kentigern is shocked, and rebukes Merlin with a triple echo: "When a man takes arms for a cause / It is the cause that strikes. / It is the cause, my son, that thou hast cast away."[40]   It is worth recalling that the title of one of Binyon's books of World War I poetry is *The Cause.*

Binyon uses these echoes sparingly; with the *VM* poet they are a mannerism.   The *VM* poet even admits a very un-Vergilian interjection.

Eya frater ait dic mortem	337. "Hey, brother," she said, "Say
virginis huius	the death of this girl."

Eya is a hearty, loud exclamation.   Columbanus[41] uses it in a yo-heave-ho context: *Extollunt venti flatus, nocet horridus imber, / Sed vis apta virum superat sternitque procellam. / Heia, viri! nostrum reboans echo sonet heia!* ("Winds whip up, the driving rain stings, /

---

[38] Binyon, 1947, 22
[39] Binyon, 1947, 33
[40] Binyon, 1947, 34
[41] Carney 190

But the ready strength of men overcomes and lays low the squall. / Hey, men! Let our resounding echo ring out: Hey!").

The virtuosic elements in *VM* consist of rendering the prose of encyclopedist Isidore of Seville and geographer Pomponius Mela into hexameters. *VM* 875-907 corresponds to Isidore's *Etymologies* XIV.v.vi; *VM* 1179-1242 to *Etymologies* XIII.xiii; *VM* 1300-1386 to *Etymologies* XII.vii.22. The subjects of these interludes are, respectively, islands, bodies of water and birds. *VM* 908-940 is from Pomponius Mela's geography (III,6,483), and is a description of the British Isles. These versifications are discussed in detail in my *Anonymity in Western Literature*.

Let us focus on *The Madness of Merlin*. In a nutshell, it is a drama of fourteen scenes, fifty-eight pages long, with a dramatis personae of eleven characters, unnamed extras and a "mob." The dramatis personae is interesting because it is titled "Characters in the Poem," and no mention is made of the extras needed for the two mob scenes. I do not take this lack of production information to mean that *MM* was not intended to be staged; Binyon's theatrical experience is a matter of record, so if he wrote stage directions and dialogue, I take the form at face value, and assume that he was writing for the stage.

No physical description of the characters is given; their delineation is accomplished to a limited extent by plot, but mostly through dialogue. Merlin, for example, is described simply as "a Welsh prince," in the dramatis personae, and in the first scene one character tells the other that a nobleman has run by, behaving irrationally, but it is his own words, from the moment he begins to speak, that shows that he is having some kind of mental crisis: "On, on, into the dark! / Why dost thou drive me on..."[42] He has been following a voice, but the voice has diminished to a whisper and then disappeared. Merlin will be portrayed as having brief periods of clarity, but there are always relapses, and he is a lost, questioning character throughout the drama.

---

[42] Binyon, 1947, 5

Guendolen, Merlin's wife, is delineated by her constant use of the first person singular. Lamenting his disappearance she says, "Yet Merlin comes not; neither comes to me, / Nor sends me a single sign."[43]   Even when she sees Merlin, dazed with his madness and half-dead from exposure from many days and nights spent in the woods, she says, "O miserable me!" and later, "Cruel Merlin, so to leave me! / What have I suffered!   What tears have I shed!"[44]   Ego is everything to her: her remedy for her husband's madness is to dress him in a robe of state.   "I put the precious, the embroidered robe, / The proud, purple robe of ceremony / Over your shoulders.   Now / Be again my Merlin, prince among men,   / Prince among princes, my prince!"   Ego and status are everything to her, and so when she finds Merlin's scabbard empty, giving credence to the report that he threw his sword away, her condemnation is instant and absolute: "For this, my desolation, / For this, my shame and the pointed fingers? / My shame?   It is your shame! / I deny you…"[45]   She denies him publicly, saying that he is a changeling: "I, Guendolen, I, Merlin's wife / I say it is not he."[46]   By contrast, Gwyndyth, Merlin's sister, is portrayed as patient and realistic.   "Things there are that are not in our experience / And abide, may-be, beyond our understanding,"[47] she says.   When Merlin is lost, she is sad, but not frantic; when he is found, she is gentle: "He has been far into a different world from ours. / Patience is all."[48]   (Gwyndyth makes her last appearance in Scene VII, however, which is an odd aesthetic decision on Binyon's part; he splits this *VM* character into two roles.   In the *VM* she is Merlin's sister and Redderch's queen, but Binyon limits Gwyndyth to the sister role, creating a new character, Langoreth, to carry on with the queen's actions.

---

[43]   Binyon, 1947, 9
[44]   Binyon, 1947, 23-4
[45]   Binyon, 1947, 25-6
[46]   Binyon, 1947, 33
[47]   Binyon, 1947, 10
[48]   Binyon, 1947, 23

King Redderch's epithet is "the Generous," with the ambiguity that the term implies. He is helpful and kind to Merlin, even when Merlin's behavior becomes violent, and he is deferential, even humble before Kentigern. On the other hand, he is easily deceived: he is blind to the faithlessness of his wife, to the jealousy of Peredur, and to Merlin's anguish, saying, "I know not of these things. The world is a good world. / The air tastes sweet, the hearts of men are kind."[49]

Queen Langoleth, Redderch's wife, has a small role, but her dialogue is vivid. Her manly ideal is not her generous husband, but her lover, the warrior Peridur; she is exasperated by the kindness Merlin is receiving, and by the influence of Kentigern. She complains to Peredur, "Battles are over. Shave your head! / There's no use for a sword's sharpness. / A madman honoured, a monk enthroned!"[50]

The monk is Saint Kentigern, who has been induced by Redderch to come to his kingdom, and is received with honor. He makes long speeches on the spread of Christian doctrine in Britain, hoping for a peaceful world; "Yet still shall the sword be needed / For the enemies of Christ are around us."[51] As mentioned earlier, Kentigern takes Merlin's defection seriously.

Taliesin is portrayed as an old comrade of Merlin's: he addresses him as *my heart's brother,* the same phrase as Redderch uses.[52] Taliesin comes to visit Merlin in his forest haunts, reminding him of the beauty of the world, and urging him to go back to his home. In the *VM* Taliesin comes to learn scientific lore from Merlin, which means, in the context of the poem, that Taliesin's questions introduce the scientific versifications.

Peredur is little more than a name in the *VM*. He is a comrade in arms of Merlin, as stated above, and after the battle tries to console him.

---

[49] Binyon, 1947, 45
[50] Binyon, 1947, 42
[51] Binyon, 1947, 30
[52] Binyon, 1947, 32;36

Solatur Peredurus eum	68.	Peredur comforted him, and
proceresque ducesque		the chiefs and the leaders;

Binyon has given him a larger, though still minor role: he is Langoreth's lover, and   Merlin's taunting antagonist.

The final echo of the *VM* in the dramatis personae is the minstrel, who is delineated more by the songs he sings than by his dialogue, but the dialogue he has is vivid: "How shall I ensnare this lost one? Wary, wary!   No cracking stick must give his ear alarm,"[53] which is much more incisive than the VM version.

Nuntius hunc scandit tacitoque	142.	The messenger climbed to
per ardua gressu		that place, up the steep
		slopes, with silent step,
Incedit querendo virum tum		He got close, seeking the
denique fontem		man, then at last the spring
Merlinumque videt		And Merlin he saw

Himilian, is described simply as a country girl.   The poem begins and ends with references to her femininity: her companion warns her that Merlin's sword is "no thing for a girl / To handle."   Later he exclaims, "A girl with a man's sword for a plaything— / It's a mad sight to see upon the moor, / And the dark coming."   She is fascinated with the sword and intrigued with the man who threw it away at her feet.   The drama ends with her announcement that she is pregnant by Merlin.

Greid, "a young peasant, her companion," is little more than a foil for Himilian: he is attracted to the sword for the money it would fetch, but changes his mind when he sees how excited Himilian is with it, and urges her to bury it and forget it.

The plot, by scenes, is as follows: (I) The peasant girl Himilian has found a sword in the grass, thrown away by a warrior fleeing a battle.   She vows to keep it.   (II) Merlin has a long soliloquy on his

---

[53]   Binyon, 1947, 20

rejection of civilization. (III) Guendolen, Merlin's wife, tells Gwyndyth, his sister, of her anger at the gossip that Merlin fled because of cowardice. Himilian enters and tells them that Merlin has been sighted. King Redderch is told, and is asked to send envoys to bring Merlin to court. (IV) Another Merlin soliloquy, containing images from the *Vita Merlini*. (V) At court. St. Kentigern arrives at the king's request. (VI) Merlin soliloquizes, then is accosted by a minstrel, who calms him with a song. He agrees to be led home. (VII) Merlin is at court, with Guendolen and Gwyndyth. They try to get him to readjust. Gwyndyth is kind and comforting; Guendolen is resentful of the harm Merlin's madness has done to her, finally exclaiming, "I deny you." (VIII) Redderch's court, where Kentigern preaches to the assembly. He is told of Merlin's breakdown in the battle. Merlin enters, and is besieged with questions and accusations of cowardice; he rushes away. (IX) The bard Taliesin accosts Merlin in the forest. They converse, and have a musical dialogue. (X) Langoreth, Redderch's queen, meets with Peredur, one of Merlin's accusers. It is evident that they are lovers. (XI) Himilian hears a mob that has captured Merlin "riding on a stag." (XII) Merlin is in confinement; Redderech, then Langoreth come; Merlin laughs, but refuses to say why. He explains, in exchange for his freedom, that Langoreth has a lover. (XIII) Merlin soliloquizes in the wilderness. (XIV) Merlin is delirious, visionary; he is attended by Himilian, who becomes pregnant by him.

The first impression one has of the plot of *MM* is of disjointedness. It should not be thought that this disjointedness has anything to do with Binyon's death, that *MM* is in any way unfinished. True, he had planned a trilogy, of which *MM* was only the first part.

> Binyon's poem was to have been in three parts, but at his death he had completed only the first...The unpublished manuscripts show that instead of pushing ahead with the other two parts, Binyon worked painstakingly on Part I, adding to

the density and physicality of the text, paring away all inessentials.[54]

In point of fact, he had moved on to the sequels, as the fragmentary drafts show.[55]   *MM* is a finished work, not only in its line-by-line polish, but also in its form, which is neatly symmetrical.   Sorted by themes, the scenes resolve neatly into an arch (granting that Scene X is only a set-up for XII).

VII (Ladies of the Court)

VI Minstrel   Priest VIII

V Priest   Bard   IX

IV   Merlin is mad   XI

III   Ladies of the Court   (X),XII

II   Merlin's Soliloquy   XIII

I   Himilian's Femininity   XIV

A theater audience, of course, would have no such overview of the work; in performance one takes in the individual lines, speeches, turns of plot, as they come.   The overall effect, I repeat, is disjointedness.

There are two reasons for the disjointedness of *MM,* and both will require some explanation.   The first has to do with Binyon's use of the *Vita Merlini* as a source, because it is not a source in the sense of a model or a *corpus vile* that is to be reworked or rearranged: *MM* is a continuation of the *Vita Merlini,* a filling-in of the gaps in that medieval epic by the addition of new episodes to the main line of its narration.   The *Vita Merlini* is thus everywhere and nowhere. Consider this passage from Scene XI of *MM,* where the peasant girl Himilian hears a disturbance offstage.   She asks, "What are they calling there? / I hear a wondering cry. (A VOICE [without])

---

[54] Hatcher 287

[55] Binyon, 1947, vii

Himilian, Himilian!   Come, / Come look. / (ANOTHER VOICE) It is the mad Merlin. (FIRST VOICE)   And riding on a stag, on a wild stag. / His hand upon the antler guides it / Up to the King's door."

The next scene opens with Merlin under close confinement, and raving, with no transition, nor with any explanation for the lack of transition at all.   We find the transition by consulting the medieval source.   The reference in *MM* to riding a stag identifies the offstage commotion as the episode in the *Vita Merlini* (ll. 451-480) where Merlin, who has been living in the forest as a wild man, goes to attend his wife's remarriage.   (My translation.)

Dixerat et silvas et saltus circuit omnes	He spoke, and he went round the groves and meadows all,
Ceruorum que greges agmen collegit in unum	And the herds of deer he gathers in one column,
Et damas capreas que simul cervo que resedit	And the does and nanny-goats likewise, and he sat on a stag,
Et veniente die compellens agmina pre se	And when the day came, driving the column by himself
Festinans vadit quo nubit guendoloena	455. Hurrying he forged ahead to where Gwendolyn was getting married.
Postquam venit eo pacienter stare coegit Cervos ante fores proclamans guendoloena	After he came there, he made the stags stand Patiently before the gates while he shouted, "Gwendolyn!
Gendoloena veni te talia munera spectant	Gwendolyn! I have come! Such gifts are looking at you!"

Ocius ergo venit subridens	Soon Gwendolyn came,
Guendoloena	smiling,
Gestari que virum cervo 460.	And is amazed that the man
miratur et illum	is borne on a stag, and that it
Sic parere viro tantum quoque	Thus submits to him, that it
posse ferarum	is possible that so great
	indeed a number
Uniri numerum quas pre se	Of animals can be united,
solus agebat	which he was driving before
	him, all by himself,
Sicut pastor oves quas ducere	Just like the sheep that the
suevit ad herbas	shepherd matter-of-factly
	drives to the pasture.

Now for the abrupt change in Scene XII of *MM,* where Merlin is in custody, obviously having had a relapse, as shown by his monologue: "Chains!   Chains for the madman! / The oxen come to trample on my mind./ Staring faces, crowding faces! / Eyes, everywhere eyes!"   In point of fact, there is a transitional passage in the *Vita Merlini,* immediately after Merlin's arrival on the stag.

Stabat ab excelsa sponsus	The bridegroom stood
spectando fenestra	looking from a high window,
In solio mirans equitem risum 465.	Looking at the "knight" in his
que movebat	"saddle," and a laugh escaped
	him.
Ast ubi vidit eum vates animo	But when the bard saw him,
que quis esset	and [knew] in mind who he
	was,
Calluit extemplo divulsit	All at once he hardened, and
cornua cervo	tore the antlers off the stag
Quo gestabatur vibrata que	On which he was carried, and
iecit in illum	threw them, whizzing, at the
	other man,

Et caput illius penitus contrivit eumque	And smashed his head in, and
Reddidit exanimem vitamque fugavit in auras	470. Left him dead, and his life fled into the air.
Ocius inde suum talorum verbere cervum	Quickly from thence, kicking the stag with his heel,
Diffugiens egit silvas que redire paravit	Fleeing, he made off, and prepared to return to the woods.
Egrediuntur ad hec ex omni parte clientes	Vassals from all over came there,
Et celeri cursu vatem per rura sequuntur	And followed the bard through the countryside in hot pursuit.
Ille quidem velox sic precurrebat ut isset	475. He, indeed, fast, thus ran before, so that he might go
Ad nemus intactus nisi previus amnis obesset	Untouched to the grove, except for the river that was in his way.
Nam dum torrentem fera prosiliendo mearet	For while the beast proceeded over the torrent with a lurch
Elapsus rapida cecidit merlinus in unda	Merlin slipped and fell in the rapid wave.
Circueunt ripas famuli capiunt que natantem	The servants ringed the banks and captured the swimmer,
Adducunt que domum vinctum que dedere sorori	And they led him home bound, and gave him to his sister.

In terms of theatrical *praxis,* one could remark that the abruptness of the transition between Binyon's Scene XI and Scene XII is good theater, and leave it at that. In terms of analysis, however, the foregoing example illustrates the necessity of delineating the cross-references between the *VM* and Binyon's drama.

Synoptic Merlins

Synopsis of Binyon's *Madness of Merlin* by scenes	Synopsis of the *Vita Merlini* by lines
	Dedication; a battle, in which Merlin, a Welsh king, has a mental breakdown. He flees. (1-74)
I. The peasant girl Himilian has found a sword in the grass, thrown away by a warrior fleeing a battle. She vows to keep it.	
	Merlin lives in the forest, having become a wild man. (75-85)
II. Merlin has a long soliloquy on his rejection of civilization.	
	Merlin soliloquizes on the hardships of his forest life. A passer-by sees him, and reports the sighting to a courtier. (86-137)
III. Guendolen, Merlin's wife, tells Gwyndyth, his sister, of her anger at the gossip that Merlin fled because of cowardice. Himilian enters and tells them that Merlin has been sighted. King Redderch is told, and is asked to send envoys to bring Merlin to court. IV. Another Merlin soliloquy, containing images from the *Vita Merlini.*	

V. At court.   St. Kentigern
arrives at the king's request.

VI. Merlin soliloquizes, then is   Merlin soliloquizes, is
accosted by a minstrel, who   overheard by
calms him with   an envoy who calms him
                                         through music,
a song.   He agrees to be led   and leads him back to court.
home.   (138-214)
VII. Merlin is at court, with   Merlin's wife and sister rejoice to
Guendolen
and Gwyndyth.   They try to get   have him back. (215-218)
him
to readjust.   Gwyndyth is kind
and comforting; Guendolen is
resentful of the harm Merlin's
madness has done to her, finally
exclaiming, "I deny you."
VIII. Redderch's court, where
Kentigern
preaches   to the assembly.   He
is told of Merlin's breakdown in
the battle.   Merlin
enters, and is besieged with   Merlin is besieged with well-
questions
and accusations of cowardice; he   wishers celebrating his return.
rushes away.   The stimulus is too much for
                                         him, and he wishes to escape;
                                         the king, however, has him
                                         bound and guarded.
                                         (219-253)

IX. The bard Taliesin accosts
Merlin in the forest.   They
converse, and have a musical
dialogue.

X. Langoreth, Redderch's queen,
meets with Peredur, one of
Merlin's accusers.   It is evident
that they are lovers.

The queen greets the king; Merlin
laughs; he is promised his
freedom if he will explain the
laugh; he says that the queen has
a lover.   Merlin, challenged by
the queen, predicts a triple death
for a courtier.   Merlin's wife and
sister beg him not to leave, but he
returns to the woods.   The triple
death prediction comes true.
Gwendolyn remarries; Merlin,
riding a stag, kills the bridegroom,
and is recaptured.   (254-480)

XI.   Himilian hears a mob that
has captured Merlin "riding on a
stag."
XII.   Merlin is in confinement;
Redderech,
then Langoreth come; Merlin
laughs,
but refuses to say why.
He explains, in exchange for his
freedom,
that Langoreth has a lover.

Merlin is confined.   He
laughs
twice.   The king offers him his

freedom for an explanation.
He offers two prophecies,

and is allowed to return to the
forest.   They beg him not to
go until spring.   He leaves, but
invites her to visit, and bring
Taliesin.   Prophecies.
(481-688)

XIII.   Merlin soliloquizes in the
wilderness.

> Taliesin (a Welsh bard) joins
> Merlin in the wilderness.
> Disquisitions on learned subjects,
> and prophecies.   Another wild
> man is discovered.   He is cured,
> and agrees to join Merlin and
> Taliesin in the woods.   More
> disquisitions and prophecies.
> Gwendolyn prophesies, too.
> Coda.   (688-1529)

XIV.   Merlin is delirious,
visionary; he is attended by
Himilian, who becomes pregnant
by him.

The disjointedness of Binyon's story line may seem less extreme
when juxtaposed with the *Vita Merlini,* but saying that only highlights
MM 's lack of continuity when considered by itself.   It is true that
MM has an arch form, but that does not dispel the feeling of
disjointedness either.   There are echoes in dialogue between scenes,
as has been noted with *my heart's brother;* a survey will tell us
whether they give the drama any unity.   Greid fears forest ghosts who
will "twist the long briars, coil by coil" in Scene I,[56] and can compare
it to Merlin's "the cruel coiling of the thorns" in Scene IV.[57]   There is
a mouse in Scene II[58] and a mouse in Scene VI, which Merlin
addresses as "Little companion, we are alone / Together, you and I,"[59]
which recalls the *VM* Merlin's comradeship with a wolf.

---

[56]   Binyon, 1947, 3
[57]   Binyon, 1947, 15
[58]   Binyon, 1947, 6
[59]   Binyon 1947, 1

Tu lupe care comes nimorum	102. You, dear wolf, companion of
qui devia mecum	the groves, who with me
Et saltus peragrare soles vix	Are accustomed to traversing
preteris arva	the woodland paths and
	meadows, scarcely do you
	cross the field,

Merlin will have a vision of "A child, a man-child"[60] that foreshadows Himilian's "Wonderful shall I be among women / So I bear a man-child..."[61]   Gwyndyth's explanation of Merlin's madness, that "It was some blinding vision from above / Estranged the world to him is echoed by Redderch's, that / The lightning comes and then is gone again / Ere a breath be taken, leaving darkness darker.   May it not be some sudden vision smote / Blinding into his mind and left him so..." Merlin himself laments his night with Himilian, and her pregnancy, "Ensnared by the wild flesh, / The ungovernable sting, / The pinnacle, the ecstasy, the fall, / Brief as the lightning, and irrevocable."   The stage directions for Scene III have Hadrian's wall in the background; in Scene VIII Kentigern uses the wall as his text.   "Rome built it. Though these many years / It has stood gapt and broken and dismanned, / Yet every stone of it remembers Rome..."[62]   Taliesin asks, "How was I guided to this solitary pool, / This splintered rock?"[63] and Merlin later exclaims "I am a stone broken off from the living rock, / A fragment that cannot rejoin its own nature..."[64]   (Gwyndyth's description of the battle, "Three champions came against us, the three sons of Mor, / And none resisted them, / But Merlin smote them, one by one, to death, / And in that instant clove the path to victory,"[65] is echoed in Merlin's description of the onset of his madness: "There

---

[60] Binyon, 1947, 79
[61] Binyon, 1947, 58
[62] Binyon, 1947, 28
[63] Binyon, 1947, 35
[64] Binyon, 1947, 51
[65] Binyon, 1947, 10

were three sons of Mor. / They were beautiful in battle. / One after the other / By this hand they fell."[66]   The dialogue, then, of *MM* has the kind of resonance that shows that it was written by a poet; remembering that *MM* is a drama, not a poem, however, I maintain that the overall effect is one of disjointedness, of plot, of settings, and of the internals of the dialogue: Binyon's avoidance of lines of regular length gives the impression that the characters are blurting their lines out, as opposed to the grand relentlessness of the *VM*'s dactyllic hexameter.   I have characterized other parameters of the *VM* as allusiveness, musicality and virtuosity, each of which elements contributing in its way to the *VM*'s unhurried continuity.   Binyon minimizes all three: it could be argued that this is a consequence of scale, that a work of fifty-eight pages cannot have the same degree of interlocking imagery as a work of 1,529 lines.   There is more,

---

[66] This echo is in turn an echo of a passage in the *VM.*

Venerat ad bellum Merlinus cum Pereduro	Merlin had come to the war on Peredur's side,
Rex quoque cambrorum rodarcus sevvus uterque.	Also the king of the Welsh, Rhydderch; both men were fierce.
Cedunt obstantes invisis ensibus hostes,	They killed the opposing foemen with their dread swords,
Tresque ducis fratres fratrem per bella secuti	As did three brothers of the leader who had followed their brother through the wars,
Usque rebellantes cedunt perimunt que phalanges.	35. Even slaying rebels and shattering their ranks.
Inde per infestas cum tali munere turmas	Off they went, through the hostile squadrons, so gung-ho,
Acriter irruerant. subito cecidere perempti.	Sharply they rushed in. Suddenly they fell, snatched away.
Hoc viso merline doles tristesque per agmen	When this was seen, O Merlin, you are afflicted and are sad, and throughout the column

It will be noted that in the story as Binyon found it, the three brothers appear to have been on Merlin's side.   By making them enemies Binyon changed Merlin's grief from a lament for fallen comrades to *Weltangst* over fallen foemen.

however: Binyon not only avoids parameters that would unify the dialogue; he writes dialogue that is disjointed in content, as we see in the very opening scene.   "Upon a bare ridge of moor against evening light stands a girl, Himilian; her eyes are fixt on the ground, and she does not stir, though a young man, carrying a faggot of furze, hails her as he mounts the slope."   The theatrical principle of suspense is created by the tension between the immobility of Himilian and the insistent calling of Greid: "What have your eyes found in the grass? / Why do you stir not, head or hand, / Himilian?   An adder is it? / Himilian!   Speak!"[67]

Himilian's answer, after repeated appeals from Greid, simply adds to the suspense: "(lifting a hand, but not her face).   Listen! Listen!"[68]   She says "listen," but she continues to gaze at something at her feet.   Does Binyon have Himilian answer at cross-purposes merely as a theatrical "shtik," to increase suspense?   Binyon, the dramatist, was certainly aware of the importance of stage "business," like the "shtik" in Scene XII, where Queen Langoreth tries to avoid meeting Merlin, because she senses that he knows of her adulterous affair with Peredur, and her evasiveness becomes progressively more panicky.   First, she tells the king to "Loose him, send him away / To the wild woods, his place."   When Redderch hesitates, she says, "I leave you now. / Enjoy this chosen company."   Merlin laughs.   The king repeatedly asks why he laughed.   Langoreth's anxiety is almost comical.   "Seek for no cause.   It is a madman's mirth... / It is but crazy babble that you'll hear... / It's idle importuning ravelled wits... / What do we here, waiting a madman's whim, / Come away!   I lose patience.   Come away!"[69]

Is Himilian's silence also a "shtik?"   First, let us recall Binyon's setting: "Upon a bare ridge of moor against evening light stands a girl, Himilian; her eyes are fixt on the ground, and she does not stir."

---

[67] Binyon, 1947, 1
[68] Binyon, 1947, 1
[69] Binyon, 1947, 47-49

Compare this setting with his description of an equally stark Chinese painting in *The Flight of the Dragon.*

> A priest meets with his disciple. The two figures, face to face with each other, are alone. Blank space of sky is over and about them. The great roots of a tree swerve upward out of the design, and a branch from the unseen stem hangs into it from above. Not only is the principle of symmetry done away with, but the unsymmetrical, the imperfect, the incomplete has become the principle of design...Space therefore, empty space, becomes a positive factor, no longer something not filled and left over, but something exerting an attractive power to the eye, and balancing the attractive power of forms and masses. But, to exert this power, space must be used broadly and with emphasis, as an end in itself.[70]

Landscape would be even more important as Binyon grew older. Consider another Binyon passage written almost thirty years later: "Here the figure of the woman...fills the eye, though the landscape is no mere background, but seems almost as if it were a projection from her mind..." This is not Binyon the dramatist, but Binyon the art critic, describing a very old (Sung Dynasty) painting of a Buddhist mystic in a winter scene, in *The Spirit of Man in Asian Art.*

> Here certainly we meet the spirit of Zen, which...coloured the Taoist conceptions implicit in so much Sung painting with a special tinge...It was like a note of music implying all the related harmonies of existence. A spray of blossom trembling in the wind seemed to be at once an apparition from a world of intenser life and a kind of secret thought unfolding in the heart of man.

---

[70] Binyon, 1909, 76

I recall one small painting of hibiscus in which only half of the blossom is visible, hovering over its reflection in the water; nothing is wholly shown, everything is suggested.[71]

Binyon wrote *The Spirit of Man in Asian Art* in 1936, when his poetry was still mainstream British. There is nothing mainstream about "Winter Sunrise" from *The Burning of the Leaves,* which was, according to his widow, his last poem,[72] unless it be mainstream Tang Dynasty, whose trademark was concrete images simply stated. For a touchstone, consider Li Bai's (701-762) famous rhyming quatrain (my translation): "Before my bed the bright moon shines. / I sense this. Frost on the ground. / I raise my head, look at the bright moon. / My head falls back, I think of home." "Winter Sunrise" is longer, but the spirit is the same: "Suddenly, softly, as if a breath breathed / On the pale wall, a magical apparition, / The shadow of the jasmine, branch and blossom! // It was not there, it is there, in a perfect image; / And all is changed. It is like a memory lost / Returning without a reason into the mind;... // And it seems to me that the beauty of the shadow / Is more beautiful than the flower; a strange beauty, / Pencilled and silently deepening to distinctness. // As a memory stealing out of the mind's slumber, / A memory floating up from a dark water, / Can be more beautiful than the thing remembered."[73]

It would seem that Binyon the poet had caught up with Binyon the theorist. It will be seen that characteristics in *MM* that appear at first to be loose ends, will instead be explicable as Binyon realizing the poetic and dramatic potential of the aesthetic ideas that he had described in Chinese and Japanese painting. Returning to the opening scene, it can at least be said that Binyon asks his audience to pay close attention to his backgrounds; as for the counterpoint between the landscape, the characters' actions and their dialogue, the germ of

---

[71] Binyon, 1936, 102-3
[72] Binyon, 1944, i
[73] Binyon, 1944, 16

Binyon's ideas can be traced back to his 1918 lecture "English Poetry in its Relation to Painting and the Other Arts":

> But the essential characteristic of poetry is its power of focussing the whole range of our sensibilities. Its primary appeal is the music of rhythmical language, but into this it fuses a world of sensation and a world of emotion and a world of thought. It plays upon all the subtle associations of the senses, the mind, the feelings. No art fuses so many elements of human experience. I think few would deny that in this human experience the world of sight—all that comes to us through the faculty of vision—plays, for art, at least, the richest part. For memory of things seen—and not only seen with the eye but dyed in a thousand associations—the poet draws for the images through which alone he can express his inmost feeling.
>
> If a poet is known by the music of his speech, he is also known by the imaginative texture of his thought. He thinks in images...
>
> It is on this side of imagery that poetry comes closely into relation with painting.[74]

Binyon would seem to have had these ideas in mind in the first scene in *MM*, once Himilian begins to speak. Greid appeals for her to come home, as evening is coming. Again she answers at cross-purposes. "It is coming out of the West upon the wind; / The Sound of Battle!... / The sound faints. Hark, it leaps up again now, / A sound of exulting, sound of anger. / The blue spears will be reddening there."[75] Binyon's polish here is remarkable. How does a poem convey a sound? By particularizing the image, in this case by having it come from the west, and having it carried "upon the wind." How does a

---

[74] Binyon, 1918, 383
[75] Binyon, 1947, 1

poet give a line declamatory "snap?" By juxtaposing words that are unlike ("faints" and "hark"), by using unusual turns of phrase ("The sound faints," instead of "The sound grows fainter"), by keeping the images physical (the sound "leaps up again" instead of "increases"), by unbalancing a parallelism ("A sound of exulting, sound of anger," instead of the classically weighted "A sound of exulting, a sound of anger"), and by demanding that the reader fill in nuances for himself ("blue" instead of, say, "steel-blue," or even "frosty blue," as he wrote in *The Sirens,* "red" instead of "scarlet"). This very vivid writing continues in Greid's next speech, after he sees the object of Himilian's reverie, a sword. "Was it this / Your eyes were fastened on? A sword! / Strange you look; bewitched you are. / Never a spot, never a smear / Of rust on it. How came it there? (HIMILIAN) He cast it at my feet. (GREID) What he? / (HIMILIAN) He that passed me on the moor. / He cast his own sword at my feet." Binyon presents still more rhetorical tricks: circumlocution ("fastened on" for "looking at"), introducing unexpected content without preparation (there is nothing in the drama, setting or dialogue, to prepare a theater audience for the sword), parallelism ("Strange you look; bewitched you are"), a surprise predicate ("you" would seem to be the subject of "never a spot, never a smear" until the next line's "rust on it" revealing that the sword is meant), avoiding conventional words ("What he?" for "who?"), and more strong imagery (an unknown man throwing a sword down).

When Greid finds that the man has fled into the woods, he gives him up for lost. "He will be lost and sinking now / With the black ooze up to his lips: / Or if he pass the mosses safe / There in the forest, when the dark thickens, / The ghosts will have him in their snares / And twist the long briars, coil by coil, / Round and round him, until he dies, / For they'd have all of us be ghosts."

This passage marks a technical advance on Binyon's part, a curing of a poetic deficiency noted in 1905 by Cornelius Weygandt, whose most famous student at the University of Pennsylvania, young

Ezra Pound, would soon attach himself to Binyon (the BinBin of the *Cantos*).

Each of these poems is in its way beautiful, but not one of them smacks of the soil, has the home-thrust of observation that brings back to keen senses the very tang of wood and tillage. Mr. Binyon, whatever his upbringing, is in his poetry no more than a city man. Although there is little detail, country-side and seashore are present to these descriptive poems in form and color, but taste and smell and sound are seldom used to bring very out-of-doors before us. A flower to Mr. Binyon is apt to be a thing of beauty, or a symbol of beauty, and nothing more; not, too, a primrose or a foxglove whose mention would make the definite appeal of a thing known and loved. So seldom does he name a bird that it is a real surprise to find that he does know a thrush and can speak definitely of his "dewy notes." I state his neglect of the little things of Nature not as a defect, but as a limitation.[76]

Weygandt's observations were true in 1905, but not in the last years of Binyon's life; first, he had expanded his palette of nature-images: instead of "bird," he now has "kestrel" and "lapwing." Second, and more importantly, however, Binyon had gone beyond the mere invocation of nature, what Weygandt calls the ability to "bring very out-of-doors before us," the ability to evoke rusticity: Binyon has made them building-blocks of his drama, as we see from his transmutation of the following *VM* line.

Hec inter frutices coriletaque	113.	This he chanted among the
densa canebat		undergrowth and the hazel
		thickets,

---

[76] Weygandt 281

In Scene IV Merlin muses that "Hazel boughs are all about me / But beyond them / I see a hill all smooth with grass / And on the top a single apple-tree." In Scene VII, Merlin is beginning to readjust to court life; the apple tree is the sign of a relapse. / (GUENDOLEN) "The mist clouds over and conquers him again.   (MERLIN)   Where is my apple-tree?   /   (GUENDOLEN)   What could that mean? There is no apple-tree. / (MERLIN)   Where is my apple-tree? / I see it, and I see it not. It's gone. / A cloud of night has taken it.   Gone, gone!"

There is a passage in the *Vita Merlini* that may have suggested the above; at least it is similar.   Mad Merlin soliloquizes.

Tres quater et iuges septene	90.	Thrice four and, you may
poma ferentes		add, seven apple-bearing
Hic steterant mali nunc non		Apple trees stood here, now
stant ergo quis illas		they do not stand. Therefore, who has snatched them
Quis michi surripuit, quo		Away from me, who?
devenere repente?		Where have they suddenly gone off to?
Nunc illas video nec non. sic		Now I see them, now I don't.
fata repugnant		Thus the fates hinder
Sic quoque concordant cum		And at the same time help,
dant prohibentque videre		since they grant and forbid [me] to see.

There is nothing abstract or symbolic about the way the *VM* poet speaks of the apple trees: Merlin is hungry, and has no apples to eat. This is not to say that the *VM* poet is primitive; on the contrary, his use of the apple tree image is simply the mirror-image of Binyon's.   The *VM* poet implies a movement from delusion to reality by the concreteness of the trees; Binyon does the opposite, moving Merlin from the here-and-now of the presence of his wife and sister to the fantasy of the non-existent apple trees.   The difference between the

VM poet's technique and Binyon's is that Binyon brings the image back, creating an echo that reminds the reader of what has gone before and that brings the reader's recollections to bear on the poetic situation. A similar instance is found in the last lines of Scene VIII.   Merlin, his return to sanity still tenuous, is pushed over the edge by the agitation of a mob.   "(MERLIN)   Who are all these that crowd round me? / Who are all these that trample on my mind / Like oxen at the ford? / Give me air!   I cannot breathe.   I must be gone. (Merlin rushes out)" The reader will recall the already-cited opening lines of Scene XII, "The oxen come to trample on my mind."

There is another scene where Binyon and the *VM* poet treat the same material: the episode where Merlin divines that Queen Langoreth has a lover.   Binyon's treatment has been cited for its comic element, the Queen's increasingly nervous attempts to evade detection, but there is more.   Binyon heightens the comic tension by King Redderch's obtuseness: not only does Langoreth have a lover, but she has just come from a passionate tryst with him.   Redderch is such a dunderhead that he does not recognize her "afterglow," saying "Stay, stay! / Surely your heart is full of happy news. / I never saw your beauty beautiful as now. / You came as if with victory on your lips, / With bosom heaving and with eyes shining, / As if your words would break / A box of incense open on the air. / Tell me this news, my queen, / Let me rejoice in it, rejoice with you."   The stage direction has: "(Merlin laughs)"

Merlin laughs, indeed; but in a live performance the audience would probably already be laughing.   This is low comedy, music-hall stuff, and the picaresque, *buffo* tone is maintained relentlessly, right up to the end of the scene, when Merlin, in exchange for his freedom, finally gives in.   The key image of the scene comes from—what else?—an apple tree.

> REDDERCH.   Now tell me.
> MERLIN.   Ask not me,
> Ask of her.

LANGORETH.   Me?
MERLIN.   Ask of her.
REDDERCH   (astonished).   Langoreth?
MERLIN.   Of her who stands before you, her who came
With bosom heaving and with eyes shining,
Who brought you happiness.
REDDERCH.   What can this mean?
MERLIN.   Ask of the apple leaf that's clinging still
Upon the loosened braiding of her hair—
See, she has plucked it out, the guilty thing.
REDDERCH.   Guilty?
MERLIN.   Ask whom she lay with under the apple-tree
In the orchard close.   That was the happy news
That made her glow with beauty in your eyes.
Poor King!
(He goes out swiftly)
REDDERCH.   I cannot believe it.   It is not true.

As recently as 1930 one E. G. Twitchett, in a lengthy and generally favorable article in the *London Mercury,* asking if Binyon was a great poet, had offered a verdict of interest here: "Mr. Binyon lacks very manifestly some qualities which we have come to regard as indispensable in poets of the first and second orders.   Like most mystics, he gives little evidence in his work of the possession of humour, or even of wit."[77]   Binyon's treatment of the apple-leaf episode is evidence for progress in this area.

The *VM* poet's version of the episode has some interesting differences.   First, the king removes the leaf from his wife's hair, and this provokes Merlin's laughter.

Iccirco risi quoniam Rodarche   "Because of that I laughed, O
fuisti   Rhydderch, because you were

---

[77] Twitchett 432

Facto culpandus simul et laudandus eodem	By that same act to be blamed and at the same time to be praised,
Dum traheres folium modo quod regina capillis	While you just now took away the leaf which the queen in her hair
Nescia gestabat fieres que fidelior illi	Unknowingly carried, you were more faithful to her
Quam fuit illa tibi quando 290. *virgulta subivit*	Than she was to you; when she went under the bushes
Quo suus occurrit secum que coivit adulter	Where her lover ran and went with her
Dumque supina foret sparsis in crinibus hesit	And while she was on her back, there stuck in her unbound hair
Forte iacens folium quod nescius eripuisti	The leaf by chance lying there, which you unknowingly took away."
Ergo super tali rodarchus crimine tristis	Therefore Rhydderch became sad concerning this misdeed
Fit subito vultum que suum 295. *divertit ab illa*	Immediately, and turned his face from her
Dampnabatque diem que se coniunxerat illi	And cursed the day which he had married her

A further difference in plot is that, whereas Binyon quickly rings the curtain down on Redderch with his mouth hanging open, in *VM* the queen goes to great lengths to destroy Merlin's credibility, which leads to several lengthy episodes.

The main difference in the two versions is one of tone, particularly as regards meter. The *VM* poet gave his readers a tale told in effortlessly-flowing dactyllic hexameter, and judging by the frequency of preference for this meter by medieval Latin authors, the medieval Latin readership must have liked the virtuosity involved in making a difficult meter look easy.   On the other hand, more than one critic of *MM* has praised Binyon's rhythmic vitality and versatility. In the   1947 review in the *Review of Books* we read:

> To judge by what we have, Binyon would have written a fine distinctive poem on this noble theme.   His verse is fresh, with a free rhythm and adjustable syllabic metre.   It expresses the new-old truths of human experience with precision and dignity, and yet with lightness and charm.[78]

It will be observed that most of the poetry is not about lightness and charm; more common throughout is

> ...a bardic speech at once primitive and sophisticated, drawing on a monosyllabic Anglo-Saxon vocabulary shorn of almost all 'poetic' and abstract words within a framework of free rhythms playing over a loose accentual base.   [Binyon] told Wilfrid   Gibson   that   he   found   traditional   metres inappropriately glib in face of the horrors of the war: 'in writing myself these days I feel a craving for language that is, so to speak, bruised & hurt or hard & rasping & rhythms to correspond.'[79]

The above statement needs refining.   First, just because Binyon's vocabulary is forceful and concrete does not mean that it is "monosyllabic Anglo-Saxon," as can be seen in the opening lines of Scene II, where Merlin makes his first entrance, staggering into the forest.   "On, on, into the dark! / Why dost thou drive me on / Into this darkening nakedness of old gaunt trees / Clutching with bony root stones in eternal sleep? / Why dost thou hunt me so, / Voice, that I

---

[78]   Jones 75
[79]   Hatcher 287

heard crying / Amid the spears and the shouting ,/ And suddenly all my strength was annulled..."

There is nothing Anglo-Saxon or monosyllabic about "annulled," regardless of the etymology of the rest of the passage. Going back to Binyon's remarks about dialogue, there is much in *MM* that is in fact hard and rasping, but there is also language that is very much in the traditional vein when describing spiritual agonies, as in Scene XIII, when Merlin has made his last withdrawal from society; "O thou maker of all things and of me, / Why art thou silent, why shuttest thyself away? / Why hast thou set me apart from all my world? / ...Am I thine Error? Am I thine Enemy?"

Binyon's dialogue is also in a traditional vein when Merlin, through his description of a peaceful, inspiring landscape, begins to emerge from his madness, only to slip back into it. "I see mountains burning afar into the dawn. / The eagles are there soaring, and streams descending: / A million flowers tremble upon their banks. / A doe suckles her fawn beneath the tree; / She has no fear. / The wind is tender, the wind is shining / In the green grass. Smell it, how sweet it is. (HIMILIAN) I see it all. Oh, hold that vision still. / (MERLIN) All is gone, all; suddenly vanishing / As if it had not been. / Down rushes the darkness / Like a black waterfall."

In addition to expressing the anguish of a mind teetering on the brink of sanity, Binyon is also giving poetic answers to theoretical questions that Binyon the art critic had posed in 1931, in *Landscape in English Art & Poetry.*

> What account does the spirit of man make of this wonderful world in which he is placed; these bountiful riches, this intricate profusion of beauties, these vast energies, these overwhelming grandeurs and terrors? What account does he make of all that wild life, not his own, which animates this earth and air? What do they mean to Man? Are they altogether outside him? Are they something to be conquered for his use, his service and his pleasure? Or are they rather to

be understood, as things having a kindred life with our own, as sharers of the universal life?[80]

Landscape merging into mindscape is the theme throughout Merlin's long monologue in his cave, which takes up the whole of Scene XIII, and his dialogue with Himilian, which continues to the end of Scene XIV, the end of the play. Binyon's imagery runs riot: "This cave is hollow like a monstrous skull; / But it houses no torment of the brain, / No obstinately knotted speculation / That blind fingers of thought / Weary to unravel." On the other hand, he invokes the vivifying power of the sun. "Penetrate earth, O sun, / Flatter the darting fly with a moment's pleasure, / Make heat within the blood of men, / Burst open the womb as the blossom, / Even in the womb / Is the unborn knocking at the door." Back and forth the images go, light versus stone. Water is added next. "I see the spring that tremblingly issues / Gliding out of the secrecy of the mountain." Himilian goes to the mouth of the cave, and sees a thunderhead. Merlin muses on water, at least "the waters of ignorance," which he believes will return him to sanity. "Can it not be tasted, can it not be beheld? / If I listen long enough, can it not be heard? / And, if I fold my hands, will it not come to me?"

I wish that I could say that the images are random, that they represent city man Binyon's letting-go before Nature, and I especially wish that it were possible to wind this analysis up without bringing in a completely new parameter at the eleventh hour, but as I read these last two scenes, I sense a shadow falling across the page. Binyon was an Oxonian who became an orientalist; he would likely, therefore, have been aware of an orientalist who became an Oxonian, James Legge (1815-1897), the pioneering Victorian Sinologist and translator of the Chinese classics, who cast a long shadow in Binyon's day (and, in Confucian studies, still does). There was something about Binyon's images that had a familiar ring; I opened Legge's great translation of

---

[80] Binyon, 1931, 3-4

the *I Ching* to his account of the trigrams that stand behind its hexagrams, and read, "heaven or the sky, water, ...the sun, ...lightning, ...thunder, ...wind."[81] Is it possible that Binyon had this grocery list of the raw materials of Chinese painting and poetry at his elbow while writing *MM*? Was he being arbitrary, or was this synthesis simply second nature to him after years of study of Chinese aesthetics? I will cite Legge's account, interspersing it with lines from *MM*. "The eight figures [represent] heaven or the sky ("There is a huge cloud towering up in heaven [XIV]"); water, especially a collection of water as in a marsh or lake ("over heath and marsh...How was I guided to this solitary pool [IX]"); fire, the sun, lightning ("O sun, kindle as thou wilt / Beneath this seeming slumber of earth / Desire [XIII]; the cloud stops the sun, that fringes it with flames [XIV]"); thunder ("It is the imprisoned thunder loosed at last.[XIV]"); wind and wood ("The wind rises, roaring [XIV]"); water, especially as in rain, the clouds, springs, streams in defiles, and the moon ("Drink this spring-water [XIV]"; earlier, Guendolen asks of Merlin's madness, "Did the bare moon entrance him in the twisted wood / Staring upon his sleep?" [VII] and Merlin, in the same scene, when asked where his sword is, replies "On the other side of the moon".); a hill or mountain ("We are alone within the mountain's heart [XIV]"); and the earth ("Penetrate earth, O sun [XIII]"). This must be more than mere coincidence, but I do not believe that Binyon was being doctrinaire here, either: in the absence of any indication to the contrary, I believe that these images were simply second nature to Binyon because of his familiarity with Oriental art.

This hypersensory imagery in *MM* dies down in the last scene, which is on the contrary remarkable for its spareness of imagery. Merlin is in the cave, being cared for by Himilian, and their dialogue is no longer rhapsodic, but that of an ailing man speaking with a caring woman. She says, "Many days, many nights. / I have watched

---

[81] Legge 11

over the trances / I have watched and waited. / None has been here but I. / (MERLIN)   Night and day, day and night, / It is all one."

Merlin has one final hallucination, then the night comes on.   At dawn Himilian addresses Merlin, "I was your joy.   Had you not joy of me?"   Merlin is world-weary and wants to withdraw from life.   "O that this night had never come to pass! / That it might turn back thither whence it came / Into the ancient dark and nothingness!"   Himilian looks forward to the birth of her child.   "My body is become a precious thing, / Fired in thy fire, and moulded in they mould. / In whom shall live the power and the wisdom / Of Merlin, prophet and prince... / Behold, the light breaks forth, / The sun rises. / The sun is risen."

The dialogue in this last scene is remarkable for its absence of landscape imagery, which may seem inconsistent with Binyon's poetry throughout *MM.*   Yet this is simply the final facet of the phenomenon of disjointedness alluded to earlier: emptiness, space, as an expressive element in art is a subject to which Binyon had given much thought.   With regard to the Chinese painting of the master and disciple alluded to earlier, he added that

> The picture is not filled; it is waiting for our imagination to enter into it, to feel the air coming out of the great heights of the sky over the bare hillside, to hear the swaying of the branches of the giant pine, to listen to the words, to watch the faces and the gestures of the disciple and his master. [82]

Binyon the theoretician amplifies the idea.

> Hollowness, emptiness—these are words, these are ideas, from which our instincts recoil; they are repugnant.   But Lao-tzŭ makes friends with the idea of Space, he makes it companionable; he dwells on the uses of emptiness.   "Clay is

---

[82] Binyon, 1909, 76-7

moulded into a vessel; the utility of the vessel depends on its hollow interior. Doors and windows are cut out in order to make a house; the utility of the house depends on the empty spaces. Thus, while the existence of things may be good, it is the non-existent in them which makes them serviceable." At once we find ourselves seeing things from a fresh angle.

Speaking of a painting called "Listening to Music," he observes that

It is hard to think of any Western painting in which the empty spaces are made as significant as they are here: one would almost say even more significant than the figures. The intervals seem brimmed with a listening silence. You feel that the artist dwelt on them, so as to draw out their eloquence. It is so to speak, space spiritualized.[83]

In Scene IX of *MM,* the Welsh bard Taliesin says, "The singer knows but half of what he sings." Although Laurence Binyon died while in midst of his Merlin project, and therefore left no after-the-fact theoretical writings, there have been several examples cited in this study that indicate that his final poems show an integration of his observations on the visual arts into his poetry, what I have called Binyon the poet catching up to Binyon the theorist. The singer knows but half of what he sings. An especially revealing passage from Binyon the Oriental art critic may shed light on the other half of *MM.*

In showing these few examples of Sung landscape, you may think I have talked too much about the world of ideas in which they were born; you may think that perhaps I have read my own fancies into them. Ignore, then, all that; regard them as they are, and for what they give you. Is it not manifest that it is no merely visual impression, no merely physical sensation

---

[83] Binyon, 1936, 76-77

that they communicate?   It is something more.   It may be
that the conscious part of the artist was absorbed in his design,
in achieving   a right relation of tone to tone, in tracing lines
that should be alive.   But whether consciously or no, he was
doing more than this, because what he put into his work comes
out from it and flows over into our minds; and we recognize
something which cannot be called intellectual only, or
sensuous only, or emotional only; it is a wholeness of spirit
which goes out, free and unafraid, into the wholeness of the
universe.   The finest landscapes...are those one can wander in,
those one can live in.

The mental landscape of *MM* is a nightmarish one, so although
the reader may find it worthwhile to wander in it, he would not want to
live in it.   Still, the commentary is valid as to the consistency and
completeness of Binyon's vision in this last drama, with which he
enriched the Merlin tradition.

As for Binyon's enriching the tradition of English poetry, an
appropriately open-ended remark is found in the 1930 *London Mercury*
article already quoted.   It is both an evaluation of the poetry of
Laurence Binyon as of that year, and a prediction of what he would
achieve with his final lyrics and *MM*.

I have seen it stated in an omniscient journal by an authority
only slightly less omniscient that "Mr. Binyon is not a great
poet."   For my part I think that I agree in the main with
all-knowledge here; provided only that the exception might be
made that great poems may be produced at any moment by
poets who are not great poets.[84]

---

[84] Twitchett 432

A Translation of the *Vita Merlini*

The *Vita Merlini* is a pastiche. Sources as disparate as Celtic legend and the scientific writings of Isidore of Seville are expertly versified, then melded into an account of Merlin's insanity, his time as a wild man and his subsequent life as a seer and recluse.

There are few clues to the date and authorship of the poem: the poet seems to make reference to events in King Stephen's reign; he had some acquaintance with the writings of Geoffrey of Monmouth; and he knew his Ovid well, even the minor works. Beyond that, everything is conjecture. The reader should not be discouraged by the uncertainties that surround the Vita Merlini, however; it is a fine poem, imaginative and polished.

I have divided the work into sections, according to the sense of the plot and the dialogue, but will otherwise let the poet speak for himself.

Merlin's Life
a medieval poem of unknown authorship
translated into modern English

A prophet-bard gone wild, the mischief done
    By Merlin, that's my story. Keep it true,
    Friend Bishop Robert. Guide what I've begun,
Critique it shrewdly as you read it through.
    Your intellectual gifts, your ministry,   *5.*
    Your leadership, make us look up to you.
Your backing of this poem – and of me –

Surpasses any prior patron's aid,
As you surpass their merits personally.
Your godly life, the talent you've displayed,   *10.*
Even your toughness, one and all admire
And all applaud the improvements that you've made.
This book should match the greatness you inspire,
But it falls short, I know.   A better pen
Than mine is what your achievements require.   *15.*
Not just the eloquence of learnéd men;
Spontaneous, unstudied, heartfelt praise
Is due you for the leader you have been.

1.

As counselor to kings in bygone days,
The fame of Merlin had spread world-wide from   20.
South Wales, where he was king.   His wild folk's ways
He regulated, and predicted things to come.

2.

But then two other chieftains had a fight
Among themselves, and war was the outcome.
Grim was the innocent civilians' plight.   25.
Duke of the North Welsh, Peredur, attacked
Gwentholy, who commanded Scotland's might.
One day the armies met: their chieftains, backed
By warrior clansmen, grappled hand to hand.
Blood flowed, men fell as swordsmen stabbed and hacked.   30.
With Peredur Merlin had made his stand,
As had Rodarch, the King of Wales.   Both brave,
With slashing swords plunged into no-man's land,
As did three brothers of the Duke, who gave
No quarter to the foe, but rushed ahead,   35.
Broke through their ranks, like madmen did behave,
Frantic with blood-lust — then, suddenly dead.
When Merlin saw this, something snapped inside,
He stopped fighting, started to howl instead.

He shrieked, "So just like that, these boys have died?   40.
   My comrades – just like that – are snatched away,
   Three who were feared both near and far?" he cried.
"O human life, that can end any day!
   O death, whose hidden, sudden power can snatch
   The fragile spirit from its home of clay!   45.
Who now will aid me, should enemies catch
   Me unawares, with these three heroes gone?
   Where can I find comrades in arms to match
Bold youths like these, when battle lines are drawn?
   Your recklessness has cost you boys the bloom   50.
   Of youth, as recklessly you set upon
Our enemies, and sent them to the tomb;
   Now you are down, your blood makes the ground red."
   Merlin, amid the fight, bewailed their doom.
The battle raged, for all the tears he shed.   55.
   The crush of fighting men, their deadly blows
   Brought death to both sides; on both sides men bled.
The Welsh rally; the tide of battle goes
   Their way, and they surge forth to sweep the field.
   They clash once more; the Scots' momentum slows;   60.
The Scotsmen waver, halt, and then they yield,
   Run for the woods, through thickets zigzag flee.

3.

   After the battle sad Merlin appealed
To his comrades to entomb the brothers three,
   Then tore his clothes and threw dust in his hair,   65.
   Rolled in the dirt, sobbed uncontrollably.
Duke Peredur tried to soothe his despair,
   But he'd have none of that, nor would be cheered.
   Three days he wept for those who had died there.
He grieved.   His appetite had disappeared,   70.
   Which made him more manic-depressive still.
   He'd howl.   Then furtively, when his mind cleared,

He stole away one night, and ran until
   He reached the forest glades, and there laid low.
   He watched the grazing creatures eat their fill,   75.
Then ran with them, ran faster than they'd go;
   Ate like them: wild roots and greens were his fare,
   Tree-fruits, berries that on the brambles grow.
He soon adapted to his forest lair,
   All summer long he lived in solitude: 80.
   Neither his kin nor comrades found him there.
None interfered with the life he pursued.

4.

   Then winter came, and killed all of the green
   Plants that Merlin depended on for food.
He prayed, lamenting, thus: "O Nazarene,   85.
   Jesus in Heaven, tell me, where and how
   Shall I live, when there's no food to be seen?
There's no grass left, no acorns on the bough.
   Thrice four and seven apple trees once stood;
   Who made them disappear?   They're not there now.   90.
I don't see them anywhere in the wood;
   Not long ago I did.   I'm teased by Fate,
   That dangles, then snatches away the good.
The apple trees' branches are bare of late;
   Without their fruit I'll starve, I'll surely freeze   95.
   Without their leaves, that cutting winds abate.
Cold rain comes pouring down and strips the trees.
   I dig for turnips growing underground,
   But ravenous wild boars rush up and seize
The few scrawny wild turnips that I've found.   100.
   Wolf, you who once raced with me wild and free,
   Half-starved you now barely stagger around,
And hunger makes us ache mercilessly.
   You lived here first, and old age first touched you:
   Gray hairs, then white, your inability   105.

To bring down game.   Surprising.   Quite a few
    Wild goats and other prey still roam the glade.
    It may be that the aging that you rue
Has made your muscles slack, and your strength fade.
    There's nothing left to do but howl, and try   110.
    To rest your bones no matter where you're laid."

5.

Deep in the thicket Merlin raised this cry,
    But with his anguish it rang loud and clear,
    And it was picked up by a passer-by
Who found the crier, guided by his ear.   115.
    Merlin ran off; the wayfarer gave chase,
    But then gave up, unable to get near.
Back on the road he then resumed his pace,
    Though brooding over the strange sight he'd seen.
    He met another not far from that place,   120.
Sent from the court of Rodarch, whose new queen,
    Ganeida, was his pride and joy; but she
    Was also Merlin's sister, and was keen
To know her brother's fate.   Relentlessly
    She sent her courtiers over hill and dale;   125.
    One of these weary scouts turned out to be
The man the traveler met along the trail.
    After the pleasantries, the question came:
    "Have you seen Merlin lurking in the vale?"
The prompt reply: "Though I don't know his name,   130.
    I saw a wild man skulk not far from here.
    I tried to talk, and at first he looked tame,
But then he took off, racing like a deer."
    The queen's man bade farewell, then trudged into
    The rugged landscape of the forest drear,   135.
And night and day he followed every clue.
    There was a fountain on a mountain slope.
    Hazels and bushes shielded it from view.

Here Merlin sat, and his musings had scope:
    He watched animals frolic in the glen.   140.
    The courtier tiptoed toward the misanthrope,
Got close; he spied the splashing fountain, then
    Saw Merlin lolling midst herbs, moss and fern,
    Soliloquizing in his hillside den.

6.

"O You who rule all, I would like to learn   145.
    Why each season differs from the other three.
    By leaves and blossoms I can spring discern;
By its fruits, summer; fall, the apple tree;
    Then icy winter sweeps all this away,
    With driving rains, then blizzards endlessly   150.
Denude the trees; the skies are sunless, gray,
    So nothing ever gets a chance to sprout,
    No apples, acorns, flowers until May.
If only all this snow that lies about
    Were turned to spring, and that the songbirds had   155.
    Returned, to let their melodies pour out!
Their sprightly courtships, their nests ivy-clad
    With chirping chicks inside, so joyfully
    Alive, would cheer me up when I was sad.
The fragrance of spring soil, the potpourri   160.
    Of blooms and turf; spring noises that abound:
    Brook water, dove-call from some leafy tree
Would soothe me to sleep, stretched upon the ground."

7.

The courtier overheard, and then broke in.
    He carried a lute with him, and its sound   165.
He hoped would calm the madman; to begin
    With, he strummed low, rhythmic chords with his thumb,
    And from behind he sang of Gwendolyn.
"Oh, Gwendolyn!   The heartfelt moans that come
    From Gwendolyn!   The tears upon the cheek   170.

Of Gwendolyn!   Her grief has left her numb.
In all of Wales her beauty was unique.
    Her skin was fairer than the lily's white,
    Or any flower of which you'd care to speak.
She had the aura of spring's glory bright,   175.
    And starlike radiance sparkled in her eyes.
    Her hair was famous for its golden light,
But now her legendary beauty dies.
    Her color and complexion bloom no more,
    Driven away by her grief and her sighs.   180.
She knows not if her husband's living, or
    If he's passed on.   There's no news that relieves
    The uncertainty of what she's waiting for.
Nor does Ganeida get any reprieves.
    She mourns her brother lost, and her heart aches.   185.
    One for her man, one for her brother grieves.
They weep the livelong day, and their woe makes
    Them wander aimlessly.   Hungry and cold,
    At times they sleep out in the weedy brakes.
The way that Dido, heroine of old   190.
    Suffered from her man's setting out to sea;
    Or, when her lover's promise didn't hold,
The way poor Phyllis mourned his perfidy;
    Briseis bewailed her absent soldier; so
    Do Merlin's sister's and wife's misery   195.
Consume them, and their tears constantly flow."
    He sang of these depressing turns of fate,
    The herald did, yet softly sang and slow.
So Merlin was entranced, and reached the state   200.
    Where his emotions freed up once again.
    He's chatting now.   His cares evaporate,
And he requests more songs from 'way back when.
    The youth responds with tunes more soothing still,   205.
    Designed to chase the madness out of men,

With lute-song lulling the unruly will.
    Delusions fade; his memory's back.   Aghast,
    He sees, he hates his time mentally ill.
His mind's as lucid now as in the past.   210.
    His feelings for his sister make him groan,
    And for his wife, when his mind cleared at last.
He asks to be led to King Rodarch's throne.
    The courtier agrees.   They leave the wood,
    And in the king's city make themselves known.   215.

8.

The queen was overjoyed.   Her brother stood
    Before her!   Merlin's wife was thrilled as well.
    Each kissed the man as often as she could,
And hugged him.   Love regained made their hearts swell.
    The king received him with trumpets and drums,   220.
    And the town rang with nobles' boisterous yell.
The noise, the celebrating crowd benumbs
    Poor Merlin, overwhelms him, and once more
    His mania returns, delusion comes.
He hankers for the life he had before.   225.
    Then Rodarch posted guards; musicians played
    Soft, lyric songs, his right mind to restore.
The king himself stood there, tried to persuade
    Him to listen to reason, and not go
    Back to his animal life in the glade,   230.
But be a king again, make the Welsh know
    Their feuding must end, pacify the realm.
    Then Rodarch talked of gifts he would bestow,
And, to persuade Merlin to take the helm,
    Had rich robes, hunting hounds and songbirds brought,   235.
    Race horses, gold and gems to overwhelm
Him, cups that master-craftsman Wieland wrought.
    Merlin declined the gifts, and spoke his mind:

9.

"Gifts like these are for men whose only thought
Is heaping up wealth, those who never find   240.
    Contentment, though they have treasures galore.
    I miss the forest life I left behind.
That is the gift I want, not these.   No more
    Enticements, Rodarch!   They are less to me
    Than Caledonian nuts I had before."   245.

10.

Seeing his gifts were useless, finally
    The king had Merlin chained up, to prevent
    His return to the woods, should he get free.
Feeling the heavy links that kept him pent
    Up, kept him far from Caledonian wood,   250.
    The bard grew sad, and all happiness went
From his face, and for days on end he would
    Stand silent, not a word or laugh the while.

11.

    The queen swept by, in the king's presence stood,
And Rodarch greeted her in courtly style.   255.
    He took her hand, guided her to a chair,
    Embraced her decorously, with kingly smile
Leaned to give her cheek a peck; in her hair
    He saw a hanging leaf.   He carefully
    Removed it, and flicked it away from there,   260.
Then chatted as befits nobility.
    Merlin saw this, and let out a guffaw.
    Onlookers asked each other what could be
The reason for this laugh.   Hoping to draw
    The madman out, the amazed King Rodarch pressed   265.
    Merlin to explain the joke in what he saw,
Adding rich gifts to sweeten his request.
    The bard said not a word, nor would explain
    His laugh, which led, at King Rodarch's behest

To more gifts heaped up, then more pleas... in vain.   270.
 He broke his silence then, and told the king:
12.
 "The greedy man only wants to attain
Treasures like these, and he'll do anything
 He's ordered to perform, a prostitute.
 My thirst is for the Caledonian spring,   275.
My hunger for its acorns, not for loot.
 Let avaricious men pick through this heap.
 Unless you set me free to pick the fruit
Of those green vales, my secret I will keep."
 Since Rodarch cannot find a way to get   280.
 Merlin to explain to him the mystery deep,
The king relents, and forthwith has him set
 Free of his chains. He's curious to know
 What made him laugh, and so his terms are met.
13.
Merlin spoke freely, being free to go: 285.
 "I laughed when you became both laughingstock
 And man to be admired, a while ago.
You took away a leaf caught in a lock
 Of your wife's lovely hair. You showed no lack
 Of husbandly concern, yet she did mock   290.
You earlier, running off the garden track
 Into the bushes with a lover, where
 She entertained the young man on her back.
By chance a leaf caught in her unbound hair,
 The leaf you saw." This broke poor Rodarch's heart.   295.
 The queen, though, putting on a careless air,
Conceals her sin, and with a brazen art
 Speaks to the king with confidence and cheer.
 "Why are you sad, beloved? And why start
To blame me, although my conscience is clear?   300.
 You listen to a raving lunatic,

And you lose face when you give him your ear.
Before you judge, I'll try a little trick
    To prove this accusation is a lie."

14.

She called the pages in, so she could pick   305..
A boy just right for the ruse she would try,
    To fool her brother before one and all.
She brought the boy, asked him to prophesy
About the boy's death, hoping he'd miscall.
    Her brother said, "O sister dear, this lad   310.
    Will die when he is grown up, from a fall."
She smiled, and sent the boy away, then had
    Him take his clothes off, put on something new,
    Rebrushed his hair and cut it back a tad,
Disguising him for the next interview.   315.
    The boy came back, with different clothes and hair,
    And stood obediently before the two.
The queen addressed her brother then and there,
    "Tell your dear sister what this boy'll die from."
    He said, "Disoriented, unaware,   320.
He'll die in a tree when his time has come."
    She told her husband of these prophecies.
    "You actually believed that I'd succumb
To temptation, based on inanities
    A madman spoke? Next time, before you heed
    Him, think how he dreamed up two destinies
For one boy, how he slandered me, to speed
    His return to the forest. Do not fear
    That I'd defile myself with some vile deed.
I fooled him twice, but now, to make it clear   330.
    That Merlin is a fraud, a third you'll see."
    She called the boy, and whispered in his ear
Her plan, that he was surreptitiously
    To put on women's clothing. He obeyed,

And came back dressed up as a girl would be.   335.
Then the queen sprang the third trap that she'd laid.
   "Hey, brother, tell me how this girl will die."
   "A river death awaits this so-called maid,"
Said Merlin, delighting his sister sly,
   Because to Rodarch he'd predicted three   340.
   Futures for one boy with this strange reply.
Therefore the king doubted what previously
   He'd heard about his wife, and he felt shame
   For heeding talk of her adultery.
The queen, relieved to have escaped from blame   345.
   Was quick to kiss and reassure her mate.

15.

Merlin, meanwhile, was making plans to claim
His freedom, and made for the city gate.
   His sister blocked his path, in tears besought
   Him, till his sanity returned, to wait.   350.
He stubbornly   refused, and gave no thought
   To anything but freedom, struggled to
   Unbar the city gate, and howled and fought
His keepers.   They gave up and let him through.
   The queen, in desperation, quickly sent   355.
   For Gwendolyn, to see what she could do.
She came imploring, but could not prevent
   His leaving.   He rejected her request
   And sullenly ignored her argument.
In grief she tore her hair and beat her breast   360.
   And scratched her cheeks, fell rolling in the dust.
   The queen saw, and her brother thus addressed:
"You're killing this girl!   How's she to adjust?
   May she remarry?   Live a widow?   Will
   You drag her to the forest, if you must   365.
Go back?   Believe me, she'll be loyal still,
   Live in the wild, as long as you're her man."

The bard responded to her nagging shrill:
16.
"To have her tag along was not my plan,
Boo-hooing, gushing tears like summer rain.   370.
Nor will I change, like Orpheus, who began
To have dreams of boys dancing through his brain,
The Styx having borne off Euridice.
Should Venus tempt either way, I'll refrain.
And as for Gwendolyn, the girl is free   375.
To find another man, again be wed.
But let her groom keep far away from me,
For if he gets in my way, why, he's dead.
Just stand too close to me, and he will meet
No friendliness, but my cold steel instead.   380.
Yet when the wedding day arrives, I'll greet
Her cordially, and keep my wrath inside.
I'll lay gifts worthy of her at her feet,
Richly enriching Gwendolyn the bride."
17.
With that, he gave them each one last goodbye,   385.
And, free at last, made for the countryside.
His wife stood in the doorway, wiped her eye,
As did the queen his sister as they gazed
After the man.   Yet, once the tears were dry,
They told each other how they were amazed   390.
At how he sensed the queen's unfaithfulness.
In fortune-telling, though, grave doubts were raised.
Three deaths for one lad?   That seemed meaningless
For years, but one day, when the boy was grown
He died three times, skeptics had to confess.   395.
A-horse, he'd left the hunt, scouting alone.
He saw, deep in the underbrush, a deer.
He loosed his dogs.   They scrambled through unknown
Terrain with frantic howls.   Trusting his ear,

Blindly he spurred after the yelping pack,   400.
Shouted to let the hunt know where he'd veer,
His horn-calls let them know he's on the track.
    There was a steep hill, rocky on each side,
    A river near it.   The stag doubled back,
Unwilling to attempt the river wide,   405.
    Instead it made for the crags up the hill.
    The young man saw the ruse, straight on did ride,
Dashed forward up the slope to make his kill,
    But drove his horse too hard: it stumbled, threw
    Him.   Off the cliff he fell headlong, until   410.
He hit the river, but landed askew,
    His foot caught in the forked trunk of a tree,
    Over the river where he'd fallen to.
He fell, drowned, and was hanged.   The prophecy
    Of Merlin had come true: he died three ways.   415.
                        18.
    Merlin, back in the woods, was living free.
Now on hard-frozen water plants he's graze,
    Snowed-on, rained-on, and bearing wind-gusts chill,
    Which he enjoyed more than his kingly days,
Bending fierce subjects by laws to his will.   420.
                        19.
    Years passed.   Meanwhile, her husband happily
    Living wild, with intent to do so still,
Gwendolyn wed again, per his decree.
                        20.
    It was midnight, the crescent moon aglow,
    A-glitter was the starry panoply,   425.
The air crisp, for a harsh north wind did blow,
    Its dry, cold breath driving the clouds away,
    Revealing heaven's sparkling, vast tableau.
Merlin observed the zodiac's display
    From a hilltop, and had these reveries: 430.

"Is this a king's death?   Near Mars a strange red ray
Portends that a pretender's come to seize
    The throne of the late monarch Constantine.
    Now his nephew Conan's conspiracies
Have gained the youth the crown, his plots obscene.   435.
    But you, Venus, always close to the sun
    And to the zodiac, what do you mean
By slicing through the ether as you've done
    With that bright ray?   Is there to be an end
    Of marriage?   Has separation begun?   440.
Gwendolyn may have found another friend,
    Since I've been gone a while, to take my place.
    I've lost, Venus.   Is that what you portend?
Our vows have disappeared without a trace,
    And all because I dawdled, while some boy   445.
    Pursued her, and now enjoys her embrace.
But I'm not jealous, and I wish her joy.
    My blessing on her, and her husband, too.
    At dawn I'll leave with gifts she will enjoy,
Just as long ago I promised I'd do.   450.

19.

    Forthwith he goes round groves and meadows all,
    Rounds up the deer and goats.   Before he's through
They're in a column.   He, astride a tall
    Stag, drives the column forward single-handed,
    Hurries them to Gwendolyn's bridal hall.   455.

20.

Once there, the column stopped where he commanded.
    He stood before the door and gave a shout.
    "Gwendolyn!   I'm here!   Deer and goats I've banded
Together, for your gift."   The bride came out,
    And was amazed to see her husband riding   460.
    On a wild stag, now tame, that round about
Wild beasts meekly submitted to his guiding,

As sheep respond to shepherds' oversight.
The groom heard the commotion, and came striding
Onto the balcony, and saw the "knight"   465.
In his "saddle."   He laughed, and Merlin knew
Who he was.   Angered by the bridegroom's slight,
The stag's antlers he snapped off, and he threw
    Them at the mocker.   They whizzed through the air
    Then struck the bridegroom's skull, piercing it through.   470.
Merlin, spurring his stag, got out of there,
    Hoping to reach his forest home, and hide.
    In hot pursuit, swarming from everywhere,
The courtiers galloped through the fields, and tried
    To cut him off, but Merlin's stag outran   475.
    Them, reached a river.   On the other side
Was safety.   The deer plunged in, faster than
    Merlin expected.   He slipped, splashing hard.
    The courtiers lined the banks, and got their man.
They led him to his sister, under guard.   480.

21.

    The captured bard was sad, wanted to flee,
    But he was kept bound, with his escape barred.
No laughter, food, drink...   His despondency
    Made his sister despondent, till at last
    Rodarch her husband saw his misery,   485.
How he'd refuse meals, preferring to fast.
    The king took pity, and ordered him led
    Around the markets, where the crowds were massed,
So the hubbub might cheer him, help him shed
    His melancholy.   At the palace gate,   490.
    There stood a ragged servant, one who pled
With passers-by to pity his sad state,
    Begging for alms to buy new clothes to wear.
    Merlin paused, gazed, as if to contemplate,
Then laughed.   He walked on, to another market square,   495.

Where a lad shopped for shoes to be re-soled.
Again he laughed, but, bothered by the stare
The market throng fixed on him, forthwith told
His minders that the daily tours would end.
He missed the woods, his habitat of old.   500.
The guards reported Merlin's wish to spend
His days in the woods, and how he laughed twice.
Rodarch, intrigued at what this might portend,
Ordered the bonds removed, and, to entice
The bard to explain the laugh, offered to let   505.
Him go back to his woodland paradise.
The answer was prompt. "The doorman we met,
So pitiful, wearing his wretched rags,
He looks as if he's broke, or deep in debt.
He begs the crowd for handouts, whines and nags,   510.
Yet secretly he's rich. He sits atop
A treasure trove of buried money bags.
That's why I laughed. You go, you dig. A "crop"
You'll find of golden coins of ancient date.
My keepers led me past a cobbler's shop.   515.
The merchant was engaged in hot debate,
The customer insisting that he throw
In extra soles, for wear he'd estimate.
I laughed at this as well. There will be no
Need for spares, or any guarantee.   520.
That young man's corpse is drifting to and fro,
Upon the sea, shoreward. You go, you'll see."
Rodarch had his men fan out on the strand,
To test again Merlin's veracity,   525.
So that, if a corpse were to drift to land,
They were to report it without delay.
They quickly carried out their king's command:
There, on the gravelly beach, the drowned man lay.
A courier rode back to tell what they'd found.   530.

Meanwhile, the beggar had been sent away.
His Majesty's men had dug up the ground,
    And found gold.   Rodarch laughed, and he gave praise
    To Merlin, who, though, was already bound
For the woods, far from hated city ways.   535.
    The queen implored him to at least postpone
    His departure until the freezing days
Of winter had passed, and spring winds had blown
    The icy white away, and brought in green,
    So he'd have fruit and warmth out there, alone.   540.
He answered sharply, and rebuked the queen,
    And was contemptuous of the winter snows.
                        22.
    "O sister dear, what do these pleadings mean?
I won't hide just because the north wind blows,
    And ice storms rage.   Nor does the falling hail   545.
    That panics flocks, scare me.   Torrential flows
Of rain the south wind brings won't make me quail.
    No, I'll head for the wilds, the meadows green.
    Facing the frost, my Spartan nerve won't fail.
I'll pass the summer in a sylvan scene,   550.
    Inhaling pure air and the flowers' scent.
    If you're concerned there'll be no food to glean,
In winter, have homes built, have servants sent
    To the woods.   They can cook and wait on me
    When it turns cold, and food supplies are spent.   555.
Before you do, build one house specially,
    Off by itself, and carefully designed,
    With doors and windows numbering seventy.
Astrology is what I have in mind.
    What do the stars foretell about the state?
    I'll need clerks to keep notes on what I find,   560.
Who're quick enough to write as I dictate.
    You, sister dear, come frequently, and so

My hunger and my thirst alleviate."
With that, he left.   His sister watched him go,
  Then set about to realize his plan   565.
  Of an observatory in the snow.
23.
As long as food held out, and Phoebus ran
  High the zodiac, he lived at ease,
  Strolled through groves and let the breezes fan
His forehead.   Then the winds grew brisk, and trees   570.
  Were stripped by downpours and by gusting gale,
  So leaf and fruit were blown down, or would freeze.
Dejectedly he'd find the forest trail
  That led to the great hall, its table spread
  With banquets that his sister without fail   575.
Provided.   Thus refreshed, he'd nod his head
  In gratitude to her, then ramble through
  The building.   He looked out the windows, read
The stars, dictating meanings he'd construe.
24.
  "O madness of the Britons!   Lavish wealth   580.
  Has crazed them, so they brazenly undo
The codes that safeguard our land's civic health.
  Caught up in civil war and private feud,
  Churches in ruin dot the commonwealth,
Abandoned by their priests to solitude.   585.
  The Boar of Cornwall's line now agitate,
  And ambush their own kin, hoping by crude
Violence they'll control the British state,
  By murder to possess the country's crown.
  A fourth will come, with cruelty and hate,   590.
Then when a warrior sea-wolf brings him down,
  He'll cross the Severn, into barbary.
  That man will then besiege Cirencester town,
Flatten its homes and walls with sparrows free.

A Gallic sea-raid.   Death by royal arms.   595.
When Rodarch dies, there'll be long anarchy,
The Scots and Welsh long suffer war's alarms.
    Till Wales be granted to the growing tooth,
    The Welsh will fight Gwent and raid Cornish farms.
No law will rein them in.   The Welsh, in truth,   600.
    Rejoice in bloodshed, and they always will.
    You foes of God, renounce your ways uncouth!
Wales will see brother fight, and brother kill,
    And blight will spread throughout the family.
    Scotch raids will strike across the Humber till   605.
They've pitilessly cut down all who won't flee.
    Their leader, though, will die as punishment.
    He'll have a horse's name, its bravery.
His heir out from our borders will be sent.
    O Scot, sheathe up the claymores that you bare!   610.
    Our folk's courage will soon make you relent.
The ruins of Acelud no king will dare
    Rebuild until the Scot has been subdued.
    The towers of Caernavon in disrepair
Until the Welsh reclaim the land, will brood.   615.
    Kaeptis will view its ruined harbor wall
    Till a wolf-toothed rich man has it renewed.
The bishop's seat of Loel town will fall
    Vacant.   The Lion's staff will bring it back.
    Richborough's sea-trade will slow to a crawl,   620.
A helmet-shipped Fleming gets it on track.
    A fifth will build St. David's walls again,
    To guard the priestly mantle from attack.
The city of legions will lose her men
    To you, O Severn.   They will face exile   625.
    Till Bear-in-Lamb comes back to claim the den.
The Saxon kings will rule those towns a while,
    Both homes and farms of those who've been expelled.

From these, three dragons.   The crown's thrice reptile.
Two hundred monks in Leicester will be felled   630.
    When Saxons seize its walls, drive off its chief.
    The first Angle that Brutus' crown has held
Will bring the desolated town relief.
    The wild men won't let bishops be ordained,
    Churches they'll fill with signs of unbelief.   635.
Then Roman cowls will cleanse what the heathens stained,
    With holy water will reconsecrate
    God's houses, and will keep them unprofaned.
Within, they will observe heaven's mandate,
    And in heavenly peace will spend their days.   640.
    The pagan race will try to violate
The righteous norm, revert to savage ways.
    They'll sell their sons to lands across the sea,
    An outrage that will make God's anger blaze.
Enslavement!   It's a crime!   It's blasphemy!   645.
    Souls God made worthy of heaven, bound and sold,
    Auctioned like cattle, stripped of liberty!
You'll stop, you scoundrel.   Like Judas of old,
    You betrayed God when first you came to power.
    The Danes will come and have their stranglehold,   650.
Then be expelled, ruling for their short hour.
    A serpent will harm two chiefs with its tail,
    Forget the oath for the sceptre's endower.
The Normans' wooden ships will thenceforth sail,
    Bearing a face in front and one behind,   655.
    With slashing swords and heavy coats of mail.
They'll strike, kill, and defeat armies aligned
    Against them, far-off peoples subjugate
    And rule, until their power is undermined.
A flying Fury will disseminate   660.
    Poison against them.   Trust, virtue and peace
    Will vanish.   Wars will rage throughout the state.

Man will betray man, and friendship will cease.
  The faithless husband will forget his bride,
  The wife forget him as her beaux increase.   665.
The church's order will be cast aside,
  Priests will bear arms, and man the barricades,
  Holy ground itself will be fortified,
Alms for the poor be lent for soldiers' raids,
  So worldly they'll become, that, wealth-obsessed,   670.
  They'll filch church funds in shoddy escapades.
Three'll bear the crown, then new ones will fare best.
  A fourth by flighty piety'll be hurt.
  Till with boars' teeth he's by his father dressed,
He'll cross a helmeted man's shade thus girt.   675.
  Anointed, four in turn will seek the heights.
  Two'll win, because they're able to subvert
The crown to start internal Gallic fights.
  A sixth the Irish walls will overthrow,
  A pious sage set men and towns to rights.   680.
I sang this to Vortigern long ago,
  Explaining at length why two dragons fought,
  As we sat by the drained pond, so he'd know.
But you, the king's deathbed is where you ought
  To be, dear sister.   Have Taliesin sent   685.
  To me, so I'll learn what he has been taught
By Breton Gildas, toward enlightenment."
                              25.
  She found sage Taliesin, but wearing black.
  The king had died.   She heard courtiers' lament
And she herself broke down.   Her knees went slack,   690.
  She tore her hair and sobbed this to her friends:
  "Weep, women, weep for Rodarch, don't hold back.
He was one of a kind.   Go to the ends
  Of the earth and his like you'll never find.
  He loved the law on which the peace depends,   695.

Prevented coercion of any kind.
   He treated holy priests with just restraint,
   And for both rich and poor, the law was blind.
He generously gave, without complaint,
   With high and low scrupulously correct, 700.
   Always true knight, true king.   He was a saint.
Now, woe is me.   You're dead, and worms infect
   You, your remains rot in an urn.
   This bed?   After your whole life being decked
In softest silk, you'll be buried in turn 705.
   Under an icy stone, be bones and dust.
   It's man's fate through the centuries, we learn.
Eden is lost.   We face death as we must.
   The glamour of earth's perishable things
   Deceives the nabobs, shames the upper crust. 710.
The bee will lure with honey, then it stings.
   Earth's glamour tricks those who are soothed.   It veers
   And strikes those who trusted its comfortings.
It cuts short what is grand, erodes the years
   As flowing water wears away the soil. 715.
   If the red rose or white lily appears,
If man or horse is handsome, but turmoil
   Ruins them, then why create in the first place?
   Leave this to God.   Those who do humble toil,
Leaving the world, are happy in His grace, 720.
   And they'll enjoy honor forevermore,
   With Creator Christ, who rules endless space.
You chiefs, high walls, and ancestors, therefore,
   Farewell.   Sweet children, farewell.   I depart.
   Now, with my brother, I'll live and adore 725.
The Lord, in black, but with a happy heart."
   She did her duty to his memory
   And left an epitaph of artless art:

RODARCH
UNRIVALLED GENEROSITY
A GREAT MAN RESTS INSIDE THIS LITTLE URN

26.

Meanwhile, Merlin saw one who'd come to see	731.
Him: he'd had Taliesin sent for, to learn	
The nature of the clouds and driving rain.	
A storm was brewing, that they could discern.	
These insights flowed from bard Taliesin's brain.	735.
"God made the world from just four elements.	
He blends them, they stay stable without strain,	
For they coexist by His providence.	
The sky, which He so grandly decorates,	
Encloses us with starry regiments.	740.
Then there's the air, through which sound resonates,	
And through which stars peep, when the weather's fair.	
The sea whose current day and night pulsates,	
Making four circuits, and thus strikes the air,	
Producing winds whose number's four as well. 745.	
Then there's the earth, firm in its strength, foursquare,	
Divided into five parts. Hot as hell,	
The middle can't be lived in. Ice and snow	
Make the extremes too cold for us to dwell.	
The rest is temperate, God made it so,	750.
And here mankind and birds and beasts all thrive.	
The clouds above give rain for us below,	
Which keeps the fruits of tree and earth alive.	
The clouds themselves are restocked by the sun,	
Whose heat gives water vapor its upward drive.	755.
Clouds fill like bags; they swell, then overrun,	
Rain gushing out in torrents, at gale force.	
Cloudbursts, snow and round hail have only one	
Origin: wet and chilly wind's the source,	

That brings the air aloft, then lets it fall. 760.
Each wind has traits it picks up from its course,
The climate it passes through, most of all.
    Above this is the starry firmament
    Which God made as the angels' dwelling-hall,
Sublime, but designed to reward time spent 765.
    In contemplation with deep peace within.
    The brilliant sun is its chief ornament,
But large or small, the way stars drift or spin
    Is so precise, each never leaves its zone. 770.
    Leaving that sphere behind, we now begin
To make out lunar light, that always shone
    Upon spirit phalanxes hovering high,
    That cheer us when we feel sad and alone.
Man's prayers pass through the air as up they fly, 775.
    Asking the Lord to grant whatever seems
    Pleasant.   Back through the air comes the reply,
Made known to us by omens, words or dreams.
    But right below the moon, bad spirits hover,
    Who tempt us, and deceive us with their schemes. 780.
When they materialize, they'll often cover
    Their forms with this or that pleasant disguise.
    In fact, women drawn to a demon lover
Bear children no one can legitimize.
    Three spirit orders, kept distinct, God made, 785.
    That bless us when descending from the skies,
Renewing earth with renewed growth displayed.
    The seas He separated, to maintain
    The pace of procreation unallayed:
He makes part boil, part freeze, and part refrain 790.
    From extremes.   Two provide our food supply,
    But that which boils was put there to restrain
Evil ones, in an abyss, circled by
    Opposing waves, that create flame from flame.

Thence descend scoundrels who God's law defy.   795.
They leave the Lord behind, and without shame
    They rush headlong into depravity.
    But there a grim judge measures praise and blame
On scales.   Each gets his due impartially.
    The second, that which freezes, washes bare   800.
    Beaches it strips by vapor-alchemy
Stirred up when Dione's star fixes its glare.
    The Arabs say this star in Pisces makes
    Gemstones, fixing on sea its fiery stare.
These gems protect whoever undertakes   805.
    To wear them, to protect him or to heal.
    Distinguishing them is simple, for God breaks
Them down by form and color, to reveal
    Their powers and to classify them right.
    The third form of the sea that like a wheel   810.
Swirls round, provides bounteous goods that please:
    The salt we extract, the fish that abound,
    Currents that bear our fleets across the seas,
Then back, whose profits suddenly redound
    To the poor man.   Rich soil along the shore   815.
    Feeds birds that thrive wherever fish are found.
The sea, indeed, is dominated more
    By birds than fish, though nature's one law rules
    Both species.   It makes fliers lightly soar,
But wetness presses down the fishes' schools   820.
    Beneath the waves, away from where it's dry.
    Fish differ, from their very molecules
On up to their behavior, which is why
    They're fascinating, healthful, doctors find.
    Red mullet won't let passion swell too high,   825.
But those who eat it, they say, will go blind.
    The thyme-fish, named for the spice, uses smell
    To trick foes of the predatory kind.

Their scent pervades the rivers where they dwell.
   All eels are female — quite an oddity! —   830.
   But they make the eel population swell
By crossing lines drawn by biology.
   For snakes will gather on the shores and hiss,
   Which for them is seductive melody
To lure the eels to rendez-vous and bliss.   835.
   Then there's the sea urchin, a half-foot long,
   That sticks to things: a ship held fast by this
Is powerless to move, it's gripped as strong
   As if it were beached.   The sea urchin's feared
   As much as the swordfish, that with its prong   840.
Can pierce a vessel that's carelessly steered
   Too close.   If caught, it stabs the hull right through:
   She sinks.   A whirlpool marks where she was speared.
The sailfish is much feared, that cuts in two
   Boats with its crest, slicing them like a blade.   845.
   It gets respect that to a sword is due.
The sea-dragon's poison makes men afraid.
   Beneath its wings its weapon's hidden, then
   Its captors die from venom that is sprayed.
The jellyfish can injure sailors when   850.
   It's touched.   Immediately one is numb
   In extremities.   They won't move again,
Left paralyzed by secretions that come
   From this creature that drifts up on the sand.
   God gave the sea to these creatures that plumb   855.
Its depths, and on its surface placed the land,
   Where people live, enjoying fertile ground,
   Abundant pasturage and vistas grand.
They say that Britain's best for all-around
   Abundance of products that are unique: 860.
   It annually bears crops that are renowned
For fragrance, the aristocrats' mystique.

Forest and meadow lush, where honey drips,
　　Wide grassland green, towering mountain peak,
Waterways for hunting and fishing trips,　　　　　　　865.
　　Ripe fruit, precious metals, even gemstones
　　Are scattered, as from Nature's fingertips.
Hot springs are there to soothe the aching bones,
　　Mineral waters which effect a cure
　　Much more drastic than a doctor condones.　　　　870.
King Bladud built spas for his paramour,
　　His consort Alaron.　The thermal springs
　　Relieve discomforts that patients endure,
Especially for women's sufferings.
　　The isle of Thanatos is found quite near.　　　　875.
　　It's snake-free, though it teems with living things.
Its soil's an antivenom, mixed with beer.
　　The Orkney Islands lie across the strait,
　　All thirty-three, out where the currents veer.
Thirteen of them their farmers cultivate.　　　　　880.
　　Ultima Thule's name comes from being last,
　　Far off from sunshine, so summer comes late.
The sunlight barely reaches, nor shines past
　　This twilight land of long, bitter-cold night,
　　Of gloom and shadows, ringed with icebergs massed,　885.
Blockading it better than warships might.
　　The island after ours that's said to be
　　Most excellent is Ireland, fertile site!
It's larger, it lacks bird and honey-bee,
　　Nor can snakes reproduce upon this isle.　　　　890.
　　If its soil's brought to lands across the sea,
All bees and snakes vanish after a while.
　　Gades, what later generations call
　　Cadiz, has gem-trees, at each root a pile
Of jewels, gum beads that drip, harden, then fall.　　　895.
　　Isles west of Cadiz, as the tale is told,

Have dragon guards that round gold apples crawl.
The Gorgon Islands near there are controlled
  By hairy women who run fast as hares.
  Argire and Cryssa, it's said, bear gold   900.
And silver common as stones Corinth bears.
  Ceylon is rich for its fast-growing grass.
  Two   crops a year in climate such as theirs,
Two springs, two summers, two grape-harvests pass
  For our one, and gemstones galore gleam clear.   905.
  Atiles Isle produces flowers en masse.
It's springtime there twelve months of every year.
  The Isles of Apples, "Fortunate," they're named,
  Because crops grow without a farmer near,
Or plows, or fertilizer.   What they're famed   910.
  For is that crops of grape and grain burst out
  Although not agriculturally tamed.
Great apple trees from tiny speeds will sprout,
  Exotic plants, not only turf and hay.
  Man's lifespan there's a hundred years, no doubt.   915.
Nine sisters rule there.   By kindly law they
  Govern those who come to them from our parts.
  Morgen, the one the other eight obey,
As they concede her beauty, knows the arts
  Of healing, and she's wise in herbal lore,   920.
  Infusing vigor into failing hearts.
She a shape-changer, too, and she can soar
  Like Daedalus, on unnatural wings
  To Brest or Chartres, even Italy's shore
She reaches through mysterious voyagings.   925.
  Moronoe, Mazoe, Glitonea, Gliten,
  Giton, Tyronoe, Thiten, all siblings,
She taught number-lore.   (That's lute-famed Thiten.)
27.
We carried wounded Arthur to her side

After the fight at Camlan, we few men.   930.
Barinthus knew the way, and was our guide,
    Steering the vessel to Morgen's domain.
    She courteously asked us to abide,
And having seen the injured monarch lain
    Upon a gold couch, wounds unwrapped, she expressed   935.
    The opinion that he could be whole again
If he stayed long with her, and convalesced,
    Although the treatment would be long indeed.
    We left him with her, hoping for the best,
Returned, with brisk winds giving us good speed."   940.

28.

    Then Merlin, groaning, answered him, "Dear friend,
    The kingdom has been torn apart by greed.
The chieftains, at each others' throats, expend
    Their energies on such barbaric acts
    That life cannot be lived, so in the end   945.
Wealth flees the country, all goodness retracts,
    And ruined citizens are refugees.
    The Saxon horde sweeps in, and it enacts
Blasphemous laws and inflicts cruelties
    On cities and temples.   God will permit   950.
    These outrages to check our fooleries.
We reap what we sow.   Thus says Holy Writ.

29.

    Scarce had he finished when Taliesin said,
    "In that case, men should understand that it
Behooves them to roust Arthur from his bed,   955.
    If he's recuperated, and return
    Him to pacify the land he once led.
Merlin replied, "That's not the way we'll earn
    Our freedom from the occupying horde.
    Long years they'll rule, no matter how we yearn   960.
For liberty, our prayers will be ignored.

But then three of us will bravely resist.
Many will die, and end foreign discord,
But it will do no good, for there exist
    Decrees of God that the Welsh won't be free,   965.
    Weak as they are, till their protagonist,
Charioted Conan comes from Brittany.
    Cadwalader with justice will unite
    The Welsh with others in their family:
Scots, Bretons, Cornishmen, with equal right.   970.
    And give their people back the captured crown.
    When Brutus' days return, our foes in flight,
They'll deal out holy justice in each town,
    And distant kings will have reason to fear,
    As victories once more give us renown."   975.

30.

Bard Taliesin addressed Merlin the seer,
    "No one will live to see your prophecies,
    No one has seen more crimes of yesteryear."
"Indeed," said Merlin. "I've seen perfidies
    Aplenty in my time, both from our kin   980.
    And from the foreigners' hostilities.
The worst was when poor Constans was done in.
    His brothers Uther and Ambrosius fled.
    At once we saw our civil wars begin,
And through our leaderless dominions spread.   985.
    Count Vortigern of Gwent mustered brigades,
    Marauding everywhere that madman led,
The helpless peasants suffered from this raids,
    Then in a coup he grabbed the reins of state,
    Most noble rivals cut down by his blades.   990.
But in so doing, he had earned the hate
    Of victims' relatives, who then began
    To torch the princes' towns, exacerbate
Unrest by having mercenaries fan

The flames, keep things chaotic, and prevent   995.
The king from reigning.   Thus, a desperate plan:
To stand against his own people, he sent
      For foreigners to help sustain his cause.
      Desperate to save his foundering government,
He'd greet soldiers of fortune with applause.   1000.
      The curved hulls of the Saxon navy came,
      Full of helmeted soldiers.   Two outlaws
Led the throng, Horsa and Hengist by name,
      And they, with unspeakable treachery
      Brought their host steel, and brought his cities flame.   1005.
For after serving the king dutifully,
      They drew him to their side, poisoned his mind,
      Warned him his subjects were not trustworthy.
They would protect the king from his own kind.
      The Saxon chiefs broke faith.   One night they tricked   1015.
      The nobles, killed them one night as they dined.
The pretext was a peace treaty.   They kicked
      The king out.   He fled over mountain snow.
      What happened was what he'd heard me predict
From there, burning and pillaging they'd go,   1015.
      To crush native resistance to their might.
      Vortimer understood his nation's woe,
How his father, deposed, had taken flight.
      He took the crown, with the people's support,
      Rode, do or die, to end the Saxon blight.   1020.
At last he won.   He drove them to their fort
      At Tanet, the Saxons' main naval base.
      In their retreat, Horsa's life was cut short,
As were many of his men in the race
      To escape our forces.   The king boxed them in,   1025.
      Besieged the remnant in that little space.
In desperation, seeing we would win,
      They tried a breakout, and reached open sea,

With frantic rowing reached their home and kin.
Having expelled the invading enemy,   1030.
    King Vortimer's prestige went far and wide
    He settled in and ruled equitably.
But Hengist's sister Rowena decried
    The outcome, and resolved to use deceit
    To avenge her brother and his losing side.   1035.
She poisoned the king, and sent word to entreat
    Hengist to muster Saxon men-at-arms
    And counterattack to inflict defeat
On Britain's yeomen. Overwhelming swarms
    Of mercenaries swept our men aside.   1040.
    They looted all, from palaces to farms,
And swept over the country like a tide.
    Meanwhile, restive guests of the Breton king
    Ambrosius and Uther, battle-tried
And war-girt, had recruitment in full swing,   1045.
    Of soldiers from everywhere, to invade
    Their native land, avenge the sting
Of conquest, and repel the Saxon raid.
    They set sail, daring stormy wind and wave,
    And landed to give their countrymen aid.   1050.
They captured Vortigern, trying to save
    Himself in Wales. They burned him in his tower.
    They turned their swords against the Angles, gave
Battle, sometimes winning against their power
    And sometimes losing. Finally, with great   1055.
    Determination and discipline, our
Men dealt them a stinging defeat. Irate,
    They showed Hengist no mercy, killed him dead.
    By acclamation throughout the whole state
Ambrosius was proclaimed the nation's head.   1060.
    He was worthy of kingship, brave and just,
    But aged only twenty, fate cut the thread.

A doctor poisoned him, betrayed his trust.
    Younger brother Uther succeeded him,
    But had no peace, because of the blood-lust   1065.
Of that nation whose name's a synonym
    For faithlessness.   Again their raiders snuck
    Across, and Uther fought, purposeful, grim,
Chasing them to the coasts from which they struck.
    He re-established peace, left wars behind,   1070.
    And also left a son who had no truck
With underhanded deals of any kind.
    His name was Arthur, and he ruled long years
    After Uther's reign had passed out of mind.
His reign began with agony and tears,   1075.
    And death of many men in long campaigns,
    For while the prince was sick, the Saxon spears
Surged forth from Anglia, led by their thanes
    Across the Humber.   The heartland was theirs.
    Too young and too naive to break their chains,   1080.
Arthur sought counsel in these grim affairs
    From priests and laymen, then sent an appeal
    To Hoel of Brittany and his confreres
For speedy aid, protection, since he'd feel
    The tug of family, one looking out   1085.
    For the other in any kind of ordeal.
Straightway Hoel assembled Bretons stout,
    Stockpiled materiel, spent time in drill,
    Then struck.   The Saxons fell back in a rout.
Over and over Hoel attacked them.   Still,   1090.
    Arthur was not behindhand, fearless clashed
    In the thick of the fight, charging until
The foemen broke and ran, formations smashed.
    He ruled with moderation, in between
    Fighting back Scotch incursions, being lashed   1095.
By Irish raids, by any nation keen

To exploit his weakness.   He subdued the lot.
Not just his neighbors.   Threats to his demesne
Across the sea, Norway and Denmark, got
    A taste of their own medicine.   He beat   1100.
    The Gauls when Frollo died, who'd got his spot
By being bought off after his defeat
    Of Roman legions who tried to invade
    His realm.   Death left a procurator's seat
Vacant.   The Romans used the accolade   1105.
    As bait, and he agreed to be their man.
    Meanwhile, that foolish Judas Modred played
His dirty game of chess, even began
    A love affair with the wife of the king.
    The king, involved with an invasion plan,   1110.
Had trusted him with guarding everything.
    But when rumors of scandal reached his ears
    He came straight home to have a reckoning.
He landed with a host of volunteers,
    And chased his nephew out, and overseas.   1115.
    That crafty fugitive sought out his peers
In villainy, the Saxons, and with these
    Legions he fought against his lord, but fell
    When Arthur brought his allies to their knees.
Oh, what mayhem for men, and what a hell   1120.
    For mothers whose sons perished on that day!
    The king himself, while fighting to repel
His foes, was badly wounded, borne away
    By ship to the nymph's palace.   You foretold
    That Modred's two sons would next join the fray,   1125.
Each one desiring to obtain a hold
    On the kingdoms, by war or murder.   Then
    The king's nephew, Constantine, employed bold
And ruthless tactics, savaged towns and men.
    When his harshness had laid everything low,   1130.

He seized the crown and ruled all in his ken.
He had no peace to enjoy his conquest, though,
 For Conan his kinsman soon after stirred
 Up rebels for another overthrow,
So now he's king, weak, feckless and absurd."   1135.

31.

While he was speaking, men came at a run,
 Excitedly relating what they'd heard:
A fountain had burst forth, a new, pure one,
 Whose waters were flowing all through the vale,
 Through meadows gurgling, sparkling in the sun. 1140.
Both men arose to verify the tale,
 And Merlin, feeling pensive, found a seat
 And praised the flowing waters and the swale,
Admired the way the spring burst from the peat.
 It made him thirsty, and forthwith he leaned   1145.
 Forward, splashed his face to relieve the heat,
Then drank deeply.   At once the water cleaned
 His innards and restored the balance to
 His system, and relieved him of the fiend
That lurked within his mind, and which would skew 1150.
 His thinking.   Now he felt himself restored,
 That he was sane again, his madness through.
Blessing God therefore, he raised his face toward
 The stars, and spoke fervently, giving praise
 For health he felt.   He thus addressed the Lord: 1155.

32.

"O King, Who keeps the night sky all ablaze,
 Yet orderly, Who keeps the earth and sea
 Teeming with life, nourishing us always
With their abundance and fertility,
 And by Whose grace my mind wanders no more,   1160.
 I'm sane, and my reason's returned to me!
A shaman, I could recite ancient lore,

And tell the future, and know of bird's flight,
Fishes' and planets' motion I'd explore,
But found it vexing, couldn't sleep at night,   1165.
Obsession with arcana held me fast.
But now I'm whole again.   My mind is right,
I'm vigorous and clear-sighted at last.
Therefore, o Highest Father, I'm your slave,
Because you've freed me from a hellish past.   1170.
I owe you for the second chance you gave,
The twofold benefits of this new spring,
Bursting from the sod with its rippling wave.
It quenches my thirst, but the greater thing
Is how it clears my mind and calms my head.   1175.
But tell me, comrade, by your reckoning
Whence came this healing fountain, that has led
Me back to myself, from insanity?"
33.
"The great Regulator," Taliesin said,
"Gave each river a healing property   1180.
To benefit the sick, keeping apart
The fountains, rivers, lakes humanity
Relies on to enhance the healer's art.
At Rome, quick-flowing Albula's a cure
For injuries, and helps the healing start.   1185.
Another spring in Italy is sure
To heal the eyes.   They call it 'Cicero's.'
The Ethiopians have a pond whose water pure
Is poured on the face, and like oil it glows.
Zama's a spring in Africa.   One sip,   1190.
And suddenly the voice melodious grows.
Aversion to wine, even one little nip,
Is Lake Clitorius' power, while those who drink
From Chios' font get groggy.   Two springs slip
From Boeotian terrain.   One helps you think,   1195.

The other takes away your memory.
A lake there whips libido to the brink;
Cyzicus' spring curbs sexuality.
    They say that drinking from Campagna's streams
    Makes barren women fertile instantly,   1200.
As well as curing the men's fever-dreams.
    In Ethiopia runs a fountain red,
    Which restores reason from insane extremes.
Leinus' spring lets childbirth go safe ahead.
    Sicilian streams will either make a maid   1205.
    Barren or fertile, as children are bred.
In Thessaly two springs' powers are displayed:
    A sheep that drinks from one will have black fleece;
    The other, white; both, wool of mottled shade.
An Umbrian lake, Clitumnus, will increase   1210.
    The size of bulls at times, and horse-hooves grow
    Rock-hard the moment the steeds cross the piece
Of sandy land that the map-makers know
    As Reatine Swamp.   In Israel's Dead Sea
    Things float on the surface, won't sink below,   1215.
But on the other hand, there's said to be
    An Indian pool, Syda, where bodies sink.
    Bodies bob on top of lake Aloë,
Even lumps of iron, heavy lead, or zinc.
    On the Marsidian fountain they do, too.   1220.
    Cliff-flowing River Styx kills those who drink,
As the land of Arcadia's witness true.
    The Idumaean fount four times a day
    By wondrous law, they say, changes its hue.
Murky at first, in an orderly way   1225.
    It goes to green, then blood-red, then it's clear.
    Downstream three months each of the colors stay,
Progressing regularly every year.
    Then there's Lake Trogdytus, whose wave flows through;

Three daily changes, sweet to sour appear.   1230.
Epirus' font makes torches burst into
    Flame, and light up again when they're put out.
    The Garamontes' fount will freeze you blue
By day, but boils all night.   It's turn-about,
    Denying access both by cold and heat.   1235.
    Hot geysers threaten many when they spout,
Brought to a boil when rushing waters meet
    Alum or sulfur, which are both endowed
    With healing properties known good to treat
The sick, artesian wells that cascade loud,   1240.
    Proclaiming the Creator's power to heal
    Through His agents, water and steamy cloud.
Also, these springs are healthful, give the feel
    Of great well-being, and cure best, I'd say,
    Not underground when slow they blindly steal,   1245.
But when they burst into the light of day.
    Subsurface streams meander, never seen
    Until a blockage is thrown in their way,
If subterranean mudslides intervene,
    Or shifting stones dam up the current, back   1250.
    It goes, until it soaks the pastures green.
You see many springs gush, and then go slack,
    Subsiding into caverns dark and deep."

34.

    Meanwhile, the rumors flew.   There was no lack
Of interest in this fountain that would leap   1255.
    From Caledonian soil, and of its cure
    Of a man long madness-ravaged, who'd keep
Company with wild beasts, and would endure
    The rigors of life outdoors.   Chieftains came,
    And saw him made whole by the waters pure.   1260.
They spoke of the land's need, and would exclaim
    That he should rule again, and be their king,

With moderation make his subjects tame.
He said, "My boys, this is the sort of thing
    I'm just too old for, now my joints are sore   1265.
    So I can scarcely walk for weakening.
I've had my happy life in days of yore,
    Rejoicing in the luxuries I got.
    My life was one of comfort heretofore.
Not far from here, in the woods, there's a spot   1270.
    Where an oak stands, ancient beyond dispute.
    Its sap's dried up, and it's starting to rot.
I saw that tree the day it first took root,
    The acorn that fell I remember clear:
    A woodpecker perched over that small shoot.   1275.
I watched it grow, as I was sitting near,
    Each twig, and I was in awe of the glen,
    Remembering the place that I held dear.
I'm old, and slower than I was back when
    I ruled the kingdom, vigorous and spry.   1280.
    The greenery of Caledon has been
So pleasing to me, that nothing can vie
    With it, no Indian gems, nor gold
    Of Spain, Greek wine from days gone by,
Sicilian crops, walled towers, nor the fold   1285.
    Of perfumed robes like those they wore in Tyre.
    No luxury can ever break the hold
That Caledon has on me.   I aspire
    To nothing more than apples, herbs and peace.
    I'll purify my flesh, set my sights higher,   1290.
That I may have life that will never cease."

35.

While he was saying this, the chieftains saw
    Above them, a "v" formation like geese,
But cranes, long lines of them, in which the draw
    Of migratory instinct made them fly   1295.

In strict order.   Merlin, asked by what law
They were impelled to navigate the sky,
    Responded, "Know that every single trait
    Assigned to creatures comes from God on high.
I've learned this living in their natural state."   1300.

36.

    "The nature of cranes, as they soar on past,
    Is to organize themselves as they migrate,
To keep together and make their strength last.
    A leader calls to keep their files intact,
    Lest stragglers keep their lines from holding fast.   1305.
When he's hoarse, a replacement's quick to act.
    They pick one crane for sentry-go at night,
    Who holds a pebble in his claw.   Attacked,
The clatter rouses the whole flock in fright.
    Their hatchlings' white wings blacken when mature.   1310.
    But eagles, famed for sharpness of their sight,
Beyond all other creatures, to ensure
    That their nestlings aren't   weaklings, hang them where
    The sun's rays are fiercest.   They should endure
Without flinching, look at the sunlight square.   1315.
    They hover over the main, mountain-high;
    Down deep their prey cannot elude their stare.
They plummet through the void, and their sure eye
    Enables them to catch fish undersea.
    She-vultures can conceive and multiply   1320.
Without their mates, however that may be.
    Though soaring high as eagles, the faint scent
    Of carrion in the nasal cavity
Guides them where they gorge to their hearts' content,
    Yet they glide slowly, as befits a bird   1325.
    With a hundred-year lifespan to be spent.
The messenger of spring, the stork, is heard
    Clacking its beak as it denudes its breast

For its nestlings' comfort, its own deferred.
When winter comes, it migrates, and won't rest   1330.
Till it reaches Asia.   Its guide's a crow.
Its chicks, long after they have left the nest,
Will feed the parent who is old and slow.
The dying swan's supreme for melody.
For sailors, it's the best welcome they know.   1335.
Up north, lute music, incidentally,
Attracts swans to the shore by its sweet tone.
The ostrich leaves its eggs buried, while she
Goes off, leaves them neglected and alone.
The sun, not mother's warmth, will make them hatch.   1340.
The heron, as sailors know, will have flown
To the clouds when a storm's about to catch
It in the open.   Mariners will note
Its flight to elude rough weather with dispatch.
The phoenix has a unique antidote   1345.
For ageing.   It forsakes its habitat
For scorching deserts where mirages float,
And in this heat it heaps up spices that
Its quick wing-flaps ignite.   The flames consume
The bird and its pyre, down to ashes, pat,   1350.
But a new bird arises, to resume
The old one's life, so on for centuries.
The cinnamolgus nests where there is room,
Makes nests of cinnamon in high oak trees.
Men use arrows to drive it off, to try   1355
To get the nests and sell them for rich fees.
The halcyon's a bird that's known to fly
Over salt-water swamps, and winters there.
While it rests, a calm seven days pass by,
With no high winds or tempests anywhere,   1360.
Producing a calm for the nesting bird.
A parrot's voice can fool you, with its flair

For imitation of a human word.
    It says "hello" and "bonjour," makes a joke.
    The pelican kills its young, it's averred,   1365.
Mourns for three days, with sobs enough to choke,
    Then tears itself open with its own beak.
    Blood coming out in waves, from that one stroke
Revives the dead chicks by that gory leak.
    The mournful cries of petrels are well-known,   1370.
    But not that they calamity bespeak,
For kings or kingdoms over which they've flown.
    And they identify people they meet
    As Greek or non-Greek.   The Hellenophone
They welcome, and with chirping, nuzzling greet.   1375.
    The others are treated like enemies,
    With wariness, alarms and wings that beat.
The sandpipers, it's said, make odysseys
    Every fifth year to mourn at Memnon's tomb,
    The Trojan War hero's last obsequies.   1380.
The hercynia bears a wondrous plume
    That glows in the dark like a burning brand,
    A light for travelers groping through the gloom.
Wedges and nails immovable by hand
    Are easy for the woodpecker to extract.   1385.
    His tapping's heard across the forest land."

37.

His speech was cut short.   Howlings of one racked
    By lunacy, who burst into the scene,
    Drowned out their talk.   His shriekings never slacked.
He frothed and raved, belligerent, obscene.   1390.
    Some men had captured him, and made him sit
    Where they could tease him, goad him, and thus glean
Some rude amusement from his jabbering fit.
    Merlin looked and remembered.   With a groan
    He said, "Time was when he was not a bit   1395.

Pathetic, but turned heads, and was well-known
 As a brave, handsome, gallant soldier true,
 Whose breeding in his every action shone.
He was, in fact, one of my retinue,
 When I had many friends, when I was king.   1400.
 We went out hunting one day, to pursue
Game in Arwystli's highlands.   A cool spring
 We found, with greenery around, and shade
 From spreading branches of oaks in a ring.
Its water was refreshing, so we stayed,   1405.
 And greedily drank of its waters pure.
 Then sat back satisfied, our thirst allayed.
We noticed, in the greenery that's sure
 To spring up near oases, the sweet smell
 Of ripe apples, tempting in their allure.   1410.
Their finder picked them quick.   He nearly fell
 As laughing he came staggering to me,
 With "tribute."   I divided them as well
As I could.   As befits nobility,
 I did without.   The heap was just too small.   1415.
 The men cheered loud my generosity,
But cheers turned into screams.   I saw them fall
 Convulsing on the ground.   Like dogs they bit
 Each other, foamed at the mouth and would bawl
Out raving nonsense, then like wolves they lit   1420.
 Out running.   Mental demons made them flee,
 Howling like wolves, and wouldn't let them quit.
I think those apples there were meant for me.
 I later learned, a woman, a sweetheart
 Had been seen there.   Now, we'd passionately   1425.
Spent years together.   Then we grew apart.
 I broke the affair off, and closed the door
 Behind me, but she used her magic art
To hex me, when her charms lured me no more.

She put those apples, smeared with poison, near   1430.
The spring I knew, to settle her old score.
I would have eaten them all, but by sheer
　　Good luck I was spared a horrible fate.
　　I ask you now to give this fellow here
Water from this spring, if it's not too late   1435.
　　For him to be cured of his agony,
　　So he can join me and recuperate
Here in the woods, living in sanctity."
　　The chieftains did so, and the man's right mind
　　Returned on drinking the spring flowing free.   1440.
He knew his friends, and rejoined humankind.

38.

　　Then Merlin said, "My friend, you must devote
　　Yourself to God's holy work, now you find
Yourself healed of the malady that smote
　　You, left you living like a witless beast.   1445.
　　But now that you're well, don't flee this remote
Seclusion just because your madness ceased.
　　Stay here with me.　A rustic recompense
　　Will soothe you.　As a sort of woodland priest.
You'll be my companion in every sense.   1450.
　　As long as we live, the other will be near."
　　The man, Maeldinus, said, "I'll not go hence,
O reverend father, but will with good cheer
　　Live with you in the woods, and dedicate
　　My thoughts to God above, and my sins here,   1455.
You as my doctor, I will expiate."
　　"Then I'll increase your number here to three,"
　　Taliesin said, "For I long to abate
My worldly business and its vanity,
　　And come back to myself, you as my guide.   1460.
　　But you, chieftains, be off!　Your soldierly
Concerns of power should be set aside

In this forest retreat.   Off with you, now."
39.
The chieftains leave, and the three men abide.
Ganeida makes a fourth.   Upon her brow   1465.
   Her late husband's crown had rested.   As queen
   She ruled her country well, all would avow.
But she preferred her brother's forest scene,
   Where she could let her spirit soar on high,
   See what's to come, explain what omens mean.   1470.
And thus it was one day she cast her eye
   Over her brother's hall and buildings, then
   With misgivings, began to prophesy.
40.
"Oxford overrun with helmeted men
   I see, who with the council will conspire   1475.
   To shackle mitred priests inside some den.
The shepherd's tower, built high, that all admire
   Will be pointlessly unlocked, to its cost.
   I see grim armies spread through Lincolnshire,
And two closed in.   The second one has crossed   1480.
   Over to bring barbarians to the walls
   And conquer the fierce band, their leader lost.
How great a crime it is when the sun falls
   A captive to the stars, their anchor true!
   I see two moons over Winchester's halls,   1485.
And acting with great ferocity.   Two
   Lions, one looking at two men, its twin
   At two, war preparations are in view.
Others rise up, and with the battle's din
   Oppose a fourth, though   none of them prevail,   1490.
   For his shield holds fast, and his weapons win
Over his triple enemies.   He'll trail
   Two of them through the north's freezing terrain.
   He'll pardon the third, which will all entail

Chaotic movement of the starry train.   1495.
   The Breton boar, an ancient oak his guard
   With swords whirling behind, two moons will gain.
I see wild beasts in combat long and hard
   With two stars.   Men of Gwent near Urien hill
   Gathered with Deireans when King Cohel warred.   1500.
The sweat that pours, the blood that has to spill
   While wounds are given to the foreign foe!
   The star that crashes into star goes still,
Taking its light away, light renewed, though.
   Alas!   How cruelly a famine hits   1505.
   And drains the people's strength, and brings them woe!
It starts in Wales, and spreads until it sits
   Across the land, forcing tribes to migrate.
   Calves scatter; the dearth no longer permits
Good Scotch cows to survive the general fate.   1510.
   Normans, go home!   Your never-ending fight
   Rages through our land.   You exterminate
The livestock and the crops, whose bounty feeds
   The folk, that you brutally confiscate!
   Christ!   Save your people from the foul misdeeds   1515.
Of the lions!   Give us tranquility!"
40.
Her comrades were amazed to find the seeds
   Of prophecy sprout so.   Approvingly
Her brother came, glad that she'd said her say.
   "Sister, will you reveal what is to be?   1520.
   Has the spirit, that took my gift away,
Given it to you?   Then speak out forcefully,
And may your gift never lead you astray."

A Close Translation of the *Vita Merlini*

"My voice stuck in my throats" is the literal translation of *vox faucibus haesit*. For two millennia, readers and translators of the *Aeneid* have recognized this Virgilian peculiarity, plural for singular, as the poet's way of making his lines fit the meter. Recognized, I should say, and overlooked, since this bit of poetic license is a small price to pay for the magnificence of the poem.

The *Vita Merlini* poet avails himself of the same device, but goes Virgil one better: his poetic license also involves verb tenses. If the passage is rolling along in the present tense, and a certain verb doesn't fit, why then he simply switches to the future tense. Previous translators of the *VM* have ignored this peculiarity of the *VM* poet, and wisely so, since rendering it literally would confuse the reader as much as Virgil's "voice stuck in my throats." The following translation stops short of being this sort of micro-translation necessary for a micro-reading of the poem, but its literalness will aid the reader who wants to get as close to *VM* as possible, short of reading it in Latin. This translation is as closely line-for-line as possible, so the reader's indulgence is asked in the matter of word order.

Vita Merlini	Merlin's Life
Fatidici Vatis rabiem, *musamque iocosam*	A prophet-bard gone mad, the laughing muse
Merlini cantare paro. tu *corrige carmen*	Of Merlin I'm preparing to sing. Correct the song, you,
Gloria pontificum calamos *moderando roberte*	Robert, glory of the priesthood, by guiding my pen,

scimus enim quis te perfudit *nectare sacro*		For we know what has anointed you with its holy nectar:
Philosophia suo fecitque per *omnia doctum*	5.	Philosophy, and it has made you learnèd throughout all [fields],
Ut documenta dares dux et *preceptor in orbe.*		So that you might give an example, being leader and teacher in the world.
Ergo meis ceptis faueas *vatemque tueri*		Therefore, may you sponsor what I have begun and protect the poet
Auspicio meliore velis quam *fecerit alter*		With better offices, if you please, than the other would have done,
Cui modo succedis merito *promotus honori.*		He whom you are succeeding because of merit, promoted to the honor.
Sic etenim mores sic vita *probata genusque*	10.	Yea, indeed [your] behavior, yea, your upright life and family
Utilitasque loci clerus *populusque petebant.*		And efficiency of your office, the clergy and laity [all] sought [it].
Unde modo felix lincolnia *fertur ad astra.*		Hence, happy Lincoln is carried to the stars.
Ergo te cuperem complecti *carmine digno,*		Therefore I would desire you to be surrounded by a song worthy [of you],
Set non sufficio; licet Orpheus *et Camerinus*		But I am not equal to the task; it would be fitting that Orpheus and Camerinus
Et Macer et Marsus magnique *Rabirius oris*	15.	And Macer and Marsus and Rabirius of the great mouth,

Ore meo canerent musis	In my mouth all should sing,
comitantibus omnes.	with the muses joining in.
At vos, consuete mecum	But you, accustomed to sing
cantare, camene,	with me, muses,
Propositum cantemus opus	Let us sing the proposed work
cytharamque sonate.	and sound ye the lyre.

*   *   *

Ergo peragratis sub multis		Therefore, having passed many
regibus annis		years under many kings,
Clarus habebatur merlinus in	20.	British Merlin was held famous
orbe britannus		in the world.
Rex erat et vates demetarum		He was king and bard of the
que superbis		South Welsh, and to the proud
Jura dabat populis ducibusque		People he gave edicts, and to
futura canebat.		the leaders he chanted the
		future.

*   *   *

Contigit interea plures		Meanwhile it came about that
certamen habere		several [chieftains] had a
		dispute
Inter se regni proceres		Among themselves, chieftains
belloque feroci		of the realm, and with a savage
		war
Insontes populos devastavisse	25.	Devastated the innocent
per urbes.		citizenry throughout the cities,
Dux venedotorum peredurus		The leader of the North Welsh,
bella gerebat		Peredur, was waging war
Contra guennoloum scocie qui		Against Gwentholy, who ruled
regna regebat.		the realms of Scotland.

Jamque dies aderat bello
prefixa, ducesque

And now the prearranged day
for war had arrived, and the
leaders

Astabant campo
decertabantque caterve

Stood forth in the field and
their bands fought it out,

Amborum pariter miseranda
cede ruentes.

30. Men of both sides falling
equally in pitiable slaughter.

Venerat ad bellum Merlinus
cum Pereduro

Merlin had come to the war on
Peredur's side,

Rex quoque cambrorum
rodarcus sevvus uterque.

Also the king of the Welsh,
Rhydderch; both men were
fierce.

Cedunt obstantes invisis
ensibus hostes,

They killed the opposing
foemen with their dread swords,

Tresque ducis fratres fratrem
per bella secuti

As did three brothers of the
leader who had followed their
brother through the wars,

Usque rebellantes cedunt
perimunt que phalanges.

35. Even slaying rebels and
shattering their ranks.

Inde per infestas cum tali
munere turmas

Off they went, through the
hostile squadrons, so gung-ho,

Acriter irruerant.   subito
cecidere perempti.

Sharply they rushed in.
Suddenly they fell, snatched
away.

Hoc viso merline doles
tristesque per agmen

When this was seen, O Merlin,
you are afflicted and are sad,
and throughout the column

Commisces planctus tale
quoque voce remugis

You mingle sad laments and
also with such a voice you
howl back,

Ergone sic potuit sors
importuna nocere

40. "Therefore was perverse fate
able to do harm,

Ut michi surriperet tantos talesque sodales	So that it might take away from me so many and such comrades,
Quos modo tot reges tot regna remota timebant?	Those whom just now so many kings and kingdoms feared?
O dubios hominum casus mortemque propinquam	O uncertain events of men, and death ever near at hand,
Que penes est illos semper stimuloque latenti	Which are in its [fate's] power, and with its hidden sting
percutit et miseram pellit de corpore vitam.	45. It smites them and drives the pitiable life from the body.
O juvenile decus quis nunc astabit in armis	O youthful elite, who now will stand in arms,
Nunc michi pone latus mecumque repellet euntes	Now a rank behind me, and with me will repel the leaders coming
In mea dampna duces incumbentesque catervas?	To do me ill, and their crushing throngs?
Audaces iuvenes vobis audacia vestra	Bold youths, your boldness
Eripuit dulces annos dulcemque iuuentam.	50. Has snatched away your sweet years and sweet youth!
Qui modo per cuneos discurrebatis in armis	You who would just rush off in arms through the wedge
Obstantes que viros prosternebatis ubique	And would anywhere lay low the men in your path
Nunc pulsatis humum rubeoque cruore rubetis	Now you hit the ground and with your red gore redden it."
Sic inter turmas lacrimis plangebat abortis	Thus among the squadrons he wept with tears—
Deflebatque viros nec cessant prelia dira	55. And he bewept the men, but the fierce battle did not stop.

Concurrunt acies sternuntur ab hostibus hostes.	The ranks rushed together, and enemies were slain by enemies.
Sanguis ubique fluit plurimi moriuntur utrinque	Blood flowed everywhere and many died on both sides,
At tandem britones revocatis undique turmis	But finally the Britons, having rallied their squadrons from all around,
Conveniunt pariter pariterque per arma ruentes	They assemble together and together rushing through the weapons
Invadunt scotos prosternunt vulnera dantes	60. They grapple with the Scots, lay them low, giving wounds,
Nec requieverunt donec sua terga dederunt	Nor do they rest until [their foes] show their backs,
Hostiles turme per devia diffugientes.	The enemy squadrons scattering through [forest] paths.

*   *   *

Evocat e bello socios merlinus et illis	Merlin calls his companions from the war and them
Precipit in varia fratres sepelire capella	He enjoins to bury his brothers in a richly-colored shrine,
Deplangitque viros nec cessat fundere fletus	65. And he bewails the men, nor does he cease to pour out his wailings,
Pulveribus crines sparsit vestesque rescidit	And he bestrewed his hair with dust and tore his clothes to tatters,
Et prostratus humi nunc hac illacque volutat.	And rolled around on the ground, now this way, now that.

Solatur Peredurus eum proceresque ducesque		Peredur comforted him, and the chiefs and the leaders;
Nec vult solari nec verba precantia ferre		Neither would he be consoled nor endure supplicating words.
Jam tribus emensis defleverat ille diebus	70.	Already he had wept for the space of three days
Respuerat que cibos tantus dolor usserat illum		And had rejected food, such agony had consumed him,
Inde novas furias cum tot tantisque querelis.		From whence [he had] new manias with such and so many conflicts
Aera complesset. cepit furtimque recedit		He had filled the air. He set out secretly and went back
Et fugit ad silvas nec vult fugiendo videri		And fled to the woods, nor did he wish to be seen fleeing
Ingrediturque nemus gaudetque latere sub ornis	75.	And he stepped into a grove and rejoiced to hide under the flowering ash,
Miraturque feras pascentes gramina saltus		And he admired the wild animals grazing [on] the grasses of the meadows.
Nunc has insequitur nunc cursu preterit illas.		Now he follows them, now he outstrips them as he runs.
Utitur herbarum radicibus utitur herbis		He lived on the roots of plants, he lived on the plants,
Utitur arboreo fructu morisque rubeti		He lived on arboreal fruits and the brambles' blackberries.
Fit silvester homo quasi silvis deditus esset	80.	He became a forest man, as if he had been dedicated to the woods,
Inde per estatem totam nullique repertus		Whence throughout the whole summer and found by no one

Oblitusque sui cognatorumque
suorum

And forgotten by his own and
by his own kinsmen,

Delituit silvis obductus more
ferino.

He went into hiding in the
woods, secluded in the way
that wild animals are.

*   *   *

At cum venit yems herbasque
tulisset et omnes

But when winter came and had
taken away the plants and all

Arboreos fructus nec quo
frueretur haberet

85.   Arboreal fruit, nor did he have
anything to enjoy,

Diffudit tales miseranda voce
querelas

With pitiable voice he
broadcast such complaints:

Celi Christe deus quid agam,
qua parte morari

"O Christ, God of heaven, what
will I do?   In what part of the
world

Terrarum potero cum nil quo
vescar adesse.

Can I dwell, when there is
nothing which I can eat?

Inspicio nec gramen humi nec
in arbore glandes

I see neither grass on the
ground nor acorns on the tree.

Tres quater et iuges septene
poma ferentes

90.   Thrice four and, you may add,
seven apple-bearing

Hic steterant mali nunc non
stant ergo quis illas

Apple trees stood here, now
they do not stand. Therefore,
who has snatched them

Quis michi surripuit, quo
devenere repente?

Away from me, who?   Where
have they suddenly gone off to?

Nunc illas video nec non.   *sic*
fata repugnant

Now I see them, now I don't.
Thus the fates hinder

Sic quoque concordant cum
dant prohibentque videre

And at the same time help, since
they grant and forbid [me] to see.

Deficiunt nunc poma michi nunc cetera queque	95.	Apples are now lacking to me, now the rest as well.
Stat sine fronde nemus sine fructu plector utroque		The grove stands without foliage, without fruit. I am irritated on both sides,
Cum neque fronde tegi valeo neque fructibus uti		When neither can I be covered by foliage, nor live on fruit.
Singula bruma tulit pluviisque cadentibus auster		The winter has taken every single thing away, and the south wind with its falling rains.
Invenio si forte napes tellure sub ima		If I chance across some wild turnips in the deep earth,
Concurrunt avideque sues aprique voraces	100.	The hungry sows and ravenous boars rush up
Eripiuntque napes michi quas de cespite vello.		And snatch away the wild turnips that I claw from the sod.
Tu lupe care comes nimorum qui devia mecum		You, dear wolf, companion of the groves, who with me
Et saltus peragrare soles vix preteris arva		Are accustomed to traversing the woodland paths and meadows, scarcely do you cross the field,
Et te dura fames et me languere coegit.		And hard hunger forces you and me to languish.
Tu prior has silvas coluisti te prior etas	105.	You inhabited these woods first; you has age first
Protulit in canos nec habes nec scis quid in ore		Brought white hair, nor do you have nor do you know what [prey] in your mouth
proicias quod miror ego cum saltus habundet		You might fling down, which surprises me, since the meadow abounds

Tot capreis aliisque feris quas prendere posses.	With so many goats and other wild animals which you could catch.
Forsitan ipsa tibi tua detestanda senectus	Perhaps that same old age of yours, to be detested,
Eripuit nervos cursumque negavit habendum	110. Has taken away your muscles and denied your participating in the chase.
Quod solum superest comples ululatibus auras	The only thing left is for you to fill the air with howls,
Ac resupinus humi consumptos deicis artus	And lying on the ground you stretch out your used-up joints."

*   *   *

Hec inter frutices coriletaque densa canebat	This he chanted among the undergrowth and the hazel thickets,
Cum sonus adquemdam pervenit pretereuntem	When the sound reached a certain passer-by,
Qui direxit iter quo sermo loquentis in auras	115. Who wended his way to where the speech of the speaker into the air
Exierat reperitque locum reperitque loquentem.	Had gone out, and he found the place and found the speaker.
Quo viso merlinus abit sequiturque viator	Merlin, when he sees him, goes off, and the traveler follows,
Nec retinere virum potuit sic diffugientem	But cannot catch the man fleeing thus.
Inde viator iter repetit quo ceperat ire	Thence the traveler resumes the way where he had started from,

Propositumque tenet casu *commotus euntis.*	120. And held to his plan, moved by the fate of the man who had run off.
Ecce viatori venit obvius alter ab aula	Lo, on the way another man came to the traveler, from the court
Rodarchi regis cumbrorum qui Ganiedam	Of Rhydderch the king of the Welsh who had taken Ganeida
Duxerat uxorem formosa coniuge felix.	To be his bride, and was happy with his beautiful spouse.
Merlini soror ista fuit casumque dolebat	She was Merlin's sister, and she was pained by the fate
Fratris et ad silvas et ad arva remota clientes	125. Of her brother, and off to the forests and faraway fields her vassals
Miserat ut fratrem revocarent. ex quibus unus	She had sent, that they might call her brother back. One of these
Obvius huic ibat set et hic sibi protinus ergo	Was the one who encountered the traveler; but going right up to him
Convenere simul commiscent mutua verba.	They met and exchanged words between them.
At qui missus erat Merlinum querere querit	But he who had been sent to seek Merlin inquired
Si vidisset eum silvis aut saltibus. alter	130. If he had seen him in the woods or meadows. The other
Ille virum talem se conspexisse fatetur	Stated that he had seen such a man
Inter dumosos saltus nemoris calidonis	Among the thorny meadows of the Forest of Caledon,

Dumque loqui vellet secum *secumque sedere*	And while he had wanted to speak to him and sit with him,
Diffugisse virum celeri per *robora cursu.*	The man had taken off through the oaks with swift flight.
Hec ait; alter abit silvasque *subintrat et imas*	135. This he said; the other went and entered into the woods, and the deep
Scrutatur valles montes quoque *preterit altos.*	Valleys he searched, and also went over the high mountains.
Querit ubique virum gradiens *per opaca locorum.*	He sought the man everywhere, stepping through the darkness of places.

*   *   *

Fons erat in summo cuiusdam *vertice montis*	There was a fountain on the height of a certain mountain
Undique precinctus corulis *densaque frutectis.*	Surrounded on all sides by hazels and tightly ringed with thickets.
Illic Merlinus consederat inde *per omnes*	140. Here Merlin sat, and from here throughout all
Spectabat silvas cursusque *iocosque ferarum.*	The forests he gazed, and [saw] the running and sporting of the animals.
Nuntius hunc scandit tacitoque *per ardua gressu*	The messenger climbed to that place, up the steep slopes, with silent step,
Incedit querendo virum tum *denique fontem*	He got close, seeking the man, then at last the spring
Merlinumque videt super *herbas pone sedentem*	And Merlin he saw sitting back on the plants

Dicentemque suas tali sermone querelas	145.	Speaking out his griefs with talk like this:
O qui cuncta regis, quid est cur contigit ut non		"O you who rule all, what is it, why did it happen so that not
Tempora sint eadem numeris distincta quaternis?		The same are the seasons, distinct in [their] fourfold numbers?
Nunc ver iure suo flores frondesque ministrat		Now spring by its command supplies flowers and leaves,
Dat fruges estas autumpnus micia poma		Summer gives fruits, autumn ripe apples,
Consequitur glacialis yemps et cetera queque	150.	Icy winter follows, and the the rest, all of it,
Devorat et vastat pluviasque nivesque reportat		It devours and ruins; and it brings back rain and snow,
Singula queque suis arcet leditque procellis		And every single thing, all of it, it keeps away and harms with its storms.
Nec permittit humum varios producere flores		Nor does it permit the soil to produce multicolored flowers
Aut quercus glandes aut malos punica mala		Or the oaks acorns or the apple trees pomegranites.
O utinam non esset hiems aut cana pruina	155.	Oh, would that there were no winter or white frost,
Ver foret aut estas cuculusque canendo rediret		That it were spring or summer and the cuckoo had returned with [its] singing,
Et Philomena pio que tristia pectora cantu		And the nightingale, who with its trusty song soothes sad hearts,
Mitigat et turtur conservans federa casta		And the turtledove preserving chaste bonds

Frondibus inque novis	And in new foliage birds with
concordi voce volucres	harmonious voices
Cantarent alieque me	160 Would sing and comfort me
modulando foverent	with warbling
Dum nova flore novo tellus	While the new earth with new
spiraret odorem	flower exhales a scent
Gramine sub viridi levi quoque	Under the smooth green grass,
murmure fontes	also fountains with murmuring
Diffluerent iuxtaque daret sub	Would flow and next to them a
fronde columba	dove beneath the foliage would give
Sompniferos gemitus	Sleep-bringing moans and
irritaretque soporem	would urge sleep!"

*   *   *

Nuntius audierat vatem	165. The herald heard the bard and
rupitque querelas	interrupted his lament
Cum modulis cithare quam	With the tones of a lute which
secum gesserat ultro	he had carried around with him
Ut sic deciperet demulceretque	That he might deceive and
furentem	quieten the maniac.
Ergo movens querulas digitis	Therefore touching the
et in ordine cordas	plaintive strings with his fingers deliberately,
Talia pone latens dimissa voce	Hiding behind, with a subdued
canebat	voice he sang thus:
O diros gemitus lugubris	170. "Oh, the desperate groans of
Guendoloene	sorrowful Gwendolyn!
O miseras lacrimas lacrimantis	Oh, the pitiful tears of tearful
Guendoloene	Gwendolyn!

Me miseret misere morientis Guendoloene	I pity the pitiful, dying Gwendolyn!
Non erat in waliis mulier formosior illa	There was no more beautiful woman in Wales than she.
Vincebat candore deas foliumque ligustri	For whiteness she would defeat the goddesses and the petal of the white flower
Vernantesque rosas et olentia lilia prati.	175. And the blossoming roses and the fragrant lilies of the meadow.
Gloria vernalis sola radiebat in illa	Spring glory glowed in her alone,
Sidereumque decus geminis gestabat ocellis	And starry ornament dwelt in her twin eyes,
Insignesque comas auri fulgore nitentes	And famous hair shining with the gleam of gold —
Hoc totum periit periit decor omnis in illa	All this she has lost, and lost all the beauty that was in her.
Et color et facies nivee quoque gloria carnis	180. Both the color and the face, also the glory of her snow-white flesh.
Non est quod fuerat multis meroribus acta	It is not what it was, driven by many griefs,
Nescit enim quo dux abiit vita ne fruatur	For she knows not where the leader has gone, nor whether he enjoys life
An sit defunctus languet miserabilis inde	Or is dead; pitiable, she languishes therefore,
Totaque deperiit longo liquefacta dolore	And she has lost everything, dissolved in lingering pain.
Collacrimatur ei paribus ganieda querelis	185. With lamentations equal to her, Ganieda weeps,

Amissumque dolet sine consolamine fratrem	And aches for her lost brother unconsolably.
Hec fratrem flet et illa virum communiter ambe	She bewails her brother and the other her husband; together both
Fletibus incumbunt et tristia tempora ducunt	They spend their time in weeping, and pass the time sadly.
Non cibus ullus eis nec sompnus nocte vagantes	There is no food at all for them, nor sleep at night, wandering as they are,
Sub virgulta fovet tantus dolor arcet utramque	190. Comforts [them] under the underbrush; such pain grips them both.
Non secus indoluit sidonia dido solutis	In the same way did Sidonian Dido suffer from the casting-off
Classibus enee tunc cum properaret abire	Fleet of Aeneas, then when he was hurrying to depart;
Cum non demophon per tempora pacta rediret	When Demophoon did not return at the appointed time,
Taliter ingemuit flevitque miserrima phillis	Thus groaned and wept poor Phyllis;
Briseis absentem sic deploravit achillem	195. Briseis thus bewailed the absent Achilles.
Sic soror et coniux collamentantur et ardent	Thus the sister and the wife lament and burn
Funditus internis cruciatibus usque dolendo	Utterly with inner torments, with sorrow without ceasing."

*   *   *

In gravibus querulis dicebat talia cantans		In heavy laments he spoke, singing such things,
Nuntius et modulo vatis demulserat aures		Did the herald, and with playing softens the ears of the bard,
Micior ut fleret congauderetque canenti	200.	So that, more tender, he might weep and rejoice with the singer.
Ocius assurgit vates iunenemque iocosis		Quite soon, the bard arises and the youth with merry
Affatur verbis iterumque movere precatur		Words addresses and asks that again he may touch
Cum digitis cordas elegosque sonare priores		The strings with his fingers and to play the earlier love songs.
Admovet ille lire digitos iussumque reformat		The other moved his fingers to the lyre and again played the requested
Carmen item cogitque virum modulando furorem	205.	Song, the same one, and with the playing drove the man
Ponere paulatim cithare dulcedine captum		To gradually put away his madness, taken by the sweetness of the lute.
Fit memor ergo sui recolitque quod esse solebat		A memory, therefore, came back to him, and he remembered what he used to be.
Merlinus furiasque suas miratur et odit		Merlin was amazed at his madness and hated it.
Pristina mens rediit rediit quoque sensus in illo		His mind of the old days returned, sense returned also to him,
Et gemit ad nomen motus pietate sororis	210.	And he groaned, moved by family feeling at the name of his sister

Uxorisque simul mentis ratione recepta	And of his wife, at the moment reason returned to his mind.
Conducique petit rodarchi regis ad aulam	And he sought to be led to the palace of King Rhydderch.
Paruit alter ei silvasque subinde relinqunt	The other deferred to him, and they left the woods forthwith,
Et veniunt pariter letantes regis in urbem	And they came equally rejoicing into the city of the king.

*   *   *

Ergo fratre suo gaudet regina recepto	215.	Therefore the queen rejoiced to accept her brother back,
Proque sui reditu fit coniunx leta mariti		And the wife was happy at the return of her husband.
Oscula certatim geminant et brachia circum		Vying with each other, they shower him with kisses, and their arms
Colla viri flectunt tanta pietate moventur		They wrap around the man's neck; they are moved by such family feeling.
Rex quoque quo decuit reducem suscepit honore		The king also received the prodigal as befitted his rank,
Totaque turba domus proceres letantur in urbe	220.	And the whole crowd of chiefs of the [royal] house rejoiced in the city.
At post quam tantas hominum merlinus adesse		But afterward Merlin saw that there were so many
Inspexit turmas nec eas perferre valeret		Swarms of people, and he was not strong enough to bear it;
Cepit enim furias iterumque furore repletus		For he started his mania, and again filled with rage

Ad nemus ire cupit furtimque	He desired to go to the woods
recedere querit	and secretly wanted to go back
Tunc precepit eum posito 225.	Then Rhydderch forestalled
custode teneri	him by posting a guard to hold him,
Rodarchus cithara que suos	And with a lute to soften his
mulcere furores	rages,
Astabatque dolens verbisque	And he stood there grieving
precantibus illum	with words and supplications,
Orabat ratione frui secumque	Beseeching him to avail
manere	himself of reason, and stay with him
Nec captare nemus nec vivere	And not seek the grove, nor
more ferino	live like a wild animal,
Velle sub arboribus dum regia 230.	Wish to be beneath the trees
sceptra tenere	when he could have
Posset et in populos ius	A royal sceptre and uphold the
exercere feroces	law over a fractious people.
Hinc promittit ei se plurima	Then he promised him many
dona daturum	gifts that would be given
Afferique iubet vestes	And he ordered garments to be
volucresque canesque	brought, and birds and dogs,
Quadrupedesque citos aurum	And swift quadrupeds, gold
gemmasque micantes	and sparkling jewels,
Pocula que sculpsit guielandus 235.	And cups which Wieland had
in urbe sigeni	sculpted in the city of Caernavon.
Singula pretendit vati	Every single thing Rhydderch
rodarchus et offert	held out to the bard, and offered
Et monet ut maneat secum	And admonished that he might
silvas que relinquet	stay with him and that he might leave the woods behind.

Talia respondens spernebat munera vates	Answering, thus the bard rejected the gifts:

*   *   *

Ista duces habeant sua quos confundit egestas	"Let the leaders have these whom their poverty embarrasses,
Nec sunt contenti modico set maxima captant	240. And are not satisfied with a moderate amount, but [whom] overabundance captivates.
Hiis nemus et patulas calidonis prefero quercus	Rather than these I prefer the grove and spreading oaks of Caledon
Et montes celsos subtus virentia prata	And high mountains, beneath them verdant meadows.
Illa michi non ista placent tu talia tecum	Those [gifts], not these please [me]; such things you,
rex rodarche feras mea me calidonis habebit	King Rhydderch. should take with you; my Caledonian
Silva ferax nucibus quam cunctis prefero rebus	Wood will have me, rich as it is in nuts; I prefer [it] to all [these] things."

*   *   *

Denique cum nullo potuisset munere tristem	246. Finally, when he could by no gift hold back
Rex retinere virum forti vincire cathena	The sad man, the king had him bound with a strong
Iussit ne peterit nemorum deserta solutus	Chain, so that he might not escape and seek the forest wilds.

Ergo cum sensit circum se vincula vates		Therefore, when the bard felt the chains around him
Nec liber poterat silvas calidones adire	250.	And that he would not be able to go to the Caledonian forest,
Protinus indoluit tristis que tacens que remansit		Right away he grieved, and sad and silent he remained,
Leticiamque suis subtraxit uultibus omnem		And took all joy from his face
Ut non proferret verbum risumque moveret		So that he might not speak a word or laugh.
Interea visura ducem regina per aulam		Meanwhile the queen was going through the palace to see her lord,
Ibat et ut decuit rex applaudebat eunti	255.	And he, as befitted a king, greeted her as she came,
Per que manum suscepit eam iussitque sedere		And took her by the hand, and bade her sit,
Et dabat amplexus et ad oscula labra premebat		And embraced her, and pressed her lips in a kiss,
Convertensque suos in eam per talia vultus		And, turning his face toward her while doing this,
Vidit in illius folium pendere capellis		He saw a leaf hanging in her hair.
Ergo suos digitos admovit et abstrait illud	260.	Therefore he moved his fingers and took it away.
Et proiecit hume letus que iocatur amanti		And tossed it on the ground, and happily joked with his wife.
Flexit ad hoc oculos vates risumque resoluit		The bard turned his eyes to this and let out a laugh.
Astantes que viros fecit convertere vultus		This made the men standing around turn their heads,

In se mirantes quoniam ridere negarat	Looking at each other, because he had refused to laugh.
Rex quoque miratur percunctatur que furente	265. The king, too, was amazed, and pressed the madman
Tam subito facti causas edicere risus	To say as soon as possible the causes of the laugh he had uttered,
Adiecitque suis donaria plurima verbis	And added many gifts to his words.
Ille tacet differtque suos exponere risus	The other was silent, and declined to explain his laughter.
At magis atque magis precio precibus que movere	But to move more and more by gift and entreaties
Instabat rodarchus eum tum denique vates	270. Rhydderch persists, and then him the bard,
Indignatus ei pro munere talia fatur	Irate, addressed these [words] to him for the gift:

*   *   *

Munus avarus amat cupidus que laborat habere	"The avaricious man loves a gift, and the covetous man works to works to have [one].
Hii faciles animos flectunt quocunque iubentur	These easily bend their spirits wherever they are ordered.
Munere corrupti quod habent non sufficit illis	Corrupted by the gift, what they have is not enough for them;
At michi sufficiunt glandes calidonis amene	275. But the acorns of pleasant Caledon are enough,
Et nitidi fontes per olentia prata fluentes	And the sparkling springs flowing through fragrant meadows.

Munere non capior sua munera tollat avarus	I am not taken by a gift; let the greedy man bear gifts away,
Et nisi libertas detur repetamque virentes	And unless freedom is given, and I may again seek the green
Siluarum valles risus aperire negabo	Valleys of the forests, I will refuse to explain the laughter."
Ergo cum nullo potuisset munere vatem	280. Therefore, when by no gift could Rhydderch
Flectere rodarchus nec cur risisset haberet	Sway the bard, nor have [the reason] why he had laughed,
Confestim sua vincla viro dissoluere iussit	Forthwith he ordered that his chains be slipped off the man
Dat que potestatem nemorum deserta petendi	And he gave the power of seeking the solitudes of the groves.
Ut velit optatam risus expromere causam	How he wishes to articulate the desired cause of the laughter!

*   *   *

Tunc merlinus ait gaudens quia possit abire	285. Then Merlin said, rejoicing because he was able to go,
Iccirco risi quoniam Rodarche fuisti	"Because of that I laughed, O Rhydderch, because you were
Facto culpandus simul et laudandus eodem	By that same act to be blamed and at the same time to be praised,
Dum traheres folium modo quod regina capillis	While you just now took away the leaf which the queen in her hair
Nescia gestabat fieres que fidelior illi	Unknowingly carried, you were more faithful to her

Quam fuit illa tibi quando virgulta subivit	290. Than she was to you; when she went under the bushes
Quo suus occurrit secum que coivit adulter	Where her lover ran and went with her
Dumque supina foret sparsis in crinibus hesit	And while she was on her back, there stuck in her unbound hair
Forte iacens folium quod nescius eripuisti	The leaf by chance lying there, which you unknowingly took away."
Ergo super tali rodarchus crimine tristis	Therefore Rhydderch became sad concerning this misdeed
Fit subito vultum que suum divertit ab illa	295. Immediately, and turned his face from her
Dampnabatque diem que se coniunxerat illi	And cursed the day which he had married her
Mota set illa nichil vultu ridente pudorem	But she, nothing moved, with a laughing face her shame
Celat et alloquitur tali sermone maritum	She hides, and addresses her husband with such words:
Cur tristaris amans cur sic irasceris ab re	299. "Why are you saddened, beloved? Why are you thus angry from the thing
Me que nec ex merito dampnas credisque furenti	And me you condemn not from [my] deserts, and you believe a madman
Qui ratione carens miscet mendacia veris	Who, lacking reason, mixes lies with the truth.
Multociens qui credit ei fit stulcior illo	Many times does the man who believes in him become more foolish than he.
Excipe nunc igitur ne sim decepta probabo	Pay attention, now, therefore; unless I am mistaken, I will prove

Quod sit delirus quod non sit vera locutus	How he is delusional, how he does not speak the truth."

*   *   *

Ut plures alii fuerat puer unus in aula	305.	There was a boy in the palace, as were many others;
Hunc cum prospiceret convoluit protinus artem		When she had seen him, right away she came up with a trick,
Ingeniosa novam qua vult convincere fratrem		Cleverly, a novel one, by which she wishes to ensnare her brother.
Inde venire iubet puerum fratremque precatur		Thence she orders the boy to come, and implores her brother
Qua moriturus erit pueri predicere morte[m]		To predict by what death the boy was to die.
Ergo frater ei soror o carissima dixit	310.	Therefore the brother said to her, "O sister dearest,
Hic morietur homo de celsa rupe ruendo		He will die an adult, falling headlong from a high cliff."
Illa sub hec ridens puero precepit abire		She, smiling at this, tells the boy to go,
Et quibus indutus fuerat deponere vestes		And to take off whatever clothes he was wearing,
Et vestire novas longos que recidere crines		And put new ones on, and cut back his long locks.
Sic que redire iubet ut eis appareat alter	315.	And she orders it thus so that he might appear different to them.
Paruit ergo puer rediit nam talis ad illos		Therefore the boy obeyed, for he returned thus to them
Qualis erat iussus mutata veste redire		As he had been ordered, to return with garments changed.

Mox iterum fratrem regina precatur et infit	Right away, again the queen besought ber brother, and she began to speak.
Que mors huius erit narra dilecte sorori	320. "Tell your dear sister what the death of this one will be."
Tunc merlinus ait puer hic cum venerit etas	Then Merlin said, "This boy, when the age shall come,
Mente vagans forti succumbet in arbore morti	Wandering in his mind, will succumb to a violent death in a tree."
Dixerat illa suum sic est affata maritum	She had spoken thus to her husband,
Siccine te potuit falsus pervertere vates	"Is it thus that the false bard was able to mislead you,
Ut crimen tantum me commisisse putares	That you would think that I had committed such a misdeed?
Ac si scire velis qua sit ratione locutus	325. And if you want to know in what state of mind he spoke
Hoc nunc de puero censebis ficta fuisse	About this boy, you will consider that it was made up,
Que de me dixit dum silvas possit adire	What he said about me while he could go to the forest.
Absit ut hoc faciam castum servabo cubile	Away with the idea that I should do this! I will keep our bed chaste,
Casta que semper ero dum flabit spiritus in me	And I will be chaste while the breath of life is in me.
Illum convici pueri de morte rogatum	330. I fooled him when he was asked about the death of the boy,
Nunc quoque convincam tu sedulus arbiter esto	Now I will prove it. You, observant, be the judge,

Hec ait et tacite puerum secedere iussit	This she said, and quietly ordered the boy to go away,
Vesteque feminea vestire sic que redire	To dress himself in women's dress, and thus return.
Mox puer abcessit iussumque subinde peregit	Right away the boy left and promptly did as he was told.
Et sub feminea rediit quasi femina veste	335. And like a woman under womanly clothes returned
Et stetit ante virum cui sic regina iocando	And stood before the man, to whom the queen in jest [said]
Eya frater ait dic mortem virginis huius	"Hey, brother," she said, "Say the death of this girl."
Hec virgo nec ne dixit morietur in ampne	"This person, whether a girl or not, will die in a river."
Frater ei movit que sua ratione cachinnum	Her brother provoked her laughter by his reasoning.
Regi Rodarcho quoniam de morte rogatus	340. Because to King Rhydderch, asked about the death
Unius pueri tres dixerat esse futuras	Of one boy, he had said that there would be three futures.
Ergo putabat eum de coniuge falsa locutum	Therefore he thought that he had spoken falsely concerning his false wife,
Nec credebat ei set contristatur et odit	Nor did he believe him, but was penitent and hated
Quod sibi crediderat quod condempnarat amantem	Because he had believed him, because he had condemned his beloved.
Id regina videns veniam dat et oscula iungit	345. Seeing this, the queen was kind and kissed him
Et blanditur ei letum quoque reddidit illum	And soothed him, and also made him happy again.

*   *   *

Cogitat interea silvas Merlinus
adire

Meanwhile Merlin is considering
going to the woods,

Egressusque domum portas
aperire iubebat

And leaving home; he ordered
the gates to open.

Set soror obstabat lacrimisque
rogabat abortis

But his sister stood in his way
with gushing tears and asked

Ut secum remaneret adhuc
tollat que furorem

350. That he remain with her still,
and that he stop his madness.

Improbus ille suis non vult
desistere ceptis

He, petulant, did not wish to
leave off what he had begun,

Set perstat reserare fores et
abire laborat

But keeps on, and works to
unbar the gates and go off,

Et fremit et pugnat famulosque
fremendo coartat

And howls and fights and
makes the servants cringe with
his howling.

Denique cum nullus posset
retinere volentem

Finally, when no one could
hold the man back who wanted

Ire virum iussit cicius regina
venire

355. To go, the queen quickly
ordered

Eius ad abcessum absentem
guendoloenam

His Gwendolyn to come to the
departed, absent man.

Illa venit suplexque virum
remanere precatur

She came imploring, and
begged the man to remain.

Spernit at ille preces nec vult
remanere nec illam

But he rejected her entreaties,
nor did he wish to remain, nor

Sicut erat solitus gaudenti
cernere vultu

Look at her as he used to, with
glad face.

Illa dolet fletuque fluit
laniatque capillos

360. She sorrowed, and tears
flowed, and she tore her hair,

Et secat ungue genas et humi
moriendo volutat

And scratched her cheeks with
her nails, and rolled on the
ground like one dying.

Id regina videns affatur taliter
illum

Seeing this, the queen
addressed him thus:

Hec tua que moritur sic pro te
Guendoloena

"This [is] your Gwendolyn
who is dying for you.

Quid faciet dabiturve viro
viduamue manere

What will she do?   Be given
to a man or remain a widow,

Precipis aut tecum quocumque   365.
recesseris ire

Which do you advise?   Or
will you take her with you
wherever it is that you go?

Ibit enim tecumque nemus
nemorisque virentes

For she will go with you, and
will the groves and will dwell

Leta colet saltus dum te
pociatur amante

Happily in the green meadows
of the grove while she claims
you as a lover."

Vocibus hiis igitur respondit
talia vates

To these words therefore the
bard answers as follows:

*   *   *

Nolo soror pecudem patulo que
fontis hiatu

"I do not wish, sister, for a
mascot which with the gaping
mouth of a fountain

Diffundit latices ut virginis   370.
urna sub estus

Sprays liquid [tears] like the
urn of Virgo after summer.

Nec curam mutabo meam velut
Orpheus olim

Nor will I change my care as
Orpheus did once,

Quando suos calathos pueris
commisit habendos

When he left the baskets he
had to have with boys,

Euridice stigias priusquam
transnavit harenas

Before Euridice swam across
the Stygian beaches.

Mundus ab alterutro veneris sine labe manebo	I will remain clean from both, without the defect of Venus.
Huic igitur detur nubendi iusta facultas	375. A proper right to [re]marry should therefore be given her;
Arbitrioque suo quem gestit ducere ducat	Whoever she in her judgement she desires, may lead her [to the altar].
Precaveat tamen ipse sibi qui duxerit illam	Let him beware, though, whoever marries her,
Obvius ut numquam michi sit nec cominus astet	Lest he ever cross my path, nor stand at close quarters,
Set se divertat ne si michi congrediendi	But let him stay away, lest an encounter with me
Copia prestetur vibratum sentiat ensem	380. Chance to happen, [and] he should feel the quivering sword.
Cumque dies aderit sollempni lege iugali	And when the day of the solemn wedding by law shall arrive,
Diverse que dapes convivis distribuentur	And the varied feasts are distributed to the guests,
Ipsemet interero donis munitus honestis	I myself will be there, giving worthy gifts.
Ditabo que datam profuse Guendoloenam	I will profusely enrich Gwendolyn when she is given away."

*   *   *

Dixerat atque vale gradiens subiunxit utrique	385. He had spoken, and, setting out, added a farewell to each,
Et peciit silvas nullo prohibente cupitas	And headed for the desired forests, with no one stopping him,

Guendoloena manet spectans in limine tristis	Gwendolyn remained gazing, sad, in the doorway,
Et regina simul casuque moventur amici	And the queen at the same time, and they were moved by the case of their friend,
Mirantur que nimis rerum secreta furentem	And they were amazed at the many secrets
Nosse virum venerem que sue scivisse sororis	390. That the raving man had known, and that he had known of the love-affair of his sister.
Mentitumque tamen pueri de morte putebant	They thought that he had lied, though, about the boy's death,
Quam dixit ternam cum dicere debuit unam	Which he said was threefold, when he ought to have said single.
Inde diu sua visa fuit vox vana per annos	Thence for a long time his statement appeared meaningless, for years,
Donec ad etatem venit puer ille virilem	Until the boy came to a man's age.
Tum cunctis patefacta fuit multisque probata	395. Then it was made plain to all, and proved for many.
Nam dum venatum canibus comitantibus iret	For while he went hunting game with his hounds and companions,
Aspexit cervum nemoris sub fronde latentem	He saw a deer hiding under the leaves of the forest,
Dissolvit que canes qui cervo devia viso	He released his dogs, who, when the deer was seen, off the course
Transcendunt complentque suis latratibus auras	They veered, and filled the air with their barking.

Ipsemet urget equum *calcaribus insequitur que*	400. He himself drove his horse with his spurs, and they followed
Nunc cornu nunc ore monens *operis que ministros*	Now with the horn, now with his mouth he directs those who carry out the action,
Increpat atque iubet cursu *ciciore venire*	He snaps and orders them to come more quickly in their course.
Mons ibi celsus erat *circumdatus undique saxis*	There was a high mountain, surrounded on all sides by rocks,
Juxta quem fluvius subtus per *plana fluebat*	Next to which a river flowed through the flatlands below.
Hunc fera transcendit fugiens *dum venit in amnem*	That way the fleeing beast veered, while it came to the river,
Exegit que suas solito de more *Latebras*	406. It sought hiding-places, as its habit usually is.
Instigat iuvenis montem *quoque tramite recto*	The youth presses on, up the mountain and in a straight course
Preterit et cervum per saxa *iacentia querit*	Goes forward, and looks for the deer in the rocks lying about.
Contigit interea dum duceret *impetus ipsum*	It happens meanwhile that while he impetuously leads, the same
Labi quadrupedem celso de *rupe virumque*	410. Quadruped slips, and the man from the high cliff
Forte per abruptum montis *cecidisse sub amnem*	By chance fell down the steep slope of the mountain right into the river,

Ut tamen hereret pes eius in arbore quadam	So that his foot stuck in a certain tree,
Et submersa forent sub flumine cetera membra	And his other members were submerged in the stream.
Sicque ruit mersusque fuit ligno que pependit	And thus he fell, and was submerged and was suspended from wood,
Et fecit vatem per terna pericula verum	415. And made the bard true by the three dangers.

*   *   *

Qui nemus ingressus fuerat ritu que ferino	Who was gone into the woods and after the manner of wild beasts
Vivebat paciens concrete frigoris alge	Was living, getting by on water-plants hard-frozen,
Sub nive sub pluvia sub iniquo flamine venti	Snowed on, rained on, facing gusts of wind.
Idque placebat ei pocius quam iura per urbes	And that pleased him more than upholding the law
Exercere suas gentes que domare feroces	420. Throughout the cities and controlling the fierce people.
Interea ducente viro labentibus annis	Meanwhile, years having passed, with her husband leading
Cum grege silvestri talem per tempora vitam	This sort of life with his forest flock over time,
Guendoloena datur nubendi lege marito	Gwendolyn was given in marriage according to her husband's decree.

*   *   *

Nox erat et nitide radiebant cornua lune	It was night, and the horns of the moon shone brightly,
Cuncta que convexi splendebant lumina celi	425. And all the lights that were shining in the arched sky.
Purior aer erat solito nam frigidus atrox	Purer was the air than usual, for cold, cruel
Expulerat nubes boreas celumque serenum	Boreas had driven out the clouds and had the clear sky
Reddiderat sicco detergens nubila flatu	Brought back, sweeping away the clouds with dry breath.
Sidereum cursum vates spectabat ab alto	The bard gazed at the stars' courses from a high
Monte loquens tacite sub divo talia dicens	430. Mountain, speaking quietly out in the open, saying such things as,
Quid sibi vult radius martis regem ne peremptum	"What does the ray of Mars mean? Does it the loss of the king
Portendit noviter rutilans alium que futurum	Portend, strangely glowing red, and that another [king] is coming?
Sic equidem video nam constantinus obivit	Thus, indeed, I see, for Constantine has passed on,
Ipsius que nepos scelerata sorte conanus	And his nephew Conan by wicked mischance
Per patrui iugulum sumpto diademate rex est	435. Is king, having assumed the crown by the murder of his uncle.
At tu summa venus que certo limite Labens	But you, highest Venus, who are gliding in a certain orbit,
Infra zodiacum solem comitaris euntem	Beneath the zodiac, you going along with the sun,

Quid tibi cum radio qui duplex ethera findit	What is it to you with the ray which divides the double ether?
Discidium ne mei sectus portendit amoris	Does it portend the parting of my love?
Talis enim radius divisos signat amores	440. For such a ray means loves divided;
Forsitan absentem me guendoloena reliquit	Perhaps Gwendolyn has left me, absent as I am,
Alterius que viri gaudens complexibus heret	And clings rejoicing in the embraces of another man.
Sic igitur vincor sic alter fungitur illa	Thus therefore I am defeated, thus another enjoys her,
Sic mea iura michi dum demoror eripiuntur	Thus my vows are snatched away from me while I delay,
Sic equidem nam segnis amans superatur ab illo	445. Thus indeed, for the lazy lover is beaten by him
Qui non est segnis nec abest set cominus instat	Who is not lazy nor absent, but is right there.
At non invideo nubat nunc omine dextro	But I do not envy; let her now marry with good omens,
Utatur que novo me permittente marito	And let her enjoy her new husband, with my blessing.
Crastina cumque dies illuxerit ibo feram que	And when the day tomorrow shall have have lightened, I will go and will bear
Mecum munus ei promissum quando recessi	450. With me my gift that I promised her when I returned."

*   *   *

Dixerat et silvas et saltus circuit omnes	He spoke, and he went round the groves and meadows all,

Ceruorum que greges agmen collegit in unum	And the herds of deer he gathers in one column,
Et damas capreas que simul cervo que resedit	And the does and nanny-goats likewise, and he sat on a stag,
Et veniente die compellens agmina pre se	And when the day came, driving the column by himself
Festinans vadit quo nubit guendoloena	455. Hurrying he forged ahead to where Gwendolyn was getting married.
Postquam venit eo pacienter stare coegit	After he came there, he made the stags stand
Cervos ante fores proclamans guendoloena	Patiently before the gates while he shouted, "Gwendolyn!
Gendoloena veni te talia munera spectant	Gwendolyn! I have come! Such gifts are looking at you!"
Ocius ergo venit subridens Guendoloena	Soon Gwendolyn came, smiling,
Gestari que virum cervo miratur et illum	460. And is amazed that the man is borne on a stag, and that it
Sic parere viro tantum quoque posse ferarum	Thus submits to him, that it is possible that so great indeed a number
Uniri numerum quas pre se solus agebat	Of animals can be united, which he was driving before him, all by himself,
Sicut pastor oves quas ducere suevit ad herbas	Just like the sheep that the shepherd matter-of-factly drives to the pasture.
Stabat ab excelsa sponsus spectando fenestra	The bridegroom stood looking from a high window,
In solio mirans equitem risum que movebat	465. Looking at the "knight" in his "saddle," and a laugh escaped him.

Ast ubi vidit eum vates animo que quis esset	But when the bard saw him, and [knew] in mind who he was,
Calluit extemplo divulsit cornua cervo	All at once he hardened, and tore the antlers off the stag
Quo gestabatur vibrata que iecit in illum	On which he was carried, and threw them, whizzing, at the other man,
Et caput illius penitus contrivit eumque	And smashed his head in, and
Reddidit exanimem vitamque fugavit in auras	470. Left him dead, and his life fled into the air.
Ocius inde suum talorum verbere cervum	Quickly from thence, kicking the stag with his heel,
Diffugiens egit silvas que redire paravit	Fleeing, he made off, and prepared to return to the woods.
Egrediuntur ad hec ex omni parte clientes	Vassals from all over came there,
Et celeri cursu vatem per rura sequuntur	And followed the bard through the countryside in hot pursuit.
Ille quidem velox sic precurrebat ut isset	475. He, indeed, fast, thus ran before, so that he might go
Ad nemus intactus nisi previus amnis obesset	Untouched to the grove, except for the river that was in his way.
Nam dum torrentem fera prosiliendo mearet	For while the beast proceeded over the torrent with a lurch
Elapsus rapida cecidit merlinus in unda	Merlin slipped and fell in the rapid wave.
Circueunt ripas famuli capiunt que natantem	The servants ringed the banks and captured the swimmer,

Adducunt que domum vinctum *que dedere sorori*	And they led him home bound, and gave him to his sister.

*   *   *

Captus item vates fit tristis et *optat obire*	481.	The captured bard became sad and wanted to go
Ad silvas pugnat que suos *dissoluere nexus*		To the forest, and fought to loosen his bonds
Et ridere negat potum que *cibum que refutat*		And refused to laugh, and would not accept food or drink,
Tristicia que sua tristem facit *esse sororem*		And his sadness made his sister sad.
Ergo videns illum rodarchus *pellere cunctam*	485.	Therefore, Rhydderch, seeing him drive away all
Leticiam nec velle dapes libare *paratas*		Joy and that he did not want to sample the meals prepared for him,
Educi precepit eum miseratus *in urbem*		Taking pity, ordered him led into the city,
Per fora per populos ut letior *esset eundo*		Through the marketplaces, through the crowds, so that by going he might be more cheerful,
Resque videndo novas que *vendebantur ibidem*		And seeing unusual things that they sold there.
Ergo vir eductus dum *progrederetur ab aula*	490.	Therefore the man was led out; while leaving the palace
Inspicit ante fores famulem sub *paupere cultu*		He saw before the gates a servant who looked very poor,
Qui servabat eas poscentem *pretereuntes*		Who guarded them, begging the passing

Ore tremente viros ad vestes munus emendas	Men with his mouth all trembling for alms to buy clothes.
Mox stetit et risit vates miratus egentem	Right away the bard stood still and laughed, seeing the beggar.
Illinc progressus nova calciamenta tenentem	495. From thence moving on, he saw a youth
Spectabat iuuenem commercantemque tacones	Holding new shoes, and bargaining for soles.
Tunc iterum risit renuit que diutius ire	Then again he laughed, and refused to go daily
Per fora spectandus populis quos inspiciebat	Through the marketplaces, to be looked at by the people which he saw.
At nemus optabat quod crebro respiciebat	But he desired the woods, which he frequently looked back on,
Quo nitebatur vetitos divertere gressus	500. To which he strove to turn his forbidden steps.
Inde domum famuli redeunt ipsum que cachinnum	From thence the servants returned home and reported
Bis movisse ferunt silvas quoque velle redire	That laughter had twice escaped him and that he wanted to return to the forests.
Ocius ergo volens rodarchus scire quid esset	Right away, therefore Rhydderch, wanting to know what it might be,
Quod portendisst risu dissoluere nexus	What might be meant by the laugh, ordered that the bonds
Ilico iussit ei concedens posse reverti	505. Be loosed, allowing him to be able to return
Ad solitas silvas si risus exposuisset	To his accustomed woods if he would explain the laugh.

Letior assistens respondit talia vates	More happily standing by, the bard answered thus:
Janitor ante fores tenui sub veste sedebat	"The doorman was sitting at the gates with thin clothes,
Et velut esset inops rogitabat pretereuntes	And as if he were impoverished was asking the passers-by
Ut largirentur sibi quo vestes emerentur	510. That they might be generous to him so that new clothes could be bought;
Ipsemet interea subter se denariorum	Meanwhile, he himself had under him hidden heaps
Occultos cumulos occultus dives habebat	Of money; they were his: he was secretly rich.
Illud ergo risi tu terram verte sub ipso	Therefore I laughed. You turn up the ground under him
Nummos invenies servatos tempore longo	And you will find the money preserved for a long time.
Illinc ulterius versus fora ductus ementem	515. From there, when I was led toward the marketplace,
Calciamenta virum vidi pariterque tacones	I saw a man buying shoes and soles for them,
Ut postquam dissuta forent usuque forata	That when afterward they might come unsewn, and have holes from being worn,
Illa resartiret primos que pararet ad usus	He might restitch them and they would resemble their first wearings.
Illud item risi quoniam nec calciamentis	I laughed at this, too, because neither the shoes
Nec superadditis miser ille taconibus uti	520. Nor the tacked-on heels will that poor man be able to use

Postmodo compos erit quia iam submersus in undis	Thereafter, because even now, drowned in the waves
Fluctuat ad ripas tu vade videre videbis	He drifts toward the shore; you go see, you will see.
Dicta probare viri cupiens rodarchus ad ampnem	Desiring to test the words of the man, Rhydderch forthwith
Circumquaque suos iubet ocius ire clientes	Orders his vassals to fan out along the river,
Ut si forte virum per proxima littora talem	525. So that if by chance they might see such a man on the near shore,
Demersum videant festina voce renarrent	Drowned, they might report with a hasty voice.
Jussa ducis peragunt nam fluvia circumeuntes	They obey the orders of the chieftain, for going around the rivers
Submersum iuvenem squalentes inter harenas	The drowned youth on the gravelly beach
Inveniunt redeunt que domum regi que renarrent	They found, and they returned home and reported to the king.
At rex interea forium custode remoto	530. But the king meanwhile, having removed the gate-keeper,
Suffodit et vertit terram reperit que sub ipsa	Dug and turned the ground and found under it
Thesaurum positum vatemque iocosus adorat	A treasure placed, and laughing he venerated the bard.
His igitur gestis vates properabat abire	When these things were done, the bard hastened to go
Ad solitas silvas populos exosus in urbe	To his accustomed forests, hating the people in the city.
Precipiebat ei secum regina manere	535. The queen asked him to remain with her,

Optatumque nemus postponere donec abirent	And to postpone his longed-for groves until departed
Que tunc instabant candentis frigora brume	The icy whiteness of winter that was upon them.
Atque redieret item teneris cum fructibus estas	And that summer might return with its mellow fruits
Unde frui posset dum tempora sole calerent	That he could live on while the seaons warmed by the sun.
Ille repugnabat verbis et talibus illam	540. He fought back with words, and with these her
Alloquitur cupiens secedere frigore spreto	He addressed, desiring to depart, contemptuous of winter:

*   *   *

O dilecta soror quid me retinere laboras	"O dear sister, why do you endeavor to hold me back?
Non me bruma suis poterit terrere procellis	Winter cannot frighten me with its storms,
Non gelidus boreas cum flatu sevit iniquo	Nor can icy Boreas when it rages with its hostile breath
Balantum que greges subita cum grandine ledit	545. And suddenly harms the flocks of bleaters with hail,
Non cum turbat aquas duffusis imbribus auster	Nor when the South Wind disturbs the waters with released rains.
Quin nemorum deserta petam saltusque virentes	Indeed, I will seek the wilds of the groves and the green meadows.
Contentus modico potero perferre pruinam	Content with little I will be able to endure the frost.

Illic arboreis sub frondibus inter olentes		There beneath the trees' leaves among the fragrant
Herbarum flores estate iacere iuvabit	550.	Flowers of the grasses I will enjoy lying in summer.
Ne tamen esca michi brumale tempore desit		Lest, however, a morsel be lacking in the winter,
In silvis compone domos adhibe que clientes		Build houses in the woods, and have vassals there,
Obsequium que michi facient escas que parabunt		That they might do me service and prepare morsels
Cum tellus gramen fructumque negaverit arbor		When the ground denies [me] grass and the tree its fruit.
Ante domos alias unam compone remotam	555.	Before the other houses, build one far off,
Cui sex dena decem dabis [h]ostia tot que fenestras		Which you will provide with sixty and ten doors and as many windows,
Per quas ignivomum videam cum venere phebum		Through which I may see fire-belching Phoebus with Venus,
Inspitiam que polo labentia sydera noctu		And I may examine the stars gliding around the pole by night
Que me de populo regni ventura docebunt		Which will teach me things to come about the people of the kingdom.
Totque notatores que dicam scribere docti	560.	And let just as many copyists, taught to write what I shall say,
Assint et studeant carmen mandare tabellis		Be there, and let them be zealous to commit my pronouncements to writing.
Tu quoque sepe veni soror o dilecta meam que		You come too, o dear sister, often, and my

Tunc poteris relevare famem *potuque cibo que*	Hunger you will be able to relieve by drink and food."

*   *   *

Dixit et ad selvas festinis *gressibus ivit*		He spoke, and went with hastening steps to the woods.
Paruit ergo soror nam iussam *condidit aulam*	565.	Therefore his sister relented, and founded the hall he ordered,
Atque domos alias et quicquit *iusserat illi*		And the other houses and whatever else he had ordered her to.
Ille quidem dum poma manent *phebus que per astra*		He indeed, while the apples remained and Phoebus through the stars
Altius ascendit gaudet sub *fronde manere*		Climbed higher, he was glad to remain under the leaves
Ac peragrare nemus zephiris *mulcentibus ornos*		And wander through the ash-groves with the soothing breezes.
Tunc veniebat yems rigidis *hirsuta procellis*	570.	Then winter came, bristling with frozen storms
Que nemus et terras fructu *spoliabat ab omni*		Which denuded the groves and lands of all fruits
Deficeret que sibi pluviis *instantibus esca*		And did away with every morsel with incessant rains.
Tristis et esuriens dictam *veniebat ad aulam*		Sad and hungry he would come to the aforementioned hall.
Illic multociens aderat regina *dapesque*		The queen often was there, and meals
Et potum pariter fratri gavisa *ferebat*	575.	And drink, too, she gladly brought to her brother.

Qui postquam variis sese recreaverat escis	He, after he had refreshed himself with various dishes,
Mox assurgebat complaudebat que sorori	Rose right away and thanked his sister.
Deinde domum peragrans ad sidera respiciebat	Then wandering around his home he looked at the stars,
Talia dum caneret que tunc ventura sciebat	While he expounded such things and then knew the future.

*   *   *

O rabiem britonum quos copia diviciarum	580.	"O madness of the Britons, whom the abundance of riches,
Usque superveniens ultra quam debeat effert		Even overflowing, carries them beyond what is seemly.
Nolunt pace frui stimulis agitantur [h]erinis		They do not wish to enjoy peace, are agitated, spurred by the furies;
Civiles acies cognata que prelia miscent		They are embroiled in civil wars and family fights.
Ecclesias domini paciuntur habere ruinam	584.	They suffer the churches of the Lord to fall into disrepair,
Pontificesque sacros ad regna remota repellunt		They drive the holy priests into remote kingdoms,
Cornubiensis apri conturbant queque nepotes		The descendants of the boar of Cornwall also agitate,
Insidias sibimet ponentes ense nephando		Laying ambushes on their own. By the accursed sword
Interimunt sese nec regno iure potiri		They kill each other; not hoping to become masters of the kingdom by law,

Expectare volunt regni diademate rapto	They want [it] by seizing the crown of the kingdom.
Illic quartus erit crudelior asperior que	590. Thence there will be a fourth, more cruel and harsher;
Hinc lupus equoreus debellans vincet et ultra	A battling sea-wolf will conquer him, and beyond
Sabrinam victum per barbara regna fugabit	The Severn, defeated, he will flee through savage realms.
Idem kaerkeri circumdabit osidione	That man will besiege Cirencester
Passeribus que domos et menia trudet ad imum	And with sparrows lay its homes and walls low.
Classe petet gallos set telo regis obivit	595. With a fleet he will attack the Gauls, but he will die by a king's weapon.
Rodarchus moritur postquam discordia longa	Rhydderch dies; thereafter long anarchy
Scotos et Cumbros per longum tempus habebit	Will grip the Scots and Welsh for a long time,
Donec crescenti tribuatur cumbria denti	Until Wales be granted to the growing tooth.
Cambrigei gewissos post illos cornubienses	The Welsh will attack the men of Gwent, after them the Cornish,
Afficient bello nec eos lex ulla domabit	600. Nor will any law control them.
Kambria gaudebit suffuso sanguine semper	Wales will always rejoice in bloodshed.
Gens inimica deo quid gaudes sanguine fuso	O people hostile to God, why do you rejoice in bloodshed?
Kambria compellet fratres committere pugnas	Wales will force brothers to fight together

Et dampnare suos scelerata morte nepotes	And to damn their own descendants to wicked death.
Scotorum cunei trans humbrum 605. *sepius ibunt*	The shock-troops of the Scots will often go across the Humber,
Obstantes que uiros periment pietate remota	And, far removed from pity, will kill those men who oppose them.
Non impune tamen nam cesus ductor obibit	Not unpunished, however, for the leader will die cut down.
Nomen habebit equi qui fiet sevus in illo	He will have the name of a horse, which will make him fierce in that.
Finibus ex nostris heres expulsus abibit	His heir will go off expelled from our borders.
Scote reconde tuos quos nudas 610. *ocius enses*	O Scot, hide your swords which you bare!
Vis tibi dispar erit nostra cum gente feroci	Your strength will be unequal to our fierce people.
Corruet urbs acelud nec eam reparabit in evvum	The city Acelud will come crashing down, nor will any king rebuild it for an age
Rex aliquis donec subdatur scotus a bello	Until the Scot be subdued by war.
Urbs sigeni et turres et magna palatia plangent	The city Caernavon, both its towers and great palaces will mourn
Diruta donec eant ad pristina predia cambri	In ruins until the Welsh go to their realms of old.
Kaeptis in portu sua menia rupta videbit	Kaeptis will see its broken walls in the harbor
Donec eam locuples cum vulpis dente reformet	Until a rich man with a wolf's tooth will repair them.

Urbs loel spoliata suo pastore vacabit	The city Loel will be empty, bereft of its shepherd,
Donec reddat ei cambucam virga Leonis	Until the staff of the lion returns the office to it.
Urbs rutupi portus in littora strata iacebit	620. The city of Richborough will lie stretched on the shores
Restauabit eam galeata nave rutenus	A Fleming with a helmeted ship will restore it.
Menia menevie reparabit quintus ab illo	A fifth will repair the walls of St. David's
Per quem palla sibi reddetur dempta per annos	By which the mantle will be returned to it, taken away for years.
In que tuo sabrina sinu cadet urbs legionum	And in your bosom, O Severn, will fall the city of the legions
Amittet que suos cives per tempora longa	625. And its citizens will be sent away for a long time;
Hos sibi reddet item cum venerit ursus in agno	They will return when the bear in the lamb comes.
Saxonici reges expulsis civibus urbes	The Saxon kings will rule the cities whose citizens have been expelled,
Rura domosque simul per tempora longa tenebunt	The homes and coutryside for a long time.
Ex hiis gestabunt ter tres diadema dracones	From these three dragons will wear the didadem thrice.
Ducenti monachi perimentur in urbe Leyri	630. Two hundred monks will die in Leicester,
Et duce depulso vacuabit menia saxo	And its walls will be empty when its chief is driven off by the Saxon.

Qui prior ex anglis erit in diademate bruti	He of the Angles who will first be in the diadem of Brutus
Restauabit item vacuatam cedibus urbem	Will restore the city emptied by killing.
Gens fera per patriam prohibebit crisma sacrare	The savage race will forbid holy baptism throughout its homeland
Inque dei domibus ponet simulachra deorum	635. And in the Houses of God will put images of gods.
Postmodo roma deum reddet mediante cuculla	Later Rome will return God by means of the hood.
Rotabit que domos sacro sacer imbre sacerdos	And a holy man will turn the Houses holy by holy sprinkling,
Quas renovabit item pastoribus intro locatis	Which houses he will renew with pastors stationed inside.
Legis divine servabunt iussa subinde	They will observe the mandates of divine law in them,
Plures ex illis et celo iure fruentur	640. Many of them will enjoy heaven by its rule.
Id violabit item gens impia plena veneno	The impious race will violate it, full of poison,
Miscebit que simul violenter fas que nephas que	And will jumble right and wrong together,
Vendet in extremos fines trans equora natos	Will sell its sons into faraway lands across the sea,
Cognatos que suos iram que tonantis inibit	And its kin, and will provoke the wrath of the Thunderer.
O scelus infandum quem conditor orbis honore	645. O unspeakable crime! Him whom the Founder of the World with honor

Celi dignatus cum libertate creavit	Created, worthy of heaven, with liberty,
Illum more bovis vendi duci que ligatum	That man is sold like a bull, and is led tied up.
Cessabis miserande deo qui proditor olim	You will cease, miserable man, who was once a traitor to God,
In dominum fueras cum primum regna subisti	Against the Lord, when first you came to power.
Classe supervenient daci populoque subacto	650. The Danes will come over, and the population being conquered,
Regnabunt breviter propulsati que redibunt	They will reign briefly and will be driven off.
His duo iura dabunt quos ledet acumine caude	Two will give orders to these, and a serpent will harm by the sharpness of its tail,
Federis oblitus pro sceptri stemate serpens	Forgetful of its agreement, for the pedigree of the sceptre.
Indeque neustrenses ligno trans equora vecti	Thence the Normans, borne by wood across the sea
Vultus ante suos et vultus retro ferentes	655. Bearing their faces before and behind,
Ferratis tunicis et acutis ensibus anglos	With iron birnies and sharp swords
Acriter invadent periment campo que fruentur	They will fiercely attack the Angles, and will kill them and will hold the field.
Plurima regna sibi submittent atque domabunt	They will subjugate many kingdoms to themselves and will rule
Externas gentes per tempora donec erinus	Far-off peoples for a time until a fury

Circumquaque volans virus diffundet in ipsos	660.	Flying all around will broadcast poison against them.
Tum pax atque fides et virtus omnis abibit		Then peace and trust and all virtue will go away,
Undique per patrias committent prelia cives		And everywhere throughout their homelands citizens will engage in wars.
Virque virum prodet non invenietur amicus		Man will betray man, no friend will be found.
Coniuge despecta meretrices sponsus adibit		The husband, his wife forgotten, will go after loose women,
Sponsa que cui cupiet despecto coniuge nubet	665.	And the wife, her husband forgotten, will marry whom she pleases.
Non honor ecclesiis servabitur ordo peribit		No honor will be kept for the church; the order will perish.
Pontifices tunc arma ferent tunc castra sequentur		Then priests will bear arms and then will follow the forts.
In tellure sacra turres et menia ponent		They will put towers and walls on holy ground,
Militibusque dabunt quod deberetur egenis		And will give to soldiers what should be given to the needy.
Diviciis rapti mundano tramite current	670.	Carried away by wealth, they will run to worldly things,
Eripient que deo quod sacra tyara vetabit		And they will snatch away from God what the holy tiara forbids.
Tres diadema ferent post quos favor ille novorum		Three will carry the crown after whom the favor will be that of the new ones.

Quartus erit sceptris pietas cui leva nocebit

There will be a fourth for the sceptre, whom flighty piety will harm.

Donec sit genitore suo vestitus ut apri

Until he will be clothed by his father so that by the boar's

Dentibus accinctus galeati transeat umbram

675. Teeth, girded, he shall cross the shadow of a helmeted man.

Quatuor ungentur vice versa summa petentes

Four will be anointed, seeking the heights in their turn,

Et duo succedent quia sic diadema rotabunt

And two will succeed because they will thus turn the crown

Ut moveant gallos in se fera bella movere

So that they will move the Gauls to move fierce wars against themselves.

Sextus hibernenses et eorum menia vertet

679. A sixth will overthrow the Irish and their walls,

Qui pius et prudens populos renovabit et urbes

One who is pious and wise will renew the people and the cities.

Hec vortigerno cecini prolixius olim

I sang of these things at greater length once to Vortigern,

Exponendo duum sibi mistica bella draconum

Explaining to him the mystic combat of the two dragons,

In ripa stagni quando consedimus hausti

When we sat together on the banks of the drained pond,

At tu vade domum morientem visere regem

But you, go home to see the dying king,

O dilecta soror thelgesino que venire

685. O dear sister, and have Taliesin come,

Precipe namque loqui desidero plurima secum

Order him, for I want to discuss many things with him,

Venit enim noviter de partibus armoricanis

For his has just come from the realms of Brittany,

Dulcia quo didicit sapentis dogmata gilde	Where he has learned doctrinal sweets from wise Gildas."

*   *   *

It ganieda domum thelgesinum que reversum		Ganieda returned home and found that Taliesin had returned,
Defunctumque ducem reperit tristesque clientes		That the king was dead and the vassals in grief.
Ergo fluens lacrimis collabitur inter amicos	691.	Therefore, overflowing with tears she collapsed among her friends
Et laniat crines et profert talia dicens		And tore her hair and spoke, saying these things:
Funera rodarchi mulieres plangite mecum		"Lament with me the funeral rites of Rhydderch, o women,
Ac deflete virum qualem non protulit orbis		And bewail with me the man whom the world has not brought forth
Hactenus in nostro quantum discernimus evo	695.	So far in our epoch, as much as we can tell.
Pacis amator erat populo nam iura feroci		He was a lover of peace for laws to a fierce people
Sic dabat ut nulli vis inferretur ab ullo		He gave so that coercion was applied to no one by anyone else,
Tractabat sanctum iusto moderamine clerum		He treated the holy priest with just moderation,
Jure regi populo summos humiles que sinebat		And he permitted high and low to be ruled by law.
Largus erat nam multa dabat vix quid retinebat	700.	He was generous, for he gave many things away and kept scarcely anything.

Omnibus omnis erat faciens
quodcumque decebat

He was all things to all men,
doing whatever was proper.

Flos equitum regumque decor
regnique columpna

The flower of knights, the
ornament of kings, the pillar of
the kingdom.

Heu michi qui fueras inopinis
vermibus esca

Alas for me!   The man you
were, unexpectedly given as
food for worms

Nunc datus es corpus que tuum
putrescit in urna

Now, and your body rots in the
urn.

Sicne cubile tibi post serica
pulchra paratur

705.   Is the bed thus prepared for
you, after beautiful silks,

Siccine sub gelido caro
candida regia membra

And thus your fair flesh, royal
limbs, under an icy

Condentur saxo nec eris nisi
pulvis et ossa

Stone will be hidden, nor will
you be anything but dust and
bones?

Sic equidem nam sors
hominum miseranda per evum

For thus indeed is the pitiable
fate of men throughout the
centuries

Ducitur ut nequeant ad pristina
iura reduci

Carried out, and they cannot be
led back to pristine laws.

Ergo nichil prodest pereuntis
gloria mundi

710.   Therefore, all for nothing is the
glory of the transient world,

Que fugit atque redit fallit
Leditque potentes

Which flees and returns,
deceives and harms the
powerful.

Melle suo delinit apes quod
postmodo pungit

The bee smears with honey
what it will afterward sting.

Sic quos demulsit devertens
gloria mundi

Thus those whom it soothes,
the glory of the world, veering,

Fallit et ingrate collidit
verbere caude

Deceives, and hits with a blow
from its unwelcome tail.

Fit breve quod prestat quod habet durabile non est	715. It cuts short what is preeminent; what it has is not durable;
More fluentis aque transit quodcumque ministrat	In the manner of flowing water it passes.
Quid rosa si rutilet si candida lilia vernent	What is a rose if it reddens, if a white lily if it flourishes,
Si sit pulcher homo vel equus vel cetera plura	If a man or a horse or many other things be beautiful?
Ista creatori non mundo sunt referenda	These matters are to be referred to the Creator, not to the world.
Felices igitur qui perstant corde piato	720. Happy, therefore, are they who persevere with pious heart,
Obsequium que deo faciunt mundumque relinqunt	And do service to God, and leave the world behind.
Illis perpetuo fungi concedet honore	To them He will grant the enjoyment of perpetual honor
Qui sine fine regit christus qui cuncta creavit	Who rules without end, Christ, who created everything.
Vos igitur proceres vos menia celsa lares que	You chieftains, therefore, you high walls and ancestral spirits,
Vos nati dulces mundanaque cuncta relinquo	725. You sweet children and all mundane things I leave,
Et cum fratre meo silvas habitabo deumque	And with my brother I will inhabit the forest, and God
Leta mente colam nigri cum tegmine pepli	Will I serve with a happy heart, with the covering of a black robe."
Hec ait atque suo persoluit iusta marito	She said these things, and discharged her obligations to her husband,
Signavit que suam cum tali carmine tumbam	And wrote the following poem on his tomb:

Rodarchus largus quo largior	730. Rhydderch the generous, than
alter in orbe	whom no one in the world was
Non erat hic modica	More generous. A great man
magnus requiescit in urna	rests in this bushel-sized urn.

*   *   *

Venerat interea merlinum
visere vatem

Meanwhile there came to see
Merlin the bard

Tunc telgesinus qui discere
missus ab illo

Then Taliesin, who was sent to
learn from him

Quid ventus nimbus ve foret
nam mixtus uterque

What wind or cloud there
would be, for both mixed

Tunc simul instabant et nubila
conficiebant

735. Were there at the same time,
and were brewing up a storm.

Hec documenta dabat socia
dictante minerva

He gave these lessons, with
Minerva his ally speaking:

Quatuor ex nichilo produxit
conditor orbis

"The Creator of the world
produced, out of nothing, four
things,

Ut fierent rebus precedens
causa creandis

That they might be the
antecedent cause of things to
be created,

Materies que simul concordi
pace iugata

And the elements joined
together in peace.

Celum quod stellis depinxit et
altius extat

740. The sky which he decorated
with stars and stands on high,

Et quasi testa nucem
circumdans omnia claudit

And surrounding everything
like a nutshell, closes it in,

Aera deinde dedit formandis
vocibus aptum

Then he gave [us] the air, fit
for forming sounds,

Quo mediante dies et noctes
sidera prestant

Through which the days and
nights show the stars;

Et mare quod terras cingit		And the sea, which surrounds
valido que recursu		the lands and with its strong current
Quatuor amfractus faciens sic	745.	Making four circuits, thus
aera pulsat		strikes the air
Ut generet ventos qui quatuor		So that it begets winds which
esse feruntur		are said to be four,
Vique sua stantem nec se		And He put, firm in its own
levitate moventem		strength, and not lightly moved,
Supposuit terram partes in		The earth, divided into five
quinque resectam		parts,
Quarum que media est non est		Of which the middle is not to
habitanda calore		be inhabited because of heat,
Extremeque due pre frigore	750.	And the two extremes are
diffugiuntur		avoided because of the cold.
Temperiem reliquis permisit		He permitted the remaining
habere duabus		two to have moderation;
Has homines habitant volucres		These men inhabit, and birds,
que greges que ferarum		and herds of animals.
Ut que darent subitas pluvias		And He put clouds in the sky,
quo crescere fructus		that they might give sudden rains
Arboris et terre facerent		By which the fruits of tree and
aspergine miti		earth might grow by soft showers,
Adiecit celo nubes que sole	755.	And with the help of the sun
ministro		
Sicut utres fluviis occulta lege		Are filled like bags from rivers
replentur		by a hidden law,
Inde per excelsum scandentes		Thence from on high, borne
ethera sumptos		aloft in the air

Diffundunt latices ventorum viribus acte

The waters pour, driven by the force of the winds

Hinc fiunt imbres hinc nix hinc grando rotunda

Hence are begotten rains, hence snow, hence round hail,

Cum gelidus madidus movet sua flamina ventus

When the wind, chilly and wet, moves its blasts,

Qui nubes penetrans quales facit egerit amnes

761. Which, penetrating the clouds, expels the streams just as it made them.

Naturam que suam zonarum proximitate

Each wind draws to itself its nature from the zone closest

Ventorum sibi quisque trahit dum nascitur illuc

To where it arose.

Post firmamentum quo lucida sidera fixit

After that is the firmament, in which He fixed the bright stars.

Ethereum celum posuit tribuit que colendum

765. He placed the aetherial sky and ordained it as the dwelling

Cetibus angelicis quos contemplatio digna

For the angel orders which, worthy of contemplation

Ac dulcedo dei reficit miranda per evum

And the consolation of God, He set up to be wondered at through the ages.

Hoc quoque depinxit stellis et sole chorusco

This He also decorated with stars and the brilliant sun,

Indicens legem que certo limite stella

Setting forth the law which a star in a certain limit

Per sibi commissum posset discurrere celum

770. Might course through the [part of the] sky entrusted to it.

Postmodo supposuit lunari corpore fulgens

Afterward he put under it the aetherial heaven shining

Aerium celum quod per loca celsa redundat

With the light of the moon, which surrounds the high places

Spirituum cuneis qui nobis compaciuntur	With the phalanxes of spirits which console us
Et colletantur dum sic aliter ve movemur	And cheer us while we are otherwise moved.
Sunt que preces hominum soliti perferre per auras	775. And the prayers of men are regularly borne through the air,
Atque rogare deum quod sit placabilis illis	And ask God what is agreeable to them,
Affectum que dei sompno vel voce referre	And to carry God's decisions back, either in dreams or by voice,
Vel signis aliis ut fiant inde scientes	Or by other signs, that they might become known.
At cacodemonibus post lunam subtus habundat	But beneath, after the moon, abounds in evil demons,
Qui nos decipiunt et temptant fallere docti	780. Which trick us, and are taught to try to deceive,
Et sibi multociens ex aere corpore sumpto	And which often, having taken on forms from the air,
Nobis apparent et plurima sepe sequuntur	Appear to us, and many things often happen.
Quin etiam coitu mulieres agrediuntur	In fact, they approach women in intercourse
Et faciunt gravidas generantes more prophano	And make them pregnant, getting children in an immoral way.
Sic igitur celos habitatos ordine terno	785. Thus, therefore, he made the heavens populated by three orders
Spirituum fecit foveant ut singula queque	Of spirits, that individually indeed they might foster
Ac renovet mundum renovato germine rerum	And renew the world with renewed seed of things.

Et mare per species varias distinxit ut ex se	And the sea he set apart by various kinds, that from itself
Proferret rerum formas generando per evum	It might bring forth the forms of things, by generating through the ages.
Pars etenim fervet pars friget et una duabus	790. For part boils, part freezes, and one [part], taking moderation
Temperiem sumens nobis alimenta ministrat	From the two, supplies us with food.
Ast ea que fervet baratrum cum gentibus acris	But that which boils, encircles an abyss with sharp peoples,
Circuit et tetri diversis fluctibus orbent	That the foul ones may be cut off by the opposing waves.
Secernit refluens ignes ex ignibus augens	It separates the world, flowing back, making fires grow from fires.
Illic descendunt qui leges transgrediuntur	795. Thence descend those who transgress the laws,
Postposito que deo quo vult perversa voluntas	Having left God behind; whatever their perverse will wishes,
Incedunt avidi corrumpere quod prohibentur	Avidly they rush in, to corrupt what is forbidden them.
Trux ibi stat iudex equali lance rependens	There a grim judge stands, balancing in equal scales
Cuique suum meritum condignaque debita soluit	To each what he deserves, and pays back as he ought.
Altera que friget pretonsas voluit harenas	800. The second, that which freezes, rolls over the sands shaved bare,
Quas secum gignit vicino prima vapore	Which it begets by itself first by neighboring vapor

Quando suos radios inmiscet
stella diones

When the star of Dione mixes
its rays.

Hanc perhibent arabes
gemmas generare micantes

The Arabs say that sparkling
gems are created by this [star],

Dum peragrat pisces dum
respicit equora flammis

While it crosses Pisces, while it
looks on the waters with
flames.

Hec virtute sua populis
gestantibus ipsas

805.   These [gems] are good for the
people who wear them,

Prosunt et multos reddunt
servant que salubres

And heal many and keep them
healthy.

Has quoque per species
distinxit ut omnia factor

The Creator distinguished these
by types, so that all,

Ut discernamus per formas per
que colores

So that we might distinguish by
forms and by colors

Cuius sint generis cuius virtutis
aperte

What might be known of their
classification and powers.

Tercia forma maris que
nostram circuit orbem

810.   The third form of the sea which
circles our world

Proximitate sua nobis bona
multa ministrat

Supplies us with many good
things,

Nutrit enim pisces et sal
producit habunda

For it nourishes fish and
produces much salt,

Fertque refertque rates
commercia nostra ferentes

And bears and bears back our
vessels bearing our commerce,

Unde suo lucro subito fit dives
egenus

Whence a poor man by his
income suddenly becomes rich.

Vicinam fecundat humum
pascit que volucres

815.   It makes the soil nearby
productive, and feeds birds,

Quas perhibent ortas illinc
cum piscibus esse

Which, they say, arise with the
fish.

Dissimilique tamen nature iure
moventur

Although different, they are
moved by the law of nature

Plus etenim dominatur eis *quam piscibus equor*	Indeed, the sea is dominated by them more than by the fish.
Unde leves excelsa petunt per *inane volantes*	From it these fliers lightly seek the heights, through the void,
At piscis suus humor agit *reprimit que sub undis*	820. But the wetness drives and presses the fish under the waves,
Nec sinit ut vivant dum sicca *luce fruuntur*	Nor does it allow that they might live while they enjoy the dry light.
Hos quoque per species *distinxit factor eorum*	Also the Creator distinguished them by their species,
Naturam que dedit distinctis *unde per evum*	And the nature He gave them, whence through the ages
Mirandi fierent egrotanti que *salubres*	They become wonderful and healthful to the sick.
Nempe ferunt mullum cohibere *libidinis estum*	825. It is said, for example, that the red mullet represses the surge of passion,
Set reddit cecos iugiter *vescentis ocellos*	But blinds the eyes of those who eat it;
At qui nomen habet timeos de *flore timallus*	But the one that has the name of timallus, after the flower thyme,
Sic quoniam redolet vescentem *sepius illo*	Because it smells so that it betrays whatever feeds on it
Protrahit ut tales oleant per *flumina pisces*	So that those fish smell all through the rivers;
Femineo sexu subtracto iure *murenas*	830. The murenas are female, contrary to the laws [of nature],
Esse ferunt cunctas coeunt *tamen ac renovantur*	All of them, they say, and propagate and are renewed

Multiplicant que suos alieno germine fetus	And multiply their young by another kind of fertilization,
Conveniunt etenim per littora sepius angues	For snakes often gather on the shores
Quo degunt faciunt que sonos ac sibila grati	Where they live, and make pleasant sounds and hissing,
Et sic eductis coeunt ex more murenis	835. And when the murenas are thus led out, they propagate as is regularly done;
Est quoque mirandum quod semipedalis echinus	There is also an amazing one, the half-foot echinus,
Herens cui fuerit fixam quasi litore navem	Sticking to where it might be, will hold a ship stuck as if
Detinet in ponto nec eam permittet abire	On the beach, in the ocean, nor does it permit her to proceed,
Donec discedat tali virtuti timendus	Until it, to be feared because of this power, releases [her];
Quemque vocant gladium quia rostro ledit acuto	And [there's the fish] called "sword," because it damages with its sharp beak
Sepius hunc nantem metuunt accedere navi	841. Often ships fear to approach where it is swimming
Nam si sumptus erit confestim perforat illam	For if it is caught, it will promptly pierce the ship,
Et mergit sectam subito cum gurgite navem	And will sink her, cut up, in a sudden whirlpool;
Fit que suis cristis metuendus serra carinis	The serra is to be feared by hulls on account of its crest,
Quas infigit eis dum subnatat atque secatas	845. By which it sticks them while it swims below, and, when they are cut,
Deicit in fluctus crista velut ense timendus	It casts them down into the waves, and its crest is to be feared just like a sword;

Equoreus que draco qui fertur habere venenum	And the sea-dragon which, they say, has poison
Sub pennis metuendus erit capientibus illum	Under its wings, is to be feared by its captors,
Et quociens pungit ledit fundendo venenum	And whenever it strikes, it harms by pouring poison;
Ast alias clades torpedo fertur habere	850. But the torpedo, they say, has other injuries,
Nam qui tangit eam viventem protinus illi	For whoever touches a live one, immediately his
Brachia cum pedibus torpent et cetera membra	Arms and feet are numb, and the other members
Officio que suo quasi mortua destituuntur	Are left as if dead, without their functions,
Sic solet esse nocens illius corporis aure	Thus it is regularly harmful by what comes out of its body.
Hiis deus ac aliis ditavit piscibus equor	855. To these and other fish God gave the deep,
Adiecit que suis plures in fluctibus orbes	And he added other continents in its waves,
Quos habitant homines pro fertilitate reperta	Which men inhabit for their discovered fruitfulness,
Quam producit ibi fecundo cespite tellus	Which the ground produces there with abundant pasturage,
Quarum prima quidem melior que britannia fertur	Of which the first and best is said to be Britain,
Ubertate sua producens singula rerum	860. Producing by its richness unique things.
Fert etenim segetes que nobile munus odoris	For it bears crops which bestow a noble gift of scent
Usibus humanis tribuunt reddendo per annum	For human use, returning every year,

Silvas et saltus et ab hiis stillantia mella	Forests and meadows and from them dripping honey,
Aerios montes lateque virentia prata	High mountains and wide green grasslands,
Fontes et fluvios pisces pecudes que feras que	865. Fountains and rivers, fish, cattle and game,
Arboreos fructus gemmas preciosa metalla	Fruits, gems, precious metals,
Et quicquid prestare solet natura creatrix	And whatever creative nature is accustomed to bestow.
Preterea fontes unda fervente salubres	Beyond that, there are healthful fountains, boiling springs,
Que fovet egrotos et balnea grata ministrat	Which comforts the sick and furnishes pleasant baths,
At subito sanos pellit languore repulso	870. But suddenly shocks them back to health, with their weakness driven out.
Sic Bladudus eos regni dum sceptra teneret	Thus Bladud, when he held the sceptre of the kingdom,
Constituit nomen que sue consortis alaron	Built them, and the name which was of his consort Alaron
Utilis ad plures laticis medicamine morbos	The waters are useful as a treatment for many diseases,
Set mage femineos ut sepius unda probavit	But especially women's diseases, as often the waters have proven to be.
Adiacet huic thanatos que multis rebus habundat	Nearby lies Thanatos, which abounds in many things.
Mortifero serpente caret tollit que venenum	876. It lacks deadly snakes, and its soil does away
Si sua cum vino tellus commixta bibatur	With venom if it is mixed with wine.

Orchades a nobis nostrum quoque dividit equor	Our sea divides the Orkneys from us.
Hec tres ter dene se iuncto flumine fiunt	They are thirty-three in number, divided by the currents.
Bis dene cultore carent alie que coluntur	880. Twenty are untilled, the others are under cultivation.
Ultima que Thule nomen de sole recepit	Thule receives its name from being 'last' from the sun.
Propter solsticium quod sol estivus ibidem	On account of the solstice, which while the summer sun does it there,
Dum facit avertit radium ne luceat ultra	Turns its ray away, nor does it shine beyond
Abducit que dies ut semper nocte perhenni	And takes away the days so that in the perennial night
Aer agat tenebras faciat quoque frigore pontum	885. The air always makes shadows, it makes the sea freeze
Concretum pigrum que simul ratibus que negatum	Solid and sluggish, and at the same time denied to vessels.
Insula post nostram prestantior omnibus esse	The island after ours that is said to be more excellent
Fertur hibernensis felici fertilitate	Than all is Ireland, with its fortunate fertility.
Est etenim maior nec apes nec aves nisi raras	It is larger, and produces neither bees nor birds exept for those seldom encountered,
Educit penitus que negat generare colubres	891. And within it does not allow snakes to reproduce.
Unde fit ut tellus illinc avecta lapis ue	890. Whence it happens that earth or stone that is removed from there,
Si superaddatur serpentes tollat apes que	If it is put somewhere else, will do away with serpents and bees.

Gadibus herculeis adiungitur insula gades	Gades Island is connected to the Cadiz of Hercules.
Nascitur hic arbor cuius de cortice gummi	A tree originates here from whose bark a gum
Stillat quo gemine fiunt super illita iura	895. Dirps, from which gems are made, over its broken sap.
Hesperides vigilem perhibentur habere draconem	They say that the Hesperides have a guardian dragon
Quem servare ferunt sub frondibus aurea poma	Who, they say, keeps golden apples under leaves.
Gorgades habitant mulieres corporis hirci	Women with hairy bodies inhabit the Gorgades,
Que celeri cursu lepores superare feruntur	Who, it is said, beat rabbits in their swift course.
Argire crisse que gerunt ut dicitur aurum	900. Argire and Cryssa bear gold, it is said,
Argentum que simul ceu vilia saxa corinthus	And silver, just as Corinth does common stones.
Taprobana viret fecundo cespite grata	Ceylon flourishes, thanks to its fast-growing turf,
Bis etenim segetes anno producit in uno	For twice in one year it produces crops,
Bis gerit estatem bis ver bis colligit uvas	Summer comes twice, spring twice, twice grapes are gathered,
Et fructus alios nitidis gratissima gemis	905. And other fruits; it is most pleasing for gleaming gemstones.
Atilis eterno producit vere virentes	Tiles produces greenery in an eternal spring,
Flores et frondes per tempora cuncta virendo	Flowers and leaves, flourshing through all the seasons.

Insula pomorum que fortunata vocatur

The island of apples, which is called "fortunate,"

Ex re nomen habet quia per se singula profert

Has its name because it produces things by itself.

Non opus est illi sulcantibus arva colonis

910.   There is no need for plows or farmers.

Omnis abest cultus nisi quem natura ministrat

All cultivation is lacking, except for what nature supplies.

Ultro facundas segetes producit et uvas

Beyond that, it produces rich harvests and grapes,

Nataque poma suis pretonso germine silvis

And apple trees grow from the close-cropped seed in the forest

Omnia gignit humus vice graminis ultro redundans

The soil produces everything, not just growing more grass.

Annis centenis aut ultra vivitur illic

915.   They live for a hundred years or more there.

Illic iura novem geniali lege sorores

Nine sisters rule there, by kindly law

Dant his qui veniunt nostris ex partibus ad se

Governing those who come to them from our parts.

Quarum que prior est fit doctior arte medendi

The one who is preeminent among them is quite learnéd in medicine,

Excedit que suas forma prestante sorores

And she is superior to her sisters in appearance.

Morgen ei nomen didicit que quid utilitatis

920.   Morgen is her name, and she has learned what is useful

Gramina cuncta ferant ut languida corpora curet

Of all herbs, they say, so that she might cure bodies lacking energy.

Ars quoque nota sibi qua scit mutare figuram

She also knows how to change her shape,

Et resecare novis quasi *dedalus aera pennis*	And cleave the air with strange wings, like Daedalus.
Cum vult est bristi carnoti sive *papie*	When she wants, she is in Brest, Chartres or Pavia,
Cum vult in vestris ex aere *labitur horis*	925. When she wants, she glides from the air in your shores.
Hanc que mathematicam *dicunt didicisse sorores*	They say that she taught mathematics to her sisters,
Moronoe mazoe gliten glitonea *gliton*	Moronoe, Mazoe, Gliten, Glitonea, Gliton,
Tyronoe thiten cithara *notissima thiten*	Tyronoe and Thiten, most famous for her lute, Thiten.

*   *   *

Illuc post bellum canblani *vulnere lesum*	There, after the war of Camlan, we led Arthur,
Duximus arcturum nos *conducente barintho*	930. Injured with a wound, Barinthus leading us,
Equora cui fuerant et celi *sydera nota*	To whom the waters and stars of the sky were known.
Hoc rectore ratis cum principe *venimus illuc*	With this pilot the vessel with the prince, we came there,
Et nos quo decuit morgen *suscepit honore*	And as it was fitting, Morgen received us with honor.
Inque suis talamis posuit super *aurea regem*	And in her chambers, she put the king on a golden
Strata manu que sibi detexit *vulnus honestum*	935. Couch, and with her hand uncovered his honorable wound.
Inspexit que diu tandem que *redire salutem*	And looked at it for a long time; finally she said that

Posse sibi dixit si secum *tempore longo*	He could recover, if he stayed with her for a long time.
Esset et ipsius vellet *medicamine fungi*	And wished to take advantage of her medicines.
Gaudentes igitur regem *commisimus illi*	Rejoicing, therefore, we entrusted the king to her,
Et dedimus ventis redeundo *vela secundis*	940. And, returning, we gave the sails to the favoring winds."

*   *   *

Tunc merlinus ad hec ait o *dilecte sodalis*	Then Merlin said, in answer to this, "O dear comrade,
Postmodo quanta tulit violato *federe regnum*	Thereafter, how much has the kingdom borne, the bond being violated,
Ut modo quod fuerat non sit *nam sorte sinistra*	So that what it was, it might not be, for by unlucky fate
Subducti proceres ac in sua *viscera versi*	The chieftains are led astray, and are at each others' throats;
Omnia turbarunt ut copia *diviciarum*	945. They stir everything up, so that the abundance of riches
Fugerit ex patria bonitas que *recesserit omnis*	Will have fled from the country, and all goodness will have receded,
Et desolati vacuent sua menia *cives*	And the ruined citizens will abandon their walls.
Insuper incumbit gens saxona *marce feroci*	The Saxon people, fierce in war, will oppress them,
Que nos et nostras iterum *crudeliter urbes*	Which again us and our cities cruelly
Subvertit legem que dei *violabit et edes*	950. Overthrow, and will violate the law of God and the temples.

Nempe deus nobis ut corrigat insipientes

Has patitur clades ob crimina nostra venire

Indeed God, so that He might correct the foolish, will allow

These disasters to come to us on account of our crimes."

*   *   *

Non dum desierat cum talia protulit alter

Ergo necesse foret populo transmittere quemdam

Et mandare duci festina nave redire

Si iam convaluit solitis ut viribus hostes

Arceat et cives antiqua pace reformet

Non merlinus ait non sic gens illa recedet

Ut semel in vestris ungues infixerit ortis

Regnum namque prius populos que iugabit et urbes

Viribus atque suis multis dominabitur annis

Tres tamen ex nostris magna virtute resistent

Et multos periment et eos in fine domabunt

[Merlin] had scarcely finished when the other spoke with these words:

"Therefore, it would be necessary for the people to send someone

955. And to bid the commander to return in a swift ship

If he has already recuperated, so that with his former powers

He may ward off the enemy and reestablish the citizens in [their] old-time tranquility."

"Not," said Merlin, "Not thus will that nation pull back

As once it has gotten its claws into our shores;

960. For it will first dominate the kingdom and the people

With its power, and will rule for many years.

Three, however, of our number will resist with great valor,

And many will die, and in the end they will beat them.

Set non perficient quia sic sententia summi	But it will do no good, because thus goes the decision of the Highest
Judicis existit britones ut nobile regnum	965. Judge: that the Britons for a long time
Temporibus multis amittant debilitate	Will lose their noble kingdom through weakness,
Donec ab armorico veniet temone conanus	Until Conan come with his chariot from Brittany,
Et cadualadrus cambrorum dux venerandus	And Cadwalader, the respected leader of the Welsh,
Qui pariter scotos cambros et cornubienses	Who will equally unite the Scots, the Welsh and the Cornish,
Armoricosque viros sociabunt federe firmo	970. And the men of Brittany in a firm treaty,
Amissum que suis reddent diadema colonis	And will give to their peasantry the lost crown.
Hostibus expulsis renovato tempore bruti	When the enemies are expelled, and the time of Brutus is renewed,
Tractabunt que suas sacratis legibus urbes	They will deal with their cities with holy laws.
Incipiunt reges iterum superare remotos	They will begin again to overcome remote kings,
Et sua regna sibi certamine subdere forti.	975. And subdue their kingdoms to them with strong battle."

*   *   *

Nemo superstes erit tunc ex hiis qui modo vivunt	"None of those now living will still be alive then,"

Telgesinus ait nec tot fera
prelia quemquam

Inter concives quot te vidisse
putamus

Sic equidem merlinus ait nam
tempore multo

Vixi multa videns et de
nostratibus in se

Et de barbarica turbanti
singula gente

Crimen quod memini cum
constans proditus esset

et defugissent parui trans
equora fratres

Uter et ambrosius ceperunt
ilico bella

Per regnum fieri quod tunc
rectore carebat

Vortigernus enim consul
gewissus in omnes

Agmina ducebat patrias ut
duceret illas

Ledens innocuos miseranda
clade colonos

Denique vi subita rapuit
diadema peremptis

Nobilibus multis et regni
cuncta subegit

Ast hii qui fuerant cognato
sanguine iuncti

Taliesin said, "Nor has anyone
seen as many fierce battles

Between fellow-citizens as we
think you have."

"Yes indeed," said Merlin,
"For I have lived

980. A long time and seen many
things, both ours, among
ourselves

And characteristics of the
foreign nation that upsets things.

The crime which I remember,
when Constans was betrayed,

And the little brothers fled
across the sea,

Uther and Ambrosius.   Wars
began from that,

985. Throughout the kingdom,
which then lacked a guide.

Consul Vortigern of Gwent,
you see, led his columns

Against every country, that he
might govern them,

Harming the helpless peasants
with miserable disaster.

Then, with sudden force he
stole the crown, many   nobles

990. Being done away with, and he
conquered the whole of the
kingdom.

But those who were related by
blood

Fratribus id graviter tolerantes igne cremare	To the brothers, taking it hard, began to burn
Ceperunt cunctas infausti principis urbes	All the cities of the unlucky princes with fire
Et turbare suum crudeli milite regnum	And to turn the kingdom upside-down with brutal soldiery,
Nec permiserunt illum cum pace potiri	995. Nor did they permit him to rule it in peace.
Anxius ergo manens cum non obstare rebelli	Constantly worried, therefore, since he could not withstand
Quivisset populo parat invitare remotos	The rebellious populace, he prepares to invite faraway
Ad sua bella viros quibus obvius iret in hostes	Men to his wars, with whom he might stand against his enemies.
Mox ex diversis venerunt partibus orbis	Soon from various parts of the world came
Pugnaces turme quas excipiebat honore	1000. Belligerent bands which he recieved with honor.
Saxona gens etiam curvis advecta carinis	For the Saxon nation, arriving in its curved hulls,
Eius ad obsequium galeato milite venit	Had come to do him service, with helmeted soldiers.
Hinc duo prefuerant audaci pectore fratres	Their leaders were two bold-hearted brothers,
Horsus et hengistus qui prodicione nefanda	Horsa and Hengist, who with unspeakable treachery
Postmodo leserunt populos lesere que urbes	1005. Afterward harmed the populace, and harmed the cities.
Postquam namque ducem famulantes sedulitate	For after serving the king dutifully,

Attraxere sibi cives quoque lite propinqua	They drew [him] to them, and also, they saw citizens
Viderunt motos leviter quo subdere regem	Easily moved to fight, by which they were able to mislead the king.
Possent in populos verterunt arma feroces	Agressive, they turned their weapons against the people.
Ruperunt que fidem proceres quoque premeditatos	1010. The chieftains broke faith and with a thought-out
Fraude necaverunt sedentes ferme vocatos	Deception they killed them all as they sat, called
Insimul ut pacem secum fedus que iugarent	Together so that they might effect a peace treaty among themselves.
Truserunt que ducem nivei trans ardua montis	And they kicked the king out over the slopes of snowy mountains.
Que sibi de regno cepi cantare futura	These things I began to prophesy to him concerning his kingdom.
Inde domos patrie peragrantes igne cremabant	1015. From there, wandering around, they burned the nation's homes with fire,
Et nitebantur sibimet submittere cuncta	And struggled to subordinate everything to themselves.
At vortimerus cum causa pericula regni	But Vortimer, when he had seen the cause of the kingdom's
Expulsum que patrem bruti vidisset ab aula	Danger and that his father had been expelled from the palace of Brutus,
Assensu populi sumpsit diadema feramque	He took the crown, with the people's assent, and attacked

Invasit gentem concives dilaniantem	1020. The wild nation tearing his citizens apart,
Atque coegit eam per plurima bella redire	And he compelled it, by many wars, to go back
In thanatum qua classis erat que vexarat illam	Into Tanet, where the fleet was, that had conveyed it.
Set dum diffugerent bellator corruit horsus	But when they were fleeing, the warrior Horsa fell,
Et plures alii nostris perimentibus illos	And many others, [killed were] they by our fighters.
Inde secutus eos circumdedit obsidione	1025. The king, following them, surrounded them with a siege,
Ilico rex thanathum terra que mari que resistens	Cutting Thanet off by land and sea;
Set non prevaluit subito nam classe potiti	But he did not prevail, for suddenly they linked up with their fleet,
Vi magna fecere viam ducti que per equor	They made a breakthrough, and, carried by sea,
Exegere suam festino remige terram	Attained their land by hasty rowing.
Ergo triumphato bellis victricibus hoste	1030. Therefore, his enemy conquered in victorious war,
Fit vortimerus rector venerandus in orbe	Vortimer became a ruler to be respected in the world,
Attrectando suum iusto moderamine regnum	Ruling his kingdom with just moderation.
Set soror hengisti successus renua tales	But Hengist's sister Rowena, bearing these events
Indignando ferens protecta que fraude venenum	With indignation, and protected by deceit, mixed

Miscuit existens pro fratre maligna noverca	1035. Poison, becoming on her brother's behalf a wicked stepmother,
Et dedit ut biberet fecit que perire bibentem	And gave it him to drink, and made him die drinking it.
Confestimque suo mandavit trans freta fratri	Immediately she sent to her brother across the straits
Ut remearet item cum tot tantis que catervis	That he might row back with all the manpower he could muster,
Quot sibi pugnaces possent submittere cives	As many as could defeat the warlike citizens.
Sic igitur fecit nam tantus in agmina nostra	1040. Thus, therefore, she did; for so great he came
Venit ut eriperet cunctis sua predia pregnans	Against our army, that he stole from everybody, loaded with loot,
Et loca per patrias penitus combureret igne	And he burned places throughout the country with fire.
Hec ita dum fierent in finibus armoricanis	While these things were going on, in Breton lands,
Uter at Ambrosius fuerant cum rege Biduco	Uther and Ambrosius were with King Biducus,
Iam gladio fiunt cincti bello que probati	1045. Already they were both girded with the sword and tested in war,
Et sibi diversas sociabant undique turmas	And were assembling different squadrons from everywhere,
Ut peterent natale solum gentesque fugarent	So that they might attack their native soil, and the nations might flee

Quod tunc instabant primam vastare paternam	Which then were oppressing their first homeland.
Ergo dedere suas vento que mari que carinas	Therefore they gave their ships to the winds and seas,
Presidio que suis concivibus applicuerunt	1050. And they landed for the protection of their fellow-citizens.
Nam vortigernum per cambrica regna fugatum	For Vortigern, fleeing through the Welsh kingdoms,
Inclusumque sua pariter cum turre cremarunt	They burned, shut up in his tower.
Enses inde suos vertere recenter in anglos	From there they turned their swords against the Angles,
Congressi que simul vincebant sepius illos	And often, when they came together, would defeat them;
Et vice transversa devincebantur ab illis	1055. And on the other hand they would be defeated by them.
Denique consertis magno conamine dextris	Finally, with great effort and with firm right hands
Instant nostrates et ledunt acriter hostes	Our men oppose and the enemy and deal them a stinging defeat,
Hengistum que necant christoque volente triumphant	And they kill Hengist and by the will of Christ are victorious.
Hiis igitur gestis cleri populique favore	Therefore by these deeds and the favor of the clergy and people
Ambrosio regnum que datur regnique corona	1060. The kingdom is given to Ambrosius, and the crown as well.
Postmodo quam gessit tractando singula iuste	Afterward he had managed it, dealing with justice,

Emensis autem per lustra *quaterna diebus*	But, the days being measured out through four terms,
Proditur a medico moritur que *bibendo venenum*	He was betrayed by a doctor and died by drinking poison.
Mox germanus ei succesit *iunior uter*	Immediately his younger brother Uther succeeded,
Nec primum potuit regnum *cum pace tueri*	1065. Nor was he able to watch over the kingdom in peace,
Perfida gens etenim demum *consueta redire*	For the faithless nation, accustomed then to return,
Venerat et solita vastabat *cuncta phalange*	Had come in their familiar formations and laid waste to everything.
Oppugnavit eam sevis *congressibus uter*	Uther fought against them in savage battles
Et pepulit victam trans equora *remige verso*	And beat them back across the water, rowing away.
Mox reformavit posito *certamine pacem*	1070. Right away he reestablished peace, struggles being put behind him,
Progenuit que sibi natum qui *postmodo talis*	And he got him a son who after all this
Extitit ut nulli fieret probitate *secundus*	Lived so that he could be second to no one in virtue.
Arturus sibi nomen erat *regnum que per annos*	Arthur was his name, and he governed the kingdom
Optinuit multos postquam *pater uter obivit*	For many years after his father Uther had died.
Id que dolore gravi gestum fuit *atque labore*	1075. This was accomplished by great woe and toil
Et nece multorum per plurima *bella virorum*	And the death of many men in several wars.

Nam dum predictus princeps langueret ab angla	For while the aforementioned prince was sick, from Anglia
Venerat infidus populos cunctas que per enses	The treacherous one came across the Humber, and by the sword
Trans humbrum patrias submiserat ac regiones	Conquered the people and all the home regions.
Et puer arturus fuerat nec debilitate	1080. And Arthur was a boy, and was not able,
Etatis poterat tantas compescere turmas	Because of his weakness and youth, to check the hordes.
Ergo consilio cleri populi que recepto	Therefore, having received the advice of the clergy and the people,
Armorico regi mittens Hoelo	Sending to Hoel, king of Brittany,
Ut sibi presidio festina classe rediret	That he might come back quickly, as a guard for him,
Sanguis enim communis eos sociabat amor que	1085. For he was bound by ties of blood and affection,
Alter ut alterius deberet dampna levare	So that one was obliged to relieve the afflictions of the other
Mox igitur collegit hoel ad bella feroces	Soon, therefore, Hoel had assembled for war,
Circumquaque viros et multis milibus ad nos	Rallying his fierce men and many soldiers,
Venit et arturo sociatus pertulit hostes	He came, and allied with Arthur drove them back,
Sepius agrediens et stragem fecit acerbam	1090. Often attacking, and he wrought havoc.
Hoc socio securus erat fortis que per omnes	With this ally Arthur was secure and strong and through all

Arturus turmas dum progrederetur in hostes	The hordes, when he advanced against the foe
Quos tandem vicit patriam que redire coegit	Which he then defeated, and compelled to return to its homeland.
Composuit que suum legum moderamine regnum	And he set his kingdom in order with moderation of its laws.
Mox quoque submisit post hec certamina scotos	1095. Right away he also conquered, after these battles, the Scots
Ac hibernenses convertens bella feroces	And the Irish, bringing wars, the fierce
Supposuit patrias illatis viribus omnes	Nations all he subdued with the forces he had brought.
Et norvegenses trans equora lata remotos	Also the Norwegians, far off across the sea
Subdidit et dacos invisa classe petitos	He subdued, and the Danes with the hated fleets were attacked;
Gallorum populos ceso frollone subegit	1100. He overcame the tribes of the Gauls at the death of Frollo,
Cui curam prime dederat romana potestas	To whom the Roman authority had given his office,
Romanos etiam bello sua regna petentes	For, fighting the Romans when they attacked his kingdom,
Obpugnans vicit procuratore perempto	He had won, and with the death of Procurator
Hybero lucio qui tunc collega que legnis	Hyberus Lucius, who then was a colleague of Legno
Imperatoris fuerat iussuque senatus	1105. The emperor, and by order of the Senate
Venerat ut fines gallorum demeret illi	Had come so that he might occupy the realms of the Gauls for it.

Ceperat interea sibi subdere regnum	Meanwhile Modred, the faithless and foolish regent
Infidus custos modredus desipiens que	Had begun to take over the kingdom for himself,
Illicitam venerem cum coniuge regis agebat	Carrying on an illicit love with the wife of the king.
Rex etenim transire volens ut fertur in hostes	1110. For the king, wishing to cross over, it is said, against his enemies,
Reginam regnumque suum commiserat illi	Entrusted his queen and his kingdom to him.
Ast ut fama tanti sibi venit ad aures	But when the rumor of such a great thing came to his ears,
Distulit hanc belli curam patriam que revertens	He deferred his concern for the war, and returning home
Applicuit multis cum milibus atque nepotem	He landed with many soldiers, and fighting
Obpugnans pepulit trans equora diffugientem	1115. Against his nephew he drove him fleeing across the deep.
Illic collectis vir plenus prodicione	There the man, full of deception, having gathered
Undique saxonibus cepit committere pugnam	Saxons from everywhere, began to wage war
Cum duce set cecidit deceptus gente prophana	With his commander, but he fell, deceived by the profane nation,
In qua confisus tantos inceperat actus	Trusting in whom he had begun such great undertakings.
O quantas hominum strages matrum que dolores	1120. Oh, what mayhem of men and sorrows of mothers
Quarum conciderant illic per prelia nati	Whose sons had fallen there in battle!

*Illic rex etiam letali vulnere
Lesus*

There the king, too, hurt with a
fatal injury

*Deseruit regnum tecumque per
equora vectus*

He left the kingdom and with
you, borne over the deep

*Ut predixisti nimpharum venit
ad aulam*

As you predicted, came to the
palace of the nymphs.

*Ilico modredi duo nati regna
volentes*

1125. Then the two sons of Modred,
each desiring

*Subdere quisque sibi ceperunt
bella movere*

To subdue the kingdoms for
himself, began to wage war,

*Alternaque suos prosternere
cede propinquos*

And to lay those near them low
with murder.

*Deinde nepos regis dux
constantinus in illos*

Then the nephew of the king,
Duke Constantine, against them

*Acriter insurgens populos
laniavit et urbes*

Rising sharply, tore into the
people and cities,

*Prostratis que simul crudeli
morte duobus*

1130. And when both were laid low
together in cruel death

*Iura dedit populo regni
diademate sumpto*

He ruled the people, having
assumed the diadem.

*Nec cum pace fuit quoniam
cognatus in illum*

Nor was he in peace, because
his relative Conan

*Prelia dira movens violavit
cuncta conanus*

Started a dire war against him
and despoiled everything

*Proripuit que sibi regiones
rege perempto*

And snatched for himself the
regions, the king being
deceased,

*Quas nunc debiliter nec cum
ratione gubernat*

1135. Those which he now governs
weakly and chaotically.

*   *   *

Hoc illo dicente cito venere clientes	When he was saying this, vassals came a-running
Et dixere sibi fontem sub montibus illis	And said to him that a fountain at the foot of those mountains,
Erupisse novvum latices que refundere puros	A new one, had burst forth and that it gushed pure waters
Qui iam manantes longe per concava vallis	Which now, flowing far through the hollows of the valley,
Girabant saltus refluo cum murmure lapsu	1140. Were swirling through the meadows with gurgling sound as it flowed.
Mox igitur spectare novvum consurgit uterque	Right away, therefore, both arose to see the new
Festinus fontem viso que resedit in herba	Fountain; Merlin, hastening, when he had seen it, sat on the grass
Merlinus laudat que locum limphas que fluentes	And praised the place and the flowing waters
Et miratur eas de cespite taliter ortas	And looked at them, springing from the turf thus,
Moxque siti captus se proclinavit in amnes	1145. Right away, taken with thirst, he leaned down to the river
Potavit que libens et tempora proluit unda	And drank freely, and washed his temples in the wave,
Utque per internos alui stomachique meatus	So that, going through his innards and stomach,
Humor iit laticis subsedavitque vaporem	The humor of the water settled the vapor
Corporis interni confestim mente recepta	Of the inside of his body, and without delay, his mind being regained,

Sese cognovit rabiem quoque perdidit omnem	1150. He came to himself and lost all madness
Et que torpuerat per longum tempus in illo	And what had lurked in him for a long time.
Sensus item rediit mansit que quod ante manebat	His sense returned to him, and he remained what he had been before:
Sanus et incolumis rursus ratione recepta	Healthy and unharmed again, his reason regained.
Ergo deum laudans vultus ad sidera tollit	Therefore, praising God, he raised his face to the stars,
Edidit et voces devoto famine tales	1155. And gave these words in a devoted utterance:

*   *   *

O rex siderea quo constat machina celi	"O King by whom the starry engine of the heavens stays on course,
Quo mare quo tellus leto cum germine fetus	By whom the sea and by whom the earth teem with offspring,
Dant que fovent que suos crebro que iuumanine prosunt	And give and foster them and with frequent help are beneficial
Humano generi profusa fertilitate	To the human race by lavish fertility,
Quo sensus rediit mentisque revanuit error	1160. By whom reason has returned and the wandering of my mind has vanished!
Raptus eram michimet quasi spiritus acta sciebam	I was taken away from myself, like a ghost I knew the deeds
Preteriti populi predicebamque futura	Of peoples in the past, and I predicted the future.

Tunc rerum secreta sciens
volucrum que volatus

Then, knowing the secrets of
things and of the flight of birds

Stellarum que vagos motus
lapsus que natantum

And the wandering movements
of stars, and the glide of
swimming [fish].

Id me vexabat naturalem que
negabat

1165. That disturbed me, and denied
me the tranquility

Humane menti districta lege
quietem

Natural to the human mind, by
the hold it had.

Nunc in me redii videorque
vigore moveri

Now I am returned to myself
and I seem to be animated with
the vigor

Quo vegetare meos animus
consueverat artus

By which the soul used to
animate my limbs.

Ergo summe pater tibi sic
obnoxius esse

Therefore, Highest Father,
slavish to you I ought

Debeo condignas ut digno
pectore laudes

1170. To be, so that worthy praises
with a worthy heart

Dicam semper agens letus
libamina leta

I may proclaim, and, happy,
doing happy sacrifices.

Bis etenim tua larga manus
michi profuit uni

For twice your generous hand
has benefitted me with one

Munere dando novvm viridi de
cespite fontem

Gift, giving a new fountain
from the green turf,

Nam modo possideo latices
quibus ante carebam

For now I possess the water
which before I lacked;

Et reducem capitis sumpsi
potando salutem

1175. And I regained by drinking it
the health of my head.

Ista set inde venit bis o dilecte
sodalis

But, o dear friend, whence
comes this twice,

Ut fons iste nouus sic effluit
atque reformet

That this fountain thus flowed
and restored

Me michi qui fueram quasi	Me to myself who was mad
vecors hactenus ex me	hitherto, beside myself?"

*   *   *

Telgesinus ait rerum		Taliesin said, "The lavish
moderator opimus		Regulator of things
Flumina per species divisit et	1180.	Divided the rivers by types
addidit ultro		and, further, gave
Cuique suas vires ut prosint		To each its powers so that it
sepius egris		might often benefit the sick.
Sunt etenim fontes fluuii que		You see, there are fountains,
lacus que per orbem		rivers and lakes throughout the world,
Qui virtute sua multis et sepe		Which by their power many
medentur		and often are helped.
Albula namque rapax rome		At Rome, for instance, the
fluit amne salubri		rushing Albula flows, with its healthful river,
Quem sanare ferunt certo	1185.	Which, they say, is a sure cure
medicamine vulnus		for wounds.
Manat in italia fons alter qui		There is another fountain in
ciceronis		Italy, which is Cicero's,
Dicitur hic oculos ex omni		It is said, which cures the eyes
vulnere curat		from every injury.
Ethiopes etaim stagnum		They say that the Ethiopians
perhibentur habere		have a pond
Quo velut ex oleo facies		Which makes the face it is
perfusa nitescit		poured on shine as if from oil.
Affrica fert fontem qui vulgo	1190.	Africa has a fountain which is
zama vocatur		commonly called Zama;
Potus dat voces subita virtute		One drink, and it produces
canoras		melodious voices with sudden power.

Dat lacus italie clitorius tedia vini	Lake Clitorius in Italy gives an aversion to wine.
Qui de fonte chios potant perhibentur hebere	Those who drink from the fountain Chios are said to become groggy.
Fertur habere duos tellus boetica fontes	The Boeotian earth is said to have two fountains;
Hic facit inmemores memores facit ille bibentes	1195. One makes those who drink forgetful, the other makes them remember.
Continet ipso lacum tam dira peste nocivum	The same place contains a poisonous lake with such a dire contagion
Ut generet furias nimieque libidinis estum	That it produces delirium, and surges of too much libido.
Fons syticus venerem venerisque repellit amorem	The fountain of Cyzicus drives away libido and the love of sexuality.
Campana regione fluunt ut dicitur amnes	In the region of Campagna there flow, as it is said, rivers
Qui faciunt steriles fecundas flumine poto	1200. Who make barren women fertile when its stream is drunk.
Idem dicuntur furias abolere virorum	The same are said to destroy the furies of men.
Ethiopum tellus fert rubro flumine fontem	Ethiopia's soil contains a fountain with a red current;
Qui bibit ex illo limphaticus inde redibit	When a madman drinks from it, thence he will be restored.
Fons leinus fieri numquam permittit abortum	The fountain of Leinus never permits a miscarriage.
Sunt duo sycilie fontes steriles facit alter	1205. There are two fountains in Sicily; one makes girls barren,

Alter fecundans geniali lege puellas	The other making them fertile according to the law of reproduction.
Flumina thessalie duo sunt virtutis opime	In Thessaly there are two rivers of abundant power;
Hoc potans nigrescit ovis candescit ab illo	Drinking from this one a sheep turns black, turns white from that one,
Ast ab utroque bibens variato vellere degit	But the one drinking from both lives with mottled fleece.
Clitumnus lacus est quem continet umbrica tellus	1210. There is a Lake Clitumnus, which the soil of Umbria contains;
Hic aliquando boves fertur producere magnos	This is said to produce big bulls at times,
In que reatina fit equorum dura palude	And in the Reatine Swamp horses' hooves harden
Ungula confestim dum progrediuntur arenas	Immediately when they go over its sands.
Asphaltite lacu iudee corpora mergi	In the Asphalt lake in Judaea bodies cannot
Nequaquam possunt vegetat dum spiritus illa	1215. Ever sink while a soul animates them,
At contra stagnum syden fert indica tellus	But on the other hand the soil of India has a pool called Syda,
Quo res nulla natat set mergitur ilico fundo	In which no thing swims, but sinks to the bottom of it.
Et lacus est aloe quo res non mergitur ulla	And there is Lake Aloe, in which no thing sinks,
Omnia set fluitant quamvis sint plumbea saxa	But everything floats, even lumps of lead.
Fons quoque marsidie compellit saxa natare	1220. The Marsidian Fountain also makes stones swim.

Stix fluuius de rupe fluit
perimet que bibentes

The River Styx flows from a
cliff and kills those who drink.

Has clades eius testatur
achadia tellus

The land of Achadia bears
witness to these deaths.

Fons ydumeus quater
inmutando diebus

An Idumaean fountain four
times in the days changing

Mira lege suos fertur variare
colore

Its color by a marvelous law, it
is said:

Pulverilentus enim viridis que
fit ordine verso

1225. For, murky, it becomes green
in an orderly progression;

Fit quoque sanguineus fit
limpidus amne decoro

It also becomes blood-red; it
becomes clear, with its
downstream idyllic.

Ex hiis per ternos unum
retinere colorem

It keeps one color of these for
three

Asseritur menses semper
voluentibus annis

Months, it is claimed, as the
years keep rolling by.

Trogdytus lacus est eius
quoque profluit unda

There is Lake Trogdytus,
whose wave also flows

Ter fit amara die ter dulci
grata sapore

1230. Three times a day it is bitter,
thrice pleasing, with a sweet
taste.

Epiri de fonte faces ardere
feruntur

Torches, it is said, burst into
flame from the fountain of
Epirus,

Extincte rursus que suum
componere lumen

And when put out light up
again.

Sic algere die perhibetur fons
garamantum

Thus the fountain of the
Garamantes, it is said, is cold
by day

Et vice trans versa tota
fervescere nocte

And in turn boils all night,

Ut neget accessum pre frigore pre que calore	1235. So that it might deny access by cold and by heat.
Sunt et aque calide multos fervore minantes	There are hot waters that threaten many by their heat,
Fervoremque trahunt dum perlabuntur alumen	And bear this heat while they flow through alum
Aut sulphur quibus est vis ignea grata medendi	Or sulfur, in which there is a fiery power good for healing.
His aliis que deus ditavit viribus amnes	God endowed rivers with these powers
Ut fierent egris subite medicina salutis	1240. That they might be a ready treatment for the health of the sick,
Et manifestarent quanta virtute creator	And that they might show forth with what power the Creator
Premineat rebus dum sic operatur in illis	Is preeminent in things while thus He works in them.
Hos etiam latices summa ratione salubres	Also these waters are healthful in the highest degree,
Esse reor subitam que reor conferre medelam	I think, and I think that they could bring a prompt cure
Nunc poturere novo sic erumpendo liquore	1245. Now, just when the liquid has burst forth.
Hii modo sub terra per concava ceca fluebant	They were just flowing under the ground in blind caves,
Ut plures alii qui submanare feruntur	Just as many others are said to do, which flow below.
Forsitan excursus illorum prepediente	Perhaps their outflowing is from a blockage
Obice vel saxi vel terre pondere lapse	Thrown in their way, whether a stone or the weight of sliding earth,

Retrogradum cursum facientes arbitror illos	1250. Making their current go backward, I think,
Paulatim penetrasse solum fontem que dedisse	Little by little penetrating the soil and giving a fountain.
Sic plures manare vides iterum que redire	Thus you see many flow again and return
Sub terram rursus que suas tenuisse cavernas	Under the ground again which kept to their caverns.
Hec ita dum gererent rumor discurrit ubique	When these things were proceeding, the rumor went out everywhere
In calidone novum silvis erumpere fontem	1255. That a new fountain had burst forth in the forests of Caledon,
Sanatum que virum post quam potavit ab illo	And that a man had been cured after drinking from it,
Tempore qui multo rabie corruptus et isdem	A man ravaged by madness for a long time, and this same man
Extiterat silvis ritu vivendo ferarum	Had lived in the woods with the manner of living of wild animals.
Mox igitur venere duces proceres que videre	Right away, therefore, the leaders and chieftains came and saw
Et colletari curato flumine vati	1260. And rejoiced with the bard cured by water.
Cum que statum patrie per singula notificassent	And when they had reported in detail the state of the nation,
At que rogaretur sua sceptra resumere rursus	And when he was asked to take up his sceptre again,
Et tractare suam solito moderamine gentem	And do deal with his people with his accustomed moderation,

Sic ait o iuvenes mea non hoc exigit etas	Thus he spoke: "O youngsters, my age demands not this,
In senium vergens que sic michi corripit artus	1265. Getting close as I am to old age, which grips my joints
Ut vix preteram laxatis viribus arva	So that I can scarcely cross the field with my slackend powers.
Iam satis exegi longevo tempore Letos	I have already had a long time of life, happy
Glorificando dies michi dum rideret habundans	Days, rejoicing while on me there smiled abundant
Copia magnarum profuse diviciarum	Resources, a profusion of great wealth.
Roboris annosi silva stat quercus in ista	1270. There stands a forest of an aged oak; the oak therein
Quam sic exegit consumens cuncta vetustas	Is so oppressed by age, which consumes everything,
Ut sibi deficiat succus penitus que putrescat	So that its sap is drying up, and it is rotting within.
Hanc ego cum primum cepisset crescere vidi	I saw it when it began to grow,
Et glandem de qua processit forte cadentem	And the acorn from which it grew falling by chance,
Dum super astaret picus ramumque videret	1275. While a woodpecker perched over it and looked at the branch.
Hic illam crevisse sua iam sponte sedebam	Here I would sit, watching it grow of its own accord,
Singula prospiciens tunc et verebar in istis	Each twig then, and I was in awe in these
Saltibus atque locum memori cum mente notavi	Meadows, and I marked the spot in my memory.
Ergo diu vixi mea me gravitate senectus	Therefore, I have lived a long time, and my old age, with its heaviness,

Detinuit dudum rursus regnare recuso	1280. Holds me back, refusing to rule again as formerly.
Me calidonis opes viridi sub fronde manentem	The riches of Caledon, staying under the green branch
Delectant pocius quam quas fert india gemme	Please me more than the gems that India produces,
Quam quod habere tagus per littora dicitur aurum	More than the gold that the Tagus is said to have along its shores,
Quam segetes situle quam dulcis methidis uue	Than the crops of Sicily, than the grapes of sweet Methis,
Aut celse turres aut cinte menibus urbes	1285. Or high towers, or cities girt about with walls,
Aut fraglascentes tirio medicamine vestes	Or robes fragrant with Tyrian unguents.
Res michi nulla placet que me divellere possit	Nothing pleases me that can tear me away
Ex calidone mea me iudice semper amena	From Caledon, always pleasant, if I'm to judge.
Hic ero dum vivam pomis contentus et herbis	Here I will be while I live, content with apples and herbs,
Et mundabo meam pia per ieiunia carnem	1290. And I will purge my flesh by humble devotions
Ut valeam fungi vita sine fine perhenni	That I may be wothy to enjoy the life without end, everlasting.
Hec dum dicebat proceres super ethera cernunt	While he was saying this, the chieftains saw up in the air,
Agmina longa gruum flexo per inane volatu	Long lines of cranes through the sky, in a veering flight,
Ordine girantes per littora certa videri	Flying in order through certain shores they could be

Possunt in exstructa liquido super aere turma

1295. Seen in a regulated formation through the clear air.

Hec admirantes merlinum dicere poscunt

Marvelling at this they asked Merlin to say

Quid certe fuerat quod tale more volarent

Why it was that they would fly in that manner.

Mox merlinus eis volucres ut cetera plura

Right away Merlin [said] to them, "The Founder of the world

Natura propria ditavit conditor orbis

Endowed the birds and many other beings with their proper nature.

Sic didici multis silvis habitando diebus

1300. Thus I have learned by living in the woods for many days.

*   *   *

Est igitur natura gruum dum celsa pererrant

It is the nature of cranes, while they wander above

Si plures assint ut earum sepe volatu

If many are there, as often in their flight,

Aut hanc aut aliam videamus inesse figuram

Either this or another pattern we see,

Una modo clamando monet servare volando

One just warns by calling to hold steady while flying,

Turbatus solitis ne descrepet ordo figuris

1305. Lest the formation be out of its customary pattern.

Aut dum raucescit subit altera deficienti

Or when he becomes hoarse, another overtakes the failing one.

Excubias noctis faciunt custos qui lapillum

Sleeping in the field at night they appoint a guard who holds

Sustinet in digitis dum vult
expellere sompnos

A pebble in its claws while it
wants to drive away sleep.

Cumque vident aliquos subito
clamore citantur

And when they see others, with
a sudden noise they are roused.

Penne nigrescunt cunctarum
quando senescunt

1310. The wings of all of them
blacken as they age.

Ast aquile que nomen habent
ab acumine visus

But eagles, who get their name
from the sharpness of their sight,

Obtutus tanti pre cunctis esse
feruntur

Of such acuity that they are
said to be beyond all,

Ut perferre queant non flexo
lumine solem

So that they can bear the direct
light of the sun.

Ad radium pullos suspendunt
scire volentes

They hang up their nestlings in
its beams, wanting to know

Illo vitato ne degener exstet in
illis

1315. If there are weaklings among
them, who avoid it.

In montis sullime manent super
equora pennis

They hover over the deep,
mountain-high,

Aspiciunt que suas uno sub
gurgite predas

And they see their prey beneath
the flood;

Ilico descendunt rapido per
inane volatu

Down they go in rapid flight
through the void,

Et rapiunt pisces ut poscit
origo natantes

And seize fish, swimming as
their species requires.

Postposito coitu sine semine
sepe mariti

1320. Avoiding coitus, often without
the seed of her mate,

Concipit et generat dictu
mirabile vultur

The she-vulture concieves and
reproduces, amazing to say.

Hec per celsa volans
aquilarum more cadaver

She, flying through the heights
like an eagle, carrion

Naribus elatis longe trans
equora sentit

She scents with wide nostrils,
far across the deep.

Quod quamvis tardo non horret adire volatu

The which she does not shrink from approaching, with slow flight,

Ut sese valeat preda saciare cupita

1325. So that she may be able to satiate herself with the desired prey.

Idem centenis robustus vivit in annis

This same bird lives strong for a century.

Nuntia veris avis crepitante ciconia rostro

The messenger bird of spring with its croaking beak, the stork

Dicta fovere suos in tantum sedula natos

Is said to protect its young so very carefully

Exuat ut proprias nudato pectore plumas

That it removes the feathers from its bare breast.

Hec cum bruma venit fertur vitare procellas

1330. This bird, when winter comes, is said to avoid storms

Et fines asie ductu cornicis adire

And to go to the borders of Asia, led by a crow.

Pascit eam pullus senio cum deficit etas

The chicks feed it when with feebleness age has taken away,

Quod depavit eum iam debuit ipsa diebus

Because it fed them in the days when it ought.

Excedit volucres dulci modulamine cunctas

The swan exceeds all birds with the the sweet melodiousness

Cum moritur cignus nautis gratissimus ales

1335. When it dies, a bird most welcome to sailors.

Hunc in hiperboreo perhibent acccedere tractu

They say that in Hyperborea it is attracted

Ad cantum cithare per littora forte sonantis

To the music of the lute played by chance on the shores.

Strucio que ponit sub pulvere deserit ova	The ostrich abandons the eggs which she puts under the dust.
Ut foveantur ibi dum negligat ipsa fovere	So that they may be cared for there while she neglects to care for them;
Inde creantur aves radio pro matre cubante	1340. Thence birds come into being by sunbeams in place of a mother.
Ardea cum pluvias tempestates que perhorret	The heron, when it fears rains and storms,
Evolat ad nubes ut tanta pericula vitet	Flies to the clouds, and avoids such dangers.
Hince illam subitos dicunt portendere nimbos	Thus sailors say that it foretells sudden rain-clouds
Sublimem quociens spectant super ethera naute	When they see it high up in the sky.
Unica semper avis divino munere phenix	1345. The phoenix is unique among birds by a supernatural gift.
In terris arabum redivivo corpore surgit	In the lands of the Arabs it arises with a renewed body;
Cumque senescit adit loca fervidiora calore	Whenever it gets old it goes to places burning with the heat
Solis et ingentes ab aromate iungit acervos	Of the sun and puts together heaps of spices,
Componit que rogum quem crebris motibus ale	And makes a pyre which with quick wing-movements
Succendit fertur que super penitus que crematur	It ignites, and it is said that on it it is burned up.
Producit volucrem pulvis de corpore facta	1351. The ashes from its body produce a bird,
Et fit item phenix hac lege novata per evum	And the phoenix in this way is renewed for centuries.

Nidificare volens fert cinnomon cinomolgus	The cinnamolgus, wishing to nest, brings cinnamon
Edificat que suum procero robore nidum	And builds its nest in a high oak.
Illinc pennatis homines abducere telis	1355. From there men with feathered weapons attempt
Moverunt cumulum soliti transmittere venum	To take away the heap, accustomed to take it away for sale.
Alcion avis est que stagna marina frequentat	The halcyon is a bird that frequents maritime pools
Edidficat que suos hiemale tempore nidos	And builds its nests in winter.
Dum cubat equora sunt septem tranquilla diebus	While it nests, the seas are calm for seven days
Et venti cessant tempestates que remisse	1360. And the winds cease, and storms hold back, to produce
Inpendunt placidam volucri famulando quietem	A placid calm for the nesting bird.
Psitacus humanam proprio modulamine vocem	The parrot's voice is sometimes mistaken for a human's
Dum non spectatur prorsus proferre putatur	While not being directly observed.
Intermiscet ave verbis et chere iocosis	It mixes "hello" and "bonjour" with joking words.
Est pelicanus avis pullos consueta necare	1365. The pelican is a bird accustomed to kill its young,
Et confusa tribus lugere dolore diebus	And mourn in grief for three days.
Denique supposito laniat sua corpora rostro	Thereafter it tears its own body with its beak,

Et scindens venas educit sanguinis undas	And, cutting the veins, lets out waves of blood,
Et vite reduces reddit rorando volucres	And the birds are quickly returned to life by the dripping.
Dum diomedee lacrimosa voce 1370. *resultant*	When the petrels resound with tearful voice
Et faciunt planctus subitam portendere mortem	And make their cry, sudden death is portended,
Dicuntur regum vel magna pericula regni	They say, of kings or great dangers to the state.
Cumque vident aliquem discernunt ilico quid sit	And when they see anyone, they make out what he might be,
Barbarus an grecus nam grecum plausibus ale	Barbarian or Greek; for the Greek with flapping of wing
Et blandimentis adeunt lete que 1375. *resultant*	And nuzzlings come forward, and happily twitter;
Circueunt alios pennis que feruntur iniquis	They circle around the others and are borne on hostile wing,
Horrentique sono velut hostes agrediuntur	And with cries of alarm, as if an enemy were approaching.
Mennonides quinto semper dicuntur in anno	The sandpipers are said, every fifth year,
Mennonis ad tumulum longo remeare volatu	To make the long flight to the tomb of Memnon
Et deflere ducem troiano marte 1380. *peremptum*	And mourn the leader lost in the Trojan War.
Fert quoque mirandam splendens circinea pennam	The radiant Hercynia carries an amazing feather,
Nocte sub obscura que fulget ut ignea lampas	Which shines in the dark night like a fiery torch
Aque ministrat iter si preportetur eunti	And shows the way if carried before the traveller.

Quando nidificat devellit ab arbore picus	When the woodpecker nests, it tears from the tree
Clavos et cuneos quos non divelleret ullus	1385. Nails and wedges which no other can tear out;
Cuius ab impulsu vicinia tota resultant	The area around resounds with his blows."

*   *   *

His igitur dictis quidam vesanus ad illos	When these things had been said, a certain madman to them
Accessit subito seu sors conduxerat illum	Came, all at once, whether fate had led him;
Terrifico clamore nemus complebat et auras	With a frightful howling he filled the grove and the air,
Et quasi sevus aper spumabat bella minando	1390. And like a wild boar he was foaming at the mouth, having threatened wars.
Ocius ergo virum capiunt secum que sedere	Soon, therefore, they captured the man and forced him
Cogunt ut moveat risus que iocos que loquendo	To sit, that he might provoke laughter and jokes by his talk.
Inspiciens igitur vates attentius illum	Looking, therefore, at him, the attentive bard
Quis fuerit recolit gemitum que reducit ab imo	Remembered who he had been, and fetched a groan from deep down
Pectore sic dicens non hec fuit eius ymago	1395. From his breast, saying thus: "This was not always his appearance.
Olim dum nobis iuuenilis floruit etas	Once, while the time of our youth was in bloom,

Pulcher enim fortis fuerat tunc tempore miles	He was handsome and strong, a knight at that time,
Et quem nobilitas regum que ferebat origo	And the nobility of kings and his origin marked him.
Hunc mecum plures que simul tunc dives habebam	I had him and many like him with me when I had wealth.
Tot que bonis sociis felix censebar eramque	1400. I was thought happy in so many good friends, and I was.
Accidit interea dum venaremur in altis	It happened meanwhile, while we were hunting in the high
Montibus argustli nos devenisse sub una	Mountains of Arwystli that we came up under one
Que patulis ramis surgebat in aera quercu	Oak whose spreading branches rose up in the air.
Fons ibi manabat viridi circumdatus herba	There was a fountain there, surrounded by green plants
Cuius erant latices humanis haustibus apti	1405. Whose waters were fit for humans to drink.
Ergo siti pariter correpti sedimus illic	Therefore, overcome by thirst we sat down there
Et fontis puros avide libavimus amnes	And greedily drank the pure water of the spring
Deinde super teneras solito conspeximus herbas	Then we saw, on the delicate greenery that usually
In rivo fontis redolentia poma iacere	Lies on the banks of a spring, fragrant apples.
Mox ea collegit qui primus adspexerat iste	1410. Right away the man gathered them who had first seen them,
Porrexit que michi subito pro munere ridens	And all at once, laughing, passed them to me, as a gift.
Ergo distribui data poma sodalibus et me	Therefore I distributed the apples he had given, and I

Expertem feci quia non suffecit acervus	Did without, because the heap was not big enough.
Riserunt alii quibus impertita fuerunt	The others laughed, with whom the apples had been shared,
Me que vocant largum cupidis quoque faucibus illa 1415.	And they call me generous, and also with their greedy throats
Agrediendo vorant et pauce fuisse queruntur	They devour them, and complain because they were so few.
Nec mora corripuit rabies miserabilis istum	With no delay, a pitiful madness seized him
Et cunctos alios qui mox ratione carentes	And all the others who, immediately bereft of reason
More canum sese lacerant mordendo visissim	In the manner of dogs bit each other by turns,
Strident et spumant et humi sine mente volutant 1420.	They howled and foamed at the mouth and rolled on the ground out of their minds.
Denique digressi sunt illinc more Lupino	Then they ran off, in the manner of wolves,
Complentes vacuas miseris ululatibus auras	Filling the empty air with pitiable howls.
Hec michi non illis velut estimo poma dabantur	I think these apples were intended for me, not for them;
Postmodo ceu diidici nam tunc in partibus illis	Afterward I learned just that, for then in those parts
Una fuit mulier que me dilexerat ante 1425.	One woman there was who had loved me before,
Et mecum multis venerem saciaverat annis	And had satisfied her passion with me for many years.
Hanc post quam sprevi secum que coire negavi	I rejected her after that, and refused her company,

Ut me dampanaret rapuit mox leva voluntas	So that she cursed me, and right away an unhinged desire seized her,
Cumque movens aditus alios reperire nequiret	And when, for all her maneuvering, she was unable to find any other approaches,
Apposuit fonti super illita dona veneni	1430. She put her gifts smeared with poison over the spring,
Quo rediturus eram meditans hac arte nocere	Where I would be returning, intending by this means to do harm
Si fruerer pomis in gramine forte repertis	If I had enjoyed the apples found by chance on the grass.
At me sors melior sic conservavit ab illis	But a better fate thus saved me from them,
Ut modo predixi set eum compellere queso	As I have just said, but I ask you to make that man
Hoc de fonte novo limphas potare salubres	1435. Drink the healthful waters of this new spring,
Ut si forte suam possit rehabere salutem	So that if by chance he can regain his health
Se cognoscat item mecumque laboret in istis	He may know himself and work with me in these
Saltibus in domino dum postera vita manebit	Meadows, in the Lord, while the rest of his life remains.
Sic igitur fecere duces sumpto que liquore	Thus, therefore, the chieftains did, and when the liquid had been consumed
Redditur ille sibi qui vecors venerat illuc	1440. He, who had come there mad, was returned to his senses.
Cognovit que suos subito curatus amicos	And, cured, he recognized his friends at once.

*　　　*　　　*

Tunc merlinus ait tibi nunc constanter eundum	Then Merlin said, "You must now go constantly
Est in agone dei qui te tibi reddidit ut nunc	In the work of God, who has returned you to yourself, as now
Ipsemet inspectas qui per deserta tot annis	You see yourself, who for so many years in the wilderness
Ut fera vixisti sine sensu turpis eundo	1445. Did live like a wild animal, dull, without sense.
Ne modo diffugias frutices ratione recepta	Nor should you flee the trees, your reason having returned,
Aut virides saltus quos iam limphando colebas	Or the green meadows that you inhabited while you were mad.
Set mecum maneas ut quos tibi surripiebat	But you should remain with me so that those days which
Vis virosa dies iterum reparare labores	1449. The man-devouring force took from you to compensate
Obsequio domini quod erit per singula mecum	As a gift of the Lord, what will be with me in every　aspect.
Ex hoc nunc commune tibi dum vivit uterque	From this point on, while the other lives, in common with you
Ergo sub hoc maeldinus ait nam nomine tali	Therefore, at this, Maeldinus said (for by that name
Dictus erat non hoc pater o venerande recuso	He had been called), "I will not refuse this, o reverend father
Letus enim tecum silvas habitabo deum que	For I will live happy with you in the woods, and God
Tota mente colam tremulos dum rexerit artus	1455. I will serve with my entire mind while my trembling members are guided

Spiritus iste meos quem te doctore piabo	By the spirit, the which I will purify, you being the doctor."
Sic et ergo faciam vobiscum tercius auctus	"Thus I too will increase your number to three,"
Telgesinus ait despecto themate mundi	Taliesin said, "Leaving the business of the world behind,
Iam satis exegi vivendo tempora vane	I have already lived long enough, for nothing.
Et nunc tempus adest quo me michi te duce reddam	1460. And now the time is here where I will return to myself, you being the leader.
Vos set abite duces urbes defendere vestras	But you, chieftains, go off to defend your cities.
Non decet ut nostram vestro sermone quietem	It is not fitting that your speech should disturb
A modo turbetis satis applausistis amico	Our quiet speech. You have applauded my friend enough."

*   *   *

Discedunt proceres remanent tres et ganieda	The chieftains go away, and the three remain, and Ganeida,
Quarta soror vatis sumpta quoque denique vita	1465. The bard's sister, making a fourth, who had gotten on with her life
Ducebat vitam regis post fata pudicam	After the king's passing, and was leading a blameless life,
Que modo tot populos indicto iure regebat	Ruling so many peoples by the laws he had enacted.
Nunc cum fratre sibi silvis nil dulcius exstat	Now, in the woods with her brother, there was nothing sweeter.

Hanc etiam quandoque suus rapiebat ad alto	Her spirit, too, carried her off to the heights from time to time,
Spiritus ut caneret de regno sepe futura	1470. So that she would often foretell the future concerning the kingdom
Ergo die quadam cum fratris staret in aula	Therefore, on a certain day when she stood in her brother's hall
Inspiceret que domos radientes sole fenestras	And saw the houses, windows shining in the sun,
Edidit has dubias dubio de pectore voces	She uttered these doubtful words from a doubtful heart.

*   *   *

Cerno ridichenam galeatis geatibus urbem	I see the city of Oxford full of helmeted
Impletam sacros que viros sacras que tyaras	1475. People, and holy men and holy mitres
Nexibus addictos sic consiliante iuuenta	Consigned to bonds, thus with the help of the Council.
Pastoris excelse mirabitur edita turris	The tower of the shepherd, built high, will be admired,
Et reserare sui cogetur futile dampni	And it shall be pointlessly unlocked, to its harm.
Cerno kaerloyctoyc vallatam milite sevo	I see Lincoln ringed by a fierce army,
Inclusos que duos quorum divelliter alter	1480. And two closed in, of which the second is torn away,
Ut redeat cum gente fera cum principe vallis	That he might return with wild people with their chieftain to the walls

Et vincat rapto sevam rectore catervam	And conquer the fierce band when their ruler has been captured.
Heu quantum scelus est capiant ut sidera solem	Alas! What crime it is that the stars should seize the sun
Cui sullabuntur nec vi nec marte coacta	By which they set, forced neither by power nor by warfare.
Inspicio binas prope kaerwen in aere lunas	1485. I see a double moon in the sky near Winchester,
Gestari que duos nimia feritate Leones	And two lions behaving with excessive ferocity,
Inque duos homines unus miratur et alter	And one looking against two men, and another
In totidem pugnam que parant et cominus astant	Aganst the same number, which prepare for war and stand at close quarters.
Insurgunt alii quartum que ferocibus armis	Others rise up, and a fourth, with warlike weapons,
Acriter obpugnant nec prevalet ullus eorum	1490. They oppose bitterly, nor does one of them prevail,
Perstat enim clipeum que movet telis que repugnat	For he withstands, and moves his shield and fights back with weapons
Et victor ternos confestim proterit hostes	And he routs his triple enemies, the winner,
Impellit que duos trans frigida regna boetes	And drives two across frigid realms of the north,
Dans alii veniam qui postulat ergo per omnes	Giving a pardon to the other who asks it, therefore through all
Diffugiunt partes tocius sidera campi	1495. Parts of the whole field the stars flee.

Armoricanus aper quercu protectus avita	The boar of Brittany, protected by an ancestral oak
Abducit lunam gladiis post terga rotatis	Takes away the moon with swords whirled behind backs.
Sidera bina feris video committere pugnam	I see twin stars in combat with wild animals
Colle sub urgenio quo convenire deyri	Beneath the hill of Urien, where the Deirians gathered
Gewissique simul magno regnante cohelo	1500. Along with those of Gwent, when the great Cohel was reigning.
O quanta sudore viri tellusque cruore	O how wet the men are with sweat, and the soil
Manat in externas dum dantur vulnera gentes	With blood, while wounds are given to the foreigners!
concidit in latebras collisum sydere sidus	Star colliding with star goes down into hiding
Absconditque suum renovato lumine lumen	And takes away its light, light having been renewed.
Heu quam dira fames incumbit ut arceat alvos	1505. Alas! What a cruel famine falls, so that it grips bellies
Evacuat que suos populorum viribus arctus	And drains the peoples' limbs of strength.
Incipit a kambris peragrat que cacumina regni	It begins in Wales and spreads over the far corners of the kingdom.
Et miseras gentes equor transire cohercet	And forces wretched tribes to cross the deep.
Diffugiunt vituli consueti vivere Lacte	The calves scatter who had been accustomed to live on the milk
Vaccarum scotie morientum clade nephanda	1510. Of Scotch cows dying from the unspeakable disaster.

Iteque neustrenses cessate
diutius arma

Ferre per ingenuum violento
milite regnum

Non est unde gulam valeatis
pascere vestram

Consumpsistis enim quicquid
natura creatrix

Fertilitate bona dudum
produxit in illa

Christe tuo populo fer opem
compesce Leones

Da regno placidam bello
cessante quietem

Go, Normans, and cease to
bear your long-term

Arms through our native
kingdom with violent
aggression!

There is nothing with which
you will be able to feed your
gullets!

For you have devoured
whatever creative Nature

1515. In its good bounty has over
time produced.

Christ!   Carry strength to your
people!   Hold the lions back!

Give the realm quiet tranquility,
war having ceased!"

*   *   *

Non super hoc tacuit
commirantur que sodales

Germanus que suus qui mox
accessit ad illam

Hoc que modo verbis
applaudens fertur amicis

Te ne soror voluit res
precantare futuras

Spiritus os que meum
compescuit atque libellum

Ergo tibi labor iste datur
leteris in illo

She was not silent after this,
and the comrades were amazed.

Her brother, who quickly came
to her,

1520. This, and with these kind
words applauding her, spoke in
this way:

"Sister, does the spirit wish
that you sing of future events,

And has stopped my mouth and
book?

Therefore to you is this work
given; may you rejoice in it!

Auspiciis que meis devote singula dicas	And with my blessings may you speak the events with dedication!"

*　　*　　*

Duximus ad metam carmen vos ergo britanni	1525. We have led this song to its end.　You, therefore, Britons,
Laurea serta date Gaufrido de Monumeta	Give a laurel wreath to Geoffrey of Monmouth,
Est etenim vester nam quondam prelia vestra	For he is yours, and formerly your wars
Vestrorum que ducum cecinit scripsit que libellum	And your leaders has he sung, and wrote a little book
Quem nunc gesta vocant britonum celebrata per orbem.	Which now they call The Deeds of the Britons, renowned throughout the world.

Conclusion and Acknowledgements

Merlin is an instantly-recognizable symbol of medievalism, the use of medieval elements in modern literature, which manifested itself in the late nineteenth and early twentieth centuries as a subset of romanticism. The primary mood of medievalism was nostalgia, either in the hortatory sense of living up to past ideals, or in the autumnal sense of regretting the end of a golden age. Tennyson's *Idylls of the King* exemplifies the latter, and "Merlin and Vivien" was a pervasive background influence on the portrayal of Merlin, so much so that in this study it has been used as a touchstone: the authors discussed here have been grouped into a Tennysonian and a non-Tennysonian continuum.

Edwin Arlington Robinson was firmly in the Tennysonian continuum, in which the plot and the dramatis personae are fixed, where Merlin is the seer who falls prey to a wily woman, where Arthur is majestic, Gawaine is light-hearted, Dagonet is joking, where Guinevere is a *femme fatale,* and in which Camelot falls because of human frailty. Robinson relies on his readers' familiarity with Tennyson in order to obviate the need for descriptive or explanatory passages, and he creates interest, even tension, by sometimes ignoring his readers' Tennysonian expectations and sometimes deceiving them. The works of Robinson's contemporaries who also wrote in the Tennysonian mode have been surveyed and discussed not only for context (as with the early dramas of Laurence Binyon and Stark Young, and poems by Sophie Jewett, Robert Buchanan and Madison Cawein, all of which are of period interest), but for the interesting nuances that some of the authors add. To the legendary architect Ralph Adams

Cram, Merlin is something of an architect: despite human frailty he intends to build a utopia.   Richard Hovey's familiarity with contemporary European culture made his Merlin somewhat Wagnerian. Despite the   Wagnerian-sounding score that Henry Hadley wrote when he set Ethel Watts Mumford's libretto to music, their operatic Merlin is no Siegfried; he is swept off his feet by the strong-willed Vivian so fast that for virtually all of his time onstage he is nothing more than a study in puppy-love.

It has been noted that the operas of Richard Wagner were specifically invoked as an important background influence by this group, but that this influence was superficial, having to do with subject matter and staging, but not with the aesthetic internals that give Wagnerian opera its force.   An exception was the case of E. A. Robinson, who adapted the Wagnerian leitmotiv into the poetics of his *Merlin* as a means of providing unity and variety.   Robinson also introduced a series of techniques for sustaining interest by giving the reader a jolt from time to time: changes of scene, flashbacks, surprises of detail.   The intricacy of the structure of *Merlin* has not been noted heretofore in Robinson criticism: this epic, and the other book-length poems of the author's maturity, have suffered from careless reading and the dismissive attitude that they are long simply because Robinson grew garrulous.   On the contrary, *Merlin* has been shown to have been as tightly written and as highly polished as the early, short lyrics.

In contrast to the Tennysonian Merlin there is the Merlin of Celtic tradition, a shadowy yet historical Welsh prince.   This inspired Mary Porter to write an exciting poem about the adventures of the young Merlin, and inspired Ernest Rhys to write an exotic poem about the supernatural appearances of Merlin that Rhys had heard of in his boyhood in Wales.   Philosophy professor and Scottish folklorist John Veitch had the historical Merlin in mind when he wrote his ruminative drama, and was explicitly anti-Tennysonian in his account of the Merlin legend.   Lambert Wilmer, the crusading American journalist and associate of Edgar Allan Poe, used the name of Merlin, but little else, in his drama. More important than any of these works in understanding the historical Merlin is the *Vita Merlini* ("life of Merlin"), a medieval Latin epic of unknown authorship, relevant to this study not only because it is closer in time to the Celtic Merlin traditions, but because it is the main source for Laurence Binyon's drama, in which Merlin goes mad in battle, runs away from society, and lives as a forest wild man. An original translation of the entire *Vita Merlini* is included, to show the work as Binyon saw it, which reveals not only differences between the Celtic Merlin and Tennyson's Merlin, but also between the Merlin of the *Vita Merlini* and Binyon's Merlin. As an example of the first, the Celtic Merlin is not an aged seer; he is a warrior-chief in his prime, a bard and clan member. This changes the plot and the *dramatis personae*: there is now the subplot of reconciliation with his wife and sister; of reconciliation with his fellow chieftains, since his mental breakdown paralyzed him in battle; and of his bardic hypersensitivity to the harmonies of music and to the discords of crowds. An example of the liberties Binyon took with his source is the role of Taliesin. In the *Vita Merlini* this Welsh bard appears merely as a "straight man" to introduce versifications of the scientific writings of encyclopedist Isidore of Seville; Binyon breaks the role into two roles, Taliesin and the saintly Kentigern, both of whom are fully delineated characters, comforters of Merlin in his insanity. Binyon also breaks the role of Gwendolyn, Merlin's sister and the wife of the king, into two roles: the caring sister and the faithless Langoreth. More frequent than the reworking of episodes of the original is Binyon's writing continuations of them, filling in the gaps of the medieval narrative.

Of especial interest is Binyon's integration of Asian artistic conventions into *The Madness of Merlin* and other poetry of his last years. In addition to letters, Binyon had a parallel career as an art critic, publishing works not only on English artists, but also, because of expertise gained from his post at the British Museum, on Oriental painting, especially Chinese and Japanese. Binyon gave excellent background information on the Buddhist, Daoist and Zhouist (in the sense of the *I Ching*) aesthetic ideas involved in painting, but he never applied his understanding of them to his own work until the last years of his life.   Their influence in *The Madness of Merlin* is pervasive, and explain the disjointedness of his drama, which is evident in dialogue, settings and plot.

What have we learned about Merlin?   Merlin is old and dispassionate, according to Wilmer; Merlin is young and passionate, according to Porter.   In Tennyson, he is Arthur's loyal servant; in Cram, he is Arthur's haughty master.   Merlin is a philosophizing elegist to Veitch, a rhapsodizing scientist to the *Vita Merlini* poet. Mumford portrays him as naive, while Blunt portrays him as jaded. Merlin is on the edge of human experience, and in anguish, in Binyon's drama; in Robinson's epic, Merlin is in anguish because he is sensitive to the dissonances and discords of normal life.

What, then, have we learned about Merlin?   That there is no uniformity in the roles he inspired?   That is something in itself: there is no uniformity in westerns or in detective novels, either, and that may be the essence of the modern Merlin, that there was a Merlin genre, as there would subsequently be lawyer shows or doctor shows on television, recognizable, although not quite definable.

Unlike these others, however, the Merlin genre has not lasted. Most of the works in the Merlin tradition are only of period interest, partly because of the mediocrity of the poets, but only partly: even the retelling by a great poet like Tennyson seems dated, with its Jezebel Vivien and its Merlin with feet of clay.   Robinson's *Merlin* and Binyon's *The Madness of Merlin* stand out as works of exceptional merit, dealing as they do with big life-questions through memorable poetry.

*   *   *

Tennyson's Merlin winds up entombed in a tree until the end of the world; the present work, which began as my doctoral dissertation at the University of Houston, might have wound up similarly entombed on the dissertation shelves of the English Department had it not been for the interest and encouragement of individuals who taught me about the audience that exists for medieval literature on both sides of the Pacific.   When I'm in Texas, medievalist Prof. Laurel Lacroix keeps me on my toes, and in Taiwan, Latinist and Sinologist Prof. Nicholas Koss does the same, not to mention the many other stimulating contacts in the Taiwan Association of Classical, Medieval and Renaissance Studies and the Medieval and Early Modern Studies Association of Korea.   Let me begin at the beginning, however.

I thank first and foremost my dear wife Florence Chen for her support and understanding — I'd even say tough-love — during this long project.   Thou art all my art.

I am indebted to Prof. Lorraine K. Stock for first drawing my attention to the *Vita Merlini,* and to Prof. Patricia Lee Yongue for suggesting Robinson's *Merlin* as a topic.

Lively conversations with Cynthia Whitten Green were seminal in bringing the medieval Merlin into focus, but the details of my indebtedness to her fine work on Kentigern will be spelled out when my micro-reading of the *Vita Merlini* is complete.

I was already indebted to Prof. Peter Gingiss for teaching me about linguistics, to Prof. Harry Walsh for teaching me Russian, and to Prof. Joyce Merrill Valdes for being a good and fair boss during my years at the University of Houston's Language and Culture Center; on top of these debts, however, I express my gratitude for their work on my dissertation committee, for their generosity with their time and erudition.

Special thanks are due to Prof. Irving N. Rothman, whose editorial suggestions were judicious and copious, and improved the work enormously.   His hand is evident on every *Merlin* page.

The hand that is evident between the lines on every *Merlin* page is its dedicatee, Prof. John McNamara, who guided *Merlin, Merlin, Merlin* from its embryonic start (as a mere squib on the *VM* poet's versifications of Isidore of Seville), through multiple rewrites, to dissertation length and on to its present reader-friendly format, leading by example — most recently the example of his *Beowulf.*   For energy and creativity, he is the youngest man I know, and something of a Merlin himself.

Michael Skupin
Houston and Taipei
March 9, 2009

References

Primary Sources

Binyon, Laurence. The Madness of Merlin. *London: Macmillan, 1947.*

Robinson, Edwin Arlington. Merlin: A Poem. *New York: Macmillan, 1917.*

The Vita Merlini. *Parry, J. J., ed. and trans. Urbana, Ill.: The University of Illinois, 1925.*

Secondary Sources

Abbott, Claude Colleer. *The Life and Letters of George Darley Poet and Critic.* Oxford: Clarendon Press, 1967.

Anon. "An Appreciation of the Poetry of Edwin Arlington Robinson." Scribner's Magazine 66 (December 1919): 763-64.

_____. "Merlin. A Poem. By Edwin Robinson." The Catholic World 106 (October 1917 to March 1918): 255.

_____. "Poets Who Adhere to Rhyme." The American Review of Revews 55 (January-June 1917): 660.

Assad, Thomas J. *Three Victorian Travellers: Burton, Blunt, Doughty.* London: Routledge & Kegan Paul, 1964.

Baker, Carlos. "Robinson's Stoical Romanticism: 1890-1897." The New England Quarterly 46 (1973): 3-16.

Barnard, Ellsworth. *Edwin Arlington Robinson: A Critical Study.* New York, 1952.

_____. *Edwin Arlington Robinson: Centenary Essays.* Athens: University of Georgia Press, 1970.

Binyon, Laurence. *Arthur: A Tragedy.* Boston: Small, Maynard and Company, 1923.

_____. *Attila: A Tragedy in Four Acts.* London: John Murray, 1907.

_____. *The Burning of the Leaves and Other Poems.* London: Macmillan, 1944.

_____. *The Cause: Poems of the War.* Boston and New York: Houghton Mifflin Company, 1917.

_____. "English Poetry in its Relation to Painting and the Other Arts," *Proceedings of the British Academy 1917-18.* London: Oxford University Press, 1918.

_____. *The Flight of the Dragon, An Essay on the Theory and Practice of Art in China and Japan, Based on Original Sources.* London: J. Murray, 1959.

_____. *Landscape in English Art and Poetry.* London: Cobden-Sanderson 1931.

_____. *The Spirit of Man in Asian Art.* Cambridge, Mass.: Harvard University Press, 1936.

_____. *Tradition and Reaction in Modern Poetry.* The English Association: Pamphlet No. 63, April, 1926.

Blunt, Wilfrid Scawen. *A New Pilgrimage: and Other Poems.* London: Kegan Paul, Trench, 1889.

_____. *The Celebrated Romance of the Stealing of the Mare / Abu Obeyd, Translated from the original Arabic by Lady Anne Blunt; done into verse by Wilfrid Scawen Blunt.* London: Reeves and Turner 1892.

Bois, Jules. "Le Poète Américain de la Conscience: Edwin Arlington Robinson." Revue Politique et Littèraire (Revue Bleu) 66 (June 16, 1928): 369-74.

Braithwaite, William Stanley. "The Year in Poetry." The Bookman (March 1917-August, 1917): 429-30.

The Camelot Project, The University of Rochester. <http://www.lib. rochester.edu/camelot/cphome.stm>

Carman, Bliss and Hovey, Richard. *More Songs from Vagabondia.* New York: Dodd, Mead, 1928.

Carney, James. *Medieval Irish Lyrics.* Berkeley: University of California Press, 1967.

Cary, Richard, ed. *Appreciation of Edwin Arlington Robinson: 28 Interpretative Essays.* Waterville, Maine: Colby College Press, 1969.

_____. "E. A. Robinson as Soothsayer." Colby Library Quarterly 6 (1963): 233-45

_____. "The First Publication of E.A. Robinson's Poem 'Broadway'." American Literature 46 (1974): 83.

_____. "Robinson on Moody." Colby Library Quarterly 6 (December 1962): 176-80.

Cassidy, John A. *Robert W. Buchanan.* New York: Twayne, 1973.

Cawein, Madison. *Accolon of Gaul and Other Poems.* Louisville: J. P. Morton, 1889.

_____. *Poems.* Fwd. by William Dean Howells. New York: Macmillan, 1911.

Cestre, Charles. *Les Poètes Américains.* Paris: Presses Universitaires de France, 1948.

Chant, Mrs. Elsie Ruth (Dykes). "The Metrics and Imagery of Edwin Arlington Robinson, as Exhibited in Five of His Blank Verse Poems." Diss., U. of New Mexico, 1930.

Clarke, Basil. *Life of Merlin.* Cardiff: University of Wales Press, 1973.

Clum, John M. *Ridgely Torrence.* New York: Twayne, 1972.

Cochran, Rebecca. "Character as Fate in Edwin Arlington Robinson's *Tristram.*" *Selected Papers on Medievalism.* 1 (1986-1987): 58-68.

_____. "Edwin Arlington Robinson's Arthurian Poems: Studies in Medievalisms?" Arthurian-Interpretations 3.1 (1988): 49-60.

_____. "Edwin Arlington Robinson's Morgan Le Fay: Victim or Victimizer?" Platte Valley Review 19.2 (1991): 54-60.

Cox, Don R. "The Vision of Robinson's Merlin." Colby Library Quarterly 10 (1974): 495-504.

Coxe, Louis. Edwin Arlington Robinson: The Life of Poetry. New York : Pegasus, 1969.

Coxe, Louis O. "E. A. Robinson: The Lost Tradition." Sewanee Review 62 (1954) 248-66.

Cram, Ralph Adams. Excalibur, an Arthurian Drama. Boston: R. C. Badger, 1909.

_____. My Life in Architecture. New York: Kraus Reprint, 1969.

Crowley, John W. "E.A. Robinson and Henry Cabot Lodge." The New England Quarterly 43 (1970) 115-24.

Darley, George. Sylvia or The May Queen. London: J. M. Dent, 1892.

_____. Selected Poems of George Darley. Ed. Anne Ridler. London: Merrion Press, 1979.

Davis, Charles T., ed. Edwin Arlington Robinson: Selected Early Poems and Letters. New York: Holt, Rinehart and Winston, 1960.

Dean, Christopher. A Study of Merlin in English Literature from the Middle Ages to the Present Day: The Devil's Son. Lewiston: The Edwin Mellen Press, 1992.

Domina, Lyle. "Fate, Tragedy and Pessimism in Robinson's Merlin." Colby Library Quarterly. 4 (1969): 471-478.

Echard, Siân. Arthurian Narrative in the Latin Tradition. Cambridge University Press, 1998.

Evans, Nancy. "Record of an Interview." The Bookman 75 (1932): 675-81.

Foy, J. Vail. "Robinson's Impulse for Narrative." Colby Library Quarterly 8 (1969): 238-49.

Flexner, Stuart Berg. I Hear America Talking: An Illustrated Treasury of American Words and Phrases. New York: Van Nostrand Reinhold, 1976.

Franchere, Hoyt C. *Edwin Arlington Robinson.* New York: Twayne Publishers, 1968.

Free, William J., "E. A. Robinson's Use of Emerson." American Literature 38 (1966): 69-84.

Galyon, Aubrey E. "William Morris: The Past as Standard." Philological Quarterly 56.2 (1977): 216-18.

Gant, Roland. "Laurence Binyon, *The Madness of Merlin.*" Poetry Quarterly 9 (1947-48): 252-3l.

Gilman, Owen W., Jr. "Merlin: E. A. Robinson's Debt to Emerson." Colby Library Quarterly 21.3 (1985): 134-41.

Griscom, Acton. *The Historia Regum Britanniae of Geoffrey of Monmouth.* London: Longmans, Green and Co. 1929.

Hadley, Henry. *Merlin and Vivian.* Poem by Ethel Watts Mumford. New York: G. Schirmer, 1907.

Hagedorn, Hermann. *Edwin Arlington Robinson.* New York: Macmillan 1939.

_____. *The Great Maze and The Heart of Youth: A Poem and a Play.* New York: Macmillan, 1916.

_____. *The Roosevelt Family of Sagamore Hill.* New York: Macmillan, 1954.

_____. *You Are the Hope of the World! An appeal to the girls and boys of America.* New York: Macmillan, 1917.

Halpern, Martin. *William Vaughn Moody.* New York: Twayne, 1964.

Hatcher, John. *Laurence Binyon: Poet, Scholar of East and West.* Oxford: Clarendon Press, 1995.

Henry, Archdeacon of Huntingdon. *Historia Anglorum: The History of the English People.* Diana Greenway, ed. and tr. Oxford: Oxford University Press, 1996.

Hepburn, James G., "E. A. Robinson's System of Opposites." PMLA 80 (1965): 266-74.

The Historia regum Britannie of Geoffrey of Monmouth. Neil Wright, ed. Cambridge University Press, 1985.

Holaday, Woon-Ping Chin. "Pound and Binyon: China via the British Museum." Paideuma 6.1 (1977): 27-36.

Hourani, Albert. Europe and the Middle East. Berkeley: University of California Press, 1980.

Hovey, Richard. The Marriage of Guinevere. Boston: Small, Maynard, 1899.

_____. The Quest of Merlin. Boston: Small, Maynard, 1898.

Hughes, Glenn. A History of the American Theatre 1700-1950. New York: Samuel French, 1951.

Humphry, James III. The Library of Edwin Arlington Robinson. Waterville, Maine: Colby College Press, 1950.

I Ching: Book of Changes. Trans. James Legge. New York: Gramercy Books, 1996.

IBDB: Internet Broadway Database. The League of American Theatres and Producers, Inc. <http://www.ibdb.com/about.asp>

IMDb: Internet Movie Database, Inc. <http://us.imdb.com>

Isaacs, Lewis M. "E. A. Robinson Speaks of Music," New England Quarterly 22 (1949): 499.

Jewett, Sophie. The Poems of Sophie Jewett: Memorial Edition. New York: Thomas Y. Crowell, 1910.

Jones, Gwyn. "The Madness of Merlin." Life and Letters To-Day 54 (1947): 74-6.

Joyner, Nancy. Edwin Arlington Robinson: A Reference Guide. Boston: G. K. Hall, 1978.

_____. "Robinson's Poets." Colby Library Quarterly 9 (1972): 441-455._

Kaplan, Estelle. Philosophy in the Poetry of Edwin Arlington Robinson. New York: Columbia University Press, 1940.

Kinkaid, James R. "Tennyson's Ironic Camelot: Arthur Breathes His Last." Philological Quarterly 56.2 (1977): 211-14.

Kunitz, Stanley and Haycraft, Howard, eds. Twentieth Century Authors: A Biographical Dictionary of Modern Literature. New York: H. W. Wilson, 1973.

Lehmann, Rosamond. "In Memoriam: Laurence Binyon." <u>Horizon</u> 7 (1943): 221-2.

Leiter, Samuel L., ed. *The Encyclopedia of the New York Stage, 1920-1930.* Westport, Connecticut: Greenwood Press, 1985.

Lippincott, Lillian. *A Bibliography of the Writings and Criticisms of Edwin Arlington Robinson.* Boston: F. W. Faxon, 1937.

Lodge, George Cabot. *Poems and Dramas of George Cabot Lodge.* 2 vols. Boston: Houghton Mifflin, 1911.

Lowell, Amy. *A Critical Fable.* Boston: Houghton Mifflin, 1922.

_____. *Tendencies in Modern American Poetry.* New York: Macmillan, 1917.

M., D. L. "The Arthurian Legend in New Guise." *Boston Transcript* III, 9, March 31, 1917.

Malory, Thomas. *The Arthurian Tales: The Greatest of Romances.* Rasmus B. Anderson, ed. Int. Ernest Rhys. London: Norrœna Society, 1906.

McCoy, Dorothy Schuchman. "The Arthurian Strain in Early Twentieth-Century Literature: Cabell, T. S.   Eliot, and E. A. Robinson." <u>West Virginia University Philological Papers</u> 28 (1982): 95-104.

Merriman, James D. "The Other Arthurians in Victorian England." <u>Philological Quarterly</u> 56 (1977): 249-53.

Monroe, Harriet. "Mr. Robinson in Camelot." <u>Poetry</u> 10 (1917): 211-13.

_____. *Poets & Their Art.* New York: Macmillan, 1932.

Moody, William Vaughn. *The Great Divide, a Play in Three Acts.* New York: Macmillan, 1909.

_____. *Letters to Harriet.* Percy MacKaye, ed. Cambridge: The Riverside Press, 1935.

Morris, Celia. "Robinson's Camelot: Renunciation as Drama." <u>Colby Library Quarterly</u> 9 (1972): 468-82.

Morris, Lloyd. *The Poetry of Edwin Arlington Robinson: An Essay in Appreciation.* New York: George H. Doran, 1923.

Moses, Montrose J. and Brown, John Mason, eds. *The American Theatre as Seen by its Critics 1752-1934.* New York: W. W. Norton, 1967.

Murphy, Francis, ed. *Edwin Arlington Robinson: A Collection of Critical Essays.* Englewood, Cliffs, N.J.: Prentice Hall, 1970.

Neff, Emery. *Edwin Arlington Robinson.* New York: Sloan, 1948.

Nelson, Lynn H. *The Normans in South Wales, 1070-1171.* Austin: University of Texas Press, 1966.

Nivison, David S. "Does it Matter how Annandale Went Out?" Colby Library Quarterly 5 (1960): 170-85.

Ó Cuív, Brian. "The Motif of the Threefold Death." Éigse: A Journal of Irish Studies Geimhreadh [Winter] 15.2 (1973): 145-50.

Ó Riain, Pádraig. "A Study of the Irish Legend of the Wild Man." Éigse: A Journal of Irish Studies. Samhrach [Summer] 14.3 (1972): 187-206.

The Oxford Companion to Canadian Literature. Toye, William, ed. Toronto: Oxford University Press, 1983.

Parry, J. J. "An Arthurian Parallel." MLN 39.5 (1924): 305-309.

Partridge, Angela. "Wild Men and Wailing Women." Éigse: A Journal of Irish Studies 18.1 (1980): 25-37.

Peabody, Josephine Preston. *Diary and Letters of Josephine Preston Peabody.* Baker, Christina Hopkinson, ed. Boston and New York: Houghton Mifflin, 1925.

_____. *The Piper, a play in four acts.* Boston: Houghton Mifflin, 1909.

Perrine, Laurence. "The Sources of Robinson's Arthurian Poems and His Opinions of Other Treatments." Colby Library Quarterly 10 (1974): 336-46.

_____. "The Sources of Robinson's *Merlin*." American Literature 44 (1972): 313-21.

_____. "Tennyson and Robinson: Legalistic Moralism vs. Situation Ethics." Colby Library Quarterly 4 (1969): 416-33.

Phelps, William Lyon. *Autobiography with Letters.* New York: Oxford University Press, 1939.

Pipkin, E. Edith. "The Arthur of Edwin Arlington Robinson." English Journal 19:3 (1930): 183-95.

Reed, Edward Bliss. "Poetry of Three Nations: Merlin." Yale Review 6 (1917): 863.

Redman, Ben Ray. *Edwin Arlington Robinson.* New York: McBride, 1926.

Rigg, A. G. *A History of Anglo-Latin Literature 1066-1422.* Cambridge University Press, 1992.

Rittenhouse, Jessie Belle. *The Younger American Poets.* Freeport, N. Y.: Books for Libraries Press, 1968.

Rhys, Ernest. *Everyman Remembers.* New York: Cosmopolitan Book Corporation, 1931.

_____. *Wales England Wed: An Autobiography by Ernest Rhys.* London: J. M. Dent, 1940.

_____. *Welsh Ballads and Other Poems.* London: Dived Nutt, 1898.

Robinson, Edwin Arlington. *Collected Poems.* New York: Macmillan, 1937.

_____. *Edwin Arlington Robinson's Letters to Edith Brower.* Ed. Richard Cary. Cambridge: Harvard University Press, 1968.

_____. *The Poetry of E. A. Robinson.* Mezey, Robert, ed. New York: Modern Library, 1999.

_____. *The Porcupine.* New York: Macmillan, 1915.

_____. *Uncollected Poems and Prose of Edwin Arlington Robinson.* Cary, Richard, ed. Waterville, Maine: Colby College Press, 1975.

_____. *Untriangulated Stars: Letters of Edwin Arlington Robinson to Harry de Forrest Smith,1890-1905.* Ed. Denham Sutcliffe. Westport, Conn.: Greenwood Press 1947.

_____. *Van Zorn: A Comedy in Three Acts.* New York: Macmillan, 1914.

Romig, Edna Davis. "Tilbury Town and Camelot." University of Colorado Studes 19 (1932): 303-26.

Rothert, Otto Arthur. *The Story of a Poet.* Freeport, New York: Books for Libraries Press, 1971.

Russell, John. "Laurence Binyon as Art Critic." Listener 5 (1944) 384.

Shand-Tucci, Douglass. *Ralph Adams Cram: Life and Architecture. v. 1. Boston Bohemia, 1881-1900.* Amherst: U of Massachusetts P. 1994.

_____. *Ralph Adams Cram, American Medievalist.* Boston: Boston Public Library, 1975.

Sharp, Robert, Archivist, Historical Manuscripst Commission, Science Library. Personal Communication. London, England. <http://www.hmc.gov.uk/archon/searches>

Shepard, Odell. "Versified Henry James." The Dial 63 (1917): 339-41.

Smith, Chard Powers. *Where the Light Falls: A Portrait of Edwin Arlington Robinson.* New York: Macmillan 1965.

Starr, Nathan C. "Edwin Arlington Robinson's Arthurian Heroines: Vivian, Guinevere and the Two Isolts." Philological Quarterly 56.2 (1977): 253-58.

Stephen, Sir Leslie, and Lee, Sir Sidney, eds. *The Dictionary of National Biography.* London: Oxford UP, 1921-1922.

Stickney, Trumbull. *The Poems of Trumbull Stickney.* Ed. Amberys R. Whittle. Foreword by Edmund Wilson. New York: Farrar, Straus and Giroux, 1972.

Stovall, Floyd. "The Optimism Behind Robinson's Tragedies." American Literature 10 (1938): 1-23.

Suss, Irving D. "The Plays of Edwin Arlington Robinson." Colby Library Quarterly 8 (1969): 347-63.

Swinburne, Algernon Charles. *The Complete Works of Algernon Charles Swinburne.* Ed. Edmund Gosse and Thomas James Wise. London: William Heinemann, 1925.

Tate, Allen. *Essays of Four Decades.* Wilmington, Delaware: ISI Books, 1999.

Thompson, W. R. "Broceliande: E.A. Robinson's Palace of Art." The New England Quarterly 43 (1970): 231-49.

Trachtenberg, Alan. "Democracy and the Poet: Walt Whitman and E. A. Robinson." Massachusetts Review 39.2 (1998): 267-80

Twitchett, E. G. "The Poetry of Laurence Binyon." London Mercury 22 (1930): 423-32.

Van Doren, Mark. *Edwin Arlington Robinson.* New York: The Literary Guild of America, 1927.

Veitch, John. *The History and Poetry of the Scottish Border: Their Main Features and Relations.* 2 vols. Edinburgh: William Blackwood and Sons, 1893.

_____. *Memoir of Sir William Hamilton, Bart.* Edinburgh: William Blackwood and Sons, 1869.

_____, trans. *The Method, Meditations and Philosophy of Descartes.* New York: Tudor, 1901.

Vielhauer, Inge, ed. *Das Leben des Zauberers Merlin: Geoffrey von Monmouth Vita Merlini erstmalig in deutscher Übertragung mit anderen Überlieferungen.* Amsterdam: Castrum Peregrini Presse, 1964.

Walker, Helen. "The Wisdom of Merlin" The Forum January 1922; 67:1:179-181.

Weygandt, Cornelius. "The Poetry of Mr. Laurence Binyon." *Sewnee Review* July 1905; 13:279-91.

Whittle, Amberys R. *Trumbull Stickney.* Lewisburg: Bucknell UP, 1973.

Whitaker, Muriel. "Laurence Binyon." *The Arthurian Encyclopedia.* Ed. Norris J. Lacey. New York, 1986.

Wilmer, Lambert A. *Merlin. Baltimore 1827. Together with Recollections of Edgar A. Poe.* Mabbott, Thomas Ollive, ed. New York: Scholars' Facsimiles & Reprints, 1941.

_____. *Our Press-Gang; or, A Complete Exposition of the Corruptions and Crimes of the American Newspapers.* Philadelphia: J. T. Lloyd, 1859.

Winters, Yvor. *Edwin Arlington Robinson.*   Norfolk, Connecticut: New Directions Books, 1946.

Young, Stark.   *Addiio, Madretta and Other Plays.*   Great Neck, New York: Core Collection Books, 1976 [1912].

_____. *Stark Young: A Life in the Arts.   Letters, 1900-1962.*   Ed. John Pilkington, Baton Rouge: Louisiana State University Press, 1975.

_____. "Merlin."   The New Republic 11 (1917): 250-51.

Yeats, W. B.   *The Variorum Edition of the Plays of W. B. Yeats.*   Ed. Russell K. Alspach.   New York: Macmillan, 1966.

語言文學類　AG0112

Merlin, Merlin, Merlin

作　　者 / Michael Skupin
發 行 人 / 宋政坤
執行編輯 / 詹靚秋
圖文排版 / 鄭維心
封面設計 / 陳佩蓉
數位轉譯 / 徐真玉　沈裕閔
圖書銷售 / 林怡君
法律顧問 / 毛國樑　律師
出版印製 / 秀威資訊科技股份有限公司
　　　　　臺北市內湖區瑞光路 583 巷 25 號 1 樓
　　　　　電話：02-2657-9211　　　傳真：02-2657-9106
　　　　　E-mail：service@showwe.com.tw
經 銷 商 / 紅螞蟻圖書有限公司
　　　　　臺北市內湖區舊宗路二段 121 巷 28、32 號 4 樓
　　　　　電話：02-2795-3656　　　傳真：02-2795-4100
　　　　　http://www.e-redant.com

2009 年 5 月 BOD 一版
定價：460 元

讀　者　回　函　卡

感謝您購買本書，為提升服務品質，煩請填寫以下問卷，收到您的寶貴意見後，我們會仔細收藏記錄並回贈紀念品，謝謝！

1.您購買的書名：＿＿＿＿＿＿＿＿＿＿＿＿＿＿＿＿＿＿

2.您從何得知本書的消息？

　□網路書店　　□部落格　　□資料庫搜尋　　□書訊　　□電子報　　□書店

　□平面媒體　　□ 朋友推薦　　□網站推薦　□其他＿＿＿＿＿＿

3.您對本書的評價：(請填代號　1.非常滿意 2.滿意 3.尚可 4.再改進)

　封面設計＿＿＿　版面編排＿＿＿　內容＿＿＿　文/譯筆＿＿＿　價格＿＿＿

4.讀完書後您覺得：

　□很有收穫　　□有收穫　　□收穫不多　　□沒收穫

5.您會推薦本書給朋友嗎？

　□會　□不會，為什麼？＿＿＿＿＿＿＿＿＿＿＿＿＿＿＿＿＿＿＿＿＿

6.其他寶貴的意見：＿＿＿＿＿＿＿＿＿＿＿＿＿＿＿＿＿＿＿＿＿＿

　＿＿＿＿＿＿＿＿＿＿＿＿＿＿＿＿＿＿＿＿＿＿＿＿＿＿＿＿＿＿＿

　＿＿＿＿＿＿＿＿＿＿＿＿＿＿＿＿＿＿＿＿＿＿＿＿＿＿＿＿＿＿＿

　＿＿＿＿＿＿＿＿＿＿＿＿＿＿＿＿＿＿＿＿＿＿＿＿＿＿＿＿＿＿＿

讀者基本資料

姓名：＿＿＿＿＿＿＿＿＿＿＿　年齡：＿＿＿＿　性別：□女 □男

聯絡電話：＿＿＿＿＿＿＿＿＿　E-mail：＿＿＿＿＿＿＿＿＿＿＿

地址：＿＿＿＿＿＿＿＿＿＿＿＿＿＿＿＿＿＿＿＿＿＿＿＿＿＿＿＿

學歷：□高中(含)以下　　□高中　　□專科學校　　□大學

　　　□研究所(含)以上 □其他＿＿＿＿＿＿＿＿

職業：□製造業 □金融業 □資訊業 □軍警 □傳播業 □自由業

　　　□服務業 □公務員 □教職　□學生 □其他＿＿＿＿＿＿
